VALLEY AT RISK

SHELTER IN PLACE

Through the eyes of an investigative reporter, *Valley at Risk: Shelter in Place* gives us a chilling and deeply personal look into the lives of people living in the shadow of an enormous amount of toxic chemicals. Harshbarger describes the human errors that led to a horrifying fatal chemical plant explosion, one that nearly became an American Bhopal. We see ordinary citizens successfully standing up to a huge chemical corporation. But even in victory, the people of the valley continue to breathe air laced with toxic chemicals. Harshbarger's novel opens windows into the chemical industry's dark past, and its living presence—what we face today.

Richard Meibers
Author *Falling Off the Wind*

The novel is compelling and insightful, and certainly a book that needed to be written.

Beverly Brooks Steenstra
Kanawha Valley (WV) resident

The characters come alive, the threat is palpable.

Joseph Wyatt
Professor Emeritus, Marshall University

VALLEY AT RISK

SHELTER IN PLACE

Dwight Harshbarger

Mid-Atlantic Highlands

Mid-Atlantic Highlands
Huntington, West Virginia

Cover design: JoAnne Thompson
Cover Image: Debbie Richardson
Interior Design: Jennifer Adkins

10 9 8 7 6 5 4 3 2 1

Printed in the United States of America

Library of Congress Control Number: 2014954645

ISBN-13: 978-0-9840757-9-9

Mid-Atlantic Highlands
An imprint of Publishers Place, Inc.
821 Fourth Avenue, Suite 201
Huntington, West Virginia 25701

www.publishersplace.org

Frontispiece poems: From Irene McKinney's poem "Deep Mining" and
Melissa Bailey's poem "City Darkness," both published in *Wild Sweet
Notes: Fifty Years of West Virginia Poetry 1950-1999*: Huntington: Publishers
Place, 2000.

To the memory of Ryan White,
and to a cleaner, safer West Virginia and the success of
People Concerned About Chemical Safety

Author's Note

This is a work of fiction. The story was inspired by events and historical accounts of the chemical industry and represents the author's opinion and commentary on matters of longstanding public concern and debate. With the exception of Mother Jones, Union Carbide's former CEO Warren Anderson, and Carbide's Hawks Nest and Bhopal disasters, which are mentioned for historical purposes, all characters, organizations, settings, incidents and dialogue are products of the author's imagination and are not to be construed as real.

Acknowledgements

Thanks to the people and groups that contributed to the development of this novel. The Morgantown Playwriting Group provided critiques of the story and opportunities to test dialogue on stage in New Works productions. Participants at Green Mountain Writers' Conferences and West Virginia University Writers' Workshops gave helpful suggestions on the story's development. Wil Lepkowski deepened my understanding of the chemical industry. Special thanks to my colleagues and students in West Virginia University's School of Public Health for their support.

Thanks to advanced readers who took time from busy schedules to read and comment on the novel: Mark Brazaitis, Jim Casto, Paula Grace, Dan Lambright, Kate Long, Maya Nye, Eliot Parker, Beverly Brooks Steenstra, Joe Wyatt, and to readers of the manuscript's earlier versions, Cindy Ashworth, John Linberg, Michael Mays, and Crystal Rhodes.

The *Charleston Gazette* provided rich and helpful accounts of the chemical industry's environmental, health and safety incidents. I'm especially grateful for the reportage of Ken Ward, Jr. *The New York Times* added important perspectives on chemical industry incidents around the world. The CBG Network's bulletins and newsletters gave visibility to international chemical incidents that sometimes stayed below the radar screen of the US press.

The successful efforts of the grassroots PCMIC, People Concerned About MIC, ended one major toxic threat to the Kanawha Valley and demonstrated that citizens can reduce the chemical industry's risks to communities. Today the citizens-based safety movement is led by People Concerned About Chemical Safety.

Special thanks to Editor Patrick Grace for his literary architecture and support, and to the staff of Publishers Place.

And thanks to family, friends and neighbors who have supported my efforts. Many of them lived with direct exposure to West Virginia's chemical plants and suffered the fatal illnesses of characters in this story.

Dwight Harshbarger
Morgantown, West Virginia
September 5, 2014

Listen: there is a vein that runs
through the earth from top to bottom
and all of us are in it.
One of us is always burning.

Irene McKinney,
"Deep Mining"

There are things in the headlight-pierced night
that should breathe only in nightmares;
Yet they are real,
living in the smog's gloom—
waiting, waiting…
dripping outside my window.

Melissa Bailey,
"City Darkness"

Prologue

Two whitewater streams join, high on a West Virginia mountain plateau seventy miles east of Jackson, to form the Vandalia River. The river drifts down from the plateau to Jackson, rolls by downtown businesses, decaying old neighborhoods below affluent homes on the hillsides, and the state capitol's gold dome.

In the late 1700s, pioneers discovered the valley's rich deposits of salt and natural gas. The development of salt wells and mines attracted settlers. Many families, including the Jacksons, brought slaves with them. The Jackson family became prime movers in building the salt industry. For two generations, they dominated local politics. The salt industry's economic power built the towns of the valley. The largest of them became known as Jackson Salines.

About the time the Civil War began, a flood wrecked local salt production. By then canals had been built around the eastern US. And railroads had arrived. With these new forms of transportation, salt mined in deposits in other parts of the country gained traction. The economic power of Jackson Salines, like a pile of salt in a heavy rainstorm, melted away.

By the turn of the century, the development of coal mining had brought renewed wealth and economic power to the valley. In the small towns and hollows of Vandalia County, miners' families lived in company built-and-owned housing and traded at company stores. When miners attempted to organize for safer operations and higher wages, they met firm armed resistance from the mine owners. Mother Jones arrived in the valley to help the miners' efforts. She led a strike for higher wages and, along with local union organizers, went to jail. During the strike armed Baldwin-Felts mercenaries on railroad flatcars fired into tent camps of strikers' families. Women and children died. Miners fought back in bloody and still-legendary union-coal company battles.

In the early 1900s, chemical companies began their first operations in the valley, processing brine and barium salts to produce sulfur dyes. With the onset of World War I, the plants produced tear gas, chlorine and carbon tetrachloride as well as other commodity chemicals. The war brought boom and then bust employment cycles, with local chemical plant employment reaching as high as 20,000. When the war ended, production shut down and jobs ended as other parts of the USA became producers of commodity chemicals.

The valley's chemical companies turned to the production of specialty chemicals. One of them, Union Carbide, prospered. Carbide built diversified operations around the world, at one time numbering over 700 facilities. At the Carbide plant in the little town of Academy, a tall chain-link fence separated the plant's expanses of asphalt paving and chemical tanks from the verdant lawns and trees of the Vandalia State College campus. The college had been founded in the late 1800s as the Vandalia Negro Academy. A small town, later named Academy, developed around the school. The families of many black teachers and staff settled there. During World War II the town became the site of a government chemical plant. Many black workers built homes in Academy. By 1976 Vandalia State had a majority of white students and soon became a university; Academy became a fully integrated community.

Union Carbide had roots that ran deep into the people and towns of the Appalachian Mountains. Carbide, people called the company. Local residents took pride in Carbide's success. Until the disaster at the company's Bhopal plant.

In 1984, at Carbide's plant in Bhopal, India, just after midnight a storage tank ruptured, releasing forty thousand pounds of deadly MIC gas into a sleeping community. People in and around Bhopal died. Initial estimates put the number of deaths at 3,000. Estimates of deaths climbed sharply to 5,000. Wind carried MIC across the countryside; estimates of deaths rose to 10,000 or more. The true number of human deaths will never be known. And there has been no attempt to count the deaths of oxen, sheep, cattle, goats, chickens and other farm animals, not to mention domestic dogs and cats, as well as birds and other creatures, domestic and wild. Children born to women who survived Bhopal have been labeled Bhopal Babies. Birth defects and health problems have plagued a second generation of survivors. Bhopal remains the deadliest industrial disaster in the history of the world; Carbide's legacy.

The Bhopal disaster began Carbide's decline. Sales slumped. Profits eroded. In 1990 Kabot AG, a German corporation, completed its purchase of the company.

In 2008, state-wide, the chemical industry employed over 13,000 people, nearly 18% of the workforce. Chemicals accounted for 46% of the gross state product. The chemical industry enjoyed an 80% community acceptance rate.

State government, with thousands of employees, became the second most powerful presence in the valley. Government officials and industry executives shared a common view: what's good for the chemical industry is good for the valley.

With the leverage of the industry's economic power and substantial campaign contributions, chemical companies successfully lobbied for minimal chemical-related environmental and health laws and regulations. Many regulatory standards contained gray areas that gave companies freedom of action. In addition, industry lobbyists worked to keep the funding of state regulatory offices low, often making regulatory enforcement difficult.

The *Jackson Chronicle* quoted a talk the governor gave to state officials: "When you find a company in violation of environmental regulations, instead of filing charges and levying a fine, ask how you can help make things better." That edition of the *Chronicle* also carried an editorial asking, "Are environmental regulators learning to look the other way?"

Chapter 1

ACADEMY, WV, AUGUST 20, 2008—The silhouette of the Kabot Agronomy plant loomed in the night sky. The interior lights of office buildings and bright amber lights strung around the tall chemical tanks beamed into the surrounding darkness. Smokestacks rose like giant torches, orange flames flaring from their tips. Industrial pumps, after three months of inactivity, again throbbed the rhythmic heartbeats of production.

Silver light from mercury-vapor street lamps gave a cold glow, even on that hot summer night, to half-filled parking lots, to the plant's massive vats and tanks, to steam releases that, like wisps of apparitions, appeared then vanished, only to be reborn. After a three-month shutdown, the hum of chemicals surging through arterial lattices of pipes, moving from tank to tank, signaled a renewal of the plant's life.

The plant's largest production unit bore the name of its product, the agricultural pesticide Desin, developed decades ago. Desin contained a powerful neurotoxin, MIC, methyl isocynate. It instantly killed agricultural pests, particularly boll weevils, Desin's number one target. Desin's toxicity didn't discriminate in its killing. For humans, one deep breath of Desin and neurotransmitters for eyes, lungs, and heart, in roughly that order, failed fast. Then death.

Desin increased the yield of cotton fields by killing boll weevils for major growers around the world, principally China, India, America and Egypt. Cotton crops spread over two and a half percent of the world's arable land. Desin became a major stream of revenue and profit for Kabot, who had purchased the plant from Union Carbide.

For three months in the summer of 2008, the Academy plant had been shut down to perform in-depth plant maintenance. Workers upgraded and installed new systems and equipment, including a new chemical tank, the residue treater, in the Desin unit. A new electronic process monitoring and safety system replaced the plant's outdated monitoring and safety technology.

Don Benson, a tall and lanky senior plant operator, his face pale from years of evening and night shift work, had marked off each day of the shutdown on his calendar. He looked down at his rotund boss, Jeff, and said, "The shutdown can't end soon enough. Let's finish training on new controls. Turn on the juice. Get going!"

For Don, the plant had a life of its own, a powerful presence. Acres of lights, familiar hums, each hum the voice of a step in processing, fluid chemicals under pressure passing through pipes and tanks. "I want to smell chemicals again." He laughed. "What some folks in town call 'odors' and phone the plant to complain about."

Jeff said, "Chemical smells mean jobs. They mean higher crop yields all around the world."

Don laughed and raised the back of his shirt collar. "Read that label—'Made in Bangledesh.' What it don't say? This shirt is made possible by cotton saved from boll weevils by Desin."

During the shutdown, an unusually large number of international orders rolled in from China and Egypt. The plant had built up its pre-shutdown inventory of Desin. Except for India, with its drought, 2008 had been a good year for cotton growers, and 2009 promised to be better. Heavy product demands had created above-plan increases in orders and shipments. Halfway through the shutdown, shipments of Desin had emptied the warehouse. Field salespeople called for more. But there was none to send.

Jeff showed Don an e-mail from a corporate vice president. 'Jeff—When are you guys going to restart production? We're losing sales. Maybe you can afford to give up your bonus, but I can't.' Jeff said, "I've got a hundred more just like it."

Sales of pesticides followed the seasonal rhythms of cotton crops. Plant, nurture, harvest. Don read Jeff's memo and said,

"They know better. Cycles of seasons get evened out by the warehouse. We stock up in the off-season and ship in-season. He oughta know that."

Jeff said, "This year's orders surprised everybody. Overwhelmed the warehouse's stockpile. We need to plan better."

Don replied, "Larvae hatch, and boll weevils attack, in warm weather. Growin' seasons are regulated by ol' Mother Nature. She's in charge, not us. Don't know why the big boys upstairs didn't think of that when they scheduled the shutdown."

During the shutdown, each day corporate directives pushed managers and employees. "Stick to the plan. Meet your completion dates for every element of the shutdown. Stay on schedule!" If Jeff, Don and the other operators heard it once, they heard it a thousand times. Everybody worked long, sometimes eighteen hour, days, often continuing through weekends.

One Monday Don said to his wife, Flora, "Yesterday you got dressed up and headed out the door. I wondered where you were going. I didn't even know it was Sunday."

The last day of the shutdown, driving through the front gate, everybody greeted the guard with big smiles. "Hey, Norm, after today, we're gonna rock and roll!"

To the plant's general manager, Otto Heidrich, stocky and middle aged, his English bearing strong accents of his native Germany, the end of the shutdown meant relief. For the past two weeks, Hermann Gans, his always nervous and overweight boss in the Agronomy division's corporate office in Connecticut, had called Otto at least twice a day. Early each morning to ask about the plan for that day's work, late each evening to ask, "Well, Otto, what have you accomplished this day?"

The morning of the first day of startup, operators returned to the large control room and their work stations. The walls had a fresh coat of beige paint. And the ratty old office chairs, with their ripped seats and armrests stained by years of coffee spills and sweat, had disappeared. At each workstation, centered in front of each console's group of screens, sat a new Herman Miller Aeron chair. An operator yelled, "Hey, my backache's as good as cured!"

Conversations about the new chairs ended as operators booted up computers. Screens filled with processing system icons, computer-generated images of operations. Icons on each screen displayed the Desin unit's chemical processing systems, steps in sequences that followed a chemical recipe. Measure and mix chemical ingredients, then cook the chemicals under heat and pressure, create the end product, Desin.

The first day of startup Don had planned to arrive at the control room by 3 PM, an hour before the start of his shift, the swing shift. But at noon Flora's congestion worsened. This time she had deep, chest-heaving coughs. When she spit up blood, they went to the hospital emergency room. After talking with her doctor, they had a prescription filled. Don tucked Flora in bed and arrived at the plant at 3:30.

Don gazed at his screens. He again viewed measures of chemical temperature, pressure, and flow through pipes and tanks. But the screens had new images, familiar but different.

"Old wine in new bottles," said Worley, a middle-aged and veteran operator who, in his bib overalls, more resembled a farmer than an operator.

The computer screens of the old electronic system had displayed graphs of temperature and pressure across the steps of Desin processing. In the new system, graphs had disappeared, replaced by icons, colored pictures and diagrams. The icons represented tanks and connecting pipes, links and relays. Rippling lines showed the flow of chemicals through the system's tanks and pipes, along with overlays of temperature and pressure for each of the processing steps. Before the start-up, Don and the other operators had gone through training on the new electronic system and learned to identify and respond to its unfamiliar computer screen images.

During training, Jeff had asked Don what he thought of the new electronic system. Don said, "Well, the old screens showed the same basic stuff, volume, pressure, and flow. But those old graphs, I knew 'em like the dashboard of my truck. The new pictures, icons they call 'em, give the same information, but they're different. Remember when I traded in my beat-up old Ford truck for a new GMC pickup? Well, this is kinda like that, like drivin' a new truck. Everything's familiar, but it takes some gettin' used to."

~   ~   ~   ~   ~

About 4:30 PM, in the hallway outside the control room, Charlie, a young day shift operator preparing to leave, said, "Hey Jeff, day shift fired up the kitchen. Desin soup's a heatin'."

Jeff turned to Don. "The day shift activated the Desin systems. Turned on the heat. Started chemicals moving."

Don said to Charlie, "Why so soon?"

"I heard this morning the big boys upstairs are pushing hard to get everything going. We done our part. The rest is up to you fellows."

Charlie handed Don a clipboard with a worksheet, the form used in the pre-startup equipment checkout, and walked down the hall. Over his shoulder he called, "Feels good to have everything up and running again."

Walking into the control room, Don looked at the form on the clipboard. Only half the boxes on its long list had checkmarks. He turned to Jeff. "What the hell is this? If those guys were flying a plane, they would've taken off without finishing the pre-flight checkout! What the hell's going on?"

Jeff said, "Let's take a look." He waved toward the operators. "Run an initial systems check, see what we've got to do." Jeff slid into the chair at his console.

Minutes later Jeff said, "They haven't done the valve lineups. I'll start on that. Don, you keep going with the equipment checkout." He yelled across the room, "Burl, double check the startup safety review. I'll bet they haven't done that either."

Chapter 2

JACKSON, WV, AUGUST 20, 2008—A light breeze drifted through an open window in the newsroom of the 1920s *Jackson Chronicle* building. The air carried scents of autumn even though leaves still held the dark green of late summer. In the soft light of early morning, on distant mountains touches of gold colored a few maple trees. The morning's warm air signaled a day of subtropical heat on the way; humid, close. Dog days, people in the Appalachian Mountains called this time of year; too hot to mow the grass, too hot to weed the garden. Watch out for rabid dogs and angry drivers.

A young woman sat at a desk in the *Chronicle's* cavernous newsroom. The scent of newsprint hung in the air. Only a stack of "To Julie Brown" notes distinguished her desk from the eleven others, all unoccupied, each with its own stack of notes. The paper's night shift had gone home. The day shift had yet to arrive. The in-between time, a rare period of quiet that punctuated the raucous life of the newsroom. Julie's time to think and write.

She ripped the top sheet from her notepad and took a last look at what she had hoped would become the story's outline, disjointed scribbles. Before her lay a stack of reports: chemical spills, toxic releases, explosions, injuries and deaths. The reports went back to the early 1900s and the formation of the Union Carbide company. They continued to the present and the safety record of the company's present owner, Kabot Agronomy. Her assignment? Pull it all together in a story on the Vandalia River Valley, the city of Jackson, and the chemical industry.

Julie wadded the sheet into a ball and threw it in the wastebasket. *Why is this so difficult?* She knew the links in the story's long chain of events. They pulsed with life, sometimes awakening her at two in the morning. The plant, what it had done to and for people of the valley. Carbide's and Kabot's impact on her mom and dad, on her boyfriend Ben's family, particularly his brother, Roger, his illness a wrenching story in her notebooks. Hospital visits and the anguish of bedside conversations as Roger passed down a one-way street; at its other end, darkness.

Julie had laid out plans for the story. She would talk with plant workers, current and retired. Around the valley, she would talk with government officials and store clerks, doctors and patients, truck drivers, bankers and waitresses. She already knew a lot about Carbide and Kabot, the jobs the companies provided, products that both improved life and brought harm, even disasters, to people and communities.

Yet, even in the face of disasters, the commerce of the company and the industry continued uninterrupted. She sensed, but could not describe, an informal government and industry consensus that made it all possible. Did quiet agreements reach beyond laws and regulations? Would that be her story?

The chain of the plant's, the industry's, history had many links in the valley and around the world. Some links were bright: agricultural products and pharmaceuticals that improved crop yields and health; chemistry to improve the quality of life.

Some links were dark: chemical explosions, toxic gas releases, environmental contamination; defective and lethal pharmaceuticals, birth defects, illnesses and deaths; chemistry that killed.

Some links were even darker: cover-ups.

And most dangerous of all, a special link in the chain, the uncovering of a cover-up. That job fell to police detectives and newspaper reporters. And with it came unknown risks.

She held her pen above her notepad, as if waiting for it to automatically leap to the page and scribble notes. A voice, her voice, small in the empty newsroom, said, "Write!" She failed to obey her command.

Julie picked up her pen and pushed away from her desk. She grabbed her backpack and walked to the employee break room. Pouring a mug of coffee, she glanced at her image reflected in the glass doors of the cabinet behind the coffee urn. Her high cheekbones, curly black hair, and year-round tan. Like her mom, she carried the African-American and Native American genes of her grandmother. The shadows below her dark eyes reminded her of how little sleep she'd had the past few nights.

She sat down and lifted a small notebook from her backpack. The leather-bound notebook, the most recent in a long chain of diaries, continued Julie's ongoing accounts of her personal history since childhood. Julie's record of her life. At home, the current year sat on a shelf in the spare bedroom she had converted to her study and workspace. Other years had been packed in crates and stored in the basement. Someday she might again read them. Or perhaps her yet unborn children might. Julie smiled and wondered if she really wanted them to read all that private stuff, her secrets? Most likely, she would. They presented the truth of her life.

Julie's notebooks contained stories of her life and the lives of her mom and dad, Arlene and Harold Brown. They expanded to include their close friends and next door neighbors, Charles and Mary Gruber, and their sons, Ben, Julie's age, and Roger, a child prodigy pianist, seven years older.

The two families lived in South Jackson, across the river from the town of Academy, site of the Kabot Agronomy, formerly Carbide, chemical plant where Charles and Arlene worked. The two families had a long-standing friendship. They shared backyard cookouts, local athletic and musical events. Roger, Ben, and Julie had attended South Jackson's public schools. As children, Ben and Julie had played together.

In 1965, Ben's dad, Charles, fair haired, athletic, had received a degree in business from the state university. Upon his graduation, Carbide hired Charles as an accountant. His father had worked his entire career in Carbide's Academy plant. After joining Carbide, Charles steadily worked his way into increased responsibilities and became manager of the department.

Mary, Ben's mother, tall, thin, and an avid reader, grew up in South Jackson. Her father had worked as a purchasing agent in state government and her mom as a substitute elementary teacher. In college, Mary majored in elementary education. During her undergraduate years, both her parents became seriously ill. Her mother, who never smoked, contracted lung cancer; her father, pancreatic cancer. Her dad died before she completed her degree. In 1964, Mary graduated from college and returned to South Jackson. She lived with her mom and taught in a local elementary school. In Mary's first year of teaching, her mother passed away. She continued to teach after her marriage to Charles. Mary stopped teaching after the birth of their first son, Roger.

Arlene, Julie's mom, curly haired, carried the dark features of her parents. She studied accounting at the local business college. Then she worked as an accountant in the financial department of Union Carbide's Academy plant. She often rode to and from work with Ben's dad, Charles, who headed the department.

Arlene had grown up in the valley. Her parents, Armen and Orville Orr, had worked in the local office of the United Mine Workers. In the 1930s, they served as union organizers in the southern coalfields.

Julie's dad, Harold, burly and soft-spoken, commuted daily to downtown Jackson. He had grown up in South Jackson. His parents owned and operated a hardware and farm machinery store. During Harold's high school years, his dad sold the store and retired. After graduation from high school in 1960, Harold attended college for two years, then joined the Jackson police force. He soon became a detective. About the time of Julie's birth, the chief selected Harold to head the department's investigations unit.

In her diary, Julie wrote—

Daddy was a cop, a detective with the Jackson police. When I was a little girl, sometimes he'd take me to work. We'd walk through police headquarters, past officers with men in handcuffs, sometimes on their way to jail cells, sometimes to court. We often stopped at the full-sized mirror on the wall behind the desk sergeant. Across its top was a printed message: "How will you look to the public?" Daddy would read the words aloud, and then speak to my reflection in the mirror. "Well, how will they see us?"

I stared at our mirror images, Daddy, in his rumpled brown suit, his large frame towering over the gangly curly-haired girl in the mirror, and answered, "Well, you look pretty good." Daddy laughed. One time he yelled to the desk sergeant, "Hey, Charlie, I believe this kid can falsify an answer and keep a straight face."

"Hire her."

Daddy tousled my curls and gave me a hug.

In his office we talked about cases he'd worked on. When calls came in, he'd hand me a stack of wanted posters and nod, the signal that he had to get down to business. I liked to study the faces of people on the posters, read about their past offenses, their qualifications I called them, and imagine their lives: A shoplifter who graduated into a career of grand theft auto; an embezzler with a Harvard MBA; a minister who became a bank robber and murderer. I imagined and wrote their stories. Even then I carried a notebook and pencil. Daddy used to kid me, "You're getting ready to write for the *Jackson Chronicle*." He was right.

About once a month, when Daddy handed me the stack of posters, he'd again tell an old joke. "After the cops arrested the famous bank robber Willie Sutton, they asked him, Willie, why do you rob banks? You know what he said?"

"No, what did he say?"

"Because that's where the money is." We laughed. I enjoyed Daddy's laugh, full, a whole belly of it.

Each night I prayed, "God, please protect Daddy from bad guys. Make him bullet proof." Wrong prayer. Shortly after I finished college, cancer got him. A few years ago it took my mom.

Nobody talks about our town's just-below-the-radar-screen cancer epidemic, the elephant in the living room, or the day-to-day intersection of the chemical industry with our lives and our bodies. What it's like to walk to school in a morning's aerosol plume of chemicals. Some days we'd breathe the odor of rotten eggs; other days we'd inhale chlorine-laced air, as if we lived in a world of over-chlorinated swimming pools. Company town, chemical valley; each chemical plant an elephant in the living room.

Cancer consumed Daddy's vigor. His burly 200 pounds dropped to 145. Near the end I sat with him each evening. Sometimes we'd talk about family. But most of the time Daddy talked about being a policeman and told me what the world looked like through the eyes of a cop. What he'd learned about people, about life.

One evening Daddy said, "Julie, a person, a family, even a company, is like the tip of an iceberg. Above the waterline is what we see. The world we know. Below the water line lurks the body of the iceberg, the world we don't know. All the risks built up over all the years. Invisible. Powerful. Coiled. Waiting to strike."

Chapter 3

ACADEMY, WV, AUGUST 20, 2008—In the control room, operators finished sandwiches from their lunch pails near 7 PM. They brought up views of the system, scanned their screens, and then toggled across them. Don continued the equipment checkout. Before the shutdown, checkout would have been a routine procedure wrapped up in an hour, two hours max. With new equipment and new electronic systems, no one knew how long it would take.

On the operators' screens, the ingredients, including MIC and catalysts, as well as pressure and temperature settings in each step of Desin production, remained the same as before. But the on-screen icons, representing measures within each of the processing steps, had changed—not a lot, but they had changed. The new icons, what did they say or signal? Each operator had to make a rapid mental translation from readings on the new system's screens to what would have been there in the old system. And hope they had them right.

Jeff said, "Hey, in a few days all this'll be history. We'll all be further along. We'll know how to drive this . . . well, like Don driving his new truck. It'll come. Concentrate on the measures, the on-screen pictures."

Operators sat erect, their eyes focused on the screens before them. Without turning from his screen, Worley said, "Hey, Jeff, these things are moving faster than I can cipher."

Don scanned his screens. "Everything looks okay to me." A moment later he added, "I mean, I *think* it looks okay."

For three days operators had struggled to master the icons and learn the new system. At the end of the third day, Worley said, "It's comin'. Thank God we've got two more days to go."

A senior manager had said to Jeff, "You boys have got the basics. Two more days of training would just be practice days. You fellows know your jobs. You might as well practice doing the real thing. Let's get production rolling."

Shortly after 9 PM, gazing at his computer screens, Don yelled to Jeff, "Something don't look right. Did they calibrate the new system?"

"Good question. Don't know. I'll call the tech people."

"And what about the EPA and OSHA inspections?" Don asked. "Weren't we supposed to get them before start up?"

Moments later Jeff told the operators, "The first shift didn't calibrate the system. We're getting incomplete readings."

"Worse'n none at all," Worley said. "What about that new residue treater? We haven't finished testing. Now it's online. Solvent's flowing in. Heat's turned on."

Looking at his gauges, Jeff said, "New systems, new tank. And same old, same old. The residue treater's still slow to heat. We got to raise the temperature."

Don stiffened. "I'm getting variable readings from the crystallizer. That could mean trouble. We need to get the crystallizer stabilized."

"The soup is cookin', the clock is tickin'," Worley yelled. "We gotta open her up! Let the catalysts flow in. Mix with the solvent. By God, that'll raise the temperature!"

Don said, "Can't do it, Worley. Not unless we override the safety interlocks. Jeff, want me to call upstairs? Ask if we can do that?"

"How many times do we have to ask?" Jeff shouted. "The big boys said OK a long time ago. We been doing it ever since. Even Otto knows. The clock's ticking. Who's got the password?"

"I'll enter it," Don said. On his keyboard, Don entered the codes disabling the safety interlocks. "Okay. Three interlocks are disabled. She's open. Temperature should perk up."

An hour later, from across the room an operator yelled, "That damn crystallizer's still acting up."

Worley said, "You fellows better come take a look at this."

Don and Jeff stood behind Worley, their gazes fixed on his screens.

"Those readings tell me I better check my systems." Don walked back to his console. Jeff joined him.

The temperature readings on Don's screens had risen sharply. Don said to Jeff, "Fifteen years as an operator, there's not much I haven't seen. But there's something about the flow, the rate the temperature's climbing. Too steep, too fast."

Suddenly one screen began flashing readings in bright red. Jeff said, "Maybe the vent's blocked."

At a quarter past ten Don adjusted his headset and microphone and then pressed his console's transmit button. "Howard, Jim, can you read me?"

Both men, making their rounds in the plant, replied in near-unison, "Loud and clear, Don."

In a steady cadence, Don said, "Desin Unit. The residue treater. Temperature's goin' up fast. Maybe a blocked vent. Take a look?"

"Ten-four."

Don pushed his chair back, eyes fixed on the center screen. Although air-conditioning cooled the control room to a steady seventy-one degrees, beads of sweat covered Don's forehead. The armpits and back of his khaki shirt had turned dark brown.

Howard jogged to the Desin Unit. Still lean and athletic at age forty-six, he ran well ahead of Jim, ten years younger but twenty pounds heavier.

Three minutes later, in the control room Don watched the bright red and ever-higher spikes of the temperature readings on his screens. "Damn! No!"

Howard arrived at the Desin Unit, a tall metal building. A few yards inside the door, he stopped in front of the new tank, the residue treater, and stood motionless. Wisps of smoke surrounded the tank and rose to the blinking red warning light on top of the tank.

Flames licked the tank's base, then crawled up its sides. Howard stared at the flames. In an instant, his thoughts flashed through twenty years of images, gauges readings, opening and closing valves, regulating the flow of toxic chemicals. Those images ended. Howard's wife, Betty, and their two daughters stood smiling at him, then disappeared. In his final moment, Howard's gaze locked on the ever larger flames.

Howard's last words, *"Oh, shit!"*

At 10:21 PM the tank exploded in a deafening BOOM! An enormous ball of fire leapt to the sky and rolled through the Desin Unit, roaring over Howard, through the building's roof and walls, incinerating everything in its path.

The fiery blast propelled Jim twenty yards backward. He sailed through the air, limbs flailing like a rag doll's. A guttural shockwave thundered through the plant, the streets of Academy, South Jackson, through the Vandalia Valley, then up the sides of mountains.

On the other side of the plant, in the control room the force of the explosion knocked operators to the floor. A moment later, Don stood, dazed. He shook his head and then helped the other operators to their feet. Worley lay on the floor beside his console, unconscious. Black smoke poured into the room. Alarms screeched and honked.

Don and Jeff put Worley's arms around their shoulders and, trailing Burl and the other operators, carried him outside.

The Desin Unit became a mass of flames that leaped into the night sky. Above them rose a mushroom-shaped cloud of thick black smoke.

Across the plant, sirens wailed.

At the moment of detonation, the power of the explosion transformed the residue treater into a five-thousand-pound steel rocket. It blasted off at lightning speed and flew straight ahead until, an instant later, the rocketing tank smashed into a wall of steel beams, bending and twisting them. At the crash site, flames leaped across the tangled maze of smashed pipes and steel.

Chapter 4

SOUTH JACKSON, WV, AUGUST 20, 2008—The evening of the explosion, Julie and Ben had a simple dinner, spaghetti and a salad, at her small single-story two-bedroom home across town from the plant. With a small inheritance from her dad, she had made a down payment on the house and secured a mortgage. She had furnished it with her parents' old furniture.

When during dinner Ben asked, "Do you want to plan on a June wedding?" Julie answered, "I'm not sure. The time never seems right." In her private moments Julie had reflected on their continued delays of wedding plans. Perhaps they had waited too long. She wondered if the two people who'd finished college ten years ago, deeply in love and planning to marry, had changed. New interests. New jobs. Shifts in values. A date for the wedding may have been the visible problem. But the real reasons lay elsewhere. In her heart, Julie wondered if she wanted to marry Ben at all.

For an hour they discussed possible wedding dates, real and potential conflicts with family events and work schedules. Julie's work on the school fire story had opened other assignment possibilities at the newspaper. Ben's new job at the plant had required him to go through a series of familiarization programs. Kabot management had asked him to attend some meetings in Stuttgart. At the end of the conversation, the wedding date again remained unset.

After dinner they watched TV for an hour. Julie said, "Let's watch the ten o'clock news in bed." Both of them were self-defined news junkies, Julie to keep up with all the news in the larger world, Ben to keep up with events that might impact Kabot.

In her bedroom, Julie turned on the window air conditioner and then the small TV perched on her dresser. They spooned their bodies as the announcer described the day's events in Afghanistan and Iraq.

Julie's stroked Ben's leg, and he pulled her close to him. About the time the national news ended and the local news began, their hugs had turned to lingering touches; at first brief, then ever longer kisses. Even after years of intimacy, starting back in high school, Julie and Ben continued to discover new pleasures in subtleties of touch and movement.

She stroked Ben's body with her hand, then her lips and tongue. They soon found themselves grasping and thrusting in a lovemaking frenzy.

Like a bystander refusing to acknowledge intimate actions taking place in front of him, the news announcer continued to report local events. Julie felt like yelling, "Hey, the main event is here!"

Their moans and gasps overpowered the news, rapidly reaching, and then ending, in a burst of movement and a frenzied climax. For a few moments they lay still, arms and legs entwined. Their breathing slowed and heart rates returned to normal. They kissed and rolled apart.

The TV newscaster droned on, "Tomorrow's weather? Another warm day on its way. Hey, it's August, what else? A low pressure system . . ."

At 10:21 PM the explosion's sudden shock wave pummeled Julie's house. Window panes rattled. Julie and Ben leaped out of bed and ran to the window. To the west, the sky glowed bright red.

A printed announcement, NEWS BULLETIN, filled the screen. Behind it, a voice said, "We interrupt our regularly scheduled news program. There has been an explosion at the Kabot Agronomy chemical plant in Academy. No details are available. Stay tuned. To repeat, there has been . . ."

They grabbed their cellphones. Ben called the plant. Julie called the *Chronicle*.

"Ben Gruber, public rela . . . hello? Hello?"

Julie managed little more than, "Hello? What's . . . ?" before she lost the connection. She placed a second call. "This's Julie Brown. No, don't hang up. I'm one of your reporters, damn it!"

Ben placed an unsuccessful second, then third call to the plant. His right foot tapped the floor as he waited. "I can't get through," he yelled to Julie.

A moment later Julie ended her call and turned to Ben. "*Chronicle* reporters only know what's on TV. The county emergency people told them to stay inside until we know more about the blast." She stared out the window at the red sky. "They said the chemicals, the smoke, may be toxic."

They hurriedly pulled on clothes. Standing at the window, Julie pointed to a black cloud formed on the red horizon and said, "Is that cloud toxic? Will it drift across town?"

Ben grabbed the TV's remote control and checked news on each of the local channels. They each carried an identical banner that scrolled across the bottom of the screen: "Explosion at the Kabot Agronomy Plant. Stay tuned for details. . . . Explosion at the Kabot . . ."

Chapter 5

B Y 10:30 PM, THE STREET IN FRONT of the Kabot plant's front gate had a traffic jam of ambulances, fire trucks, emergency responders and official vehicles. They arrived with sirens wailing. Police officers, firemen and emergency officials jumped out of the vehicles, ran to the gate and pounded on it while speaking into cell phones. "This is Emergency One . . . Kabot, open up . . . hey, open the damn gate!" Acrid black smoke fell over the front gate. First responders coughed.

Inside a small guardhouse on the other side of the gate, a uniformed Kabot security guard looked out at the emergency responders. In silence he shrugged his shoulders and pointed to the plant's administration building.

A hundred yards beyond the guardhouse, in the depth of the plant's tanks and buildings, the fire raged. On the perimeter of the Desin Unit, wearing white hazmat protective suits, Kabot firefighters hosed water and flame retardant chemicals into the fire.

In downtown Jackson's Metropolitan 911 Emergency Services, a uniformed officer sat at a console. He spoke into the microphone attached to his headset. "Kabot, this is Metro 911. What do you have down there?"

In the Kabot plant's security office, on the first floor of the administration building, that night's communications officer, wearing headphones and a microphone, sat at a communications console. "Metro 911, I haven't got instructions. . . . uh, we have an emergency in progress."

In the front seat of South Jackson's largest fire truck, the chief, Randall Kirby, gray hair and a large belly, his face beet red, sat erect. He pressed a button on the radio console. "Kabot, this here's Chief Kirby. Open up!"

The Kabot communications officer answered in an even and unhurried manner. His voice, like the chief's, rolled in the soft gentle twang of the Appalachian Mountains. "Sorry, Chief, we're not authorized . . ."

With his eyes on the plant's leaping flames, Chief Kirby slammed his hand on the truck's dashboard. He yelled into the truck's radio, "Damn! What the hell's going . . . is it the Desin Unit?"

"Sorry, Chief, we're not authorized . . ."

Fifteen minutes later, outside the front gate a crowd of county emergency responders, fire and law enforcement officials paced back and forth. They looked through the heavy wire gate into the plant grounds, yelling "Open up." Some first responders pressed against the gate.

In the heart of the plant, flames leaped high into the night sky. Kabot emergency vehicles raced through the plant's streets. The plant's company of firefighters yelled commands, manned hoses.

The Metro 911 officer transmitted, "All units, we still don't have . . . let's find out before we roll in."

Kabot's communications officer transmitted a request to 911. "We need an ambulance, uh . . . immediately. . . . We have a burn victim."

The dispatcher at 911 answered, "What happened?"

The communications officer replied, "I can't give out any information."

A large black SUV arrived at the front gate. The emergency responders gathered around it. On each of the front doors, in gold letters above an official seal, were the words "State Fire Marshal."

Marshal Bricker jumped out of the vehicle. A beefy, tall man in his middle years, he added even more height with his wide-brimmed Stetson hat. First responders, including Chief Kirby, surrounded him. The chief shook Marshal Bricker's hand. The first responders all talked at once. "Can't find out . . . another Bhopal? . . . Get on 'em, Marshal. . . . won't open the damn gate!"

Bricker unsnapped the leather phone case attached to his belt, removed his cell phone, and punched in the plant's emergency number. "This's Marshal Bricker. What the hell's . . . ?"

The plant communications operator interrupted, "Sorry, Marshal, not authorized to . . ."

"Not authorized, my ass! Gimme your boss-man. . . . Hello? Hello?" Bricker held his phone at arm's length, glaring at it as if the instrument had failed him. "Bastards!"

The dispatcher transmitted, "Kabot, we have reports of a dark cloud, moving west . . . tell us what that is?"

The Kabot communications officer replied, "I can't give out any information."

Deep in the flames, the muffled boom of another explosion sent ripples into the rising smoke. Responders coughed as a gust of wind blew thick black smoke through the front gate; many of them donned the masks of portable respirators.

Bricker placed another call. "This's Marshal Bricker. Gimme Deputy Holt." A few seconds later he said, "Curly, they're not giving us anything. What have you got?"

"Marshal, looks like a cloud of somethin' is movin' west. . . ."

"It's from the Desin Unit."

"Damn . . . could be MIC!"

Bricker recoiled. "MIC? De-con-tam . . .? Curly, we need to decontaminate?"

As clocks ticked toward 11:30, now over an hour after the explosion, at the front gate Marshal Bricker, agitated, huddled with first responders. He waved one arm toward the fire and the other toward the town.

Chief Kirby climbed into the cab of his fire truck and listened to radio transmissions.

Metro 911: "Do we need to decon . . . decontaminate ourselves? The chief thinks it's the Desin Unit. Methyl isocyanate. Same as Bhopal. Still trying to confirm . . . hold on . . . all units, we believe it *is* the Desin Unit."

Kabot: "My supervisor told me to alert the community. Will keep you informed."

Metro: "Can you confirm it is the Desin Unit?"

Kabot: "I'm only allowed to tell you we have an emergency."

Nearby, Bricker's deep bass voice punctuated the noisy cacophony of emergency personnel chatter, truck engines, bursts and whines of the fire itself. He turned to the county's director of emergency services. "Screw 'em . . . it's been an hour!"

The EMS director punched numbers into his cell phone, talked for a minute, and then ended the conversation with, "That's right. The whole damn valley. My order. *Shelter in place!*"

Immediately a wave of sirens wailed through the valley, penetrating homes and lives.

Chief Kirby pressed his truck radio's transmit button. "All units, shelter in place! Shelter in place! Mobile units, drive the streets. Wake folks up, tell 'em, loud and clear. Shelter in place! Tell 'em! Tell 'em! Tell 'em!"

At the eastern and western ends of the valley, the red and blue lights of police cars flashed at interstate roadblocks. Behind them sat the massed headlights of tens, soon hundreds, of stopped vehicles.

Again speaking into his phone, Marshal Bricker said, "That's right. And if the governor don't like it, he can call me . . . in about a week!"

In unison, the radios of emergency vehicles chanted, "All units, interstate's shut down. State Route 18's shut down . . ."

Throughout the valley, only police, fire and utility vehicles moved. Streets and highways became ribbons of flashing red, blue and yellow lights.

Above the plant, the giant plume of black smoke flattened like a layer cake and spread over the valley.

Through the early morning hours, on the streets and highways near the plant, only emergency vehicles moved. On city streets, no traffic other than police cars, blue lights flashing, moved.

At the break of dawn, throughout the valley, instead of the hum of commuter traffic, stillness settled over the valley. One hotspot section of the plant, the Desin Unit, continued to send up a stream of dark smoke.

At 5:20 AM the Metro 911 officer transmitted his final communication. "All units, we have an all clear . . ." then said in a rising tone of disbelief, a question more than a statement, ". . . except for *the Desin Unit*?"

Chapter 6

A T THE MOMENT THE BLOCK WORDS SHELTER IN PLACE filled
Julie's TV screen, an announcer said, "Emergency order,
shelter in place! Stay inside, seal doors and windows. Emergency
order, shelter in place! Stay inside, seal doors and windows.
Emergency order . . ."

After she and Ben made their phone calls, she stared at the TV
screen as if it would soon reveal a secret. Julie's heart pounded.

Ben grabbed Julie's hand and pulled her toward the door.
"Come on. Hurry!"

They ran to the basement.

Ben opened a closet door, looked in, and then slammed it shut.
He jerked open the drawers of cupboards and ran his hands
through them. "Where the hell are they?"

Every home in the valley stocked masking tape. Residents lived
in the shadows of chemical plants, lived with the daily possibility
of unexpected leaks and spills. "Highly improbable," plant engineers always said. But now an even more improbable event, an
explosion, had happened. The unlikely event that public officials
had consistently reassured residents would not happen. But having
said that, some of them, with a wink and a smile, added, "But
just in case, stock up on masking tape."

Julie sat on the floor. She heard an inner voice say, "Ben's
looking for rolls of masking tape. Remember? You put them . . ."
She couldn't finish the sentence, couldn't remember where. Then
she remembered: in the cabinet beside the washing machine. She
tried to tell Ben. Her lips moved, but no words came. Julie sat mute.

As if Ben spoke from the distant end of a long tunnel, his
voice echoed, "Found 'em."

He removed two large rolls of masking tape from the cabinet and tossed one to Julie. It bounced off her shoulder and fell to the floor.

Ben ran to one, then to another of the basement's ground level half windows, applying tape around them.

"Come on, honey, MIC, that shit's poison!"

Julie managed to say, "Uh . . . can't . . ." She put her hands over her face and began to weep. "No . . . no . . ."

SHELTER IN PLACE! SHELTER IN PLACE! As if powered by a jackhammer, the words pounded themselves into Julie's consciousness.

~   ~   ~   ~   ~

SOUTH JACKSON, WV, JULY 15, 1985—The shelter in place announcement transported Julie to a Sunday morning in her childhood. A month earlier she had finished third grade. That morning Julie had a summer cold. Her mom had said, "You're nine, Julie. Old enough to take care of yourself while I go to church."

Julie thought about all the things she could do with her little dog, Sparkle. After her mom left, she smiled at Sparkle and said, "We'll start with morning tea." Sparkle watched attentively while Julie prepared mint tea.

The emergency sirens began, one of them so close its wail hurt her ears. She put her hands over Sparkle's ears. Across the valley, more sirens, then echoes ricocheting off the mountains. Sparkle whined.

Julie ran to the living room and turned on both the radio and the TV. Different voices, same message: "Emergency order, shelter in place! Jackson and the Vandalia River Valley. Upstream to Gilbert, downstream to Tornado. Shelter in place! Stay indoors. Seal doors and windows. . . . Emergency order: shelter in place! Jackson and Vandalia River Valley . . ."

Moments later a fire truck slowly drove down her street, loudspeakers mounted on top. An amplified metallic voice commanded, "Shelter in place! Stay indoors. Seal doors and windows. Shelter in place! Stay indoors, seal . . ."

At school, church, and once in a while around the dinner table, Julie's family had talked about what to do if—well, when—the city issued a shelter in place. Other families had the same conversations. Her parents had been through shelters-in-place before. But she hadn't. At school the teachers held drills. Pupils would go to a protected area, usually the boys' or girls' locker rooms, and put masking tape around the windows. The teachers always acted scared. At home, her daddy had said, "Go to the basement. Seal all the doors and windows. Use tape, towels, anything that will stop poison gas from coming in. Then all we have to do is wait."

She asked, "What do we wait for?"

"A single long blast of the siren. That's the all clear."

"That's all?"

"Oh yeah, better pray to stay alive."

Julie once asked, "Hey, if the gas is already inside, wouldn't we be sealing ourselves in, like a tomb?"

Her daddy had grumbled, "Just do it."

That Sunday morning, fingers shaking, Julie called the church. No answer. Had everybody gone to the church basement? She dialed her daddy's office. Busy. She managed to dial both numbers again. No luck.

Now the fire truck was in front of her house. "Emergency order: shelter in place! Jackson and the Vandalia River Valley towns, shelter in place! Stay indoors. Seal doors and windows. Emergency order . . ."

Shaking, she picked up Sparkle, ran to the basement door, turned on the light, and leaped down the steps. In the basement, Julie carried Sparkle into the closet where her mom stored their winter coats. She slammed the door shut. Darkness. "Everything'll be all right, Sparkle." Her shaking worsened. Her heart felt like it was trying to pound a hole in her chest.

Along the floor Julie spotted a long thin line of light. Light! Air! A crack at the base of the closet door; it could leak light and air. "That crack could kill us! Seal doors and windows . . ."

Julie found the overhead light cord and pulled it. A dim single bulb dangling from the ceiling lit the closet. She pulled two coats off hangers and threw them along the crack. She sat on the floor and held Sparkle close.

Her daddy's overcoat hung above her. She put her head inside it, breathing the scent. Old Spice, her daddy. She held Sparkle against her chest and rocked back and forth, back and forth. The walls of the closet closed in. Darkness enveloped her.

Sparkle barked. Julie heard her mom, far away: "Julie? Julie? Sparkle?" She tried to answer but had no voice. Then Sparkle began a constant stream of high-pitched yelps, her way of saying, 'I'm in trouble.'

Lots of the Browns' neighbors became ill from the gas, aldicarb. They went to Jackson Area Medical Center's emergency room. Some of them had to stay overnight, a few for a week. Everyone later learned that aldicarb, though diluted by the time it reached distant neighborhoods, for plant employees and residents near the plant had a dangerous level of toxicity.

A few days later Sparkle began to vomit. Julie and her mom took Sparkle to the vet. "The toxic chemical from the other night," the vet said. He prescribed an antidote. It helped, but not a lot. Sparkle's running and playing days were over. Two months later she died.

~   ~   ~   ~   ~

The morning after the shelter in place, at the plant Arlene and her co-worker Bill sat in the plant's coffee lounge. "Just *aldicarb*," Bill said in a sarcastic voice. His double chin wobbled as he tapped on the newspaper and gestured, "Almost as toxic as MIC!" He sipped his coffee and passed one hand over his bald head. "After Bhopal, for five months . . . no production . . . testin' and testin' our systems, testin' everything! Then top management says 'hey, let's rock and roll—use MIC again! *Now this*."

Arlene said, "I heard management wouldn't tell emergency squads what gas'd leaked! A toxic gas plume rollin' through the valley and those squads were workin' for hours in the dark. Why wouldn't they . . ."

Bill interrupted her, relief in his voice. "Thank God aldicarb breaks down . . ."

"Emergency rooms were jammed. A couple of our people are still hospitalized," Arlene said.

Bill gave a quick laugh. "Lucky we're not linin' up to shake hands with St. Peter," then after a pause, "and folks from Bhopal."

Later that morning Charles sat at his desk reviewing financial reports. Arlene rapped on his open door. He looked up.

"Charles, you need to sign these. Authorize purchases." She handed him two forms.

"Let's see. What're we . . .?"

"Portable respirators. Oxygen masks. Need 'em posthaste. Yesterday, in that aldicarb leak, we ran into a problem. Men could've died. One fellow's still in the hospital."

Charles read the contents of the requisition and signed the forms. "Hard to believe we didn't have . . ." Then he asked Arlene, "Doesn't anybody check on these things? I mean, that sort of thing is Plant Safety 101."

At the onset of the aldicarb leak, a maintenance crew of six men, khaki work clothes and hard hats, had stood near a chemical storage tank. A white cloud of gas suddenly spewed from the top of the tank and spread into the plant. The men ran into a nearby control building.

They rushed to a tall cabinet with "Emergency" printed in large red letters on its doors. They swung the doors open. Two portable respirators lay on a shelf where there should have been six.

Men yelled, "Respirators! Where're the respirators?"

They opened the room's other cabinets. No respirators. Two of the men put respirator masks over their faces, took quick breaths, and then passed the masks to two others. This rotation of breathe, pass, breathe, pass, continued.

One of the crew took a deep breath from the respirator and picked up the desk phone. He pressed a red button. As soon as someone answered, he exhaled, "Emergency! Building twelve. Need four respirators, NOW!"

~   ~   ~   ~   ~

Three days later, walking along the corridor to his office, Charles passed small knots of employees in animated conversations. He placed his briefcase on his desk and began to remove papers.

A moment later Arlene stood in his doorway. "Have you seen this morning's paper?"

"With these financials . . . didn't even have breakfast this morning. What'd I miss?"

"Last night. Here, our plant. Another gas leak. At least this time, no shelter in place."

"I had a meeting in Adamsville. Spent the night there. Mary called, told me something happened but everything was all right."

"Something happened? It sure did!"

Like a student who'd just returned to school from an absence and eagerly sought to catch up on events, Charles said, "What? Fill me in."

"Butyol and sulphuric acid. Rotten-egg stench . . . multiplied by a hundred. No, a thousand! Eyes burned. Made us sick."

"Y'all okay?"

"Mmm, I guess so. I mean, what do you do when every breath is rat shit? Julie was up half the night. I didn't get much sleep. At 2 AM, she asked me, 'Mom, are we gonna die?' "

"Want to take the day off?" Charles motioned to the chair beside his desk.

Arlene sat down and took a deep breath. "Thanks, no. Julie went to school. If I was home," she gave a wan smile, "I'd have to deal with Harold."

"Is he still sick?"

"Worse, he's mad. Harold loves his garden. Tomatoes, beans, squash. This morning's paper says local produce may be coated with chemicals; don't eat 'em. He's actin' like it's my fault. You'd think a cop would be more understandin'."

Charles picked up a ballpoint pen, stared at it, and repeatedly clicked it open and closed. "People used to, well, they knew we could handle toxic . . . dangerous stuff. Till now, I thought so, too. Then after Bhopal, I thought we had it fixed."

"I guess everybody was wrong."

Later that day in a near-empty break room, Charles and Arlene served themselves coffee, then sat at a table.

Charles sipped his coffee and said, "We'd almost put Bhopal behind us. Now two leaks in three days. Red flags are goin' up on Wall Street."

"What does that mean?"

"Rumor is, General Chemicals may try to buy us. Should say, take over the company . . . a *hostile takeover.*"

"*Hostile?* What'll corporate do?"

"Fortify the castle. Hire attorneys. Sell assets. Maybe buy back stock. Raise the drawbridge."

"*Sell our plant?*"

"Could come to that."

"What'll *we* do?"

"Our job's to help defend the castle."

"You mean," Arlene paused, looked away for a moment, then looked at Charles, "help 'em sell the plant? Right out from under us?"

"We're Carbiders. Once a Carbider, always a Carbider."

~   ~   ~   ~   ~

The radio in the basement continued to announce, "Shelter in place, shelter in place . . ." While Julie sat on the floor, immobile, Ben worked at a frantic pace to seal windows andeliminate the possible entry of toxic gas. Taping the basement's small windows, he intermittently stopped and glanced at Julie. When he finished the last window, he sat down beside her, "Are you . . .?"

Her voice weak, detached, Julie said, "Shelter in place. Shelter in . . ."

Ben put his arms around her. "Hey, honey, it's . . ."

She pushed him away. Julie slapped her cheeks. In a voice resembling a coach, she spoke as if giving instructions to another person, "Wake up, Julie, wake up!"

Ben took her hand. "It's okay, sweetie. It's okay."

Julie looked at him, wide eyed. In a loud voice she said, "No, Ben, not okay!"

"Easy, Jules, easy."

Memories of the dark closet loomed in Julie's thoughts. She yelled, "Kabot . . . Carbide . . . pesticides! This valley. Your dad, my mom. *YOU!*"

"Julie . . ."

"Is this another Bhopal, Ben? Better check the news. How many deaths here, tonight?" Then Julie screamed, "Another Bhopal? *Is it?*"

Chapter 7

A T SUNRISE, JULIE HAD BEEN AWAKE for hours. When Ben stirred, she whispered, "Ben?"

"Mmm." Ben rolled over to face her.

"Sleep okay?"

"I kept waking up. Thinking about the plant." Ben sat up. "I should get moving. Need to get there early."

Julie stretched then sat up. "What's going to happen?"

"Happen? Well, if you want to, you know, I could stroke your back, pull you toward me . . ."

"I mean today at the plant. What's going to happen?"

"Sorry. Just trying to start the day with a little humor." Ben's voice became firm. "Today, we'll start cleaning up the mess. I'll help do spin control for a whirling dervish."

"Spin con . . . *you'll* do spin control?"

"That was the call last night. Part of my job."

"Spin control . . . you'll, I mean you, Ben Gruber. You'll tell the truth? Right?"

"The truth? Sure . . . well, keep in mind, it's PR. . . . maybe a small exception or two, some things I can't, we can't . . . well, yeah, *most* of the truth. Kabot may be facing major liabilities."

Julie sat up, gazed at Ben, then spoke in a controlled, firm voice. "*Liabilities? Most of the truth?* Have we—you and me— have we changed our commitment?"

Ben sat up. "What do you mean?"

Julie's voice became louder. "Way back. What we promised each other. Remember? To live the truth. Tell the truth. You and me. In here. Out there."

"I'm always truthful with you."

"In here . . . *out there*. Your job. PR. Spin control for Kabot's . . . *screw up*! At 2 AM I talked to staff at the paper. One man died in the explosion. Another airlifted out. He may die. The Desin Unit, MIC, Ben. What if MIC had been released?" She glared at Ben. "But you'll do your spin control. Hey, no problem, boys. Ben Gruber's on the job."

"That's not fair."

"Fair? Where do you draw the line, Ben? Truth here, lies there . . . tell me, how does it work?"

"Honey, it's a day job."

"No, it's *life*, Ben!" She turned away from Ben for a moment, then again faced him. "Do I know you?" She stared at him. "Life! Truth! You, me, Ben, we live it." Julie threw off the covers and stood beside the bed. "Or do we?"

Julie ran to the bathroom and slammed the door.

A few minutes later she walked into the bedroom to find Ben getting dressed.

"This isn't working, Ben."

"What isn't?"

"You and me." She sat on the bed, her voice now soft. "I have loved you for a long time. But in recent months I've found myself asking, 'Do I know this man?' It would be all too easy to say your job and my job came into conflict. The truth is, you can blithely accept an assignment to place spin control on an explosion that threatened your life and mine; threatened the whole valley." Her face reddened and her voice rose. "I could never, never do that. And I'm angry that you can. A huge chasm separates us. Try as I might, I'm unable to get across it."

Julie walked to the bathroom and returned. In her right hand she held a toothbrush. In her left hand she held aftershave. She held them out to Ben. "Take these. I think it's time for you to leave."

Ben slumped and seemed at a loss for words. "OK . . . but," his voice rose, "see you tomorrow?"

"Leave, Ben. We can talk in a few days. For us, I don't know if there is a tomorrow."

Later that morning Julie recalled a talk she and her mom once had, a mother-daughter talk. "Years are passing, Julie. When do you and Ben plan to marry, have children?"

Julie thought about her life and Ben. How the time for marriage never seemed right; how she and Ben had found satisfaction in work, friends, and for Julie, running. But they'd developed divergent interests. Julie enjoyed independent films. Ben liked high tech studio productions. Julie liked jazz and symphonic music; Ben liked rock. When local productions of stage plays or traveling companies came to town, Julie bought tickets, then found she had to convince Ben to come with her. Without intending to, they had developed independent lives.

Until the explosion, Julie couldn't put her finger on what had changed. She had been satisfied to take the easy route, enjoy what she could with Ben and let the remainder stay below the surface. But she knew it had all changed. She doubted there would be children with Ben.

She had the same unsettled feelings about life in the valley. Something seemed wrong with it, too. She couldn't put her finger on that either. But she would.

Chapter 8

SOUTH JACKSON, WV, SPRING 1994—During Julie's junior year in high school, she and Ben often studied together. One afternoon they studied at her house for a biology test. Biology? Julie later laughed at the irony in that. Her mom had gone to the supermarket. She and Ben sat side-by-side on the couch. They had the place to themselves.

How did their study session changed from plant biology to human biology? With little warning their books dropped to the floor. Clothes soon followed. They put their tongues where they belonged, in each other's mouths. Their hands explored each other's bodies. She pushed Ben back, stretched her body over his, and soon felt him enter her. A little known part of her came alive. She pulled at Ben, twisted and turned on him, until a paroxysm of release spread through her. She heard their voices yelling. Then a sudden nothing fell over her, like the end of a thunderstorm.

Later they dressed, fixed a snack and took it to Julie's bedroom. Then they snacked in bed, mostly on each other, until they heard Julie's mom downstairs. A friend once told Julie, "You never forget your first time. That's a truth you can take to the bank."

Each time Julie thought they had slaked their sexual appetites, they would grow hungrier, needier. Whenever one of them touched the other, a simple brushing of arms, an accidental touching of knees, set off a carnal nuclear chain reaction. When Ben's or Julie's parents went out for an evening, they got together. In bed.

Following graduation, she and Ben enrolled at the university. They lived in dorms their first two years, then with friends in apartments their junior and senior years. Ben majored in business; Julie studied journalism.

But even with their sometimes overpowering physical chemistry, at times Julie wondered about their future. Ben loved the challenges of business: How to set and achieve business objectives; small companies, big corporations, it didn't matter. They all fascinated him. He'd sometimes talk at length about his dad's work and all the benefits Carbide, Kabot and other companies had brought to the valley.

Julie sometimes challenged his benefit calculation, suggesting he calculate the full equation. Include all the costs of production, not just the benefits. For example, the human and financial costs of water pollution, abandoned plant sites, brownfields of contaminated soil, the health impact of airborne and waterborne chemical pollutants.

Ben subtly, skillfully, changed the subject. If she persisted in her questions, he became angry.

Julie always needed to know more. Ben needed to know just enough to answer a question. Julie dug beneath the surface. Ben stayed at ground level. If they talked about a company, Julie asked, "Who are the principal investors? How does the company impact the community? The environment?" Then she had questions that went up one level. "Who owns the environment, anyway?" For her, these remained important questions. Now, looking back, she wished she had insisted they deal with them. But in their passion, the questions always melted away.

The summer after graduation they returned to the valley. Ben got a marketing job with Jackson's First National bank. Julie spent three months searching for work. Then a weekly paper, the *Mountain Tribune*, hired her. Julie reported on local events and sold ads in the Beckley, Oak Hill, and Fayetteville area. Five years later, when the *Jackson Chronicle* advertised an opening for a reporter, Julie applied. The day of her interview, she gathered her *Tribune* stories into a folder. During the interview she reviewed her work with *Chronicle* senior reporters and managers. Just as Julie's daddy had predicted, the *Jackson Chronicle* hired her as a cub reporter.

In 2007, Kabot Agronomy advertised an entry level opening in public relations. Ben applied for it and got the job. For him, going to work at Kabot, following in his dad's footsteps, seemed a dream come true.

But for Julie, the recent explosion made Ben's joining Kabot more like a nightmare. Carbide had trod a path from Jackson to Bhopal. Kabot's footprints marked a similar trail through the valley. And no matter who owned the Academy plant, too many times the community had been terrorized by the emergency announcement, "Shelter in place! Go inside. Seal all windows and doors. . . ."

At a high school reunion, Julie talked with her friend Harriet about Ben and Kabot. "Julie, have you thought about splitting from Ben? From the valley?"

"Sure, I could move away. But I'd be no different from the coal miners who lost their jobs to mechanized mining. They moved north to jobs in auto plants. Detroit. Flint. Pontiac."

Julie didn't address Harriet's other question, about splitting from Ben.

Harriet told a joke that had made the rounds. Buster said, "Hey, did you hear? The governor resigned." Boomer says, "No! What happened?" Buster answers, "The Ford plant is hirin' again."

Julie said, "All those people that moved north didn't stay up there. Families returned to the mountains. Some to jobs in Chemical Valley. Others to no jobs. The pull of place. I know myself well enough to know that, like them, if I moved away I'd be drawn back, like the snap of a rubber band. Better to stay here. Home, where I belong."

Chapter 9

IN THE AFTERMATH OF THE EXPLOSION, the managing editor of the *Chronicle*, Harrison Wilde, asked Julie to meet with him. After many delays—he had a busy schedule, and she was working on stories that required her to make calls and travel around town for interviews—they finally got together.

Harrison's office more resembled a storage room than a business office. Shelves filled with books and papers, old copies of the *Chronicle*, lined the walls. Bronze plaques and framed awards had been jammed between the stacks. The scent of newsprint hung in the air.

Over coffee with other reporters, Julie had learned that Harrison joined the *Chronicle* as a copy-boy not long after finishing high school twenty-five years ago. He later moved into advertising and sales and then became a reporter. A couple of years into the job he uncovered a state road kickback scandal. His stories led to arrests, then trials, and sent four officials to prison. He continued to do investigative reporting before moving into his present position of managing editor.

Harrison knew first-hand the wrenching pain of changes in the newspaper business: the transition from the old methods of typesetting and printing to newer, more efficient electronic print systems. He did the tough work of reorganizing operations for the digital age; new equipment, computerized operations, and staff reductions, including the pain of terminating long-term colleagues and friends. He conducted the strident and emotionally demanding labor negotiations that had followed seismic shifts in the newspaper business. During a heated contract negotiation session, a union steward who'd been a former Golden Gloves boxer, grabbed Harrison and threw a roundhouse punch that knocked him unconscious. Harrison didn't press charges, a decision that led to the calming of the negotiations and, not long afterward, a contract agreement.

After a former editor's sudden death from a heart attack, Harrison became concerned about his health and began a routine of daily workouts. He occasionally joined Julie and other employees for a local 5K race. A little over six feet tall, he'd dropped over twenty pounds to a svelte 170 pounds. His tanned face complemented his gray eyes.

Harrison's infrequent editorials, never simple, usually controversial, impacted school boards, governors, mayors, town councils and members of Congress. Lots of folks disagreed with him. Letters threatening his life became just another routine part of his workday. Harrison's editorials calling for an end to Jackson's de facto school segregation led to bussing that ended the practice. But old customs die hard. One night a bomb exploded on Harrison's front porch.

Harrison's leadership came at a price. Two years after the bomb, his wife left him and filed for divorce. They had no children.

During Julie's first year at the paper, Harrison often stopped at her newsroom cubicle. "Just checking in, wondering how you're doing."

When they met in his office a few days after the Kabot explosion, he asked, "Are you still working on your school fire story?"

"I believe it's wrapped up." Her heart rate jumped to a higher speed. Had she missed something?

Harrison raised his eyebrows. "No loose ends?"

Her voice hesitant, Julie replied, "I don't think so."

Harrison looked her in the eye. "The mayor's coming down hard on the paper."

Julie managed a smile. "Doesn't surprise me. Each time I talked with his people, one of them would make a point of telling me that people in City Hall, meaning the mayor, didn't like my stories."

"What're you working on now?" Harrison leaned back in his chair and put one foot on his desk.

Julie shrugged. "The usual. You know, the valley's flower show, other human interest stories we can wrap around ads."

"Right. We have to sell newspapers. But enough. I asked you to meet with me to tell you that you're through . . ."

Julie felt a sudden jolt pass through her. She yelled, "Enough? Through? What're you telling me?"

Harrison raised one hand. "Easy, Julie."

She bristled. "I went through hell reporting that West Elementary School fire. Late nights. Meals missed." Her hands and her voice trembled. "Did you call me in here to fire . . . ?"

Harrison raised both hands. "Hey, slow down, Julie."

Her face red, Julie yelled, "You can't be serious."

"I am. But you've got it all wrong." He grinned.

In rapid fire staccato she said, "I do? Then what's right? Tell me."

"Let me complete my sentence. You're through with flower shows. Your school fire story was first class. I'm proud of the way you stood your ground against City Hall."

Julie's tone softened and her body relaxed. "Sorry. The explosion's got me. . ." Julie took a deep breath. "I've been at the *Chronicle* for five years. You just gave me my first compliment."

"This is a hard business."

~   ~   ~   ~   ~

The morning five months ago when Harrison had called Julie into his office to talk about the West School fire remained a watershed event in her newspaper life. He sat behind his desk, the morning edition of the *Chronicle* spread before him, open to her first story on the fire. He looked up. "Truth, Julie, that's what it's all about!"

"Yes, I know."

"Do you?" he asked in a tone of voice suggesting uncertainty about her answer, perhaps about her.

She wondered, *Now what?* Julie then said, "There's something in my story that's not true?"

Harrison extended one hand across his desk toward Julie and said, "Imagine I'm holding a torch." He paused and then said, "You take it."

"Take it? Is this some kind of game?" She looked at his hand.

His baritone voice deepened. "Go on, take it!" He thrust his hand closer. The pupils of his eyes seemed to expand over their gray irises, black eyes with a stare that bored into her. "This is no game."

"I feel kind of foolish." Julie reluctantly mimed accepting the imaginary torch.

"Forgive the hokey drama, Julie. But I am serious about the torch of truth. The *Chronicle's* masthead says it: 'Carrying the torch of truth.' The paper has carried it for a hundred and forty years." He sat down.

Julie stared at Harrison. "What are you telling me?"

"Leaving aside the fact that over the years the *Chronicle* has made government more transparent, a little more honest, what do we have to show for it? Debt. Mounting bank loans. On TV, so-called news programs peddle slick half-truths. And make fortunes. Jackson's own WJTV, owned by a card-carrying member of the Tea Party, wants to buy the *Chronicle*. And you know what? We may have to sell."

Julie sat up, her back rigid and straight, and said, "Sell the *Chronicle*? Say it ain't so."

"I'm leveling with you."

"What do you want from me? This paper, reporting, has become my life. But I can't do much about the *Chronicle*'s bottom line."

Harrison's eyes flashed. He leaned forward. "The hell you can't. Your stories on the school fire: you missed the snake in the grass!"

Julie's mouth fell open. Her eyes widened. "Missed the . . .? I wrote about the faulty fire alarm."

His voice rising, Harrison asked, "Why? Why didn't the alarm work? If that fire had happened four hours later, kids could've died."

A cavern opened below her stomach and her innards fell into it. She had been so proud to have identified the faulty fire alarm that she'd missed the obvious question: *Why didn't it work?*

Harrison's voice boomed across his desk. "Carry the torch, Julie, carry it! That alarm *should have been,* even worse, *may have been,* inspected. Either way, it's a matter of public record. Somebody's at fault. Find the snake."

Julie felt bereft. She'd taken so much pride in that story. But it had fallen short, had not been the whole truth. "And if I can't?"

He gave her one of his giant-sized belly laughs. "You better find a bigger story, fast. Or you're out of a job. I'm out of a job. And the *Chronicle* joins the Tea Party."

That afternoon Julie went to City Hall. She began digging into the details of school fire-safety inspections. Who, what, where, when? She found records indicating that the West Elementary School inspections had been completed. But the reports looked like they'd come off an assembly line. That sameness—did it mean an inspector, bored after hundreds of inspections, used a routine or boilerplate way of writing up findings? Or might it signal perfunctory reports on inspections half done, or even worse, never done?

Julie showed a batch of West School safety inspection reports to an older woman, Margaret, in the city records office. Margaret and Julie's mom had attended church together. "Margaret, these inspection reports all look pretty much the same. Do you have any idea why?"

Margaret looked around the room as if to make sure no one could hear her, then in a soft voice said, "Julie, they was pencil whipped." She pointed to one of the reports. "And this one, I believe they never . . . I'm not sayin' the inspector faked it, but . . . sometimes they wanted to play golf, or something."

Her words brought home a fundamental feature of the valley's, of the Appalachian Mountains', culture. Cut some slack, look the other way. Forgive. And the corollary to forgiveness, be nice.

Julie wondered, but decided not to pursue, whether, long before the school fire, Margaret had known about the shoddy and falsified inspections. Had she and others in City Hall looked the other way when safety inspectors cut corners? How far up the chain of command did people know the truth—that perfunctory or omitted inspections and flawed or falsified reports had been condoned? But Julie cut Margaret some slack.

Then Julie began to organize her findings, construct her story. The fire alarm that later failed hadn't been tested. Some inspection reports were incomplete. A false report had been filed on the alarm that would have detected the fire.

In a second round of stories that looked into the quality of safety inspections conducted by City Hall, she reported the whole truth. How the City's fire code enforcement, or more accurately, the lack of enforcement in and following school inspections had become acceptable and commonplace.

Immediately after the *Chronicle* published Julie's new series of school fire stories, management shakeups took place at City Hall and in the county schools. School safety inspections improved to meet rigorous standards. Julie took pride in the fact that, as a result of all this, schools became safer places for kids and teachers. And the *Chronicle* sold a lot of newspapers.

One morning a few weeks later, Harrison showed Julie reports reflecting circulation increases that followed her second series of stories. He beamed a wide smile. "Hey, Julie, you *did* impact the bottom line."

~   ~   ~   ~   ~

Harrison stood in front of the window. The sky had darkened. Beyond the river a thunderstorm brewed above the mountains. He spoke toward the window. "Julie, I want you to start on the Kabot story today. You'll work with Bob Samuelson. He's been around the block a few times. The two of you will report day to day on the explosion."

After a flash of surprise mixed with pride, Julie thought of Ben and his work at Kabot. His words the morning after the explosion, "I'll do spin control." She had a hunch she knew what Harrison wanted, but asked anyway. "Give me a little guidance. What do you want me to do?"

"Take a long hard look at the Kabot Agronomy plant in Academy. Its history. Its operations. If MIC had been released, would the valley have been another Bhopal? Are there alternatives to MIC? If so, why aren't they used? What are the products they produce here? How do those products make a difference, for better or for worse, in our lives? What are Kabot's positive contributions to the valley? Jobs, career opportunities that keep young people in the valley. Support for civic and philanthropic causes. Summer camps for kids.

"And the dark side of the valley's marriage to Carbide, now Kabot. Chemical releases, explosions, fires. Shelters-in-place. Injuries and deaths. The chemicals that've seeped out day after day, lingered in the water, the air, often undetected. Unless they produced an odor we could smell, or one that made us sick. And in the background, cancer. The valley's rates of cancer."

In a voice of disbelief, Julie said, "You want me to do *what*?"

"I don't know when we'll use the larger story. And you'll do briefer, more immediate stories on events that'll come in the aftermath of the explosion, on the investigations yet to happen. Though, I guarantee you, we'll use the big one. In this business, everything hinges on . . . well, timing is everything." Outside, storm clouds had darkened the afternoon sky. Lightning flashed.

"Julie, you bring fresh perspectives to the news. You're good." He paused, looked at her and said, slowly, "You can be better. I want to see you develop, stretch yourself. The Kabot story will be a challenge. Already, when asked about the explosion, Kabot executives and our politicians are giving us the old razzle dazzle. Dancing around the truth. We need a straightforward and candid assessment. From you."

Julie's pride in herself as a reporter kicked her in the butt. She wanted to accept Harrison's challenge, jump in. But she knew what life at the paper was like. Demands never let up. Every morning a new edition, a new major story. Readers don't want old news. The paper had to give readers more than the superficial sound-bites of TV.

Julie heard her inner voice say, "The sun is rising. Grab the challenge." Than another voice said, "Opportunities are never as good as they appear."

"In the meantime, Harrison, my current stories, the flower show, another robbery at a branch bank, I keep doing them?"

Straight faced, Harrison answered, "Of course."

Julie jerked back in her chair and stared at him.

Harrison leaned forward and laughed. "Sorry. Please forgive the misguided humor of an editor. You're through with flower shows. I'll assign your current stories to another reporter and keep you freed up to work on this . . . this, what do you want to call it? A series of in-depth stories?"

What to call it? How should she know? "Keep it simple. Call it an assignment."

His smile disappeared. "Let's call it what it is: investigative reporting." He leaned across his desk, suddenly resembling one of her old journalism professors. "You've got it, kid . . . Julie. Your first assignment as an investigative reporter."

"I want to do it, but I wonder if I'm ready."

"Hey, you've already done it. That's what your school fire stories became. You didn't call it investigative reporting. But I did."

"Harrison, my boyfriend . . . well, my former boyfriend, works at Kabot. Two days ago I broke off the relationship. He's in PR, doing spin control on the explosion. I want you to know about the relationship, even though it has ended. But, who knows, it might influence me. Isn't that a journalism conflict of interest?"

Harrison again turned to the window. Sheets of rain now pelted it, water running down the panes. Then Harrison opened a desk drawer and brought out a file folder. He removed a sheet of paper and handed it to Julie. "Read this paragraph."

Anti-corruption Resource Center: A conflict of interest arises when an individual with a formal responsibility to serve the public participates in an activity that jeopardizes his or her professional judgment . . . one that primarily serves personal interests and can potentially influence the objective exercise of the individual's official duties.

Julie recalled ethics discussions in her college journalism courses. She handed him the sheet of paper. "I guess I should go back to writing stories to wrap around ads." She picked up her backpack.

Harrison stood and walked to the window. He looked out for a moment, "That's one helluva storm." He then turned to Julie. "Let me come at this from another angle. When I was new to the newspaper business, gay men hid their homosexuality. When, as it sometimes happened, a man in a position of public trust, a mayor, a minister, a senator, and so on, was discovered to be gay, reporters dug into his finances, his family life, his policy decisions, his legislative actions. Had he deceived his wife? Used his position to tilt the playing field, passed along favors to a lover? Or might he have been blackmailed by a special interest group who found out about his homosexuality? A well-known public figure, Massachusetts Congressman Barney Frank, was gay. Some people knew about it, and privately lots of people wondered about it. Had his then-secret life impacted his objectivity as a congressman? Barney Frank decided to end the secrecy, come out of the closet. Since then other public figures have followed his example. As they became transparent about their sexual preferences, possible conflict of interest issues were put in a new perspective. They largely melted away, became problems in living. And we all have them."

"What are you telling me?"

Harrison returned to his desk chair. He leaned forward and looked Julie in the eye. "A fundamental problem in most conflicts of interest is *transparency*. Or the lack of it. For example, there's no problem in public television's *News Hour* or CBS's *60 Minutes* doing an investigative story on a company that's a major sponsor," he paused, "*if* they disclose the company's sponsorship. That puts the story in a transparent relationship. It's when they don't disclose the relationship, and later we find out, that there's a problem. Did reporters, editors, hold back what they should've disclosed? Transparency, Julie. It's basic. You've taken that step."

"Now read this." He handed her another page. "From a course on the Internet."

In real life, especially at the community level, it is almost impossible to avoid all conflicts of interest. A small town reporter, for example, may cover a city council meeting at which local property taxes are discussed, taxes that may directly affect the reporter. The journalist's job, in that case, is to set aside his own interest and report the issue dispassionately. Jonathan Donley, *Community Journalism Examiner*.

"The valley's a small place. We all have friends. Families. You've heard of six degrees of separation? Here in the valley it's more like two. Your relationship with . . . what's your boyfriend's name?"

"*Former* boyfriend. Ben. Ben Gruber."

"Right . . . Ben."

"Did you live together?"

"No."

"Still, your relationship with him creates a possible conflict of interest because of Ben's employment at Kabot." He looked down at the newspaper on his desk and then looked at Julie. "You've been transparent about Ben. In turn, I'll be transparent about your relationship with the senior editors, colleagues, and the publisher. There's no denying that it presents a degree of risk for the paper. But with transparency, it's a risk we know. One I'm willing to take. That is . . . if you are."

"Yes, I want to do it." Julie wondered if this would mark a new trail for her life.

"Then investigate the explosion. Investigate Kabot. Get the facts. Report them, report *all* the facts. Then connect the dots. Give us as much truth as you can get your hands on."

Julie sat back in her chair. The tension lines that in recent years had etched themselves across her forehead disappeared.

"Later today we'll meet with Bob. I want you to tell Bob about your relationship to Ben and Kabot, make it transparent. Going forward, I want you to keep Bob informed. About your reporting and your personal life if it involves Ben. Keep me informed, too.

"You'll meet with me each morning, 8 AM. I'll review your progress on the Kabot investigation. I'll challenge you. Question every dot you plan to connect. You may come to hate me, but by God, you'll write the facts of the case."

"My mom worked at the plant. Neighbors work there. Do you really feel I can be objective?"

"I want to say yes. But the truth is, I don't know. You don't know either . . . not yet. The question is, do you want to find out? Think about it. If you want to accept the assignment, be here to-morrow morning at eight o'clock."

At 8 AM the following morning, Julie walked into Harrison's office.

Chapter 10

THE NEXT MORNING, AFTER HER MEETING with Harrison, Julie finished her final follow-up article on changes at City Hall after the school fire. She reflected on her interviews with teachers, custodians, students and families around town, city inspectors, lawyers, visits to the school, archive research. The next round of action had already begun. *Chronicle* editorials. Management changes by local officials.

Then Julie clicked on her computer's send command. With a familiar whoosh, the article leapt into cyberspace. "Your message has been sent." She took a deep breath and relaxed.

She appreciated Harrison's later stopping at her desk and saying, "You put a lot of time, energy, and shoe-leather into the series. Good work." A year ago Julie had asked Harrison for assignments to more important, even controversial, stories. He'd counseled, "In time, Julie, in time. No matter how you assess the importance of a story, high to low, small story, big story, each one is a round of practice, getting you ready for the big one that's on its way." Until this morning, the school fire story had been the big one. The Kabot explosion story dwarfed it.

Her phone rang. "Julie Brown."

"Hi Julie, it's Ben."

Ben rarely called during the workday. He and Julie respected the independence of each other's professional lives. Since the explosion and their breakup, they'd been even more distant.

"Can you meet me for dinner at the Capitol Café?"

"Capitol Café? It's pretty pricey. What's the occasion?"

"You'll see. Trust me."

Julie felt apprehensive about accepting the invitation so soon after their breakup. But she decided to treat it as Ben's honest attempt to tell her about something important.

Julie walked the two blocks from the *Chronicle* to the café. The storm had moved on, leaving behind warm, humid, sticky air. Her thoughts meandered from Ben to curiosity about the evening ahead to her just-finished article. How she might have written it differently, perhaps better? Preparation, practice, for the big one to come? She remembered the story of a young violin student, with his violin case tucked under one arm, lost in the streets of downtown Manhattan and late for a lesson with the master violinist, Itzhak Perlman. On Fifth Avenue, in desperation the student stopped a woman and asked, "How do I get to Carnegie Hall?" She first looked at his violin case, and then answered, "Practice, practice, practice."

"Hey Julie, over here!" Julie looked up to see Ben standing beside the restaurant's front door.

They hugged, more as friends than lovers. Julie pushed away as Ben, attempting to keep his arms around her, said, "You feel like a champion runner. Champion reporter, too."

"Champion runner? Once upon a time. Champion reporter? You can hold the flattery, Ben."

They walked into the restaurant. The strident noise of the street disappeared, replaced by the sound system's quiet music, Duke Ellington and his orchestra. The room's cool air bathed her hot skin.

"So, what's up? Why the mysterious phone call?"

He raised a hand. "Everything in due time."

The restaurant, a white-tablecloth establishment, seemed another world to Julie. Known for its delicious and pricey meals, it had a clientele of lawyers, business executives, people who belonged to the country club. The café had a soft pastel decor, a place for quiet conversations. The soft strains of Ellington's "Prelude to a Kiss" floated across the room. In the corner to her right Julie saw a cushioned banquette, empty. In the center of the banquette's table a sign read, "Reserved." Soon they sat there side by side.

"A bottle of your best chardonnay," Ben said to the waiter. He turned to Julie and gave her a big smile. "So much to tell."

In spite of their break, Julie still reflexively thought of Ben as part of her life. "Me, too. Wait 'til you hear what Harrison . . ."

Ben interrupted, as if what he had to say couldn't wait. "Otto Heidrich asked me to meet with him this morning! A fellow who used to work with Dad was there, too. My first anniversary at the plant. Mr. Heidrich congratulated me and told the other fellow I had, in his words, 'A magic pen that turned dark to light.' And, hold on, folks," Ben paused, his eyebrows raised in an expectant look while the waiter poured the wine, "he said I'm being promoted. To assistant director of public relations. And with the promotion comes a nice raise!"

"Promotion? And raise? I'm proud of you!"

Ben flashed a wide smile. "Then, get this. Otto . . ."

"Otto?"

"Otto. No more Mr. Heidrich! Otto is putting me on the team that's managing PR on the explosion! Here's the whole story."

~   ~   ~   ~   ~

Driving to work, Ben listened to a CD of Roger's bicentennial concert. He drove along the route he'd traveled as a child when, on special occasions, his dad would take him to work. Downtown, he passed the Bluebird Diner, small businesses and the Rialto theatre, on its marquee, *Gran Torino*. Then he drove along State Route 18 past chemical plants and across the bridge. Like a gray snowfall, ashes from the fire covered the streets of Academy. A light rain began, darkening the ashes. Rivulets of black water formed below curbs and ran into storm sewers.

He arrived at the plant to find a police car parked near the front gate. Two uniformed officers stood between the gate with two demonstrators, a middle-aged man and woman, each carrying a placard. On one, "Kabot – End MIC." On the other, "Stop poisoning our kids."

At the plant's front gate an older guard waved. "Mornin', Mr. Gruber." He pointed to the demonstrators. "Me and your daddy had to deal with folks like them after Bhopal twenty-five years ago."

Ben smiled and waved. "Guess we've got our work cut out for us. All over again."

He parked in front of a three-story office building, its once-white brick now wearing a covering of ashes on top of industrial grime. In the plant, well behind the administration building, fire-fighters hosed water and chemicals on the still-smoldering ashes of the Desin Unit.

Walking the corridor to his office, Ben passed clusters of employees in animated discussions. He took papers from his brief-case and sat down at his desk. In the center of his desktop was a memo on letterhead stationery: "Otto Heidrich, General Manager, Kabot Agronomy Academy Plant."

The message, handwritten, said, "Ben, please meet with me in my office at 9:30 AM today."

Ben took a legal pad out of a desk drawer. At the top of the first page, he wrote, "Explosion, damage control." He jotted some notes on the pad.

Thirty minutes later Ben walked upstairs to Otto Heidrich's office. He waited near the desk of Mr. Heidrich's administrative assistant, Susan. She seemed a holdover from the 1950s. Middle-aged, never married, dressed in a business suit, a blouse with a high collar, her hair pulled back into a tight bun. Susan motioned for Ben to take a seat near the open door of Mr. Heidrich's inner office.

In the metallic tones of a speaker-phone, a voice came from inside the office. "*Das kann ich nicht glauben*, cannot believe it! *Gott verdammt*, Otto, we expect *kontrolle!*"

Susan rose, gave Ben an apologetic smile, and gently closed the door.

A few minutes later, she stepped inside her boss's office as he said, "*Danke*, Hermann. *Auf wiedersehen*," followed by the thump of a telephone receiver being dropped into its cradle.

"Mr. Gruber's here."

"*Ja*. One minute."

Susan said, "He'll be right with you, Ben."

Ben didn't intend to eavesdrop on the conversation but could not avoid it. Otto said, "I am sorry, John. The explosion has changed everything."

"Otto, I need that . . ."

"You must live with your past, John. I cannot appoint you. Not now. Not ever." After a pause he called, "Susan, please send in Ben."

Otto's office had a minimalist decor. A modern desk, a few chairs around a conference table, on each wall a framed print of an abstract painting, along with many Kabot awards; a lean, even ascetic, modern decor.

Otto Heidrich, stocky, balding, his dark suit a contrast with Ben's business-casual work attire, walked briskly around his desk. He approached Ben with his hand outstretched. With enthusiasm in his German-accented voice, he said, "Good morning, Herr Gruber. Ben!"

Otto turned to the man sitting near his desk. "John, if you want, we can talk more tomorrow. But my decision . . . well, corporate's decision, stands. I am in no position to overturn it."

Delbarton's ruddy face bore a look of disappointment. In his mid-sixties, bald and overweight, he wore khakis. A yellow polo shirt tightly stretched around his middle, above its pocket the Kabot Agronomy logo. He nodded. "You have to do what you have to do."

Otto turned to Ben. "Your first anniversary, Ben. If I may, congratulations!"

"Thank you, sir." Ben laughed. "And good morning."

Otto laughed and waved a hand toward John, "Please say hello to Dr. John Delbarton." He and Ben shook hands.

"Dr. Delbarton now enjoys the luxury of retirement. John, didn't you work with Ben's father?"

"Yes, way back when . . ." he paused as if acknowledging a passing memory, then waved one arm toward the plant, "when all this was Carbide. And Ben's dad and I were younger. Ben, I remember you as a boy. Once in a while your daddy would bring you to work. And earlier, your brother . . . uh . . . Roger. An amazing pianist."

"Thank you, sir. We were proud of Roger. Well, we still are."

"I knew your dad. He was a loyal Carbider." Then he spoke more softly. "Even when the company sold the plant out from under us."

"Dad always said, 'Once a Carbider, always a Carbider.' "

Delbarton's voice again became firm, full bodied. "Right. Once . . . always . . . we were . . . ah, dedicated."

Otto beamed a wide smile. "Like father, like son. For a moment, let us leave aside the tragedy of two days ago. On this special day, Ben, we celebrate your first year with us." He picked up an envelope lying on top of his desk.

"On behalf of Kabot, a small anniversary gift." Otto handed the envelope to Ben. "Promotion to assistant director of public relations!" With vigor, Otto shook Ben's hand. "A modest salary increase will appear in your next paycheck." Nodding toward the envelope, he added, "It's all in there."

Ben beamed a bright smile at the envelope, as if greeting a new person who had joined their group.

"John, this young man is *prachtig*, fantastic. His magic pen turns dark to light."

"Doesn't surprise *me*," Delbarton said.

Otto continued, "And Ben, you're in the graduate program next door at State, am I correct?"

"Yes, sir."

"Your pen will become even more magical!" Otto paused, then in a solicitous tone continued, "I understand your *freundin*," Otto laughed, "forgive me, your girlfriend, works for the *Chronicle*."

"Yes. Though, we're taking a break from each other."

Otto laughed. "Yes, yes, of course. More time for work!" Delbarton and Ben laughed with him.

Then in a tone that signaled serious business, Otto said, "Ben, your first anniversary arrives at a difficult time for our plant. Please, sit." He gestured to the conference table and nodded to Delbarton to join them.

"I am a man of few words, Ben. With the demands of the explosion, we need fresh vision in our approach to community relations, to managing the difficulties we face."

Delbarton added, "That's an understatement."

"In your field, I believe you call it damage *kontrolle*, Ben. We need that, need your skills, to repair, *kontrolle* our damage. And I feel you, Herr Gruber, Ben, can be a great help to us. I would like you to join our explosion public relations team."

"Mr. Heidrich, I . . ."

"Please, call me Otto."

"Uh, Otto . . . I'm honored!"

"In Germany I would say, *Ich habe vertrauen* . . . I have confidence, much confidence, that you can help us clean up Kabot's public face. Will you do that?"

~ ~ ~ ~ ~

Julie knew that the assignment, perhaps more than the promotion, meant a lot to Ben. He'd worked hard for it, tried in his own way to get himself ready for the big one to come; at Kabot, and before that, at the bank. But somewhere deep in Julie's consciousness, a small red warning light flashed.

Ben smiled, "Hey, the credit card companies can stop sending reminders about my credit limits." His face became somber. He spoke slowly. "Honey, I hope that, maybe, maybe, you'll reconsider what you said the other night. Julie, I'll put aside enough to . . . well, if things change between us, maybe to make a down payment on a home. Big enough for us. And for a family."

"A family? That's history, Ben. Not the future."

Ben's face fell. "You never know. Things change." Ben raised his wine glass in a toast. "Here's to Kabot! And us."

Julie raised her glass. "Here's to Kabot."

They sipped their wine.

"What's your news, lady reporter?"

Julie stared at her wine glass, then looked up and said, "Today Harrison asked me to lead the Kabot story, to investigate the explosion."

Ben's face lit up. "A promotion for you, too!"

Julie's red warning light flashed brighter and then began to blink. "I'm not sure you understand . . ."

Ben leaned toward her and put his hand on her arm. "Hey, Miss Reporter, I mean Miss Investigative Reporter, here's your explosion story, start to finish. Pass it on to your team. Kabot had a plant shutdown. Put in new tanks. Then a plant startup. A tank malfunctioned. Boom! File the story. Roll the presses!"

Julie pulled back. "If it were that simple . . ."

"If? That explosion is already yesterday's news. I just saved you a ton of work."

The red light flashed faster, ever brighter. "Ben, it's . . ." Her stomach tightened.

In an excited voice, Ben said, "Hey, it's an ill wind that blows no good. That explosion's an opportunity, for me and for you."

Quietly, Julie said, "I just want to find out, and write, the truth."

Ben waved his hand, "Jules, me and you, we're in the game."

"In the game?" The red light became hot.

Ben's voice rose, "We're players!"

"Players?"

"Sure, you know, like in Major League baseball. We're in the starting lineup. Or at the casinos, we're like high rollers. Players!"

Julie leaned back in the booth. For a moment she stared at Ben. "Are we players on the same team?"

Ben's face fell. He gave her a puzzled look.

Her face sober, and in a voice emphasizing each word, Julie said, "A man died, Ben. You're acting like you won the lottery." Julie had always accepted Ben's ambition, for it paralleled her own. But this?

They sat in silence until Julie ended it. "Let's call it a night. I'm meeting Harrison early in the morning."

"Hey, this is a celebration. We haven't even ordered. . . ."

"Sorry, celebration's over." Julie slid out of the banquette and stood. "Maybe we'll try it another evening."

Walking away, she heard Ben say, "But honey . . . wait, the night's still young."

Outside, darkness had fallen. Not a hint of a breeze. The late air seemed warmer and more humid than when she had walked to the restaurant. And now it carried a slight odor of chlorine. Her walk to the parking lot was hot and sweaty. Julie felt, as her dad used to say, "Clammy. Chlorine clammy." Chemical valley, clammy valley . . . . The words reverberated in her thoughts.

Driving home, Julie reflected on the discussion with Ben. In hindsight, it seemed unreal. Only an hour ago Julie had looked forward to their enjoying a meal, celebrating hopes and dreams, even with their now separate lives. It seemed as if, for each of them, the final pieces in a jigsaw puzzle had fallen into place.

Except she found the last piece of the puzzle didn't fit properly; when she tried to wedge it in, the puzzle cracked.

Chapter 11

JULIE COMPILED HER NOTES AND WROTE about Roger's life many years after the actual events. She pieced together, like a patchwork quilt, fragments of memories. She had talked with Charles, Mary, Ben, and her mom and dad; Roger's friends and classmates. They had guided her entries as she stitched together Roger's story.

On Julie's sixteenth birthday, Mary had asked Julie why she felt compelled to write about Roger's life. "I loved Roger. What happened to him was unfair. In spite of it, he gave so much of himself to me, to all of us. It's a way to keep a little of him with us, and honor him."

~ ~ ~ ~ ~

On a warm day in June 1976, Roger's dad, Charles, his white shirt wrinkled, necktie loosened, left his office. He drove out of the plant parking lot, past the large sign bearing the Union Carbide logo, a blue oval with *Carbide* in white letters, then through the plant's front gate.

The security guard smiled and waved. "Night, Mr. Gruber."

With an effort, Charles returned the smile. "Good night, Norm."

In the car's rear-view mirror, images of the plant's buildings, chemical tanks, and tall smokestacks grew ever smaller. He passed the campus of Vandalia State College. Its lush green stood in sharp contrast to the industrial grays of the Carbide plant and, downstream, mile after mile of more chemical plants. He drove across a bridge spanning the Vandalia River, and soon through downtown South Jackson.

On the car's radio, Barry Manilow sang, "I Write the Songs." Charles' thoughts drifted away from financial ledgers, revenue projections and invoice payments, and toward Mary, Roger and Ben. In a few minutes, all the problems of work would become Carbide's problems.

He drove past the Rialto Theatre, on its marquee *Rocky* and *All the President's Men*. Patriotic bunting festooned the downtown storefronts. Windows displayed signs announcing bicentennial events. One sign announced the Jackson Symphony's Bicentennial Concert, "With guest piano soloist, our own Roger Gruber."

A fellow at work had said to Charles, "Roger's only seven years old? That boy's making a place for himself in music. You gotta be proud."

When he and Mary talked about Roger's future, she often fretted, "What lies ahead for him?"

Charles replied in a confident voice, "Roger will live a full, maybe cautious, but full life. We'll guide him."

Charles drove along the tree-lined streets of South Jackson's hillside residential neighborhoods and then down Oak Street to his home. The radio's music ended. A somber voice announced, "And now for the news. In a Phoenix, Arizona hospital, Don Bolles, investigative reporter for the *Arizona Republic*, lies near death after a bomb exploded beneath his car." Charles turned off the radio.

Entering his driveway, he glanced through tips of branches at the gabled roofline of his home, an old Victorian. Home. His face and shoulders relaxed. Mary called it a safe place in an unsafe world.

Charles entered the front door. "Mary?"

Mary, thirty, attractive, tall, her brown hair in a ponytail, cradled a baby in her arms. She walked into the front hall. "Hey, Charlie." Roger, age seven, thin, pale, his hair neatly combed, walked beside her.

She embraced Charles then looked at the baby. "Give your daddy a smile, Ben."

Charles kissed Ben, then knelt and hugged Roger. "Hey, Rog, how you doin', buddy? Soon as I change clothes, let's go out back and toss a baseball, okay?"

Roger smiled, "Yes!"

"Just be careful," Mary said.

Charles put his hand on Roger's shoulder. "We always are, right, Rog?"

The following morning Charles, Mary and Roger ate breakfast at the kitchen table. For Charles, the usual, cereal, fruit and toast. Mary nibbled toast and bottle-fed Ben. Roger, wearing a t-shirt with the bicentennial logo, spooned small bites from a bowl of Cheerios and stared at his baby brother.

Charles read the the *Chronicle's* page one story: "Elvis coming to town: July 22 concert." He turned to Mary. "Did you see this announcement, the concert?"

"I did." She turned to Roger. "I'll need some help today, Rog."

Charles pointed to the story and said to Mary, "Want to go to the concert?"

Mary kept her eyes on Roger while answering, "Sure. They may already be sold out."

"But Mom, Billy asked me to play baseball. I promised."

"Sweetie, we've been through this a thousand times."

"But Mom . . ."

Charles folded his paper. "Son, now that Ben's arrived, your mom needs help."

Enthusiasm in his voice, Roger said, "Last night you tossed me grounders and hit me some high fly balls. I got most of 'em!"

Charles beamed with pride. "Yep, you're pretty good, Rog. But you know, buddy," Charles said, his face becoming more serious, "we've talked about this many times. You, we, have to be . . . careful."

Roger slumped in his chair.

Mary added in a bright voice full of pride, "And don't forget, Fourth of July's just around the corner. The symphony concert. Practice, honey, practice."

Roger raised a spoon full of milk and cereal above his bowl, then slowly turned it and watched the milk drip into the bowl. "Mom, I can play 'Stars and Stripes' in my sleep."

"What about 'Rhapsody in Blue'?"

In a voice of resignation, Roger replied, "Okay."

Charles gave Roger a stern gaze. "I know it's tough, Rog. But we all have to play the hand life deals us." His gaze softened. "Remember last week, that little cut on your arm?"

"Uh-huh."

"Seemed like the bleeding would never stop. Then that bruise . . ." Charles pointed to a large purple-blue splotch on Roger's thigh.

"I ran into a table."

"For most people, it would be a little thing, son. But for you, little things become big. That makes them big for your mom and me, too."

Mary added, "Remember what Dr. Bennett said. You've got a condition. . . ."

Roger gazed at a spot on the floor. "I know, Mom. I'm a bleeder."

"Honey, it's not your fault. You were born a hemophiliac— your blood's missing an ingredient. It doesn't clot the same as other folks' blood." She leaned over and gave Roger a hug. "But if you take your medicine, and you're careful, you can do most anything."

"But not baseball, huh?"

Charles put his paper aside. "Rog, there's not a seven-year-old in town, not in the Vandalia Valley, maybe the state, who plays piano as well as you. You have a gift, son. We're proud of you."

He looked at his wristwatch. "Well, Carbide's waitin'. The plant won't run itself. Gotta wrap up our monthly financials today." Charles stood, began to walk away, and then stopped and turned to Mary. "Forgot to tell you, honey, they asked me to look over financial reports from Bhopal."

"In India?"

"Right. You remember, our sister plant. They make Desin, the same pesticide we produce here. We're knocking boll weevils outta cotton fields down south. They're knockin' 'em outta cotton fields in China and Egypt. And till the drought in India, they knocked those critters outta the fields there, too. The Bhopal plant's been going through some rough times. I gotta check on sister's financial health."

Charles stood, kissed Mary, gave Ben's arm a light squeeze, and then hugged Roger.

"Bye, Charlie. Love you."

"Love you, too."

"Bye, Dad."

"Bye, Rog. I love you, big guy. Listen to your mom. Practice for that concert." He turned to Mary. "Call me after Doc Bennett checks Roger. See y'all tonight."

Chapter 12

HARRISON STOPPED BY JULIE'S WORKSPACE at the *Chronicle*. "Making progress . . .?"

"Mmm . . . I think so. What I'm learning is unsettling. Do you know Kabot's history?"

For an instant he looked like an eighth grader facing a pop quiz in history class. "Some of it."

"I'm learning things about Kabot I don't much care to write about." Julie hesitated and mentally ran through the many ways she'd rehearsed what she needed to say. She mustered her courage and blurted out, "I'm not sure I'm the right person to do this story."

Harrison stepped inside her work space. "Any particular reason?"

Already Julie had made discoveries of, if not company secrets, little known facts. Facts that Kabot's PR machine—with Ben's help, she assumed—wanted to keep as far as possible from the public. "I'm uncovering the dark side of the plant and the corporation."

The gaze of Harrison's gray eyes bored into her. He waited nearly a full minute before he spoke. In a near whisper, he said, "Julie, two men died. We could've had another Bhopal. Right here. In the Vandalia Valley." His voice became louder. "Next time, that disaster might actually happen. What you write could help prevent it. Do the right thing. Keep digging, writing. Show me, show all of us, what you're made of." He walked away.

Later, when Julie described her conversation with Harrison to her friend Harriet, she said, "Dammit, I know what I'm made of." Then later she wondered if she knew the full answer, the whole truth.

A few minutes later Harrison returned. He leaned into Julie's workspace. "Forgot to tell you, the chief called a meeting of senior staff for 10:30 in the conference room. I'd like you to join us. OK?"

She sat up. "Uh, sure." Julie asked herself, *Me? With the editor in chief and senior staff?*

Harrison said, "Hey, relax. Won't take long. We'd like to scope out our coverage of the explosion and give you a chance to update us on where we're headed with this story."

A few minutes before 10:30, Julie walked into the conference room. Around the long oval table sat the senior reporters and editorial staff, seven men and three women, two African-Americans, and most of them at least ten years older than Julie. Harrison, a stack of papers in front of him, sat at the head of the table. Beside him sat Kirby Flemington, a few years older than Harrison, the editor-in-chief. Behind Julie came two more senior reporters, one of them Bob Samuelson, who had counseled her on development of the school fire stories.

Julie stared for a moment at Flemington. Tanned, athletic, and dressed as if he would play golf as soon as the meeting ended. The Flemington family had owned the *Chronicle* since the mid-1930s. "Grandpa bought the paper in a fire sale," he sometimes said with a smile.

Bob, wearing his usual button-down shirts and a narrow necktie, late fifties, had been at the *Chronicle* for thirty years. Julie had learned that his wife died last year and he had a son who lived in Phoenix. She had the impression that Bob drank too much. But then, so did lots of reporters.

Julie took a seat at the table. Bob sat down next to her.

Julie wondered how many times in her decade at the paper she had walked past the conference room. But she'd never attended a meeting there. She sat opposite a wall of windows; the other walls, oak-paneled, had framed photos of events in the valley's and the *Chronicle's* histories: former editors of the paper, campaign visits by presidential candidates, including William Jennings Bryan, Hoover, Roosevelt, Truman, Kennedy, and the first Bush. Jackson Salines salt production; paddlewheel steamboats pushing barges of timber and coal, and a few showboats.

Harrison asked for everyone's attention and then summarized what he knew thus far about the Kabot explosion and fire in the plant's Desin Unit. He concluded with, "Yes, MIC was present and in use in the Desin Unit. Might MIC have been released? I don't know. Anybody know?" No one did.

"One man is dead, another in critical condition," Harrison said. "Burns over 80% of his body. Ten employees hospitalized at Jackson Area Medical Center. Two are still there but expected to be released today or tomorrow."

Harrison handed out copies of a single-page document. "Look this over." He paused and looked around the table. "An editorial we're developing on how the chemical industry, including Kabot, has failed to police itself. So-called watchdog agencies, state and federal, haven't stepped in. If you have suggestions, send them to me by 2 PM this afternoon."

Around the table people nodded and a few muttered, "Okay, sure, will do." Bob Samuelson said, "We leave editorials to you guys."

"Two more things. First, Julie Brown," he waved one hand toward her, "will be working with our senior staff, attending meetings." He laughed, "Who knows, Julie, you may want to join us."

Julie sat up, her back suddenly rigid and straight. She laughed, "You may not want me."

"Julie will work with Bob on the Kabot explosion. I've asked her to take the lead on an in-depth Kabot story. I want you to work with Julie and Bob."

Around the table, heads turned toward Julie and nodded. A woman and a couple of men offered lukewarm congratulations.

Harrison did a slow turn, gazing around the table, taking a moment to look at each person. Then, in the voice of a disappointed dad speaking to a teenager, Harrison said, "I trust your support will be more enthusiastic."

Kevin, a member of the editorial staff, said, "Harrison, Julie's personal life is none of my business. But doesn't she date a Kabot manager? Is there a conflict of interest?"

"Thanks for asking about that. I meant to bring it up. Yes, her former boyfriend, underscore *former*, works there. They used to be a couple. They're not anymore. Julie has been candid and transparent about it with me. They haven't lived together. They're no longer dating. I believe she has what it takes to lead the development of the story. Along with Bob, I'll vet her work. Every morning." He paused. "I repeat, the Kabot explosion: Julie will investigate. Write an in-depth story." Then in a voice resembling a military commander issuing an order, he said, "Work with her."

Kirby Flemington beamed a smile and said, "Welcome, Julie."

Around the table, many people spoke at once. "Thanks for the clarification. Good luck, Julie. Okay. Let me know if I can help."

"Now," Harrison said, "back to Kabot. My second point. Since the explosion, we've had a blizzard of press releases from Kabot. Every public statement they've made? Every press release?" He again paused, and like a searchlight, passed his steely gaze around the table. He held it for a moment on Julie. "I'll bet you ten to one they're hedging the truth. Their publicity reads like Spin City." Another pause. "No takers?"

Around the table people closed their notebooks as if the meeting had ended. People stood and walked out the door.

Did she miss something? Julie stood to leave.

Harrison remained seated. "Julie, stick around for a minute?"

Kirby said, "See you later. Go get 'em, Harrison. You too, Julie."

Julie sat down. Harrison slid a photo across the table to Julie: a man in his late sixties, balding, overweight. "This is Dr. John Delbarton. He's a retired Carbide executive. He was a key executive in the management of the Bhopal plant prior to the disaster. He lives in Jackson. Talk with him."

Harrison and Julie walked out the door. He said, "By the way, there's a meeting of the citizens group, End MIC, tonight. At Vandalia State. Check the time. I think it's in the Student Union."

"I'll be there."

Chapter 13

JULY 4, 1976—Light breezes of warm air drifted through the valley. In Jackson, the sounds of the city, so strident during the bright sun of the day, became muted beneath a golden sunset, then the soft pastels of dusk. As dusk deepened, through the windows of office buildings in downtown Jackson interior lights glowed red, white and blue. A banner spanned the width of the First National Bank building: "America—our first 200 years!"

Along Vandalia Boulevard, closed to traffic, hundreds of pedestrians walked to the amphitheater, newly constructed for this special celebration. The amphitheater nestled between the river and downtown.

Onstage the musicians of the Jackson Community Orchestra warmed up. Wearing white blouses and shirts and dark slacks, the musicians played single notes, held them for long intervals, then moved into trills and arpeggios; a cacophony of sounds waiting for the conductor and musical scores that would transform their efforts into orchestral harmony. Above the stage hung red, white, and blue bunting and a wide banner, "1776 - 1976."

The first chair violinist, the concertmistress, stood. She played and held a single note. The musicians followed her lead, each of them playing and holding that note, stopping, making small tuning adjustments, starting again. Then she sat down. But for the distant sounds of traffic, a quiet fell over the musicians and the audience. Waves created by a passing tugboat and barge lapped rhythmically against the shore.

Applause rippled through the audience as the conductor walked to center stage. She mounted a low rise dais, nodded to the audience and then turned to the orchestra and raised her baton. With the crisp movements of a drill team, musicians raised their instruments. The audience stood as "The Star Spangled Banner" echoed through downtown and across the river.

The orchestra played selections from Aaron Copland's *Appalachian Spring*. Then the conductor turned to the audience. "For two hundred years our nation has lived a dream called America. Seven years ago, our nation had achieved an age of one hundred and ninety three. That's the year our soloist, Roger Gruber, was born. By age two he was plunking notes on a toy piano. A year later he graduated to his family's piano. One more year and he began to stun his family with renditions of recordings he had heard on his family's hi-fi. He has gone on to astound his teachers, and all of us, with his amazing talent. Tonight as we celebrate our nation, we're proud to honor our young soloist, Roger Gruber, already a legend in the Vandalia Valley. The orchestra and Roger will play George Gershwin's very American composition, 'Rhapsody in Blue.' " Then with a wide smile, her arms wide, "Please welcome our guest soloist, Roger Gruber."

Applause echoed through downtown Jackson. Roger, coatless, white shirt, walked to the piano at center stage. The conductor stepped off the podium and shook his hand. A moment later, the grand piano loomed over Roger, poised and erect on the piano bench. Viewed against the large instrument, he appeared small, even inconsequential.

The conductor raised her arms. Her right hand held the baton high, ready. Silence fell across the amphitheater; the audience, ready. The musicians raised their instruments, ready. With a small flourish of the baton, the conductor pointed the baton at the clarinetist, who answered with the plaintive opening call of "Rhapsody in Blue." A long moment later, the orchestra leapt into the composition's powerful rhythms, trumpets and trombones blaring, followed by a suspenseful pause. Then Roger began to play. His notes rolled up the keyboard then leaped into the depth and energy of the piece. His solos, electric and bold, then, like his diminutive physical presence, a near whisper against lilting strings and roaring brass. Roger's hands seemed to belong to a world apart. His solos rose over the orchestra and then, like an ethereal spirit, enveloped the audience.

At the end of the finale's climactic burst, for the briefest of moments, silence. Roger, the conductor, musicians, and audience seemed locked in place by the final note of "Rhapsody in Blue." The conductor lowered her arms. Roger and the musicians relaxed. The audience erupted in applause that became a standing ovation. "Bravo, bravo," rose above hundreds of vigorously clapping hands; an emotional thank you for Roger's gift.

In the years to follow, the Gruber and Brown families played the concert's audio and video recordings countless times, each time recreating, reliving, the magic of the concert and Roger's performance. The concert's sounds, colors, and images became indelibly etched in Julie's thoughts, the memories she created. So real, Julie felt that she'd been there.

For her, the repeated renderings of those powerful moments created, in the good times, a place of tranquility, a place to visit. A place to recall and enjoy family stories, collective memories of that night. In times of trouble, the concert became Julie's refuge, a quiet and personal shelter in place.

Chapter 14

ACADEMY, WV, SEPTEMBER 18, 2008—The *Chronicle* had carried a brief news item announcing a meeting that evening of the citizens' group End MIC in the student union at Vandalia State University.

That evening Julie Brown entered a room jammed with local residents. Many wore work clothes, men in khaki shirts and blue jeans, women in faded cotton slacks and blouses.

Julie stood near the entrance. The man in the photo walked down the corridor to the auditorium. As he neared the entrance, she approached him. "Dr. Delbarton?"

"Yes?"

Julie extended her hand. "I'm Julie Gruber."

Delbarton hesitated and gave Julie a puzzled look. Then he smiled and shook her hand. "Right, the *Chronicle.* I read your articles on the school fire. The fire inspections. Nice work. School kids need an advocate like you."

"Thank you." Julie paused and then said, "Dr. Delbarton, I'm writing an article on Kabot. Could we find a time when I could talk with you?"

He appeared surprised. "We can talk now."

Julie waved one hand at the crowd gathering in the auditorium. "I'd like a place where we can speak privately. And, if you have time, speak at length."

He laughed. "I should meet with an investigative reporter?"

Julie didn't laugh. "I'm just a reporter. I'd like to learn about the Academy plant. Carbide and Kabot."

"And if you turn up some dirt, I'll find myself in the paper, won't I? And maybe in court."

Julie stiffened. "Are you worried I may be another Erin Brockovich?"

"Uh . . . no offense intended, Miss Brown."

"None taken. Please, call me Julie."

He smiled, "And I'm John."

Julie smiled and tried to look inviting, "Can you find a time to meet with me?"

"Well . . . I guess I can. Julie, do you know Brownie's?"

~   ~   ~   ~   ~

The next day, shortly after 1 PM, Julie parked in front of Brownie's Diner. The front of the diner resembled a railway dining car with its rounded and shiny aluminum exterior, windows across its wide front. A large rectangular building had been erected behind it.

Inside the diner, she walked past the old lunch counter and toward the larger back section with its tables and booths. On the walls hung autographed pictures of long-gone sports figures, most of them local. A few stars from baseball's past, including Cincinnati's Ted Kluszewski, the Cardinals' Stan Musial, and in an ornate frame, Boston's Ted Williams; politicians, too, senators, and a couple of governors; Presidents Franklin Roosevelt and John Kennedy. On the shelves in a glass case, bowling and softball trophies won by Brownie's teams.

Behind the cash register hung a photo of the restaurant's founder, Brownie, who had passed away twenty years ago. In the photo he wore the cap of the baseball team he idolized, the St. Louis Browns. To the right of the photo, a glass case housed an official replica of the 1944 National League pennant, the only championship the team ever won. Julie recalled her dad talking about Brownie and his stories of the Browns' rise from a last place finish in 1943 to pennant winner in 1944. "And they did it with the league's lowest team-batting average," he said. "They took risks. They stretched singles into doubles. Led the league in stolen bases. Never passed up a chance to score. That's the way to live. Go after what you want!"

In a back booth sat John Delbarton, in a tan sport-coat and green polo shirt. His face looked more florid than when they'd first met. "Here, Julie," he said, waving.

Beside the booth stood a middle-aged, wiry waitress, her plucked eyebrows replaced by painted thin arcs, as if she'd asked a question and expected an answer. She wore a tan blouse with "Helen" stitched above its left pocket. Helen made a comment to the Kabot man, and they laughed.

Julie joined Delbarton in the booth. She removed photos and papers from her backpack and stacked them on the table. Today's edition of the *Chronicle* lay in front of Delbarton on the booth's tabletop.

Helen served them coffee. She winked and nodded. Delbarton removed a flask from his coat pocket and added whiskey to his coffee. He looked across the booth at Julie and said, "Add some spice?"

Shaking her head no, Julie said, "Thanks for taking time to meet with me."

Delbarton laughed. "I hope I don't read about myself in a *Chronicle* exposé."

Julie stared at him for a moment and then said, "I protect my sources, Dr. Delbarton. No exceptions."

He frowned in a look of disbelief. "None?"

"After the school fire stories, the mayor leaned hard on the *Chronicle*. His people leaned on me to name sources. People who'd given me insider information. I didn't, the *Chronicle* didn't. No names. No exceptions, Dr. Delbarton."

He relaxed and smiled. "OK, I hear you."

"Dr. Delbarton, when . . ."

Delbarton interrupted her. "I'll try this one more time. Please, Julie, I prefer to be called John."

Julie smiled. "Sorry. Thanks. Sometimes I get carried away. John it is. John, I'd like to start with your Carbide years."

"Sure. Fire away."

"When you were at Carbide, you knew about MIC, about Bhopal?"

"Knew about?" Delbarton looked away. "Everyone knew, still knows, about MIC." He looked her in the eye. "Julie, I was in charge of the Bhopal plant."

"You were . . .?"

"The plant had an on-site manager in Bhopal. He reported to me. Within the corporation, I was responsible."

Julie sat back in the booth. "I didn't know that."

"When it happened, I was here . . . at home. Getting ready to shut down the Bhopal plant. But I suppose you'd have no way of knowing. And what I'll tell you was never reported. Truth is, the people over there failed to . . ."

"*You*? I never heard your name associated with . . ."

Delbarton gave a quick laugh. "To the world Kabot yelled, *Sabotage!* A disgruntled employee was to blame. But lemme ask you this. Ever wonder why that so-called guilty employee was never named? Never prosecuted?"

"But why blame you?"

"Happened on my watch. Lots easier to blame me, then shuffle me off to a back room. Keep me, excuse my French, inside the tent pissing out. Outside the tent, I might piss in. I could be dangerous. In a few words, I knew too much.

"After Bhopal, *everybody* talked about our moral responsibility." A sardonic laugh. "It felt like we were pinned in a vise . . . on one side, the law. On the other side, the balance sheet. Those jaws squeezed tight. Moral *res-pon-si-bility.* As if talking about it would set us free."

"And?"

"Nothing but rhetoric. Bottom line? We had to do two things." Delbarton jabbed his forefinger on the table. "One, protect profits." Then he spoke louder, jabbing his forefinger again. "Two, stay out of jail. Not sure which was harder."

Julie began to speak, stopped, and stared at Delbarton.

"The Bhopal plant was our Academy plant's sister. We designed it, we built it, we developed the operations, we trained the people. For many years, Bhopal's business was strong and profitable. Then in 1984 came the Indian drought. We, I, recommended to corporate that they shut down operations at Bhopal. Close the plant, at least in the short term. Here's what happened."

Chapter 15

J ULIE MADE NOTES WHILE DELBARTON TALKED. She wrote fast, attempting to capture detail and a sense of being present in the Bhopal discussions at Carbide's Academy plant.

~ ~ ~ ~ ~

Dr. John Delbarton, then in his early forties, ruddy face, receding hairline, white shirt and necktie, chaired a meeting of plant executives, including Ben's dad, Charles. The eight men, from early to late middle age, sat around a rectangular table. An Indian executive, Raju, sat to the immediate right of Dr. Delbarton.

An executive at the far end of the table asked, "Dr. Delbarton, that corporate memo about our plant, Bhopal. Are we going to . . . ?"

Delbarton held up one hand. "Yes, yes, but hold on . . . first I want to hear from . . . Charles, would you summarize your financial analysis?"

Charles distributed a report to each member of the group. "Well, as all of you probably know, the drought in India has pretty much dried up our pesticide business."

An executive added, "And our bonuses." Laughter rippled around the table.

Charles continued, "The details are in the report. My conclusion? Bottom line, it doesn't make financial sense to keep the Bhopal plant running. That is, unless . . ."

Delbarton interrupted, "They get a good rain?"

Laughter, except for Charles and Raju.

"Unless, somehow, sales increase. And yes, without sustained rainfall, and even now it may be too late, that looks unlikely. The

Bhopal plant has already laid off over 300 workers. They're waiting on our go-ahead to put the place in mothballs. That's probably the right . . ."

"Perhaps," Raju said, his voice carrying a mixture of British and Indian dialects, "for the company. But I worry that . . . you must understand, to many of us, each worker, even the plant, has a spirit, what you call a soul."

The men sat in silence.

Delbarton ended it. "They have souls?" He laughed. "So do our shareholders, Raju." After a pause he said, "Now, about the . . . the closing. Take it step by step. First, follow up on plant safety."

An executive said, "The boys in India are checking it out. Some systems are already primed to shut down. Everything should be fine."

"*Should be?*" Delbarton looked around the table, his gaze connecting with each man. "Think carefully about this. Three years ago, at the Bhopal plant, a phosgene leak sent twenty-four workers to the hospital. One month later they had a leak of methyl isocyanate —MIC. I don't need to tell you about its toxicity. Safety in Bhopal's been a problem, one I'll be glad to get rid of."

"Pardon my grammar," the executive seated beside Charles said, "but our record here ain't so hot either."

The door opened. Rose, matronly, in a white food service uniform and hairnet, entered. She pushed a cart with carafes of coffee, a plate of rolls, and a steam tray. "Thought you boys might get hungry."

"What do you have for us, Rose?" Delbarton asked.

"Meatballs and my special rolls."

Two of the executives whispered to each other. One of them laughed.

"I heard that," Rose said. "Raju's food is special. The beef's for you boys." She pointed to one end of the steam tray. "Raju, that's lamb; it's just for you."

Leaving the room, Rose flung a look of disapproval at the executive who had laughed.

In the moment of silence that followed, Delbarton opened a file and read. He gave a nonchalant wave toward the food cart and muttered, "If you're hungry, help yourself."

Men walked to the cart, poured coffee, and put rolls on small plates.

When everyone had returned to the table, Delbarton held up a multi-page document. "Anybody hear about this report? From corporate. They're worried about us and . . ." he read from the document, ". . . I quote, 'a runaway reaction that could cause a catastrophic failure of the Academy plant's MIC storage tanks.' Do any of you know who wrote this?"

"Probably one of that bunch that's supportin' Mondale," an executive said. Around the table executives laughed.

Delbarton raised his right hand, "Okay . . . about the Bhopal closing, I'll talk to corporate. Raju, you talk to the boys in Bhopal. Make *damn sure* they can get her production-ready if and when needed in the future."

"I shall."

"And everybody, when you break the news to folks down the hall, remember, they helped build the Bhopal plant, trained the people. She's our sister plant. Go easy."

Picking up notebooks and files, the men muttered, "Sure. Okay. Understand." The meeting ended.

~   ~   ~   ~   ~

Delbarton sipped his drink then said, "The two most dangerous times in a plant's operation," he paused then spoke slowly, "are start-up and shut-down. Rare events. Once a plant is up and running, the daily life of processing operations becomes routine. But getting there, the start-up, is not routine. And neither is a shut-down."

"It's not like you practice at it," Julie said.

"That's right. Usually shut-downs happen no more than once a year. There are manuals and set procedures that are supposed to be used."

"I never heard your name associated with Bhopal."

"To the outside world, Carbide blamed a disgruntled employee. The company tossed out that explanation to the public. And with the media it stuck. But let's get serious: there's no way one employee could've carried out such a complex operation. It was a whole system. Poorly maintained. Repairs not made. All the things my people said they had done, but had not. I should've checked on them more closely, I should've trusted them less. But I had never studied management. I studied chemical engineering. I was an engineer, not a manager."

Chapter 16

DELBARTON BEGAN TO DESCRIBE TO JULIE events of the Bhopal disaster. He quickly stopped and asked, "Do you have a recorder with you?"

"Yes." She reached into her backpack and placed a small digital recorder on the table.

"I recommend you use it. Otherwise you'll never capture everything I'm going to tell you."

Julie turned on the recorder, and Delbarton told the story of the Bhopal disaster.

~ ~ ~ ~ ~

BHOPAL, INDIA. DECEMBER 3, 1984: The city of Bhopal had a population of more than one million people. In the days leading up to the disaster, all over the city signs proclaimed the religious festival of Ishtema. Decorations lined the streets and gave a new life to the city. Street vendors sold food and flowers. Pilgrims arrived from distant towns. Crowds celebrated, people worshipped. Bhopal brimmed with color, music, laughter, and prayer.

Night fell. The streets emptied of all but the flowers and festive litter of the day's celebration. The homes and shanties of the city darkened. In the center of downtown, the hands of an ornate gilded age clock showed five minutes past midnight.

Just a few yards outside the front gate, shanty neighborhoods abutted, crowded, the tall chain link fence around the plant. Though smaller, the plant was a near copy of the Carbide plant in Academy, West Virginia.

The plant sat idle, its front gate partially open. On a flagpole near the central building's front entrance, the flag of India and the corporate flag of UCIL, Union Carbide India Limited, fluttered in a light northwesterly breeze. The mercury vapor lamps illuminated the flags and the plant's headquarters building, along with chemical tanks, connecting conduits and pipes, smoke stacks, and parking lots.

Beyond the plant's central building lay smaller buildings connected to lattices of pipes, storage tanks, vents, and smokestacks. A worker walked beneath a maze of complex plumbing. He paused to read a gauge and record a measurement. He moved on, repeatedly pausing and recording measurements.

From a building deep in the maze of pipes and tanks, plumes of opaque gas began to flow from doors, windows, vents. The gas hovered along the ground. A worker ran out a side door of the building and into the path of the gas. He fell, twitched, and then lay motionless, quickly dead.

The wail of the plant's emergency siren rose and, halfway to its peak, stopped, flattened, and then tapered to a low moan before falling quiet.

Cries erupted from the headquarters building. Workers in khaki uniforms ran out the main entrance screaming, in a mixture of Indian and English, *"Help! Madada! Run! Calane! HELP!"*

Abruptly they stopped, looked at the flags, and ran into the wind. Their cries grew ever louder as they ran through the plant's front gate, then into the streets of shanty neighborhoods surrounding the plant. Those cries of alarm gave the city of Bhopal its lone warning of the approaching danger.

Like a sinister spirit, the gas drifted through the plant's fence. A goat grazing near the fence collapsed, then lay still. The gas rolled into the shanties of surrounding neighborhoods

People awakened coughing, their throats and eyes ablaze. Frantically they rubbed their eyes, screamed in pain, gasped for breath. Parents lifted children from their beds and carried them into the streets. There they found people, like themselves, crying, screaming, eyes burning, coughing. At first a few, then in ever larger numbers, people fell to the pavement, writhing for a moment, then stilled by death.

In shanties and homes, people lay askew in beds and on floors. Others sat in living rooms, their now sightless eyes aimed at television sets. A comedian's voice paused, an audience laughed, late night television as usual, except would-be watchers by the hundreds could no longer see and enjoy the show.

Confused and frightened, residents ran through the streets, desperate to outrun their invisible attacker. Coughs and screams filled the air. People fell in their tracks.

As homes emptied, crowds in the streets grew larger. Crying and screaming in pain, people jogged then ran, gaining momentum, moving away from the plant. The crowd grew larger, ran faster, and became a screaming stampede, pushing aside children and the elderly. As people fell, the crowd trampled them to death.

Auto and truck drivers lost consciousness. Without pilots, their vehicles drove into the crowd, crushing fallen victims before crashing into buildings. Cars pinned people against walls. Trucks skewered others.

The crowd numbered in the thousands. People raced to stay ahead of the gas. Many lost the race.

Hours later the first rays of sunlight illuminated streets and yards littered with the dead and dying. Around the world, television and radio newscasts told viewers and listeners, "In Bhopal, India, shortly after midnight, poison gas from a Union Carbide chemical plant swept through the city, killing residents in its path. The number of dead is as yet unknown . . . ."

Rescue workers moved among victims. They placed stethoscopes against chests, listened, signaled to one of the stretcher-bearing teams behind them, and moved to the next body. Behind them, teams of stretcher-bearers carried survivors to ambulances. A large number of teams carried the dead to flatbed trucks.

A rescue worker hovered over the body of a young girl. He placed a stethoscope on her chest, signaled to a rescue team, then yelled for help. A white-coated medic pushed the worker aside and began mouth-to-mouth resuscitation. He bolted into a stiff upright position, gasped, and reeled backward. His limbs gave a final convulsive jerk, then movement ceased.

The following day at the Bhopal airport a private jet landed. Carbide executives, led by CEO Warren Anderson, stepped off the plane. Anderson, tall and athletic, gray hair, in his sixties, led the group into the airport terminal.

A crowd of reporters met them. "Mr. Anderson, what happened at the plant? How will Carbide respond? Who is at fault? How many people have died?"

Anderson and the executives, now with a police escort, pushed through the reporters and a stunned, weeping, and angry crowd.

Chapter 17

IN A LARGE OPEN FIELD BEHIND A TEMPORARY FENCE, hastily erected pole tents extended to the horizon. Beneath the tents lay bodies neatly placed in rows.

Already, along the makeshift fence lay hundreds of pictures, all sizes, framed and unframed. Bhopal's victims: men, women, boys and girls; families, portraits, informal snapshots. Lives snuffed out. Sprays of flowers punctuated the pictures. The number of pictures and the intensity of putrid odors grew. The number of dead soared into the thousands.

With security guards surrounding him, Anderson arrived at the site. In the distance ambulances and flatbed trucks rolled in, bringing more bodies. On the distant horizon, workers erected new tents and added rows of corpses. In the hot sun, a plume of the stench of death rose from the tents. It hovered over the field of bodies.

At the edge of the field, Anderson turned to an Indian official. "Safe to go in?" The official nodded yes. Anderson strapped a cloth mask over his mouth and nose and then walked into the tents and among the bodies. He talked quietly with officials. One of Anderson's aides turned his head and vomited.

Ahead of Anderson, beneath one of the tents, a little girl, about age six, dressed in pink pajamas, lay still in a row of corpses. Then her fingers twitched and her eyes opened. She sat up and looked around, dazed. She shook her head back and forth, then shrieked, "Aiieee, aiieee!!" Medics, one carrying a portable oxygen mask and tank, ran to her.

A senior officer in the Bhopal police, papers in his hand, approached Anderson.

"Mr. Warren Anderson?"

Anderson nodded yes and remained silent.

"I have a warrant for your arrest."

Anderson recoiled. "On what charge?"

The officer slowly waved his right arm toward rows of bodies. "What is your name for this?"

Anderson stared at the officer but said nothing.

"Sir, you are charged under criminal sections of our law with culpable homicide, grievous assault, assault, and killing and poisoning of animals." The officer paused and then continued, "Personally, I call it the murder of my daughter."

Chapter 18

ONE DAY LATER, IN A CONFERENCE ROOM in UCIL Bhopal's administration building, executives sat around a rectangular table. The room's dust and sparse furnishings reflected months of disuse. Warren Anderson sat at the head of the table.

Outside UCIL's front gate, a crowd gathered. Weeping people screamed and made threatening gestures toward the building. In a rhythmic cadence they chanted, " Murd-erers! Jus-tice! Anderson, murd-erer!" Then, "Hear us, Car-bide, hear us, Car-bide . . . ."

Anderson glanced out the window. He turned to the executives. "We're not deaf . . . and we have a business to run. Now, what's the legal situation?"

Outside the fence surrounding the plant, the crowd's chanting became ever louder, soon escalating to a roar. The crowd pushed against the closed front gate. The force of the crowd slowly unified into the undulations of a single body that pushed in powerful waves against the gate. Each wave rocked the gate in ever larger swings, back and forth, back and forth, until it fell into the plant parking lot. In a mixture of cheers, jeers, and screams, the crowd rushed into the plant's campus.

In the conference room, executives watched the menacing crowd approach the main building. They made their way to the building's rear entrance where limousines waited, engines running. As the crowd entered the plant's main building, the limousines sped away.

At the Bhopal airport the limousines drove onto the tarmac and stopped next to Carbide's twin-engine jet. Like a frightened animal ready to leap to safety, the jet's engines emitted high and deafening screams. Anderson and the executives walked briskly to the waiting plane.

In the airport terminal, a large and angry crowd of demonstrators overwhelmed security guards, forced open the departure gate, and ran toward the plane.

The executives rushed up the plane's air-stairs. At the moment the crowd reached the plane, the stairs rose and folded into the fuselage. The door closed.

With police cars clearing a path through the crowd, the plane rolled to the end of the runway, then turned. The pilot opened the throttle, revving the engines while brakes and wing flaps held the craft in place. In a surge of power and sound, the plane hurtled down the runway.

By then the crowd had massed on the runway, waving and yelling defiantly, as if they could stop the approaching plane. The jet picked up speed, rolling ever nearer to the crowd. People dove to the tarmac seconds before the jet rose over them. The jet's engines assaulted the crowd with an earsplitting blast.

Immediately upon his return to the United States, Warren Anderson accepted an invitation to address a joint assembly of the U.S. Senate and House of Representatives. He concluded his brief speech with a pledge to renew Carbide's, and the industry's, commitment to safety, ". . . to ensure that there will never be another Bhopal. *Never!*"

Members of Congress burst into loud and sustained applause. Then as one body, they rose to give Anderson a standing ovation.

In the coming days, around the world newspaper headlines carried an ever darker story: "Bhopal deaths, 5,000 and rising." Indian public health officials soon estimated the total number of deaths as even higher.

In later months, these news headlines appeared around the world: "Indian court indicts Carbide CEO." Then, "India presses the United States for extradition of Carbide's Anderson."

Extradition never occurred.

Anderson soon retired as CEO of Carbide. The efforts of prosecutors in India and America slowed and then eventually ended.

Anderson disappeared from public view. Years later Greenpeace located him living comfortably in his gated estates in Florida and on Long Island.

Chapter 19

DELBARTON SAID, "AFTER THE BHOPAL DISASTER, as I told you earlier, Carbide didn't know whether to fire me or take a chance on me to stay on board, accept my paychecks, and keep quiet."

Julie scribbled some notes. "And you stayed on? Kept working at Carbide?

"Yes, even though inside Carbide they hung the disaster around my neck. Top management said 'You should've known this or that.' Should've, should've, should've. As Jack Kennedy said after the Bay of Pigs invasion, 'Success has many makers, failure has but one.'"

Julie's pen fell from her hand to her notepad. "My God, seven months later, after seven months of Carbide's public announcements about system tests, with safety reassurances that it can't happen here . . . it *did* happen here."

Delbarton smiled. "The aldicarb release. Shelter in place. People jammed hospital emergency rooms."

"I was a little kid. Home alone. I hid in a basement closet. I remembered pictures of all those little kids in Bhopal. Children's corpses laid in rows."

In a tone of dismissal, Delbarton said, "Bhopal children. Old people, young people. Dead by the thousands. Not the first time. Won't be the last. What happened reminds me of what's been called *the disappeared*. Julie, was Bhopal different from what happened in the Soviet Union? Nazi Germany? Chile? Argentina? *The disappeared*."

"Those were political . . ."

"You die by the hands of the state, you die by the hands of a corporation. There's a difference?" Delbarton sipped his coffee. "Dead is dead."

A quizzical look on her face, Julie said, "You've lived with Bhopal for nearly twenty-five years." Her words carried an implied question: *How had he done that?*

"Yes. But I've had company." Delbarton patted the flask in his coat pocket. "Twenty-five years? Julie, you have to recognize that in a publicly traded company, memory goes back only three months. To the last quarterly earnings report. Twenty-five years? Let's see, four quarterly reports per year, times twenty-five years. Bhopal was a hundred quarterly reports ago. In the meantime, Carbide sold the company to Kabot. Bhopal? Kabot says they're not responsible."

"So who is responsible?"

"Nobody. Corporate magic. A wave of the balance sheet and presto chango, the problems disappear."

Julie jabbed her pen on her notepad. "But the problems are alive! The illnesses of survivors. And now a new generation of children, Bhopal babies. Birth defects. Illnesses. Deformities."

"Alive? If you call that living."

Softly, Julie asked, "Are you able to sleep at night?"

Helen walked to the booth and poured more coffee. She gave a subtle nod to Delbarton.

He winked at her as he added whiskey to his coffee. "Life goes on."

For a moment they sat in silence. Then Delbarton pointed to the lead story on the front page of the *Chronicle.* "Did you see this?" He read aloud, "Citizens' group seeks Kabot injunction to stop MIC production."

"I wrote it."

"That citizens' bunch has high hopes." Delbarton laughed. "David against Goliath."

"Maybe David will win again."

"After Bhopal, I thought I could, too. But I became a scapegoat. Carbide, and now Kabot, let me hang in the breeze." Delbarton took his flask from his jacket and poured more whiskey into his mug. "The other day I asked Otto Heidrich for an appointment. Nothing fancy. Purely ceremonial. Could I represent Kabot? Say, at a trade show, a conference? Anything! I just wanted to hold my head high. Again. Like the old days. I told him I'd even pay my own expenses."

"Will he let you do it?" The eagerness in her voice surprised Julie. She discovered she had begun to root for John Delbarton.

"He said no." Delbarton sipped his drink. Then, staring at it, he said, "I should've reminded him I know where the company's skeletons are buried."

"John, I want to learn about Kabot. Can you, will you, help me? Point me toward the bodies?"

"Let me give it some thought. Let's meet in a couple of days. Okay?

"Yes, that'll work."

Chapter 20

SOUTH JACKSON, WV, SEPTEMBER 1981—Beneath a cloud-less blue sky, the bright sunlight of autumn intensified the oranges, reds and yellows of the trees in the Grubers' backyard. In the widest part of the yard, two small teams of boys Roger's age played touch football. Roger stood at the line of scrimmage holding a whistle, serving as the game's referee.

Mary walked out of the kitchen to the back porch steps and yelled, "Roger, supper time. Come wash up. Billy, your mom called. She's waiting supper for you."

The boys ended their game. Like two little piles of leaves blown apart by a gust of wind, the teams fragmented. The boys shuffled across the yard to return home. "See ya. Tomorrow? Play again?"

Charles, Mary, Roger and Ben, now four, sat around the dinner table. Heads bowed, the family held hands while Charles said a blessing. He ended it, "And Lord, we give special thanks for Roger's new medicine. We pray it'll help him. Amen."

Mary turned to Roger, "Have some chicken. Potatoes, too, honey."

"Not hungry."

She turned to Charles. "I sure hope that new medicine works."

Charles turned to Roger. "Rog, I know those injections are no fun." He raised his voice. "But that new medicine's gonna work." Mary had told him how Roger's body had reacted to the serum. Nausea, vomiting.

"Shhh . . . I just got Ben to sleep." Mary looked at Ben and then spoke softly to Roger. "Dr. Bennett says the medicine will put a missing ingredient into your blood, honey. Improve clotting, re-duce bruising." She turned to Charles. "Thank goodness Carbide's insurance covers the cost. . . . Do you know how much . . . ?"

"I know, honey, I know."

"Otherwise, what would we . . .? Well, I'd have to go to work . . ."

Roger's head turned back and forth, parent to parent, as if watching the volleys of a tennis match.

"What did Doc Bennett call the new medicine?"

Mary answered, "Z-Factor."

Roger laughed, "Z-Factor-Z, gonna heal me!"

Mary laughed. "This bread's better than your poetry, sweetie." She passed the bread to Roger. "Have some."

"Son, with this new medicine, you'll soon be rough housing with your friends."

Her voice reflecting concern, Mary said, "Honey, he doesn't have to rough house."

"Roger," Charles laughed, "you'll bounce up, be off and run-nin'."

"Charlie, maybe he should take it easy awhile."

"Or maybe not. Right, champ?"

Chapter 21

JACKSON, WV, JULY 1983—With the boys in the back seat, the Grubers drove to Roger's medical appointment in Jackson. Roger's body, too thin for a thirteen-year-old, and pallor contrasted with six-year-old Ben's tanned face and lithe body. During the trip they talked little.

Charles turned on the radio. "Earlier today, in London, President Ronald Reagan became the first American president to address a joint session of Parliament. Afterward President Reagan said . . ."

Mary turned off the radio. "We've got enough to think about."

Charles parked near the main entrance of the Jackson Area Medical Center. A gray sky dulled the modern building's glass and brick walls. The family walked the short distance to the entrance. Holding Ben's hand, Roger shuffled at a slow pace.

After checking in, they sat in the pediatric waiting room. Ben found some comic books and offered one to Roger. He opened it, stared at the first page, and sat in silence. At low volume, the sound system played Donna Summer singing "MacArthur Park."

Mary held Roger's hand. "You're . . . everything's going to be okay, sweetie."

Soon a nurse entered the room. She gave Roger a warm smile and ushered everyone into a consultation room.

"Roger, let's get ready for Dr. Bennett." She pointed to the examining table. "Have a seat up here." She patted the table's sheeted and cushioned top. "Would you take off your shirt?"

Roger removed his shirt and sat on the edge of the table.

The nurse inspected the red rash on Roger's chest. "Okay, let's check your temperature." Roger opened his mouth to accept the thermometer. When, a moment later, she removed the thermometer, Dr. Bennett, his girth filling his white coat, entered the room.

"Morning, everyone." He smiled at Roger and gave his leg a light tap. "Hi, Rog."

The nurse handed Dr. Bennett a folder containing Roger's medical records and charts. He scanned the top pages, then turned to Roger. "How are things going at school?"

They talked for a moment about Roger's seventh grade courses. Then Dr. Bennett said, "Let's take a look at you, pal." He first examined the rash on Roger's chest, and then put his stethoscope on Roger's back. "Okay, Rog, take a few deep breaths. . . . that's it. Good. One more."

Dr. Bennett spoke to Mary. "Any problems with the Z-Factor injections?"

"No problem giving them. One each Sunday and Wednesday. But the side effects—he gets weak and nauseous, sometimes throws up."

"That's a common reaction." Dr. Bennett put his hand on Roger's arm. "Hang in there, buddy. In time, your body will adapt to the injections."

Dr. Bennett asked Mary, "How long has he had the headache and fever?"

"Four . . . no, five days. I thought it was the flu. Then I saw the rash and that dark spot on his ankle."

"Any other symptoms?" Dr. Bennett gently probed the underside of Roger's jaw.

Although Mary spoke to Dr. Bennett, she gazed at Roger. "He hasn't been eating well. I told him, Roger, you're just going to dry up and blow away."

After Dr. Bennett completed Roger's examination, the nurse said, "Come on, boys, let's go have a soft drink. My treat. Your mom and dad can talk with Dr. Bennett." She ushered Roger and Ben to the waiting room.

Dr. Bennett sat down. Mary and Charles leaned forward in their chairs. Dr. Bennett said, "It's too soon to be sure about this, but Roger's symptoms fit an illness showing up around the country. Well, around the world, too. Mostly in Africa."

Mary's body jerked into a stiff, upright position. "Africa? Roger has an African illness? Can you cure this . . . this . . . what is it?"

"First, please keep in mind that I don't know for sure about Roger's diagnosis, if his illness is the same as the African disease. We're still learning about it. We need to do more tests with Roger."

Her voice shrill, Mary asked, "Well, tell us, what *do* you know?"

"In the USA, the disease first began to show up in homosexual men."

"No, no!" Mary grabbed Charles' hand. She began to cry. "My Roger isn't . . . that . . . what you said!"

Dr. Bennett sat up in his chair and spoke in a soft voice. "I know, Mary." He glanced at a medical journal on his desk and then looked at Mary.

"At first the medical articles called it GRID, Gay Related Immune Deficiency. We're not sure why, but in recent months there've been a lot of new cases reported among men who weren't, aren't, gay, many of them hemophilic. This led to a new name for the illness, Acquired Immunodeficiency Syndrome—AIDS. But giving it a new name didn't mean we knew more about it. AIDS appears to stem from a virus, what's known as the human immunodeficiency virus, or HIV. It attacks the immune system. And when the immune system doesn't work right, lots of things go wrong. Often, AIDS develops. We're still learning about the disease."

Mary gasped. Charles put his arm around her.

"We'll do more bloodwork. Roger's symptoms could be from some other cause. An opportunistic infection."

The color drained from Charles' face. He asked, "And in the meantime?"

"The blood tests won't take long. There's a new antibiotic that might help." Dr. Bennett took a prescription pad from the pocket of his white coat. He wrote a prescription, removed it from the pad, and handed the small piece of paper to Mary. "Please call me in a week and let me know if the antibiotic helps. And let's continue with Z-Factor."

Mary stared at the prescription. "Is my son's future on this piece of paper?"

Dr. Bennett patted her hand. "It's a prescription, Mary. No more, no less. If it doesn't help, we'll find a something that does."

"How much time do we have?"

Dr. Bennett declined to answer. Finally he said, "I don't think it's like that."

Chapter 22

SOUTH JACKSON, WV, MARCH 1984—On a bright cool Saturday morning, in front of the Bluebird Diner in downtown South Jackson, Roger, sixteen, thin with purple blotches on his cheeks, sat behind a card table. Ben and Julie, now nine, robust faces reddened by the chilly air, stood beside him. The diner's plate glass window reflected their sharply contrasting images. A light breeze lifted strands of Julie's curly hair.

A sign taped to the front of the table, and an identical sign in the front window of the Bluebird, announced, "Tickets. Bhopal Benefit Concert. 8 PM Tonight. McKinley High Gym." A rectangular sheet of white poster board had been taped from the top to the bottom of the diner's front window. On it, a large thermometer had been drawn. Above the thermometer, "Bhopal Benefit Fund: Goal = $100,000." The red interior of the thermometer stood at $82,000.

Mary turned to Ben and Julie. "There's a pay phone in the diner. If the wind picks up, call me."

She hugged Roger. "Honey, I'll be back in an hour. I don't want you out too long in the cold."

In a near whisper, Roger replied, "I'll be okay."

~ ~ ~ ~ ~

Charles left for work early Monday morning. The liability claims, legal technicalities, and stressful uncertainties growing out of December's Bhopal disaster continued. Each day brought new photos and video footage documenting the escalating tragedy at Bhopal. Bhopal-related events filled his work schedule.

All these demands piled on top of the routine financial management issues of the plant: the reports on the financial health of the business, all the things that, before Bhopal, had been Charles' full time job. In addition, he now had to prepare new reports on the plant's finances in case it had to be sold.

Late one afternoon Mary called to ask Charles to pick up Roger's medicine on the way home. At the end of their conversation she said, "Charlie, the boys and I hardly see you anymore."

"I'm doing the best I can, Mary. I don't like it either. But I've got to do what I've got to do."

Crossing the bridge over the Vandalia River, Charles turned on the radio. "And now for news from around the nation. There is a growing controversy in Kokomo, Indiana, where school officials have banned thirteen-year-old Ryan White, a hemophilic boy who has contracted AIDS, from attending school."

Charles gave a start, as if he'd received a surprise slap on the back. He sat erect and gripped the steering wheel white-knuckle tight.

"School officials are receiving widespread community support. Ryan White's family and civil liberties groups are protesting. . . ."

On the other side of the bridge, he pulled over to the road's shoulder and stopped.

"At a press conference yesterday, when asked about the Ryan White case, President Reagan had this to say." Then Reagan's rich baritone voice said, "Medicine has not come forth unequivocally and said, this we know for a fact, that it is safe. And until they do, I think we just have to do the best we can with this problem. I can understand both sides of it."

Charles leaned his forehead against the top of the steering wheel. "Dear God . . ."

Chapter 23

TWO DAYS LATER JULIE MET JOHN DELBARTON at Brownie's. They walked to the back booth where they had met on their last visit.

Delbarton gazed at Julie for a moment. "There's a lot to tell. Some of it not very pretty." He looked away for a long moment. "I was going to say, some of it has little to do with the explosion." He shrugged. "At least on the surface it doesn't. But when you look a little deeper, maybe everything that touches the history of Carbide has to do with the explosion."

Julie said, "We reported in today's paper that an unnamed Kabot manager said Kabot would rebuild the damaged Desin Unit and go back to MIC-based pesticide production. I'm still amazed by how quickly Kabot made that decision. Almost as if they shrugged and said, 'What else would you expect?' So automatic."

Delbarton smiled. "What's good for Kabot is good for the valley."

"John, I need to learn who I'm dealing with. Please, share what you know. Tell me."

"Okay. Bear with me." Delbarton signaled to Helen and said to Julie, "Brownie's BLT is terrific. Want one?"

"Sure."

He ordered two bacon, lettuce and tomato sandwiches and another round of coffee. "I read somewhere that you lose a year of your life for every pound of bacon you consume." He laughed. "If that's true, I should've died a thousand years ago." Julie laughed with him.

"The plant was built for WW II production of synthetic rubber. Carbide operated it for the government. Then after the war they bought the plant. By then the company was thirty-five or forty years old. In the early 1900s, three small chemical companies had merged into Carbide.

"All that to say, by World War II, Carbide had a platform of management practices in place; a management culture. That's what I want you to understand. They had developed Carbide's ways of doing business. Those ways were solidified, nailed down, during one of their first big projects, the 1930 Hawks Nest hydroelectric project. A dam and a river diverted through a tunnel. At the other end it drove Carbide's electrical turbines. In many ways, the project was a huge success. It produced hydroelectric power, all right. But building it produced a disaster. Over seven hundred, maybe as many as two thousand, men died there. Mostly black. Nobody knows the total number of deaths. Acute silicosis. The deadliest industrial disaster in American history. That's when the Carbide way of managing took hold. Look away from the problems. Cover up."

"My Grandpa Orville worked for Carbide at Hawks Nest," Julie said.

Delbarton sat back and took a long sip of his drink. "Tell me about that."

Chapter 24

DURING HER CHILDHOOD, JULIE RECOUNTED, with her mom and dad both working and her dad often out in the evening on investigations, her grandma often came to visit. Sometimes she stayed overnight, cooked a meal or two. Always spending time with Julie. Memories of the many evenings when her grandma read to her at bedtime remained alive for Julie, special moments.

~ ~ ~ ~ ~

SOUTH JACKSON, WV, OCTOBER 1987—At age eighty-seven, Julie's Grandma Armen retained much of the vibrant appearance and energy of her earlier years. Her once deep black hair, still curly, had become salt and pepper gray and complemented her tan face and dark eyes. One of her smiles, when flashed around a room, still turned heads. But she moved at a slower pace; her energy often flagged by mid-afternoon. Her voice had weakened.

Julie looked forward to Armen's visits. "Grandma, will you read to me tonight?"

One evening, as Armen opened *To Kill a Mockingbird,* Julie interrupted her. "Uh, Grandma? Before you read . . ."

"What is it, Julie?"

"I've been thinking about you and Grandpa Orville."

Armen beamed a bright smile. "I'm honored, Julie. I know your grandpa would be, too."

"There's so much I'd like to . . . I wish I'd known Grandpa."

"He would have enjoyed you, Julie." Armen laughed. "And he would have loved you something fierce."

"Last visit, you told me that Grandpa Orville worked for Carbide. Like Mom, and Ben's dad, Charles, next door. You said he worked on Carbide's tunnel at Hawks Nest."

"Yes, I remember."

"Why'd they dig a tunnel?"

Armen leaned back in her chair. She closed her eyes for a few seconds, then placed *To Kill a Mockingbird* on the bed. "Why'd they dig . . .? A hydroelectric project, sweetie. To generate power for Carbide plants downriver."

"Did Grandpa work in the tunnel?"

"No. He worked mostly above ground. He was a deputy sheriff for Carbide. Today they'd probably call him a company security guard."

"What sort of work did he do?"

"Your grandpa went to Hawks Nest early in the summer of 1930. Or, as we used to say, 'nineteen and thirty.' He'd lost his job, just like millions of men all over the country. We were entering the Great Depression. An Army buddy from World War I offered him a job working as deputy sheriff for Carbide in the company's tunnel construction project. In those days companies could deputize employees as law officers."

"Did he carry a pistol, like Daddy?"

Armen laughed. "No. Most of the time he carried a blackjack. Usually in a holster, like a pistol. Your Grandpa Orville told me that when he got there, his boss gave him a deputy sheriff's badge and a blackjack and sent him out on the job. I'm not sure he ever used his blackjack. He had a way of talking to people, getting them to do what he wanted done."

"Daddy says that's best."

"Your daddy's right. Remember when your daddy drove us to Hawks Nest?"

"Yes."

"We stood on the overlook and looked down at the dam and the river. Far, far below. So tiny."

"I remember steep mountains on both sides of the river!"

"You have a good memory, Julie. Well, when your grandpa got there, the dam's construction was well under way. The project gave jobs to thousands of men in hard times. Men came from all over the South to work to work there, unemployed miners, share-croppers, loggers. Most of them black. Wages were low. But low wages were better than no wages.

"Grandpa Orville arrived about the time the company started digging the tunnel. Today the opening to the tunnel is inside the wall of the dam, on the north shore of the river. From the overlook we saw the top of it.

"The tunnel is over three miles long. During construction, there were four entrances: one at the upper end, one at the lower end, and two that started in the middle. Each of the middle en-trances opened shafts that went in opposite directions, toward crews digging from each end."

Julie exclaimed, "That's like working blind!"

"The mountain was near solid rock. Men used drills, jack-hammers and dynamite to tunnel through it. The tunnel started out thirty-six feet in diameter. That's as high *and* wide as your house is tall."

The immensity of the tunnel sparked Julie's imagination. "Huge!"

"Carbide learned that the rock inside the mountain contained valuable deposits of silica. They used silica in the production of metal alloys in a downstream plant. So they expanded the size of the tunnel to forty-six feet in diameter: over fifteen yards high, fifteen yards wide. The tunnel became a silica mine. A year and a half later, when the shafts finally broke through and connected, imagine this: they were only inches apart!"

"Wow!

"When they finished the dam, the river backed up and water filled the lower valley. Then, according to a schedule, the company opened and closed an underground gate, diverting water into the tunnel. The river flowed through the tunnel to the power house. There, the force of the water turned large electrical turbines. It generated electricity for factories and is still pumping out power."

~ ~ ~ ~ ~

One evening as Julie sat at Armen's bedside, in a weak voice Armen asked, "Julie . . . do you remember when we talked . . . about your grandpa's work at Hawks Nest?"

"Yes."

"There's another part to the story. I've waited, thinking I'd tell you when you were grown up." Armen laughed. "But at my age there comes a point when waiting has to end. Truth is, I don't know how much longer I'll be around. Sweetie, I need to tell you the rest of the story."

Julie took her Grandma Armen's hand. "Please tell me. I want to hear it."

"I'll tell it the way your grandpa told me. As close as I can come to his words." Armen cleared her throat and spoke in a lower voice.

~ ~ ~ ~ ~

HAWKS NEST, WV, JULY 1930—When I arrived at the tunnel, the first man I met was a supervisor. He had white dust all over him, head to toe, and carried a baseball bat. I offered to shake hands. He stepped away, gripped the bat with both hands, and jabbed it at me. "Another deputy? How many of you boys does it take to keep them niggers in line?" He held up the bat. "All I need is this."

Early the next morning, shortly after sunrise, my boss, Bullhead, took me to the camp for colored workers, rows of shacks with two-man wooden bunks and straw ticks. He said, "Orville, watch and listen, learn how to be a shack rouster." Bullhead stuck his head in the door of the first shack, slammed his blackjack against the doorframe, and yelled, "Off your ass and on your feet, boys, this ain't church camp."

One morning a worker, a colored man, walked up to me and said, "Uh, deputy, looks to me like Hazen, over there," he pointed to a man lying in a bunk, "looks like he dead."

Every day we'd discover another one or two men, dead. Mostly in the shanties, sometimes in the woods. We learned later that the dust was hardenin' men's lungs, like mixin' concrete deep in their chests. The rock dust from tunnel drilling, heavy with silica, was killing the men.

Men worked in air thick with silica dust and no respirators or masks to protect them. Some days you couldn't see fifteen feet ahead. Each day men got out of their bunks coughing. The kind of cough that reaches deep down in a man's lungs. Brings up thick white phlegm, sometimes laced with blood.

Folks say it's an ill wind that blows no good. Weeks later, the company asked me to carry bodies to an undertaker fifteen miles away. Paid me for each body I transported on the sly. Nobody was supposed to know. Those were hard times. I needed the money. The undertaker buried hundreds of men in his family's cornfield. Unmarked graves. Just to keep going, I began to drink corn liquor, tellin' myself "What the heck?" I needed the money.

~   ~   ~   ~   ~

Armen paused and closed her eyes. She opened them and said, "My daddy had worked in the tunnel. About the time I met your grandpa, my daddy died of the same lung disease that was killing workers. Orville and I wanted to bring a stop to the deaths. We suspected the tunnel's dust was killing the men. But we needed proof. We got the first autopsy done. A young man who went to work in the tunnel at age seventeen; at age eighteen he was dead. The autopsy confirmed silicosis killed him. Acute silicosis. Finally, we had medical evidence about what was killing those men. When company men at the tunnel found out what we'd done . . . well, we were lucky to escape with our lives. Your grandpa's old Army buddy had put the company first and tried to kill him. A friend stepped in and got him first. The truth brings risk, honey."

Armen reached for Julie's hand, clasped it tightly and brought it next to her cheek. "Later, your grandpa and I worked as organizers for the union. Like my daddy did. Difference was, my daddy had to work in secret. We didn't."

She remained silent for a moment. "Memories of men who died from tunnel dust haunted your grandpa. Daytime in his thoughts, nighttime in his dreams. Haunted me, too. We spent the next thirty years working to make things better for men working underground."

"I'm proud of you and Grandpa."

"There was a lady from New York, a poet. She wrote about the men who died at Hawks Nest. About their suffering and death. The grief their families had to bear. How it didn't have to happen. Then she asked a question I still think about: What three things must we never do?"

"I don't know. What?"

Armen spoke slowly. " 'Forget. Remain silent. Stand alone.' "

They sat in silence. A distant church bell rang.

"People's memories are short. They forgot about the men who died at Hawks Nest. The few who remembered stood alone. And they remained silent."

"For people to remember, stand together, speak out, somebody has to . . ." Armen's voice faded to a near whisper, "bear witness . . . to the truth." She closed her eyes but kept a firm grip on Julie's hand. Armen opened her eyes and cast a warm gaze on Julie. "I hope life brings you opportunities to bear witness to the truth. And I hope you won't stand alone."

Julie hugged her grandma. "I promise, I won't forget. Or remain silent."

Chapter 25

ACADEMY, WV, SEPTEMBER 19, 2008—Most of the customers had left Brownie's diner by the time Delbarton told Julie about his recent meeting with Otto.

~ ~ ~ ~ ~

Carrying a small complimentary flight bag from KLM's first-class section, Otto walked briskly down the corridor to his office. Delbarton laughed. "He had a way of walking that employees called a strut." Otto greeted Susan, then nodded toward Delbarton's newspaper. "Anything of interest?" Otto waved for his subordinate to follow him into his office.

Delbarton said, "Today's Kabot story is full of what I assume you already know. Another worker died. And the Chemical Institute's investigation team is getting ready to come here. I know a couple of the people. Worked with them years ago. One of them poked around the plant after the Bhopal disaster. You'd have thought Bhopal happened here, not halfway around the world. Then he showed up again, this time with a team, seven months later when we had that aldicarb release. I thought they'd never leave us alone."

Otto waved toward the chair on the other side of his desk, motioning for Delbarton to sit. Walking around his desk, he rifled through unopened envelopes, then sat down. He placed two tumblers on the desk, brought out a bottle of scotch from a desk drawer, and poured two fingers of scotch into each glass.

Otto raised his glass. "Cheers."

"Welcome back." Delbarton took a gulp of scotch.

Otto lowered his glass without drinking.

"I trust you had a good visit to Germany. And a smooth trip across the pond."

"*Gut* visit. No, *nicht eine gute* return trip. Atlantic storms."

"Sorry to . . ."

Otto interrupted, "John, I have soon to meet with investigators. My time it is limited. Is this to be another rehash of Bhopal? Of the accusations?"

Delbarton took a long drink of his scotch. "No. I just want to finish our conversation, the one we started the day of young Gruber's first anniversary, the conversation about my future."

"Finish? What could possibly remain?"

"Carbide hung Bhopal around my neck. A tarnished necklace. Kabot has made sure I've worn it ever since."

Otto swiveled his chair a half turn, his back to Delbarton, and for a moment gazed out the window. "Our private version of corporate blackmail, is that it?" He turned to face Delbarton. "How much do you want? No guarantees. But give me your price."

Delbarton looked down and shook his head no. He looked up. "Otto, this is not about money. Carbide, then Kabot, paid me well to wear that necklace. This is about . . . it's about my good name. My reputation."

"Reputation? And just how might . . . you are seeking a position?"

"I'm not here to ask for a job. I'm too old for that."

"Then what . . .?"

Delbarton hesitated and then spoke slowly, as if he had carefully chosen each word. "A resurrection. I want a resurrection, a rebirth, an appointment that'll again let me hold my head high."

Otto sat back in his chair and raised his eyebrows. "Resurrection? For example?"

"I want to stand with my peers. Like the old days." Delbarton paused, then said, "You could appoint me a Kabot representative to, say, an international trade congress."

Otto flashed a smile that alternated from benevolent to deprecating. "A modern day Lazarus." He refilled Delbarton's tumbler. "And in exchange for this new life?"

Delbarton took a long drink. "I'm a plant insider. A credible source of information. I know about Carbide neglect leading up to Bhopal. It happened on *my* watch. Neglect by *my* people. Jumping forward to the Kabot explosion, I know about the workaround. The one nobody talks about. It happened on *your* watch. I know about the safety violations on your watch that caused the explosion. And could've caused another Bhopal. If CI investigators were to ask me how long those violations, and workarounds, had gone on, had been quietly approved by your managers *and by you . . .*"

"I doubt if investigators will seek your opinion."

Delbarton leaned forward and looked Otto in the eye, his voice firm. "But you don't know that for sure. And I might very well seek *them* out. Quietly, of course." Delbarton took another drink of scotch. "My proposal? You give me an appointment. One that is mutually acceptable. And if I'm asked about plant safety, either here or at Bhopal, well, I have nothing to add to what's already known."

Otto snapped, "Bhopal was nearly twenty-five years ago."

"So what? Think about it. Workarounds. At Kabot, here and now. At Bhopal, there and then. And in between, over two decades of explosions, leaks, injuries, and deaths."

Otto shrugged. "I doubt . . ."

"Otto, I can create a paint-by-the-numbers picture of this plant's mismanagement. One so clear even a cub reporter could connect the dots. Carbide to Kabot, different owners, same problems. Years of chemical leaks and releases. Now health risks *fill* this valley. Kabot's PR people do 24-7 spin control. Fortunately, most local folks don't want to hear about the high rates of cancer among people living near the plant. They're happy to have jobs." Delbarton's voice rose. "And now Kabot just killed two men in the Desin Unit. If that residue treater had crashed into the tank of MIC, right now the valley would be going through its own Bhopal disaster. Probably worse."

As if executing a military maneuver, Otto stood, walked to his office door and opened it. "Good day, John."

Delbarton finished his drink. He rose slowly and walked toward the door. "Print, television, Internet. Good copy for journalists, don't you think?"

Otto extended his hand, perfunctorily shook John's hand and, continuing to hold it, turned and guided him out the door. "Yes, yes, your request warrants consideration, John. I will contact you."

"I look forward to . . ."

Otto executed a quick about-face and shut the door.

~   ~   ~   ~   ~

Julie searched Delbarton's face for clues to his feelings and wondered how to describe what she saw: The absence of expression? The face of a man who had been kicked around for twenty-five years? The adult version of an abused child? A man who no longer reacted to the cuts and bruises of life? Then she wondered, twenty-five years from now, will this be Ben?

Chapter 26

JACKSON, WV, MID-SEPTEMBER 2008—Dressed for running, Julie arrived downtown shortly after 6 AM. She parked in the *Chronicle* garage, then walked to the employees' locker room and put her work clothes in a locker.

In the brisk morning air, Julie ran east along Vandalia Boulevard looking down on the river. The deep green surface of the water reflected occasional flashes of blue sky. A tug pushed six barges fully loaded with coal down the river toward her. Behind it waves rolled to the shore, crashing like miniature ocean breakers. A crane swooped low along the shoreline. Julie ran past the governor's mansion and the capitol's manicured lawns, the oak and maple trees now dressed in the bright red and gold of autumn. She recalled Harrison's comment, "The capitol's well-tended exterior contrasts with its venal interior life."

Later, showered and sitting at her desk, Julie made calls to local officials and emergency responders. She asked questions to get more details on what happened the night of the explosion.

Mid-morning, in the *Chronicle's* coffee break room, staff members, including Julie and Harrison, watched as the screen of the room's TV set flashed a printed message: "Live newscast, Kabot Agronomy." The message faded and the face of a local TV newsman filled the screen. "This is Jonas Alford. I'm in the town of Academy at the Kabot Agronomy plant where, two days ago," he paused and looked into the camera, "there was a tragic, fatal explosion. Joining me this morning are Otto Heidrich, the plant's general manager, and Ben Gruber, public relations. Gentlemen, will you please update us on the developments since the explosion?"

The camera turned from Alford to Otto and Ben. Otto wiped sweat from his brow. "*Danke,* Jonas. My associate, Ben, will speak." Otto gestured toward Ben and stepped aside.

The bright sun reflected off the sheet of paper Ben held. He turned the paper at an angle and squinted as he looked towards the camera.

"Good morning. I'm Ben Gruber. This morning I will give a brief update on the explosion." Ben looked at his paper, then toward the camera. "First, let me say, the company deeply regrets the loss of . . . uh," Ben looked at his paper, "How . . . Howard Wilson, a member of the Kabot Agronomy family."

In the *Chronicle* coffee room, a reporter said, "Right. Remember ol' what's his name?"

Harrison looked at Julie, who kept her eyes on the screen.

On television, Ben continued. "And we wish . . ." he paused and again looked at his paper.

"Careful, Ben. Get it right." A quick laugh, fast suppressed, rippled around the room. Someone said, "What is this, amateur hour?"

". . . Uh, wish Jim Morris a speedy and full recovery. Along with the Chemical Institute, Kabot is conducting an investigation into the causes of the explosion. The company is committed to full cooperation with federal and state investigators."

Julie left the room.

One hour later Julie's phone rang. "Julie Brown."

In an excited voice, Ben asked, "Did you see our announcement on TV?"

"Yes."

His voice eager, tense, Ben asked, "Did I do OK?"

The TV images and sounds, staff comments and laughter raced through Julie's thoughts. *Did he do OK?* Julie held her phone before her, looked at it, then held it to her ear and said, her tone flat, expressionless, "Ben, next time, do your homework. And rehearse."

"There wasn't time. I'd hardly read through the announcement before Otto put me in front of Alford and the TV crew."

"Fill me in. How did that happen?"

~   ~   ~   ~   ~

Arriving at work that morning, as he approached the plant's front gate Ben passed a small group carrying hand-lettered signs. END MIC. STOP THE KILLER MIC. BHOPAL—WILL IT HAPPEN HERE? An elderly black woman, two middle-aged men, one black, one white, and a young white woman carried the signs. Sweat darkened their shirts and blouses.

Between the marchers and the gate sat two Vandalia County Sheriff's cars, motors running, windows partially open, smoke drifting out. Two officers wearing aviator sunglasses, smoking cigarettes, sat in each vehicle. The officers' gazes tracked the group's movements.

In the gatehouse, on the plant's side of the front gate, a security guard kept a steady watch on the marchers.

In the plant's administration building, walking down the long corridor to his office, Ben sensed an absence of the staff's usual banter and occasional laughter. Instead, the low murmur of voices punctuated a pervasive silence. When Ben arrived at his office he found a note taped to his door. "See me immediately. Otto."

Ben walked into the anteroom next to Otto's office. Susan nodded to Ben and pointed toward Otto's open door. "He's waiting." Ben entered Otto's office.

Holding papers, Otto stood behind his desk, walked around it and handed Ben a single page. "Read this. Come, walk with me."

Walking along the corridor to the building's front entrance, Otto said, "The local TV news requests an update on the explosion. Your boss is not here to write it, or to brief them. I wrote the statement in your hand. You will read it. You are not to answer questions."

Ben and Otto walked through the building's wide glass doors. They stood facing a bright hot sun and a small TV crew with a camera, the letters WJTV printed on each side. Ben recognized the round face of Jonas Alford, the only member of the crew wearing a necktie. Alford anchored the station's ten o'clock news.

Alford nodded to Otto and Ben and shook hands with them. "Boys, ol' Mother Nature's hot this mornin'. Let's get to it." He turned to the crew. "Run it, Smitty."

The camera turned toward Alford, who straightened his necktie and wiped beads of sweat from his face. On the front of the camera, a red light came on.

~   ~   ~   ~   ~

"You know the rest of the story. I read the announcement to Alford and the camera. You don't have to say anything, Julie. I know, I know, I muffed Howard Wilson's name." Ben paused. "I *knew* his name. And had it right there on the paper in front of me. But I looked up and suddenly went blank. I tried to read the name on the paper but the sun glared . . . couldn't read it. Howard's family probably watched the news. I feel terrible."

Julie's thoughts returned to last night's aborted celebration. Now Ben's PR debacle. Julie slumped in her chair. Her brain labored to process Ben's description of his TV announcement.

"Jules, I know it didn't go well. But that's what happened. I mean, that's *how* it happened."

Ben deserved better. But he'd jumped into bed with Kabot. "Maybe you'll get another chance."

"I hope so." Ben's voice brightened. "Can I see you tonight?"

The question she had hoped to avoid had arrived. She hesitated for a moment, then said, "No. I have a lot on my plate. So do you."

Chapter 27

SOUTH JACKSON, WV, AUTUMN 1983—Early morning, Roger and Ben stood with a small group of students on Oak Street waiting on the school bus. When it arrived, the students formed a queue to board. In front of them, a larger older boy feigned fear and, raising his arms, jumped away from Roger. "Ooohhhh." He and a buddy laughed.

Ben stepped between the boys and Roger and glared at the older boy. "Come on, Rog, let's get on the bus."

At South Jackson's McKinley High School, the slate roofs on the school's three tall brick buildings, built in the high-ceilinged style of an earlier era, paled under the blue sky's bright sun.

At noon, students milled around the campus, some clustered in small groups. Roger walked slowly toward a group of boys. The boys turned and watched him approach. But when Roger neared them, the group, as if a single animal, slowly moved away. The tallest boy in the group turned and yelled, "Hey, queer, go home and play your piano."

Across the lawn, students became silent and gazed at Roger. He shuffled to the steps of the main entrance and went inside.

That afternoon Mary and Charles drove to McKinley High. Last week the principal had called and asked them to meet with him.

"He's missed a lot of classes, Charlie. But he's studying. His grades are holding up. But maybe he's got some problems we don't know about, you know, beyond grades." Since receiving the call, Mary had talked with Charles about little else. "He's bright, Charles. But his illness, the medicines, they're sapping his strength."

"Honey, it's going to be all right. Roger's a smart kid. I don't know why Mr. Holmes wants to meet with us, but I'm sure he wants to do the right thing." Charles smiled, "Maybe the teachers have figured out some ways to help Roger in his studies."

Charles and Mary walked along a hallway in the school. They stopped at an office door bearing a small sign, "Mr. Holmes, Principal," and gently knocked. A woman called, "Come in, it's open."

A few minutes later, Mr. Holmes, mid-forties, stocky, suit and necktie, welcomed Mary and Charles to his office. He motioned to two chairs on the other side of his desk.

After a few minutes of light conversation, Mr. Holmes said, "Thank you for coming to meet with me. I share your concern for Roger's health. Please know that Roger is in my prayers."

Mary whispered, "Thank you."

Mr. Holmes rearranged a stack of papers on his desk, then spoke slowly. "Our teachers and Roger's fellow students are concerned." He shook his head from side to side. "We know so little about AIDS. Parents are worried, too."

Mary sat erect. "They're worried? You think Roger's not— we're not . . . ? He loves his friends. This school. He needs all of you."

"And we love Roger, Mrs. Gruber. But . . . please know this is hard for me . . . ."

Charles' posture stiffened. "Hard? What is?"

"Mr. Gruber, across the country, so far, over seven thousand cases of AIDS have been reported, and already half of them've died. I pray for Roger's health, but AIDS is staring us in the face. We all know about the . . . the Kokomo, Indiana schools and Ryan White. I . . . we . . . have to be realistic. People are scared."

Mary wiped away a tear. "Yes, I know about Ryan White. Roger's friends have stopped coming over. Now their parents avoid us."

Charles said, "Mr. Holmes, you asked us to meet with you. Do you have a suggestion? Something to help us?"

"Please understand, I have to think about what's best for Roger and the school. I've talked with the teachers . . . and many students."

Charles leaned forward. "And?"

"The school year is almost over. During the summer, we'd like you to consider, when school starts next fall . . ." Mr. Holmes paused as if searching for just the right words. ". . . Uh, keeping Roger at home."

Mary slumped in her chair. She brought her hands to her face and sobbed.

In a voice of disbelief, Charles asked, "Stay home his senior year?"

"Mr. Gruber, I'm sorry, but . . . yes."

Charles leaned forward. His face reddened. "If AIDS doesn't kill him, this will."

"Please understand, Mr. Gruber . . ."

Charles jumped to his feet and placed his hand on Mary's shoulder. "Come on, honey."

Visibly shaken and suddenly pale, Mary rose. She clutched the edge of Mr. Holmes' desk to steady herself, then gripped Charles' arm. The couple walked to the door.

Mr. Holmes followed them. "Wait! Please consider . . ."

Without looking back, Charles and Mary departed. The drag of Mary clutching Charles' arm slowed his fast strides. Mary sobbed as they walked to the school's front door.

"How, Charlie, how'd this happen?" Her voice quivered. "And why?"

Chapter 28

SOUTH JACKSON, WV, SEPTEMBER 15, 2008—A few days later Julie and Ben met at Wung Fu, a Chinese restaurant in South Jackson. They'd gone there on dates in high school and still enjoyed the restaurant's ambience. They sometimes talked about their first date and the hanging curtain that Mr. Chan, the owner, had pulled around their table. He had bowed and smiled. "Special place for beating of the heart."

The egg rolls continued to be rated as the valley's best. Long ago, at the end of a meal at Wung Fu's, Ben had first told Julie he loved her. She looked back on that evening as if watching an event speeding into the vortex of the past, into her history. Uncertain then about how to reply to him, Julie had asked, "Get enough to eat?" Ben had answered her in what had become a private joke, replayed each time they ate at Wung Fu. "Yes. But an hour from now I'll be hungry."

They ordered egg rolls and dinners, moo-shoo gai pan, broccoli with pork, steamed rice, and hot tea. "Do you want to talk about Kabot? What happened after your TV spot with Jason Alford?" Julie asked.

"Let's let it go. Not now."

During dinner their talk bounced from the newspaper's softball team to the indictment of a state senator to a new restaurant in town. Nothing stayed in focus long enough to sustain a discussion. Each topic generated brief comments, then silence.

After one of the lengthy silences, Julie felt the words, "Get enough to eat?" form. *Times have changed. We have changed, too.* Instead, she said, "Hard to believe."

"What is?"

"The plant explosion. A fire raging. Kabot wouldn't give out information. Not to emergency response crews. Not to anybody. Now I'm told they're doing the same thing with the Chemical Institute. And no one over there returns my phone calls. You know anything about that?"

Ben ran his chopsticks through the rice remaining on his plate. Then for a moment he stared at it. "A little . . . I'm . . . it's a tangled web."

"And maybe some nasty spiders. Is there a reason you didn't answer my question?"

"I'm just . . . I'm just learning about it."

"Maybe I can make it easy for you. The *Chronicle* has a copy of an internal Kabot memo. From a woman in corporate PR. It contains her expert advice on a PR strategy for managing fallout from the explosion, how to execute spin control. In short, in the memo she said, 'Clam up.' Is that what you're just learning about?"

Ben leaned forward and at the same time tilted his chair on its front legs, an unstable position. Her past reminders that on the tile floor the chair might scoot out from under him had gone unheeded. Even after, years ago, his chin had hit the table and a front tooth punctured his lip.

He said, "I don't know how to tell you this, except just to say it. The truth is, I was in the meeting with her."

"You were there?" Julie said in a tone of disbelief. "With her?"

"Damn right!" Ben's face reddened. In the past, Julie had seen Ben's pride surface, spurring him into saying things he later regretted. "I heard it all, first-hand."

"You didn't!" Even as she said that, she felt some guilt, knowing he wouldn't be able to stay quiet about it.

Ben took a gulp of now-cooled tea. "We're on opposite sides of the explosion, but since you have the memo, here's the truth."

"Yes, the truth. Let's hear it."

~   ~   ~   ~   ~

Otto called a joint meeting of senior staff and the explosion PR team. The executives, including Ben, sat around a long conference table. To Otto's right sat two visitors. First, an attractive woman, early thirties, curly blonde hair, large brown eyes, the only woman in the room. "Her eyes reminded me of an electronic scanning device," Ben said. "Though I don't know what she was looking for. Just checking us out, I guess."

Beside her sat the other visitor, a middle aged man, heavy around the middle, salt-and-pepper hair, dark blue suit and necktie.

Otto gave a perfunctory smile to the visitors, then glanced around the table. He nodded toward the man. "I believe most of you know Martin Bean, our corporate attorney. Some of you know Anna Oberhaupt from corporate public relations." He pronounced Anna in the Germanic manner, "Ah-nah." "What you may not know is that Anna began her Kabot career ten years ago at our headquarters office in Stuttgart. Her father and her grandfather worked at Kabot. You might say," Otto gave a brief chortle and his eyes widened, then, as if a switch had been thrown, his expression flattened, "you might say Anna has Kabot genes. Her home now, I am most pleased to say, is Danbury, Connecticut, where she works in our divisional headquarters.

"I asked Anna and Martin to join us to share their recommendations about how to best deal with the explosion. Anna, please begin."

Anna stood. "I am saddened by the deaths of our fellow workers, Howard Wilson and Jim Morris." Around the table men nodded. One of them closed his eyes, then made the sign of the cross. Anna's voice carried traces of German, with the English pronunciation of the letter 'w' as a 'v'. "Otto has visited their homes. Martin has talked with their wives."

Martin interrupted. "Sorry to intrude, Anna." He looked around the table. "In case anyone asks, our attorneys will be following through with Howard's and Jim's families. You may tell people they can rest assured that Kabot will make more than adequate provisions for the two families. Each in seven figures."

Anna walked to the front of the room. "Our longer term challenge is to learn from this tragedy. Improve our operations. Most importantly, in the future, to prevent a similar accident. In our meeting today, however, our concerns are more immediate. We will put the explosion in perspective. Discuss how best to move forward. How best to reassure employees and their families. To say to them, as well as to people living near the plant: What happened was an accident. Tragic? Yes. But a rare event.

"You and I know that our engineers will design and build new safeguards. As that is done, we must remind everyone of our safe practices. Our *continuing* safe practices. And say very clearly, this cannot, *will not, ever,* happen again."

Anna walked to the window and then turned to the group. "We may need to remind everyone in the valley of a simple fact. The valley's future," she held up her left hand, "and the future of Kabot Agronomy," she held up her right hand, "are one and the same." She clasped her two hands together.

"I will be working with the people in PR to develop a media program to do all of this. In a few days Otto will have materials, print and electronic, ready to send out. To the media, to civic and church groups. To schools."

Anna picked up a whiteboard marker. "Now for a more immediate question. How do we deal with our critics, such as the *Chronicle*?" Her gaze moved around the table from face to face. She laughed. "I said, 'such as.' I will be direct. How do we deal with the *Chronicle*?"

Anna turned to the whiteboard and printed in large red letters, '*Marginalize!*'

Otto asked, "What do you mean by . . ."

Anna smiled. "Good question, Otto. What I mean can be simply stated. But," she smiled, "it is not easy to do. Here is a start." On the whiteboard, after '*Marginalize*,' she printed, 'the *Chronicle*.' To marginalize our critics, the *Chronicle* and perhaps other media outlets, we, you, all of us, must volunteer nothing. I mean that literally." She tapped the marker on the whiteboard. "*Volunteer nothing.*" She gazed around the table and made eye contact with each executive.

"Now, marginalize. How do we do this?" She paused as if waiting for an answer. "We begin by taking away the grist for their news-mill. The grist they most need. Kabot Agronomy news.

That means, first, no interviews. Second, no off the record conversations with reporters. Third, you must guard your casual comments. At home, around town. The *Chronicle* and other media are to receive only, I repeat, *only*, press releases or public statements that we have written and reviewed."

The men around the table nodded.

Anna turned again to the whiteboard. With a blue marker she printed, 'End MIC' and then faced the executives. "Now, the so-called citizens group, End MIC? How do we marginalize them?" Like a classroom teacher waiting for students to answer, she looked around the table. "In the real world, we cannot control the actions of End MIC or its members. What *can* we do?

"First, we alter the environment in which the group lives. Quietly, informally, we will discourage employees and their families from attending their meetings. Second, we will set up *our own* community meetings. In those meetings, we will control the agenda, the discussion. We will help local residents understand how much Kabot cares about the community. We will teach how the community's interests are one and the same as Kabot's interests. Our PR people will lead this effort. Third, and I do not have hard evidence to support this, we believe the End MIC group may already have been infiltrated by out-of-town radicals." Around the table men stirred. "I will keep you informed as we learn more."

The conference room door opened. An older woman in a white uniform, a net over her white hair, pushed a cart of coffee and pastries into the room.

Anna said, "I see it is time for a short break."

Otto added, "Ten minutes, everyone. Then promptly, back in your seats, please."

Side by side, Anna and Ben poured coffee and selected pastries. Otto stood beside them and smiled. "I will watch the PR team make its pastry choices." Anna and Ben pretended to debate the value of croissants and cinnamon rolls, and then, joined by Otto, laughed.

At the end of the coffee break, the group reassembled around the table. Otto said, "Martin, please share with us your legal strategy. What it is and how we are to carry it out."

Martin remained seated. "First, greetings from the corporate legal department. Since the explosion, our thoughts and hearts have been with you. And with the families of the people who were injured. And of course, with the families of Howard and Jim."

He glanced at his notes. "You may remember that after the 9-11 attacks Congress passed new national security laws. Among other things, those laws authorized placing security restrictions on information that could be useful to our nation's enemies. One law in particular, the Maritime Security Act, is relevant to our discussion today. The Maritime Security Act deals with the security of shipping ports, including the contents of shipments, shipment arrivals and departures. The provisions of the Act are directly relevant to Kabot Agronomy and today's discussion."

Otto raised his hand. "Martin, it is hard for me to understand this. We are inland, far from the sea. How would maritime security be relevant to our plant?"

"Thank you, Otto. That question may be in everyone's thoughts." Martin glanced around the table. "This plant has a port."

Martin stood, walked to the window and pointed toward the river. "Over there. A half mile away. The Vandalia River." He paused. "Kabot Agronomy has shipping docks." He again pointed out the window. "Right there. The plant receives large quantities of chemicals for production. Some volatile, some toxic. From that fresh-water port, we ship large quantities of products, including many, like Desin, that are toxic. In the wrong hands, the chemicals we bring into the plant, as well as the end products we ship, can be dangerous. They could be used by terrorists to threaten our national security."

Otto asked, "Martin, are you saying that we must hire guards to police our shipping docks?"

"Not necessarily, Otto. One or two video cameras might be sufficient. What I *am* saying, however, is that under the law, our production operations, and all of this plant, are connected to that port." He pointed toward the river. "A port owned by, used exclusively by, this plant. Our legal opinion is that in the interests of

national security, this plant can, indeed *should*, classify and withhold information on all MIC-related operations. This includes the
manufacturing of products like Desin, as well as the receipt and
storage of dangerous chemical ingredients such as MIC.

"An investigation team from the Chemical Institute will soon
be here. They will poke their noses into records. They will interview many of you, what one of my colleagues calls an industrial
witch hunt." Around the table men laughed.

"You are to be hospitable to investigators. Cooperate with
them. But," Martin paused and smiled a broad smile, "our hospi-
tality has certain limits. Starting today, our legal team will review
all files and records related to the explosion. We will review those
files for their relevance to national security. As needed, some, perhaps many of them, will be classified as security sensitive. Those
records will be out of bounds for investigators. Closed and sealed.
Not to be disclosed except as approved by Otto and my office. Or,
in rare instances, as required by a court order."

After the meeting Otto called a few people, along with Anna
and Martin, into his office. "Brilliant strategies," he said. "Martin
and Anna have given us brilliant strategies." Everyone agreed.

~　~　~　~　~

Julie interrupted, "Brilliant, Ben, brilliant? Who are these people?"

Ben forked the last piece of broccoli into his mouth and slowly
chewed it. He laughed nervously. "These people? Otto, Anna,
Martin, me . . . ."

"So . . . I hear you, Ben. You're running with the big dogs."

Ben stared at his now-empty plate.

"What's that running behind those dogs—a pack of lies?"

They finished dinner in silence. Ben picked up a fortune cookie
and stared at it. "I'm not sure I want to know what's in here." He
tossed the cookie on the table. "Maybe this was a bad idea. There
are things I need to keep to myself." He signaled for the check.

Driving home, Julie heard her daddy's voice. "The quality of
a relationship decreases as the number of secrets increase." She

wiped away a tear. Ben had drifted into another way of life. Had he passed a point of no return?

Chapter 29

ACADEMY, WV, SEPTEMBER 2008—On the phone's fourth ring, a resonant voice answered, "Dr. Henderson."

"This is Julie Brown. I'm a reporter for the *Jackson Chronicle*. I'm writing a story on the Kabot plant explosion, and I'd like to talk with you. Is there a time when I could come to your office?"

"Me? What the hell do I know? The plant blew up. That's the whole story."

"Professor Henderson, your office, the Vandalia State campus, is next door to the plant. And, if the phone directory is correct, you live in Academy, not far from the plant. I would like to get your perspective on the explosion."

~   ~   ~   ~   ~

Two hours later, Julie rode the elevator to the fifth floor of State's faculty and administration building. She knocked on Professor Henderson's office door. Inside the office a stereo played a piano concerto. One she remembered hearing Roger practice. She knocked again, this time with more force. No answer.

A man with an armload of books stepped out of the office next door. "He's in there. Drives us crazy sometimes with his loud music. Let me do it." With the heel of his hand he pounded on the door.

"Come in," a voice shouted over the music.

Julie opened the door. "Sorry to interrupt, Professor Henderson . . . Julie Brown, *Jackson Chronicle*."

Henderson opened the door and motioned for her to enter. She walked into his office. Julie had read about Professor Henderson, once a decathlon athlete on the 1972 US Olympic team. A tall

126

man, his body moved with an athlete's fluidity and grace. She glanced at a framed photo of Henderson throwing the javelin. His hair had grayed and he'd added a little weight.

Shelves of books lined the walls, and stacks of papers occupied most of his desk. Beyond his fifth floor office window, a bright sun lit the chemical tanks and buildings of the Kabot Agronomy plant. Immediately below her, shadows from fluffs of clouds dappled the landscaped gardens, lawn and trees of the campus.

The campus green ended at the heavy wire fence separating the college's and plant's properties. Beyond the fence sprawled Kabot's asphalt and labyrinths of pipes and tanks. To Julie's right, a gate closed across a road that circled the perimeter of the plant. A heavy chain and padlock secured a closed gate.

Pointing down to the gate, Professor Henderson, in a loud voice that rose above the music, said, "Know what that sign says?"

Julie shook her head, no.

"Just a minute." Henderson walked to the stereo player on the bookcase behind his desk and turned down the music's volume. "The sign announces, in big letters, all caps, EMERGENCY ROUTE —DO NOT BLOCK GATE."

"But there's a chain locking the gate shut."

"Welcome to Kabot Agronomy."

Professor Henderson walked to his desk and sat down behind it. "Please, Miss Brown, sit down." Then he turned and for a moment gazed at the stereo speakers. "Listen, Julie Brown, *Jackson Chronicle*. Listen." Then he turned and brought the volume up to its earlier level.

A puzzled expression on her face, Julie looked at one of the stereo's speakers.

Professor Henderson yelled, "Do you know that piece?"

"Yes, it's . . ."

"Beethoven's Third Piano Concerto." The professor turned down the volume.

"I'm familiar with it. A boy I once knew played . . . Professor Henderson, I came to ask you about . . ."

As if he hadn't heard her, in a firm voice Henderson asked, "Miss Brown, what if that piece was," his words slowed and he emphasized each syllable, "*the last music you ever heard*?"

"Uh . . . why would it be the last . . .?"

"Because you went deaf, like Beethoven."

"I know about Beethoven's deafness."

"That concerto was Beethoven's last composition before he went deaf, the *last!*" As if he'd never heard Julie. As if he'd forgotten something, Henderson half rose from his seat and gestured towards the window. Then, as if he'd remembered it, he dropped back into his desk chair and pointed toward the window. "I was at home, over there, a few blocks from here, listening to that music, when the plant blew up. The explosion could've blasted me to hell and back. Could've been *the last music I ever heard*. Me and Beethoven, we'd have something to talk about in the afterlife, Miss Julie Brown, *Jackson Chronicle*."

"Professor Henderson . . ."

"Knocked my windows out. And me on my ass. Flames . . . like they were in my front yard! Forget the story. Forget the newspaper. Go to church. Give thanks you're alive, Miss Julie Brown, *Jackson Chronicle*."

"Uh, Profess . . ."

He looked toward the window and spoke in a loud voice. "An hour later, an hour—hear me, Kabot! Hear me, county emergency services! On TV and radios we received shelter in place announcements. A fire truck came down my street, loudspeakers on top of it, a man yelling, '*shelter in place*.' Blasts of the town's emergency siren. I ask you, does MIC wait an hour to kill?"

Julie hurriedly made notes.

"Now the rumor's going around that MIC detectors on the fence lines had been turned off. Do you know about that? Is it true?"

"I'm not sure . . . I need to . . ."

Henderson leaned forward across his desk. "Kabot. Safety rules. Safety procedures on top of safety procedures. Then when it blows? Amateur night. Keystone Cops."

"Professor Henderson, would you rather I come back at another time?" Julie stood.

Henderson took a deep breath. "Sorry. All this has upset me. I get carried away. I apologize. Please, sit down."

Julie sat.

After another deep breath Henderson asked, "Okay, as a reporter you must be close to what's happening. Over at Kabot, what's the buzz?"

"Well, sir," Julie hesitated, uncertain about where to lead the conversation. "The employees are grieving over the deaths of the two employees, Howard and Jim."

"News reports say Kabot plans to rebuild the unit. Restart production."

"Yes, at the paper we believe that's their plan."

"My sources tell me Kabot has no stockpile of MIC in its plants in Germany. Zero risk for fellow Deutschlanders. Is that true?"

Julie had heard the same thing from Bob Samuelson. "We think so."

"Is it true that we have, right here in South Jackson, 90% of the entire MIC supply in America?"

"I don't know. I do know that we have a lot . . . ."

"Maybe you should find out, nail that down, Julie Brown, *Jackson Chronicle*."

In a tone of exasperation, Julie said, "Professor Henderson, I didn't come here to pick a fight. I'm trying to figure this mess out. I wondered what you experienced the night of the explosion. That's what brought me here."

Henderson interrupted her. His face relaxed and his voice softened. "What I experienced the night . . . my house shook. Flames. I feared for my life." He turned and gazed out the window for a moment, then turned to Julie. "Have you ever feared for your life?"

"Yes, sir, I have." At home, alone. The basement with Sparkle. "As a child. A Carbide gas release. Shelter in place."

"Then you know what I felt. My advice to you, Julie Brown? Find out the truth behind the explosion. Dig for it. Get it. Write it."

"Yes, sir, I intend to. . . ."

"Or don't. Kabot has called the shots in the valley for a long time. Let the politicians, even your paper, spout Kabot's party line. No doubt the paper will enjoy a prosperous future. And you'll enjoy a long career at the *Chronicle*." Then softly, "That is, if you can live with yourself. . . . Sorry, how you live is none of my . . ."

The desk phone rang. "Hello?" Henderson listened for a moment and then smiled. "Fast-breaking news, John, I'm still alive."

Julie stood and started to leave.

With a wave Henderson signaled for Julie to stop and then motioned for her to sit. To the caller he said, "There's a young woman here, Julie Brown, who works at the *Chronicle*." Henderson listened for a moment and then handed the phone to Julie. "Say hello to Dr. John Delbarton. He says he knows you."

"John. This is a surprise." She listened for a moment. "Day after tomorrow, 2 PM? Let me check." Julie flipped open to her daily calendar. "That's fine. See you then."

Chapter 30

ACADEMY, WV, OCTOBER 1, 2008—At two o'clock the next afternoon, Julie and John Delbarton entered Brownie's as the last of the lunch crowd left the diner. Glasses and dinnerware clinked as the busboy cleared the tables.

Delbarton pointed to the rear of the room and a table given privacy from the larger dining room by a chest-high partition. "Brownie used to call that partitioned area his conference room. We can have some privacy there."

On the floor beside Julie sat her backpack. Delbarton had placed his briefcase on a chair beside him. They placed an order for club sandwiches and chips with the waitress, Helen.

Julie's phone rang. She glanced at and answered, "Hi, Mary." She listened for a moment, then said, "Can I call you later this afternoon? I just started an interview." She paused. "Thanks, love you, too."

In a booth across the dining room, a young couple sat side by side. Helen served them sandwiches and soft drinks. Then she brought coffee to Delbarton and Julie and stood attentively in the entry near their table, as if she had been invited into the conversation. She kept an eye on the dining room and the young couple.

"I've read a little about Kabot history," Julie said. "And I visited the corporate website. It's like one long press release. I hope you'll help me wade through all that. I want to know the truth, not the company image Kabot has manufactured. I want to understand who Kabot is. How they came to buy and operate Carbide's old Academy plant."

Delbarton added whiskey to his coffee. He took a deep breath and a long drink from his mug. "Well, about the time my great granddaddy signed on with the Army of the Confederacy, over in Stuttgart, Germany, Gerhard Kabot, dye maker, and Karl Weber, salesman, started a dye making company."

He opened his briefcase. He removed a folder filled with loose photos and placed it on the table. "I thought these might be helpful." He spread a few of the photos on the table. The photos had yellowed, and some had been printed on a heavier print stock. The top photos showed Kabot laboratory buildings and a small factory. Above the buildings was the Kabot logo.

```
            K
            A
    K   A   B   O   T
            O
            T
```

Delbarton said, "By 1893 Kabot had built a good business producing dyes for textiles. More importantly, their chemists had discovered, pioneered, new methods for doing that." John pointed to a photo of the interior of a chemical lab. Men in white coats stood along a countertop with glass beakers in metal frames; beneath the beakers were the flames of Bunsen burners. Above the counter was a long metal hood to catch and remove vapors.

Helen walked to the table. She picked up the photo and studied it. "Looks sorta like my old high school chemistry lab."

Delbarton and Julie laughed, their eyes on the photo in Helen's hand.

"They learned how to produce synthetic dyes from coal tar, right?" Julie asked.

"Right. Cheaper and faster than Mother Nature's methods. But Mother Nature still had a role in the process. They figured out how to test dyes by exposing them to bacteria. Some dyes, the ones with the right formulas, survived, held their color. Over time Kabot chemists learned to match up different dyes with different bacteria."

"Right from the beginning, smarter than Mother Nature." Julie laughed.

"With the growing mass production of textiles world-wide, this was a major innovation. Good business. In 1899 Kabot hit the jackpot with its development of a new pain reliever. Before that, people chewed the bark of willow trees or drank willow-leaf tea. It contained salicin. Some companies produced salicylic acid as a pain reliever, but it was hard to digest. Kabot chemists added a couple of acetyl molecules and got it right: digestible, pain relieving, acetyl salicylic acid."

"I was a journalism major, John. Don't go too far on the technical side."

"Me too, honey," Helen said. "I mean about the technical side. I never went to college."

Helen looked across the room at the young couple, now in the midst of a passionate kiss. "Look at that. Not decent." She yelled across the room, "Hey, easy over there." The couple looked at Helen and then embraced again.

"One of Kabot's chemists perfected the process. They even tested the product on humans, a first for over-the-counter pharmaceuticals. By 1900 the new pain reliever was sold in tablet form around the world, no prescription needed." Delbarton laughed. "Put hangovers on the run." Delbarton raised his mug in a mock toast to Kabot. "Last year, just in the United States, we swallowed twenty-four billion of them." He laughed. "I did my share."

Helen leaned behind the partition and blurted, "Sweetie, I live on 'em." She and Julie laughed.

"Before I forget, in the mid-1930s, after Hitler came to power, Kabot rewrote its history of pain relievers. The chemist who did the original work was a Jew. They removed his name from the discovery. Gave credit to his assistant."

Delbarton continued, now as serious as a classroom lecturer. "In 1908 the Kabot lab produced a new reddish orange dye. It contained a sulfa compound. They tested it against bacteria that caused pneumonia."

"Sulfa drugs," Julie said with the confidence of a student who had done her homework.

"You're way ahead of me," Delbarton said. "Then, for some reason, Kabot held on to the new drug. Didn't release it. Labs in French companies developed sulfa drugs and went on to save thousands of lives. Then Kabot joined in and became a sulfa drug producer."

Delbarton slid the photos aside and placed new ones on the table. Julie and Helen looked at photos of the muddy trenches of World War I battlefields. Vast expanses of open fields and shattered tree trunks, no-man's land, separated the trench lines of the two armies. "Battlefields in France and Belgium."

A photo showed artillery cannons firing. Others showed battlefield explosions as the shells reached their targets, soldiers dismembered and dead. In one photo, in an attack on the German front lines, a company of Allied soldiers climbed out of their trenches and advanced into the unprotected no-man's land. Then photos of men cut down by German machine guns.

Delbarton pushed the photos toward the end of the tabletop alongside the others. On the table he placed another photo of the trenches of the two armies. Small signal flags stood along the German lines. In a light breeze the flags waved and pointed across no-man's land toward the Allied troops.

The next photo showed German forces wearing early models of breathing protection, gas masks, and opening canisters. Gas streamed out and flowed toward French lines. Delbarton said, "Kabot was one of the leaders in developing warfare's first poison gas. World War I. Chlorine. Delivered by canisters and artillery shells."

Then in silence Julie and Helen gazed as the former Kabot executive slowly placed a series of photos on the table. With each of them he paused. Julie saw soldiers gasping for breath, imagined their cries. Troops abandoned their positions, climbed out of trenches and ran in retreat. Overhead views of body-strewn Allied lines, thousands of soldiers dead. Then close up photos of soldiers, their bodies in twisted positions, mouths agape.

Delbarton took a long drink from his mug and then pointed to the aerial photos of troops of the front lines, countless Allied soldiers dead and dying. "The first time the Germans used chlorine gas, six thousand Allied troops choked to death." He paused and slowly repeated the number, "Six thousand," as if to convince himself it was true. "The gas opened a five-mile-wide gap in the Allied front lines."

In the center of the table Delbarton held up a photo of a mud-splattered French soldier sitting in a trench, mouth gaping open, eyes bulging as he attempted to inhale life-giving air into lungs that no longer worked. In silence, Delbarton, Julie and Helen stared at the photo.

Julie said in a near whisper, "He wanted to live."

Delbarton cleared his throat, "Kabot made it tough for the Allies to get drugs and anesthetics. But we got even with them. In 1918, the US government seized many of Kabot's trademarks. A Canadian company, Circle Pharmaceuticals, got the rights. Kept them until Kabot bought Circle in 1994. For most of the twentieth century, when people bought what they thought was a Kabot pain reliever, they really bought a Circle product."

In the booth across the room the young couple was again kissing passionately.

Julie made some notes. Helen walked to the coffee maker and returned with a fresh pot. She refilled her companions' mugs and poured one for herself. She called across the room, "Excuse me, y'all want some coffee?"

The couple sat up and shook their heads no, then returned to their interrupted kiss.

Helen sat down in the booth beside Delbarton. "Kids . . . what are you gonna do?"

On the table, Delbarton placed photos of a poverty-ridden village in Africa. Half-dressed children lay ill on straw tick mattresses. In the background of the photos rose pristine colonial buildings flying the British flag.

Delbarton pointed to the sick children. "Sleeping sickness, the scourge of Africa. After the war, Kabot developed a drug to combat it. Offered it to the British."

Julie interrupted, "I read about that. They offered the drug at the low price of . . . African colonies for Germany."

"Right. Kabot played hardball. They still do. The Brits refused the deal. Kabot held the drug. People continued to suffer and die from sleeping sickness. Later, other labs developed effective drugs."

Helen banged her mug on the table. "Stick it to the little guys."

Delbarton slid the photos aside. Across the tabletop, clusters of photos formed a mosaic. He brought out 1920s photos of the streets of economically depressed cities in Germany. Men stared at the camera, their faces gaunt, their clothes unwashed.

"The Great Depression that we knew here in the 1930s began over there in the twenties. The post-WWI German reparation payments to the Allies triggered inflation that wrecked the economy."

A photo showed a man in a white shirt and necktie pushing a wheelbarrow filled with Deutschmarks through the entrance to a grocery store. Delbarton commented, "A million Deutschmarks for a loaf of bread."

"Drove Grandma and Grandpa outta Germany," Helen said. And then she added, "They came to America, praise the Lord!"

On the table, Delbarton placed photos of political candidates and supporters in the streets of Munich and Berlin. Then photos of political posters pasted to walls, men carrying placards: Social Democrats, Centre Party, Communist Party, and the National Socialists, the Nazis. Some posters had large photos of candidates, Field Marshal Hindenberg, Heinrich Bruning, Ernst Thalmann, Adolf Hitler. And party symbols, prominent among them the swastika.

The tabletop's photos showed a chronology of political change, from the turn of the century to WWI to the rise of Nazism.

Delbarton laughed. "Who knows, Helen? If your people had stayed over there, they might've been Nazis! Or, come to think of it, were they? Are you Jewish?"

"No. But don't laugh . . . some of my people . . . I got pictures of 'em . . . arm bands with that twisted cross, swasti . . . swasti-something."

"Swastika," Delbarton said. He gathered the photos into a single stack and pushed it across the table to Julie. "You keep the photos. I doubt I'll need them anymore."

Julie answered in a voice of surprise, "You doubt . . .? Well, sure, thanks."

"Two more things." Delbarton handed Julie a slip of paper. "First, here are some phone numbers. People at the plant who want to talk about the explosion." He handed her a second sheet of paper. "Here's the electronic address of a website. Kabot tried to shut it down. The site was too hot for museums, even Harvard, to handle."

Julie examined the second slip of paper.

In a firm voice, Delbarton said, "You didn't get any of this from me."

Helen again looked at the young couple. They had angled their bodies into a near prone position. The boy's hands moved inside the girl's blouse.

Helen jumped up. "Hey! Not in here!" She stomped across the room and leaned into the couple's booth. "Oh, no! Get out of here. Find a place by yourselves. Someplace with a bed!"

Chapter 31

SOUTH JACKSON, WV, JULY 1985—Sunday morning. The valley's air, warm and humid, lay still. A putrid rotten egg odor laced the air and mingled with scents of yesterday's mowed lawns and fresh rose blooms.

Charles had worked all day Saturday. The German chemical and pharmaceutical company, Kabot Global, had entered into negotiations with Carbide to purchase the Academy plant. Charles' finance department had prepared a mountain of reports, all part of due diligence.

Sitting at the kitchen table, Charles said, "It's good to have a day with you all. Do nothing. Relax." He sipped coffee and read the front page of the *Jackson Chronicle*. Ben, seated beside him, laughed as he read the Sunday comics. "Dad, Dad, you gotta read Blondie. That Dagwood is so dumb."

Mary removed a tray of cinnamon rolls from the oven. She set it on the table beside the *Chronicle*.

"Mmm, the rolls smell great!" Charles placed a hot roll on a plate.

Mary touched his shoulder. "Nice to take a break from Sunday school . . . Roger's sleeping in."

Without missing a beat, Ben asked, "Can I sleep in tomorrow?"

Charles laughed. "Tomorrow's your day to mow the yard, ol' buddy. If it's this hot, you'll need to get an early start."

Mary placed a roll on a plate and handed it to Ben. "Take this up to Roger?"

Plate in hand, Ben walked toward the stairs. He stopped and turned to his parents, his face troubled. In a hesitant voice, Ben

said, "Mom . . . Dad . . . uh, something I've been . . . do you think
. . .?" Then in a quick burst, "I don't think Roger's medicine is
working."

Mary answered, "Dr. Bennett said we'd have to give it time,
sweetie."

The sudden wail of a nearby emergency siren blasted into the
room.

Ben stopped, as if frozen in place. Mary stood motionless.
Charles held his coffee cup as if suspended between the table and
his lips.

From a distance came the sound of a second siren. Than a moment later, farther away, came the wail of a third one.

Charles rushed to the counter and turned on a portable radio.
"Maybe something at the . . . ."

An announcer said, ". . . and windows. Repeat, Vandalia Valley
Emergency Services has issued a shelter in place. There is a toxic
gas leak at Carbide's Academy plant." Mary, Ben and Charles stared
at the radio, their gazes riveted on its small speaker. "Stay indoors.
Seal your doors and windows. Repeat, Vandalia Valley Emergency
Services has issued a shelter in place. There is a toxic. . . ."

"Ben," Charles yelled, "go turn off Roger's air-conditioner.
Hurry, go, go, go!"

Ben tossed his plate and roll on the table. He ran up the stairs
two at a time.

Charles ran through the house and out the front door.

Mary ran behind him. "Charlie, it's a shelter in place! Don't go
out there. The basement!" She yelled up the stairs, "Boys, come
down. Quick!"

Moments later Mary, Ben and Roger joined Charles in the front
yard. They gazed north toward the river and the plant. Along the
street, neighbors stood in their yards and, like the Grubers, looked
toward the plant.

Mary said, "Charles, what are you looking for? It's a gas leak.
There's nothing to see." She pointed to the front door and tugged
at Charles' arm. "Charles, boys, inside! Now!"

Charles took Ben and Roger by the hand and pulled them toward the front door. Once inside, he slammed the door shut.

A fire department panel truck, speakers mounted on top, drove along Oak Street toward the Gruber home. "Shelter in place! Everyone, go indoors! Stay indoors! Seal windows, seal doors. Wait for the all-clear. Shelter in place! Everyone go indoors! Stay indoors!" The announcement faded as the truck continued down the street. "Seal windows, seal . . ."

Charles carried Roger piggyback down the steps to the basement and gently lowered him to the couch. He joined Mary and Ben in hurriedly applying masking tape around doors and ground-level windows.

Charles turned on the basement radio. A news announcer said, "Authorities at Union Carbide's Academy plant said the shelter in place is a protective step, that residents should not worry . . . ."

Mary yelled at the radio, "Well, *I'm* worried. Is this another Bhopal? What's happening to our town?"

Chapter 32

JACKSON, WV, NOVEMBER, 2008—Julie arrived early morning at Harrison's office for their daily meeting.

Harrison stood as she walked in. "Hey, how about you briefing me over a pastry and a mug of Henry's coffee?"

"Sounds good."

A chilly November breeze pushed from behind as they walked to Henry's Books, an independent bookstore with a coffee bar and pastries. The coffee shop enjoyed a brisk business that morning. Customers occupied most of the tables. Harrison ordered two croissants and coffee while Julie located a small table for two, racks of books behind them.

Julie sat at the table and checked e-mail on her smartphone. From the other side of the entry, in the books section, she heard Ben's voice.

Ben laughed. "How many letters? I asked all the employees to write them. There may be twenty or thirty a day. Maybe more. Employees and families writing to the *Chronicle*, the governor, local officials. The letters should show we have lots of support in the community." His voice fell silent for a moment.

Harrison arrived with two cups of coffee and two banana nut muffins. "I was just thinking about . . ."

Julie waved a hand to caution him and then put her index finger to her lips.

Harrison sat down, a puzzled look on his face. He scanned the room, then mouthed the question, "What's up?"

Julie put her hand to her ear and pointed toward the entrance to the book section.

Ben said, "Must be driving the *Chronicle* nuts." He paused and then laughed. "I called her at work: 'Hey Julie, think your investigation will wrap up its findings before the Chemical Institute completes theirs?'" He paused, silent for a moment, then continued, "What was her answer? It's hard to say. She ignored me." He laughed.

During Ben's next pause, Harrison whispered, "Who's he talking to?"

Julie shook her head from side to side and shrugged.

Ben said, "What else will she write about Kabot? Who knows?" A pause. "Good question. Maybe I can find out. I'll let you know. Bye, babe."

Two words. Those last two words. Like a passing storm's final bolts of lightning followed by a sudden wind. Julie's face blanched. She jumped up and rushed to the rear of the coffee bar and into the women's restroom.

A moment later Ben, his eyes on his cell phone as he placed another call, walked through the coffee bar and out the front door.

From the restroom doorway Julie watched Ben leave. Then she returned to the table and sat down, tears in her eyes.

Harrison shook his head. "I'm sorry."

"Ben is history. But history can still hurt."

Chapter 33

JULIE RETURNED FROM HER EARLY MORNING RUN in brisk late autumn air laced with traces of chlorine. The limbs of trees over South Jackson's streets carried traces of last night's snow flurries.

Still in her sweaty running clothes, Julie sat at her kitchen table. Beside her sat a middle-aged woman. She had the stout body of a woman who'd done manual labor, worked with her hands, and the confidence of a woman who knew how to handle hard work.

A few days earlier Julie had called the church she had attended with her parents. She wondered if Millie, the church secretary, would remember her. After Julie's parents had passed away, she rarely attended church. Christmas, Easter. Weddings. Funerals. In recent years there'd been fewer and fewer weddings and more and more funerals. Each funeral seemed to bring an ever-smaller number of mourners as Julie's parents' generation dwindled. With each funeral, Julie felt her connection to the church weaken.

Millie welcomed her call. "So good to hear your voice, Julie."

Julie asked if Millie knew anyone who might be looking for work. Millie did and connected Julie with Bertha.

Julie brewed a pot of coffee. She and Bertha sat at the kitchen table. Julie remembered Bertha, stout and strong, not hesitant to speak her mind, from elementary school, where she'd once been one of the custodians. Bertha once caught her writing chalk graffiti on a school's brick wall.

"Let me get this clear, Miss Julie. What is it you want me to do?"

"Each day, Bertha, come in for a couple of hours. I'd prefer mornings, but I'll leave the time up to you. A key will be on the sill above the back door. Straighten the place up. Vacuum. Once a week clean the bathroom fixtures and the kitchen."

"Sure, I can do that. More if you need it. My man's out of work."

For a moment Julie thought about Bertha's offer. "How about cooking dinner one night a week?"

Without hesitation, and with a smile, Bertha said, "I'd like that. I mean, I'll do it if you enjoy my cookin'."

Julie smiled. "I'm sure I will."

Bertha stood. "I'd like to go to the basement. Have a look at your washer and dryer. My momma had to use an old wringer washer and a clothes line. The new machines is nice. I'm glad we got 'em. Gonna check cleaning supplies, too. Maybe tidy up things down there." Bertha left the table and walked to the basement, each of her footsteps a heavy clomp on the wooden steps.

Julie went into her bathroom and turned on the shower.

Thirty minutes later, wearing a bathrobe and a towel around her still-wet hair, Julie sat at the kitchen table with a bowl of cereal. She'd opened the *Chronicle* and spread it across the table.

After a light rap on the back door, Ben walked into the kitchen. She looked up from her cereal and newspaper.

Ben gave Julie a hug. Julie recoiled, stiffened. He didn't have ad lib entry privileges anymore.

Julie said, "This's a surprise."

Bertha entered the kitchen from the hallway. She carried a basket of clothes to be laundered.

Ben glanced at each of the women and laughed. "Just flew in from Connecticut. My arms sure are tired."

Neither Julie nor Bertha laughed. They stared at Ben.

Ben nodded toward Bertha and asked Julie, "House guest?"

"This is Bertha. She's going to help out around the house. I've been going flat out. Need a little support."

"Hi Bertha, I'm Ben."

Bertha nodded and walked down the basement steps.

Then Ben looked at Julie. "Bertha's going to do *your* job?"

"My job? I work at the *Chronicle*. Remember? This is my home. How I run it is my . . ."

"Sorry, honey, it's okay. I just keep thinking, I'll soon have my MBA. And I'm moving up at the plant. I still believe we'll, you know, put things back together. I want us to save our money. And maybe, down the road, tie the knot. Buy a large home. Kids. You know, make a dream come true."

In her head, Julie heard Ben's phone call at Henry's Books. His final words, "Bye, babe," blasted through her thoughts. Julie's cereal spoon banged as it fell to the table.

"You can drop the 'honey.' Next time knock and wait on me to answer the door. Your barging in pass has expired." Julie paused to watch the assurance in Ben's face evaporate. "Dream come true? Go back to bed, Ben. Dream again."

Ben looked at Julie with surprise. His face reddened and he turned to leave.

Julie said, "By the way, I heard another worker died from the explosion."

"How'd you . . .?" He opened the back door and called, "See you around."

Bertha clomped up the steps and entered the kitchen. "Miss Julie, you want these ironed?"

Chapter 34

THE FOLLOWING EVENING, ON THE OTHER SIDE of the plant's front gate, Julie drove past a group of people carrying placards. LOVE THY NEIGHBOR—END MIC. KABOT IS UNSAFE. STOP ANOTHER BHOPAL. MIC—A KILLER. A young woman approached Julie's car and extended her hand, holding a handbill. Julie took it. "END MIC—PUBLIC MEETING TONIGHT! 6:30 PM, Vandalia State Student Union, Room 305."

Julie parked and walked into the Student Union. Rock music filled the air. Students sat or stood at tables, talking and studying. She walked up the steps to the meeting room.

She entered Room 305. More than thirty people, about half of them African-Americans, had come to the meeting. Some stood and chatted. Others sat around classroom tables and desks. On the whiteboard at the front of the room was printed in large letters, "Meeting—END MIC." The room hummed with the buzz of animated conversations.

As the meeting started, Julie took a seat in the rear.

A woman about Julie's age stood and faced the group. Julie remembered her from running events; sometimes as a runner, other times helping with management of a race. Her soft voice carried the accent of the Appalachian Mountains. Her face seemed to invite others into conversations, even trust.

"Hi, everybody. I'm Karen Hill. Thank y'all for coming. Please take a seat. It's OK if you'd prefer to stand." After most people sat down, she continued, "Many of us are neighbors. And we all live in the valley. As upsetting as the Kabot explosion has been, and is, it's a wake-up call. To take action. Working together, we can *end* the use of MIC, *end the presence of MIC* in the Vandalia River Valley."

A tall, muscular young man in a football jersey said, "I was in the dorm when the plant exploded. Scared me. Like we'd been bombed. Scared everybody."

A ruddy-faced, middle-aged man in a John Deere cap said, "I thought a plane had crashed. Later I smelled an odor. Then I could taste it."

An older, well-dressed African-American woman in her mid-sixties seated at a table raised her hand and then spoke to the group. "I'm Angela Washington. A grade school teacher in Academy for thirty years. I live here, not far from the plant. Bhopal is still fresh in my memory. When it happened I was a young mother in my second year of teaching . . . . I wanted, we all wanted, to protect our children. Get MIC out of our back yard. We organized and, like now, we picketed Carbide. We held meetings like this one. The company said, over and over, 'We share your concerns. We're testing our systems. They work. We're safe . . . *you're safe.* We have the best engineers in the world. They know what they're doing.'"

She paused, stood up, and looked around the room. "All those reassurances. Carbide was wrong! Seven months after Bhopal came the aldicarb release. Many of us, our families, went to the hospital. We redoubled our efforts. Held protest meetings. Spoke out. Politicians joined our meetings. The president of Carbide even came." She paused and for a moment looked down. Then she looked around the room. "But *nothing happened.* No change. Except now, a quarter of a century later, many of us," her voice became louder, "right here in Academy, people living around the plant, have chronic illnesses. Cancer. Blood problems. Liver problems. We've seen children born with birth defects, others with severe learning disabilities. Like children in Bhopal. Though, thank God, here it's been on a smaller scale."

She began to weep, stopped, then put her hands on her desk to steady herself. "Sorry. I watched a neighbor child die of cancer. It's hard for me to talk about what's happened over the years."

She managed a weak smile, "When I do, I have to stop. I'll do that now." She sat down but added, her voice again forceful, "We must do *something*. We owe it to our children, to our grandchildren."

An elderly woman raised her hand and said, "The night of the explosion, when I went to bed I prayed I'd be alive in the morning. And I was. Maybe an answered prayer. Now I pray that Kabot'll get rid of the poisons. Or put their big boys and their families down here in Academy with us. Let them feel what it's like to live next door to a tank of MIC."

Around the room people applauded.

A middle-aged man in a sports coat and polo shirt rose and stood beside his desk. "I was on the faculty here at Vandalia State when Bhopal happened. We were scared. The solution to our problem? Hard to believe today, but we told Carbide we wanted them to be like Kabot over in Germany. Maintain no stockpile of MIC. Make the stuff only as needed." He laughed. "Be like Kabot? The joke was on us."

A man yelled, "But that plant means jobs. For me, maybe for you, too."

"Jobs don't mean much when you're dead!" another man called out.

A woman in the rear of the room said, "We have to do what they won't do . . . protect our community, our children." She began to cry. "And yes, ourselves, too."

A man yelled, "I only know one way to do that!"

Angela said, "We failed the last time around."

Karen asked, "What's your one way?"

"Is anybody here a lawyer?" No one spoke or raised a hand.

With a determined look on her face, Karen said, "Then let's find one."

Chapter 35

JACKSON, WV, NOVEMBER 2008—Julie joined the senior staff and Harrison for a lunch meeting in the conference room. The *Chronicle* had provided inexpensive box lunches, clear plastic containers labeled ham and cheese, turkey, veggie. In addition to a sandwich, each container had a bag of chips and two cookies. An ample supply of soft drinks sat atop a credenza.

The room buzzed with chatter. Bob Samuelson sat next to Julie. She had just briefed him on last night's End MIC meeting when Harrison rapped gently on the table and said, "Let's get started. Go ahead and eat. I don't know about you, but I'm hungry."

Kirby Flemington entered the room and took a seat at the table. The sounds of crackling plastic sounded around the table as people opened box lunches.

Harrison said, "Bob and Julie, please bring everyone up to date on Kabot."

Bob leaned toward Julie. "Go ahead, Julie."

"A little history, Harrison, everybody." She glanced around the table. "Some of you were here when the things I'll talk about happened. Please tell me if I need to correct my information. Some of you were not here back then. When I finish, I hope we'll all be on the same page."

Julie shuffled the notes in front of her. "In 1984, after Bhopal, Carbide suspended all MIC production. For seven months they upgraded and installed new safety systems. Spent millions." She opened a June 1985 edition of the *Chronicle* and held up the front page. The headline read CARBIDE TO RESTART MIC PRODUCTION. "And by the way, today is the 24th anniversary of the Bhopal disaster.

"Not long after they resumed production, a major toxic leak occurred. Another shelter in place for the valley." She held up a *Chronicle* front page from July 15, 1985, and read the headline aloud. "Carbide leak hospitalizes 135." In the center of the front page a photo showed paramedics strapping oxygen masks to victims lying on stretchers. Next to the photo a map of the Vandalia River valley had been printed with a heavy border around the affected areas of Academy, South Jackson and Jackson.

Bob said, "Only seven months after Bhopal. I wrote the story. I went to the new Carbide headquarters building, Danbury, Connecticut. Lovely place. Lots of woods around it. A five-story rectangular building with adjoining figure-eight loops of offices, everything covered with a continuous dark glass shell.

"They held a news conference I attended. A Carbide executive stood behind a podium. A reporter asked, 'Aren't Carbide computers set to predict the course of gas leaks?'

"The executive said, 'Yes, sir, our computers at South Jackson are programmed to predict where gas emissions might go. . . .'

"I jumped in and asked, 'Then why . . .?'

"He didn't let me finish my question. He said, 'But the computers weren't programmed for aldicarb.'

"I asked, 'A toxic gas leak—you couldn't predict its direction?'

" 'We can't program for every possibility.'

" 'How would you describe Carbide's plant safety today?'

" 'Last year, world-wide, we operated over seven hundred facilities. So few employee injuries that Carbide was, is, among the safest companies in the industry.'

" 'What about Bhopal? Eight months ago Carbide killed . . . two, five, ten thousand? Now a toxic leak in the Vandalia River Valley. Lots of people live there. How's all this figure into your safety record?'

Bob smiled. "The man's fingers drummed on the podium. He had a grim look on his face but answered me with a thin veneer of politeness. 'Look,' he said, 'you're moving millions of pounds of chemicals around. There are bound to be problems. You have systems. You train your people . . . hopefully those systems work. . . .'

"I couldn't resist saying, 'And sometimes they don't.'"

Harrison said, "After you returned, you wrote a great story, Bob."

Bob continued, "Then in 1994, after Kabot bought the plant, another explosion. Killed two workers."

"And the government fined them two million dollars," Julie added.

A man seated across from Julie said, "For a global corporation with billions in revenue, two million is chump change."

Julie said, "Folks in the valley may remember that fine. The explosion, too. But here's what people may have forgotten. At the plant, Carbide in 1985 and Kabot in 1994, after explosions, they installed new equipment and then failed to thoroughly test it. Too eager to get business up and running. Their people jumped in and started production before the plant was ready."

Bob said, "And now, after a shut-down, they've done the same thing again. Started up too fast. And more lives have been lost. *Déjà vu* all over again?"

"The larger Kabot corporation has its own history," Harrison said. "I've asked Julie to look into it. But for now, we need to think about the Academy plant's history, its culture—how they do business. The company Carbide built and Kabot bought. Now Kabot has layered its ways of operating on top of Carbide's culture. The question we, and by *we* I mean everyone in the valley, face is this: Has the joining, the combination, of these two companies magnified their underlying problems? And in the process, increased risks for people in the valley?"

Bob laughed. "You mean like recessive genes in in-breeding?"

"Great analogy," Harrison said, joining the laughter.

Julie said, "More recently, Kabot has had a string of safety failures and OSHA citations. Before the explosion, OSHA was about to issue a finding that Kabot had ignored its own safety studies on the Academy plant's operations."

"And nobody has stepped in, held their feet to the fire," Harrison said.

"Carbide," Julie said, "and now Kabot has friends in high places." She passed photos around the table. One showed Otto shaking hands with Dick Cheney; another showed Otto seated at a black-tie dinner for John Kerry.

"The *Chronicle* could've, should've done more," Harrison said. He opened a folder and removed some papers. "We've got a lot to cover. Bob, Julie, are you about finished?"

"Almost." Julie turned to Bob and in a lowered voice said, "Bob, the toxic leaks?"

"Okay." He glanced around the table. "A quick summary. Academy plant, 1985 and 1994 we've already talked about. Other incidents. In 1990, an acid leak and a community wide shelter in place. In 1993, a chlorine leak, another shelter in place. In 1994, sulfur chloride leak, shelter in place. In 1996, toluene leak, shelter in place . . ."

Harrison interrupted. "We get the picture. Thanks, Bob."

His voice louder, Bob spoke faster. "Then in 1999, shelter in place. In 2001 . . ."

"We get the picture."

". . . Ten workers hospitalized."

Kirby said, "Thanks, Bob, Julie. You're on the right track."

Harrison held up his hand for Bob to stop. "Bob, you and Julie write all this up. Leaks. Explosions. Shelters in place. The Academy plant's history. We'll run it, front page."

Julie leaned forward. "Just one more, Harrison, 2006. Bob?"

"You may remember. We ran a story on a 2006 EPA report. It said Kabot had released over three hundred tons of pollutants in the valley, most of them toxic. Including MIC. Kabot and our politicians worked damned hard to bury that report."

"Connected to that," Julie added, "statistics on cancer rates here are above the national average. But even those get weakened, washed out, because they are based on the valley or the county, based on large geographic areas. But walk the streets of Academy. Talk to people who live near the plant. Home after home, families who've lost loved ones to cancer."

Bob added, "When I asked the health department people, 'Why not do a study on cancer rates in Academy?' they said, 'We don't have the staff. And people move. We can't follow up.' Then a secretary told me the real reason. Kabot attorneys called and said that studies of that nature singled out Kabot, placed unwarranted, special and prejudicial attention on the company. They asked, 'What about all the other companies? Do you want us to take legal action to protect Kabot?'"

"Chemical Valley," Harrison said.

"Cancer Valley," Julie added.

Chapter 36

A FEW DAYS LATER JULIE WALKED along River Street in downtown Jackson to meet Ben for late-afternoon coffee at Henry's Books. Turn-of-the-century buildings and gas street lamps reflected an earlier era. The state capitol, destroyed by fire nearly a century ago, once stood at the north end of the street. The branches of maple and magnolia trees, a few of them still bearing colorful autumn leaves, arced over the street.

She had asked Ben to join her for coffee. Could she find an opening, a way to loosen his uncritical view of Kabot? Then she asked herself, *Do I still care?*

Ten minutes after they sat down, they had entered a discussion about Kabot and the history of the plant.

"And not just this explosion, Ben, as bad as it was. From Bhopal through today, the Academy plant, whether owned by Carbide or Kabot, has had a long history of leaks, spills, and explosions, accompanied by citations and fines. And serious illnesses and deaths among employees as well as people living close to the plant."

"The spills and explosions are water over the dam, Julie. And I don't think it is fair to blame Kabot for the illnesses of local people. Who knows what kinds of unhealthy lives they've led?"

Blame the victim, she thought. In the short time it had taken her to sip a half-cup of Henry's house blend, Julie sensed the futility of her hope for changes at the plant, or changes in Ben. She asked, "When, Ben, when, will it end? After each toxic spill, each explosion, Kabot's top people, like Carbide before them, delay and appeal. Delay and appeal. Why not admit there is a problem? Enroll support, push to fix it!"

"You don't understand corporate liability, Julie. Any, repeat, *any* admission of liability opens the door to massive numbers of injury claims. There's an ocean of legal sharks out there. Trial lawyers waiting to eat Kabot alive."

"But if Kabot's top management denies culpability, and their people follow suit, how's anything ever . . ."

"Not to worry, Jules. We have the best engineers in the world. They're working every day to make things right."

Julie's mouth opened as if to speak and then closed. She stared at Ben. Did she know this man? Had she ever really known him?

Ben stood to leave. "I have to go. We haven't seen much of each other lately. I miss you."

His words brought Julie a rush of memories, the good times, and twinges of the pain that comes with loss. "Sometimes I miss you, Ben. But you're on another path. It's not my path."

Julie stood. From her backpack, she lifted a copy of the next morning's *Chronicle*.

Ben stared at the front page's headline, "Citizens Group Files in Federal Court," and below it the lead story, "Seeks Kabot Injunction to Stop MIC Production." By Julie Brown.

Chapter 37

THE NEXT MORNING, AFTER HER MEETING with Harrison, Julie sat at her desk making notes. Her phone rang. Her phone's caller ID announced Ben Gruber.

"Hi Ben. What's up?" A moment after her question, Julie had a flash of humor and laughed as she said, "Having second thoughts about Kabot?" Immediately she wished she'd kept her thoughts to herself and her big mouth shut. *Dumb question,* she thought. Even worse, it implied an intimacy she'd tried to end.

Ben didn't laugh. "When I got to the front gate this morning, the number of people carrying signs, you know, demonstrators, had increased. A lot. Seems like more of them are here every day. Maybe winter will drive them away."

"Maybe you should listen to them."

"I had just sat down at my desk when Otto barged in. His face was beet red."

Julie chuckled. "Don't tell me. He wants to admit Kabot's guilt and enroll support in fixing the plant's problems."

"Not funny, Jules." He paused for a moment. "Otto waved a copy of this morning's *Chronicle* in my face. 'This story,' he said, '. . . your *freundin,* ah . . . your girlfriend. You could have at least warned us.'

"Maybe I should've. But I didn't. I said, 'Sorry, I didn't know.'

"Otto was hot. He yelled, 'You didn't . . . you and she are, shall we say, close? And you didn't know?'

"I pushed back. 'We don't live together. We're not even dating these days. Julie's a reporter. She writes what she writes. I'm not part of that.'

"He said, 'You are wrong, Ben. Her work reflects poorly on you. On all of us.'

"I told him, 'Otto, it's what she does for a living.'

"'What she does for a living?'

" 'Otto,' I said, 'I appreciate your . . .'

"He interrupted, 'You appreciate? Then appreciate this. I will hear from corporate. They will remind me in no uncertain terms that we, you, are to put loyalty first, Ben. I'm telling you now. *Loyalty first . . . if . . .* you want a future at Kabot.' He slammed the paper on my desk and walked away."

After a long pause, Julie said, "Loyalty, Ben. He's right about that. My question is, who and what are you loyal to?"

Click. Ben abruptly disconnected the call.

Chapter 38

EARLY SATURDAY MORNING JULIE WALKED into her kitchen. Every dish had been put away, and the sink, the floor, even the inside of the refrigerator had been scrubbed. The room had a new presence, squeaky clean. She poured a cup of coffee, admired her tidy kitchen, and felt a wave of gratitude for Bertha.

She opened her mom's old cookbook to the recipe on brownies and imagined the finished product. Already she could taste them. Something had been lightly written in pencil below the recipe. She angled the page to put the pencil marks, the indentations, in the sunlight. She tried to read the words now faded from the page. "R- - - - l i k - - t - - se." She remembered. The brownies had been favorites of Roger. "Roger likes these."

Julie melted chocolate, then poured it into a mixing bowl along with the sugar, flour, chopped walnuts, and milk. She turned on the oven, 350 degrees, then turned on the mixer and let it run at a slow speed. The machine's gentle whirring brought back memories of home, her mom preparing her childhood desserts. "Mom, can I lick the bowl?" Church socials. Evenings when life seemed simpler. Putting away the cookbook, Julie again squinted at the penciled entry below the brownies recipe. A remnant of people, those years, a simpler life, now gone.

Julie poured another mug of coffee and sat down to read the front section of the *Chronicle*. When she finished, she turned off the mixer and poured the ingredients from the mixing bowl into a baking pan. She put the pan in the oven and set the timer. Soon the kitchen filled with the rich chocolaty aroma of baking brownies.

Shortly before noon, showered and dressed for jogging, Julie put half of the brownies on a plate. She covered them with clear plastic wrap and carried the plate out her back door.

Julie walked across her back yard to the home of her neighbors, Don and Flora. Don worked at the plant. Flora had been ill and, Julie learned from a neighbor, had just come through surgery. Don and Flora had helped Julie move into her home last year. Then Julie had become so involved in work that she'd lost track of their lives. She hoped the brownies would help put things back on track.

She knocked on the back door. Don, holding a cup of coffee, opened it. "Hey, Julie."

"Hi Don." She handed him the plate of brownies.

"Hey, how'd you know? Flora loves brownies." He paused. "Well, she used to. Come in."

Julie followed Don into the kitchen. "How's Flora doing?"

"Doc says about as well as we can expect, whatever the hell that means." He motioned for Julie to sit at the kitchen table. "I just made a fresh pot of coffee. Want some?"

"Sure. Thanks. Do you think Flora'll feel up to having a brownie?"

Don poured coffee for Julie, then joined her at the table. "Maybe. Been a week. They took out one lung."

The insides of Julie's stomach constricted, and her face cringed.

"After they took out that lung, they discovered the cancer'd metastasized. Put her on chemo."

"Sorry. I didn't know." Julie sipped her coffee. "Lung cancer? I don't remember Flora smoking. Did she?"

"Never. But got lung cancer anyway. Same as Mrs. Sturbutzel over on Maple Street. And at church, Harry Simpson and Jim Hunter. And they thought smokin' was a sin!"

"My dad never smoked. Add him to your cancer list."

Don turned and stared out the window into the darkness for a moment. "At church, the preacher says the Lord'll provide. He just don't say *what*."

Don walked to the counter and poured himself more coffee He brought the carafe to the table, filled Julie's mug, and sat down. "You go through life tryin' to do the right thing. Then one day, out of the blue, a monster grabs ahold. Don't let you go 'til he's sucked the life outta you."

"Throw a stick in any direction, you'll hit somebody with cancer," Julie said. "Chemical Valley."

"And good ol' Kabot makes sure nobody talks about it. At least not in public. Chemical Valley? I call it Cancer Valley."

Don took a brownie from the plate and handed the plate to Julie. "Join me?" Julie took a brownie.

After taking a big bite of his brownie, Don said, "Hey, Julie, good brownies."

"Thanks." Julie took a bite. "Don, can I ask you something?"

"About?"

"Kabot. The night of the explosion."

The smile on Don's face disappeared. In its place, and in his voice, was apprehension. "Yeah?"

"I'm doing a story on the explosion. I was wondering, in your work at the plant, where were you when . . ."

Don slammed his mug on the table. Coffee splashed out of it. "You've been a friend and a good neighbor, Julie. But don't think a batch of brownies is gonna buy Donnie's true confessions!"

"The brownies are for Flora. I'm just trying to get a line on the truth."

Don's voice became louder. "Here's my truth, nearly forgot to mention it. Flora's upstairs dyin'."

"Sorry, Don, I . . ."

Don stood and looked toward the doorway into the hall, then turned to Julie. "I thought I heard Flora. Finish your coffee. Just let yourself out." He walked a few steps toward the stairs, then stopped. "Thanks for the brownies. Hope Flora'll get to enjoy them."

Chapter 39

A COLD WINTER WIND BLEW the last of autumn's leaves along River Street. The street's canopy of branches, once providers of summer shade, had become skeletal, like a large tent with its canvas taken away.

Julie and Ben joined other customers in the coffee bar of Henry's Books. Julie put down her backpack and said, "When you called a couple of nights ago, I'd been trying to reach you."

"You had? I was in my apartment." Ben's face tensed; worry lines appeared.

"Your line was busy. I tried, off and on, for an hour. You must've turned off your cell phone. I tried it, too, but no answer."

"Oh, I forgot. Otto called. He was concerned about, well, about your articles and the *Chronicle*. He'd heard some rumors of steps the governor might take on chemical safety. When pressure builds up, he needs someone to talk to."

"Ben the therapist?"

"I suppose so. In a way." Julie shook her head. His voice lacked conviction.

"Two hours?"

Ben sipped his coffee and looked away. "Let it go, Julie."

"That's what you want, isn't it?"

"Jules, I didn't come here to argue with you. I'm reminded again that we're becoming two separate . . ."

Julie leaned toward him. "You got it, Ben. We are. Two separate people. Period."

Ben toyed with a spoon. "Otto's on me to put out fires. You and the *Chronicle* are fanning the flames. How're you finding out all the . . ."

"I'm a reporter, Ben. Remember? It's what I do."

"Right. A reporter. And a negative one. So negative."

"I don't make the news. I just report the facts."

"What about all the good Kabot does? Medicines that heal. Pesticides for crops. Contributions to museums, the Jackson Symphony. Summer camps for kids. Remember those camps, back in the Carbide days? You and me, we were there."

"What about MIC, Ben? Small leaks, day in, day out, never reported. Are those leaks connected to high rates of cancer around the plant? Around South Jackson? Or are other chemicals doing it? And, oh yes, Kabot engineers keep telling us we're safe. Then we go through one shelter in place after another. The truth, Ben. I'm just telling the truth. I don't massage it. I don't spin it. I just tell it."

"You think anybody really cares about MIC? Do you? *Jobs.* That's what people care about, jobs! You and your damned truth!"

Julie stood and picked up her backpack. "My damned truth?" Her breath came in quick gasps. Her heart pounded. Julie walked out of Henry's coffee bar. She checked her pulse: 101 beats a minute.

Julie walked to the river, then along the shoreline for a more than a mile upstream. She walked around the capitol and nearby state office buildings. Julie looked at buildings that housed environmental protection and workplace safety offices. "Wake up!" she yelled at the closed windows.

After she returned to her office she checked her heartbeat: 60 beats a minute. Life became normal again.

Chapter 40

IN HER MORNING SESSION WITH HARRISON, Julie summarized her meeting with John Delbarton: A discussion of Germany in the 1930s—rampant economic inflation, collapse of the economy, and the rise of National Socialism, the Nazis, and Hitler.

Julie looked at her notes. "Then John pointed me toward electronic archives. Files on Kabot's business dealings with Hitler and the Third Reich; photographs, letters and news articles. Not exactly buried, but stuck away in little-known electronic locations. Not hard to find, *if* you know where to look. Mostly World War II archives. And files from the Nuremberg trials."

Harrison's face lengthened with concern. "Go slow with all that, Julie, particularly the Nuremberg trials. Kirby keeps reminding me that people in the valley own Kabot stock. And that lots of American companies did big business with the Third Reich in the run up to the war."

Julie leaned across his desk, "How about IBM, Harrison? Does Kirby want to ignore their contributions to the Third Reich? Hitler couldn't have pursued his 'final solution,' criminalizing, tracking and executing Jews, without IBM." She paused, then said, "IBM computers and punch cards made the Holocaust an efficient operation. Oh, and before I forget, until 1940, the German Luftwaffe's aviation fuel came from Standard Oil."

With a long face, Harrison said, "I know. It's a tangled web."

"So? Do you want me to whitewash Kabot?"

Harrison raised one hand. "Easy, Julie. My question, and Kirby's question, is why do you want to dig into that part of Kabot's history?"

"Kabot is the company we're dealing with, Harrison. Their history is the company's genetic heritage; it's who they are. I'm going to write about what I've learned. If your editing waters it down . . . or if you and the publisher take me off this story . . ." Her voice faded. Julie closed her eyes for a moment. "Harrison, if you or Kirby stop me, I'll find another way to tell the story. You and the editor-in-chief can . . ." In a quiet voice, Julie said, "People need to know who they're dealing with. When local people worry about explosions and toxic releases, they need to feel they can trust Kabot to protect them. Can they?"

"I didn't say . . ."

Julie slapped her hand on her notebook. "Then you and Kirby better fasten your seat belts. You know IG Farben?"

"I know about IG Farben. World War II. A German industrial conglomerate."

"A cartel. IG Farben made Hitler's conquest of Europe possible, made the launch of World War II possible."

Julie reached into her backpack and pulled out a large folder bulging with papers and photos.

Outside Harrison's door, Bob Samuelson waved to get Harrison's attention. When Harrison looked up, Bob pointed toward Julie then himself. He mouthed the words, "Talk to her."

Harrison ignored him. Bob continued to pace back and forth in front of the door.

On Harrison's desk, Julie placed photos of the streets of Munich and Berlin in the late 1920s. Shop windows were boarded shut. Men stood in employment lines and in breadlines.

"A little context. Germany's reparation payments to the Allies after World War I led them to print money, creating rampant inflation. Soon the economy collapsed. The Great Depression struck early in Germany. Millions unemployed . . ."

Julie opened a file of Kabot chemical plant and laboratory photos. "During WWI Kabot joined other large chemical companies to form a cartel, IG Farben, to protect the industry. In 1925 they incorporated Interessen-Gemeinschaft Farbenindustrie AG. Translation?"

Harrison interrupted, "Community of interests of dye making corporations, chemical companies."

Julie flashed a look of surprise. She grinned. "Excellent translation." She continued, "IG Farben became the largest chemical company in the world and the world's fourth largest industrial corporation, after General Motors, U.S. Steel, and Standard Oil of New Jersey."

Harrison glanced out his office door. Bob continued to pace and wave. Harrison ignored him.

Julie placed more photos on Harrison's desk. "The early 1930s, the streets of Munich," she said. Photos showed men carrying placards supporting candidates and political parties; photos of signs and posters with political party symbols, prominent among them, the swastika; pictures of Field Marshal Hindenberg and Adolf Hitler. In one photo, Hitler gave a street corner speech to a small crowd. Then, in successive photos, he spoke to ever larger crowds.

"In the 1933 German elections," Julie said, "IG Farben was the single largest contributor to the Nazi party. Farben was a prime mover in bankrolling Hitler's rise to power." A photo showed Hitler speaking to a filled-to-capacity stadium.

"Here are pictures of the dividends paid by Kabot's political investments." Julie placed a new series of photos on Harrison's desk. In succession, German SS troops herded well-dressed families wearing Star of David armbands into the beds of covered trucks. Crowds of Jews jammed railway station passenger platforms. Armed SS troops marched them into cattle cars.

Julie handed Harrison multiple typed pages paperclipped together. "Here. I just finished writing this. Kabot and the Third Reich."

Harrison laid the document on his desk beside a stack of books. He stared at the books.

Julie said, "It still needs some work."

Harrison, distracted, muttered, "Right, cartels."

"Hello? World to Harrison. Are you there?"

He looked toward the outside corridor and Bob, who smiled eagerly, as if pleased that he finally had Harrison's attention.

Then Harrison turned toward Julie. "I'm listening."

"Could've fooled me. Did you know all of what I talked about?"

"No, not all of it. But I was listening."

"An occupational disease of editors, Harrison? Is that what I'm seeing? You act like you're listening, but you don't listen?"

"When I *act like* . . . then I *am* listening."

"You're an *apparently* active listener . . . who doesn't . . ."

Outside Harrison's office, Bob shrugged, waved his arms in the air and walked away.

Julie stood. "Forget it." She put her notebook in her backpack. "I have work to do. There are people at the *Chronicle* who *do* listen. They actually listen."

"Julie, please sit down."

She remained standing and glared at Harrison.

In a soft voice, Harrison said, "You're right. I wasn't listening. I'm sorry."

"Planning an editorial? Mentally composing your grocery list?"

"No." He fumbled with a pencil. It slipped from his fingers and dropped on his desk. He straightened a stack of papers. "I was thinking . . ."

"Something interesting, I hope," she said, unable to keep the sarcasm out of her voice.

Harrison's face reddened. "Thinking . . . about you."

"Me? You vet my work every morning. What more is there to think about? I mean, about me?"

Harrison started to speak and then stopped. Words seemed to form behind his lips, then disappear. "Just wondering . . . about you. Who you are. What you care about. How you live your life away from work."

"Here's my life in a nutshell. In the morning, I get up and go for a run. Then I go to work. Sometimes, late in the day, I unwind with another run. I used to see Ben, but I don't anymore. Then I go to bed. I get up, go for a run. I work. Grab a meal when I can. I run and I work. There you have it. The dull but productive life of this reporter."

Julie picked up her backpack and walked two step toward the door. She stopped and set it down. "Sometimes I . . ."

Harrison's face brightened. "Sometimes you what?"

Julie hesitated and then said, "Sometimes I wonder about you, too."

Harrison smiled. "My life's about like yours. Busy as hell. Work, workouts, more work. Productive. But nothing to write home about."

Julie smiled. "Maybe we both need to make some changes."

Harrison flashed a wide grin. "You're right." He waved a hand. "Come on, let's go get something to eat."

"You're on."

They left Harrison's office and walked down the corridor. Behind them, Bob ran out of his office. He yelled, "Julie, call me?"

Julie waved and nodded to him.

Julie and Harrison went to a small restaurant, Harley's, on a short and little-traveled side street in downtown Jackson. The owner, Harley Williams, middle-aged, African American, welcomed Harrison and introduced himself to Julie.

"This man," he pointed to Harrison, "made all the difference in my family. Our son got to go to a good school, an integrated school, because of Harrison and the paper. Today my son's a doctor."

"Your son has done well because he's smart. And because you and your wife steered him in the right direction."

Harley shrugged and then looked at Julie. Nodding toward Harrison, he said, "Ditch him. He never learned to take credit for anything. Go find yourself a rich man."

They laughed.

Harrison asked Julie if he could order for them. "Sure."

They each enjoyed one of Harley's pulled-pork barbecue sandwiches, cole slaw and all the sweet tea they could drink. During dinner Harrison talked of what his dad, a paper and printing supplies salesman, had taught him about the newspaper business. The *Chronicle* had been a customer. His dad helped him get his first job as a copy boy at the *Chronicle*. "I wish I could've gone to college, wish I could've afforded it. But I got married early.

Then I found out, hey, life's a great big school. I could learn a lot if I just paid attention. I enjoyed my newspaper learning so much I let my marriage slip. After the bomb on my front porch, my wife took off with another man and headed for Florida."

Julie talked about her dad's work as a cop, a Jackson police detective, and her mom's work at Carbide. The independence they'd instilled in her. She also spoke about Ben's family next door, about Roger, his life, the discovery that, somehow, he had contracted AIDS. The growth of her relationship with Ben as Roger's health slowly deteriorated. Then Roger's death. "Since the plant explosion, Ben's work and my work have put a giant trench between us. Ben values opportunities not just to walk in his father's footsteps, but somehow to do more, do better, to be even more loyal than his dad to the plant. Maybe I'm doing a version of the same thing; trying to be my version of a detective. Warning the valley about the dangers of what many people call a threat to the community; a threat from a known but un-convicted offender, Kabot."

They walked back to the *Chronicle* building and stood in front of the main entrance.

"I've got to check on the press run for tomorrow morning. Thanks for joining me. I enjoyed getting to know more about you." Harrison extended his hand.

Julie took his hand and said, "Thanks. I enjoyed learning about you. And I really liked Harley's food." Then she suddenly found her other hand and arm move around him in a warm hug.

They looked into each other's eyes and their faces came ever closer.

"Excuse me," a man said. They abruptly pulled apart. The man walked between them and through the *Chronicle's* front door.

After the man passed into the building, Harrison said, "Sorry. I wrote the paper's no fraternization rule. Now I'm breaking it."

"That's OK. Forget it," Julie said. "My fault."

Later she surprised herself. She didn't want to forget it.

Chapter 41

THE FOLLOWING MORNING JULIE DROVE to the plant and parked outside the front gate. She counted thirty people, including Karen Hill and Angela Washington, carrying END MIC signs and slowly walking back and forth on the town side of the plant's front gate. The group of END MIC demonstrators continued to grow larger.

Julie made notes and stepped out of her car and took a photo of the demonstrators. Getting back into her car, she glanced at a narrow macadam road that curved around the outer side of the plant's boundary, the tall chain link fence. She remembered looking down on it from Dr. Henderson's office. Curious about where the road led, Julie drove the short distance to the road. Then she continued on the road for about fifty yards until she found herself facing the metal-frame gate, shut, across the road, the one she'd seen from above. Dr. Henderson had pointed down to it from his office window. The gate resembled many she'd seen on local farms. The gate's right and left sides, on hinges attached to steel posts, had each swung halfway across the road.

The two halves of the gate met in the center of the road. A padlocked chain secured the gate shut. On the chain hung a sign. Julie got out of her car to read the sign. Printed block letters declared, "EMERGENCY ROUTE." Below those words were the command, "DO NOT BLOCK GATE." She photographed the gate and its sign.

An emergency route? For evacuation? Julie pondered the implications of a locked shut gate blocking an evacuation route at a plant that had just gone through a fatal explosion. She thought about the sign's admonition, "DO NOT BLOCK GATE."

Julie drove to Jackson and parked at the *Chronicle* building. In the twenty minutes it took her to get there, she thought only about the gate and its sign. A locked gate on an evacuation route seemed logically impossible. Yet there it stood. She imagined a security guard flipping off a safety engineer and clicking the padlock shut.

After arriving at work, Julie shared the photo with Harrison and Bob. Their reactions of disbelief paralleled hers.

Julie then made calls to set up interviews. Some people wanted to talk right then, and she immediately began posing questions and doing interviews. Each call branched to other contacts, more calls and interviews. She kept telling herself, "Just one more." That only led to another one, then another, and so on. About 8:30 PM, she finally said, "Enough!" and pushed away from her desk.

Driving home, when Julie passed the red and green neon lights of the South Jackson Tavern, she remembered she had not eaten since early morning. Magically, a car vacated a parking place near the tavern. The soft glow of the tavern's lights warmed the cold evening air.

Julie pushed open the front door and entered the dimly lit tap room. Customers, many of them neighborhood folks Julie knew, occupied stools along the length of the room's mahogany bar. From behind the bar, the owner, Shorty, an oxymoron for such a tall man, served customers drinks and bowls of peanuts. In front of Shorty, decorative handles marked the different brands of draft beer. Behind Shorty stood shelves of liquor, the bottles' mellow shades of amber deepened by soft backlights. Behind the bottles, a wall of mirrors gave depth to the colors and reflected the faces and actions of people in the taproom. Lively conversations, like passes of a football, moved up and down the bar, sometimes ricocheting off the mirror and across the bar.

Julie spoke to a few friends as she walked through the bar and the adjoining space beyond the bar that had been set aside for games of darts. Julie passed two two-man teams, their eyes fixed on the board on the opposite wall.

In the small dining area, she scanned the six Formica-topped tables, three of them occupied. Each table seated four and had a small container of condiments with an attached menu. She walked to an empty table and sat down. A waiter came to the table, and she ordered a hamburger, fries, side salad and a draft beer.

Waiting to be served, Julie watched the dart game. She soon found herself, even though a distant spectator, involved in the game. She listened to the pock-pock of darts penetrating the surface of the dart board and the cheers and groans of the players. Something about the game held her attention, something more than the game itself. Then she recognized one of the players, her neighbor Don.

About that time, Don looked her way and nodded. Julie gave a small wave.

At the end of the game, Don slowly walked to Julie's table and, his voice hesitant, said, "Hi, Julie."

"Don." Julie's voice, maybe her face, too, she worried, might have signaled apprehension.

"Can I . . . I mean, is it OK if I . . . sit for a minute?"

Julie smiled and extended her hand toward the empty chair on her right. "Please, join me."

Don sat down. Behind him, the pock-pock and cheers of the game began again.

"How you doing, Don?"

"I feel sort of . . . uh, well . . ." Don's face became drawn. "I'm sorry, I didn't mean to be short with you the other evening. Flora's cancer, and the explosion, it all gets to me sometimes." He paused. "But, hey, the brownies were really good." He smiled. "Thanks!"

"My favorites. Glad you enjoyed them. I hope Flora's doing okay."

"I wish. The truth is, doc says it's just a matter of time. Hospice people, they're at the house twenty-four hours a day, seven days a week."

"I'm sorry. Flora's been in my thoughts and prayers."

"After work today, I sat with her. Remembered better times. You ever watch somebody waste away?"

"My dad. It was rough. But mom and I had each other."

"Me and Flora never had kids."

"Do you have anybody to talk to?"

Don frowned. "The preacher, if you call scripture readin' talk. A fellow at work. But he was in the middle of the stuff you asked me about."

"I asked you about?"

"Remember when you brought the brownies, you asked me . . . where I, you know, where I was the night of the explosion?"

"Sorry," Julie said. "I didn't intend to add to your burden."

Don gave a faint smile. "You didn't add nothin'. That burden was . . ." Don stared at the floor, then looked at Julie. "I feel like I'm gonna bust, Julie. I gotta do *somethin'*. Drinkin' don't help."

"People say I'm a good listener."

"I'm sorely tempted," Don nodded, "and I thank you. But I worry, you know, about you bein' a reporter and all."

"I understand."

Don pointed to Julie's near-empty glass. "Want another?"

"Sure. Thanks."

Don held up his empty glass and signaled for two beers.

From the dart game, a player called, "Hey Don, you comin' back?"

"In a minute. Go on without me. Mike can take my place."

Don turned to Julie. "Lemme ask, if I tell you somethin', can you keep it . . . uh, just between you and me?"

"Sure." Even as she spoke, Julie recognized the limits on what she'd just said. She added, "Unless . . . does it bear on the explosion?"

Don gave a brief laugh and tilted his chair back. "Oh yeah, it bears on the explosion, all right."

"Then, like you said, I'm a reporter."

The waiter arrived with two beers. "Y'all want anything else?"

Don and Julie shook their heads no.

"Julie, would you tell, you know, tell that I said it?"

"I'll keep my source, you or anybody else, confidential. No one will know."

"God knows, I need to . . . but I worry . . ."

Julie hesitated for a moment and then said, "Don, you have to decide if you want to unload what you're holding in. If you tell me, I'll protect you."

"There'll be no connection to me?"

"I'd go to jail before I'd let anyone know where I get my information."

Don looked once around the room, slowly scanning the tables.

"Then get out your notebook. Listen up! I only want to say this once."

Julie thought about asking Don if she could use the tape recorder in her backpack, but decided against it. She removed her notebook from her backpack and made notes as Don talked.

"The shutdown, installin' new tanks and electronic systems, took too long. Seemed like one thing or another was always goin' wrong. Time passed. International orders kept comin' in, stackin' up. When it came time to test those new tanks and new systems, do the tests EPA and OSHA told us to do, top management cut it short. They yelled, 'We got orders to fill. Fire 'em up!'

"Long as I can remember, old or new, that one tank, the residue treater, always heated up too slow. When they yelled, 'Fire 'em up!' the tank stayed true to its past. Slow, slow, slow. So, uh, I did what I'd always done to speed the startup. Like one ol' boy said, 'Hot-up that tank.' Speed the heatin' with chemical catalysts. To do that I used a workaround."

Julie paused in her note-taking. "A work-a-what?"

"A workaround. You know, when somethin' don't work right, you *work around* it."

"What'd you *do*?"

"I disabled safety locks. Three safety locks. I bypassed safety controls."

Julie's hand shook. She made hurried notes, attempting to capture all Don said. "You disabled safety locks, bypassed . . .?"

"Then I started chemicals flowing; catalysts to jump start, speed up, heating."

"Isn't that against . . .?"

"Sure. But we'd done it since God was a small child. Everybody knew. Us operators. The managers, all the way to the top."

"The managers?"

"Right up to Otto." Don looked away and remained silent for a moment. "After I added methomyl, she started heatin' up, fast." Don slapped the table. "Too fast." Don again slapped the table, this time harder. "The temperature started to spike!" Don slapped the table a third time.

"A graph on my computer screen crossed the red danger line. I radioed out in the plant to Howard and Jim. Asked them to check the tank, find out if the vent was blocked."

Don paused again. "In the control room, the warning horn began to blare, 'Honk, honk, honk.' God, in my sleep I can still hear it.

"Howard and Jim ran to the Desin Unit. Howard ran ahead of Jim. He went into the building." Don became silent. He folded his arms, rested them on the table, and then lowered his forehead to his arms.

He looked up. "Ever wonder how you'll be remembered?"

"Yes."

"I know what I'll remember about Howard, remember forever. His last words, '*Oh shit!*'

"The tank exploded. Engineers say it turned into a 5,000 pound steel rocket. Blasted across the unit, smashed into tanks, pipes, and steel girders." He stopped. When Don next tried to speak, he started, stopped, and then started again, speaking slowly. "That tank . . ." Don's voice cracked and wavered. "That tank almost crashed . . ." He squirmed in his chair. ". . . Almost crashed . . . into a tank of . . . of . . ."

"A tank of what, Don?"

"*MIC*! A tank holding *fourteen thousand pounds of MIC*! If that steel rocket had flown a path a few degrees to the right . . . sweet Jesus, we would've had another Bhopal right here in the valley!"

Julie and Don, now alone in the dining room, stared at each other. The room's only sound was the distant pock-pock-pock of darts hitting the dartboard.

Julie said, "We dodged a bullet."

"Tell that to Howard."

Chapter 42

THE NEXT MORNING JULIE HURRIEDLY PUT ON jeans and a sweat-shirt for her early morning meeting with Harrison. She skipped her shower.

"You okay, Julie? You look tired."

"I'm okay. And, yes, I'm really tired. Only a couple of hours of sleep last night."

"Why? What happened?

"It's a long story. Well, two stories. Story one—my conversation with Don, a control room operator at the Kabot plant. I'd worked late at the office. On my way home I stopped at a tavern in South Jackson for a hamburger and a beer. Don came to my table. We talked about what happened at the plant the night of the explosion."

"Tell me about it."

Julie spoke at a slow pace, flipping the pages of her notepad back and forth, confirming the details of what Don had told her.

Harrison frowned as Julie described the workaround and the disabling of three safety locks. He interrupted, "Does he realize . . . Julie, do *you* realize how volatile this material is? Criminal charges could be filed against Don, his boss. Right up the chain of command."

"I didn't mention any possible legal issues to him. I wanted the story. And Don wanted so badly to talk, to unload. He said, 'I feel like I'm gonna bust if I don't tell *somebody.*' "

"Did Don mention the Chemical Institute? His reporting what he told you to the investigators?"

"No. Let me finish, then let's talk."

"Okay. Keep going."

"As I said, the night of the explosion Don was surprised that they were starting up production so soon. One tank, the residue treater, was slow to heat. After the workaround, the temperature in the tank rose, then sharply spiked. Nobody knew why. Jeff, Don's supervisor, thought the tank's vent might be blocked. Don radioed two men out in the plant, Howard and Jim, and asked them to check the vent."

Julie stopped and stared at her notes. "I wrote so fast, I'm having trouble reading my scribbles."

"Take your time."

"Okay, here we go. Howard ran ahead of Jim. He entered the Desin Unit building. Howard radioed to Don that there were flames around the bottom of the tank."

"The tank, the residue treater?"

"Yes." She studied her notes in silence. She stopped and looked up at Harrison. Her voice broke as she said, "Don asked me, 'Ever wonder how you'll be remembered?' Then he said, 'Howard's last words in this life? *Oh, shit.*'"

Harrison mumbled, "Oh, shit. After airline crashes, airplane's black boxes have recorded pilots saying the same words immediately before a crash." He shook his head sideways.

"That's most of what Don told me. I couldn't sleep. I finally got up and started writing."

"I do the same thing. My former wife used to tell me that's what kept me halfway sane. Stay with it, Julie. Finish writing the story."

"I will." Julie put her notes in her backpack. "But it may be a while." She slumped in her chair.

"You said there were two parts to the story. I've heard part one. Is part two a problem?"

"Bingo."

Harrison leaned toward her. "Do you want to tell me part two?"

Julie wanted to tell him, yet something inside her pulled at her words, kept them inside. "No . . . I don't want to tell you. But I feel like Don. I'm gonna bust if I don't tell *somebody*."

"Okay. I'm somebody. Tell me."

Her voice so soft that Harrison had to lean forward to hear her, Julie said, "Near midnight, Ben called. 'I've been thinking,' he said . . ." She took a deep breath. "He slurred his words a little. And sounded angry. Maybe he'd been drinking."

"You don't have to tell me. . . ."

"Hey, my conflict of interest makes me a risk. You said you wanted me to keep you posted on the truth about Ben, about our relationship . . . well, our past relationship." Her voice rose. "Heads up, Harrison, I'm keeping you posted." She pulled a tissue from her pocket and wiped her eyes. "Ben said, 'I met an interesting woman, Julie, an interesting woman.'"

She paused, then asked, "Harrison, remember when we sat in the coffee bar at Henry's? Around the corner from Ben's phone conversation? And heard his final words, 'Bye, babe'?"

"Yes."

"Last night I told Ben I knew about his new love interest. Ben said, 'You know?' as if he didn't believe me. 'Yes, I know,' I said, working hard to contain my voice. 'Who is she?'

"'Does it matter?' he said. 'Somebody I met at work.'

"I told him, 'You're right. It doesn't matter.'"

Harrison straightened a stack of papers on his desk. "Is that all?"

"Most of it. It helps to get it off my chest. Like Don, I was gonna bust if I didn't. Thanks for listening."

Harrison walked to the window and looked out. "I'm divorced, Julie. I've been there."

"You can tell Kirby and senior staff on the *Chronicle,* any risk from my conflict of interest just shrunk to zero. You've heard the whole truth, in spades."

"I have never worried about that."

"My grandmother and I used to talk about truth telling. Truth, I've searched for it, wanted to know it. Suddenly, I'm not so sure. Too much pain."

Harrison walked to the other side of his desk, near Julie. "The truth business. It's our business. It's what we do, it's who we are. Nobody ever said it was easy."

Julie shrugged, wiped away a tear and looked up at him. "Maybe I should, I don't know, go sell shoes. Work in a bank. Something. *Anything.*"

"You could, but you won't. You've got journalism in your blood. Real journalism, the kind that keeps you asking questions till you get all the answers."

Julie put her notebook in her backpack. She stood and walked toward the door. Then she turned and walked to Harrison. She slowly extended her arms. "Hold me?"

Harrison put his arms around her and patted her on the back in a hug of friendship.

Julie pulled him next to her and held him tightly. Their bodies pressed together. She looked up and closed her eyes. The short distance between them shrank in the prelude to a kiss.

From the other side of the door came a loud knock. They jumped apart. A man's voice said, "Harrison? The mayor is on his way to see you."

Chapter 43

JULIE'S BOSTON FLIGHT HAD LANDED mid-morning. By flying on Thanksgiving Day, she had no problem making a reservation. She took a cab directly from Logan airport to Cambridge and the Harvard Square Hotel.

Immediately after she checked in at the registration desk, the only other person in the lobby, a stooped elderly man in a threadbare overcoat and carrying a well-worn leather briefcase, approached her. In a soft voice he said, "Miss Brown?"

"Yes." Julie looked at the man. She guessed him to be at least eighty; frail, thinning gray hair.

"I am Isaac Saslow."

Julie extended her hand. "Mr. Saslow. It's nice to . . . well, I'm honored to meet you."

"You are too kind. I hope I can be of help to you."

"Thank you for meeting with me. I'm confident you will. Where would you like to go to talk?"

His eyes looked across the hotel's empty lobby to the coffee shop. "If it's all right, let's get a booth in the coffee shop. As you can see, most people are elsewhere today. We can talk there in privacy."

"I have a room, if you would prefer to . . ."

He interrupted her, his voice louder. "No. Please. The coffee shop will do nicely." He led Julie through the noisy coffee shop and its few patrons, students, some laughing, others arguing, to a booth at the rear.

After a waitress took their orders, sandwiches and coffee, Saslow opened his briefcase and placed a folder filled with documents on the table. "These are copies of what I have. People at

180

Harvard said they wanted to place the papers in a permanent collection, then later declined. I'm preparing the papers to be a collection I will make available electronically. The Internet is a wonderful museum; to be sure, a different sort of museum. Nevertheless, wonderful."

For the next two hours Saslow took Julie through the documents. Later, sitting at the small desk in her room, Julie slowly did a second lengthy review of the documents. She fell asleep at her desk, awakened, and finally forced herself to drop into bed.

Julie awakened to a crisp winter morning. She dressed in her running gear and jogged from Harvard Square to the Charles River, across Longfellow Bridge, past the Hatch Shell to the science museum, then along the west side of the river past MIT and returned back to Harvard Square. Only a few miles, but enough to clear her head and start her heart pounding.

Over a light breakfast, Julie again reviewed the documents. At 2 PM Mr. Saslow met her in the coffee shop. She asked him questions, testing some of her observations. He answered in helpful ways. Walking to the cab stand in front of the hotel, Julie thanked him for his contributions. "The truth about Kabot, Mr. Saslow, you've helped me know it."

When she handed her suitcase to the cab driver, Mr. Saslow said, "Miss Brown?"

She turned. He stepped forward and gave her a warm embrace, which Julie returned. "Thank you for spending Thanksgiving with me."

"Thank you, Mr. Saslow." Julie got into the back seat of the cab and departed for Logan Airport.

She took an early evening flight from Boston to Washington and then the last flight from Washington to Jackson. Julie disembarked into a near-empty terminal. A man sweeping the floor exchanged smiles with her.

~   ~   ~   ~   ~

A few days earlier, Harrison had resisted when she first broached the trip to him. "That's a lot of travel expense. And what'll you have when it's done?"

"I'll have, we'll have, a deepened understanding of Kabot. Its culture. 'We cannot ignore our history,' Lincoln said. You, me, every person, every company, including Kabot, lives its history. Those are the building blocks of who and what we are. They're put in place early. For Kabot, the years leading up to World War I, the development of poison gas, the use of it in warfare without any ethical considerations. Pioneers in high-profit chemical warfare. World War II: IG Farben, in bed with Hitler and the Third Reich; stealing chemical plants from countries conquered in Hitler's blitzkrieg. At Auschwitz, Kabot tested pharmaceuticals on concentration camp prisoners; built a synthetic rubber factory there using imprisoned Jews as slave labor. Ethics? A foreign word in the world of Kabot. Now, today, here in the valley, we live in the shadow of Kabot and their history. During and after the explosion, they have violated their own published principles. Can they be trusted?"

"Julie, how could I, how could anyone, answer that question?"

"It's not an academic question, Harrison. It's real. We've created a world awash in chemicals. Knowing Kabot's history, do you trust them to take all, repeat *all*, necessary safeguards to protect the valley? MIC isn't the only threat. And don't forget, Harrison, seven months after Bhopal and Carbide's repeated assurances that we were safe, the plant had a major toxic chemical leak. It sent over a hundred people to the hospital. There've been decades of shelters in place. Not long ago at the DuPont plant a hose ruptured and sprayed a man with phosgene. Killed him. At Kabot and at plants up and down the valley there's more than phosgene. Just for starters, sulfuric acid, hydrochloric acid, potassium cyanide, methylene chloride, and huge tanks of chlorine near highways and towns."

"You're going beyond our readers."

"Then we have to help them understand what we're facing. Think about it. America lives according to the Eleventh Commandment: thou shalt kill annoying insects and worship weed-free lawns. We live in a world of pesticides and herbicides. When the chemical plants producing them make mistakes, somebody dies; sometimes a lot of somebodies.

"Who is Kabot, Harrison? Can we trust them? My trip, and understanding Kabot's history, will help us answer those questions."

~   ~   ~   ~   ~

Arriving in Jackson, Julie claimed her suitcase. Wheeling it through the parking lot to her car, she thought about the man sweeping the floor and their exchange of smiles. Home. Chemical risks notwithstanding, it felt good to be in the valley. Julie again recognized the powerful emotional pull of her place in the mountains.

Chapter 44

HARRISON WOULD HAVE TO WAIT on her trip report. Julie had a more immediate priority. One final effort, she counseled herself, one more shot at teaching Ben a few things he should recognize in his employer. And if she failed? Well, at least she'd made the effort. Inside her a voice yelled, "Wake up, Ben. This is not about us. See your company for what it is. Know the truth about Kabot!" Then another voice asked, "Hey Julie, why do you care?" Julie muttered to the voices, "We go way back. He deserves to know."

Julie called Ben. She made a special effort to sound positive, upbeat. "Hey, want to meet at Wung Fu for dinner?"

"Wung Fu?" He paused, then said, "I have to work late today."

"No problem. I'll wait."

"I promised some friends I'd meet them for a workout."

After another round of her invitations and his evasions, Julie said, "I get the idea, Ben. You don't want to do it." She paused and then said, "What do you have to lose? Come on, Ben, I'll buy."

Ben remained silent, then said, "Okay . . . seven thirty?"

"Fine. See you at seven thirty."

At Wung Fu, Mr. Chan led them to a familiar table. When they sat down, he again pulled curtains around their table.

"Nice to be alone," Ben said. He gently grasped her hand and laughed. "An evening of romantic events?"

Julie pulled her hand away. "Events, to be sure." She laughed. "But not romantic."

When the egg rolls arrived, Julie had just placed a stack of photos on the table. She barely had time to bring out a second stack before the waitress served the rice and main courses.

In the past few days, Julie had dug deep into the *Chronicle*'s archives. And in Internet searches she had followed branching pathways into a remote and little-known website that held Mr. Saslow's documents as well as others.

Ben ate as Julie showed him copies of Mr. Saslow's photos and related materials. She provided a running commentary to campaign posters and photos of Hitler giving street corner speeches. "The 1933 election in Germany, Ben." She felt her lower lip quiver with a childlike anxiety. She remembered the anxieties of the times in her early childhood when she would give a recitation to one of her mom's groups, feeling that she had put herself at risk. She clamped her upper teeth on her lip, then reached for an egg roll and took a bite; chewing helped.

She continued, "In the 1933 election, IG Farben became the single largest contributor to Hitler's Nazi party. Farben, Ben. That's Kabot, in bed with the Nazis."

Ben looked at the photos. For the first time Julie noticed two furrows rise between his eyebrows. He picked up a photo. Hitler stood on a Munich street corner speaking to a group. "My boss says that when Kabot joined other companies to form IG Farben, Kabot disappeared," Ben said.

"Do you believe him?"

"Until now I hadn't thought about it."

In a voice that carried a sting, she said, "Well, think some more about it." Ben's face became the Ben she'd known in sixth grade. The teacher had asked to see his homework. He hadn't done it.

Julie knew the standard argument advanced by Kabot. She'd read it a hundred times. In 1925, facing a disintegrating German economy, Kabot, BASF, Hoechst, and other chemical companies had merged to form IG Farben. Once merged, Kabot said, the identities of Kabot and the other companies disappeared.

"The story about Kabot's disappearance into IG Farben is corporate camouflage. The truth? Within Farben, Kabot remained an intact company; heathy, whole and fully functioning as Kabot.

She placed photos on the table: the blitzkrieg, the Luftwaffe and the German army overrunning Poland, Czechoslovakia, Holland, most of Europe. Photos showed German troops occupying cities. At gunpoint, SS troops marched professors out of university buildings and into the canvas-covered beds of trucks. In one photo, a professor, bald, thick glasses, one arm raised in surrender, stared at a soldier pointing a rifle at him. His face seemed to ask the question, *"Warum?"* Why?

"As the German army captured refineries and chemical plants . . . IG Farben came right behind them, taking over operations; committing corporate theft." She placed more photos on the table.

Ben studied the mosaic, examining one or another of the photos, always picking them up by the edges, as if he had to be careful not to get too close to the images.

The next photo Julie put in front of Ben showed a long view of railroad tracks. In the distance the rails' perspective converged at a fence and gate. Behind the gate sat low-rise buildings. Then she showed him a close-up photo of the gate. In an arch above it was a greeting in tall iron letters: *Arbeit Macht Frei.*

Julie said, "The front gate of Auschwitz."

"I remember some German from college: *Work makes you free.*"

"Right. Tell that to six million Jews. Welcome to Auschwitz."

Julie opened a file of photos of workers' barracks and industrial buildings. In one photo, a factory was under construction. "Farben built a chemical factory, the Buna Werke, at Auschwitz to manufacture synthetic rubber and synthetic oil. Kabot actually built and operated the factory. The Waffen SS, the armed wing of the Nazi party, leased concentration camp prisoners to IG Farben, to Kabot, as slave labor. The average life expectancy of factory workers in the Buna was three to four months. Farben paid workers' meager wages directly to the SS. The SS had grown from 120 brown-shirted German thugs in 1933 to, late in the war, eight divisions of misfits, the psychopaths of Europe, commanded by Heinrich Himmler. The SS operated independently to do Himmler's and Hitler's bidding, not within the German army."

She pointed to a photo of an officer in polished knee-high boots and SS uniform striding along a construction site. "That's Himmler inspecting the Buna Monowitz factory's construction."

Then Julie showed him a photo of an executive, a handsome man in his forties. She said, "The man responsible for the construction, Ludwig Von Freir. A decorated Nazi." she paused and watched Ben as she said, "Von Frier was a former Kabot senior executive. More about him in a minute."

Ben winced, not much of a wince, Julie thought, call it a micro wince; undetectable by anyone who didn't know him well. In her thoughts a voice whispered, "My God, it bothers him. Wait'll he finds out the rest."

Julie held up a photo of prisoners, including undernourished children in ragged pajama-like uniforms of prisoners. Half-starved, they walked from concentration camp barracks to the Buna Monowitz factory. A man resembling the hands-over-his-head professor from the earlier photo walked among them.

"This is Block Ten, Auschwitz." Julie showed Ben a photo of a squat three-story brick building with a peaked roof. Across the building's front, narrow rectangular windows overlooked five concrete steps leading to a front door of thick wood.

Then she opened photos taken inside the building. Women prisoners stood in a queue awaiting inspection by doctors in white lab coats. "For their experiments, Farben purchased women prisoners from the SS." As if a vise had begun to close around her vocal chords, Julie's throat tightened. She sipped her tea, still too hot, but she kept on sipping. "One of the physicians, Dr. Fritz Ronk, a former medical school professor who became a Nazi, injected diseases into prisoners. Then he treated the sick prisoners with experimental drugs, *from Kabot*." Ben winced again. "Most of the infected prisoners soon died." She paused and took a deep breath, trying to center her consciousness, settle her thoughts.

"At the Nuremberg trials, prosecutors produced a letter from Ronk to Kabot. He wrote, 'I have thrown myself into my work wholeheartedly. Especially as I have the opportunity to test our new preparations. I feel like I am in paradise.'"

Julie pushed a photo of a handsome young man, wavy black hair, dark eyes, an engaging smile, toward Ben. Then a second photo of the same young man, this time in a white lab coat. He smiled at children in pajamas as he gave them pieces of candy. The vise around Julie's throat tightened again. In a scratchy voice, she said, "Dr. Joseph Mengele. The Auschwitz children trusted him. They called him the candy man.

"Mengele performed crude experiments on little kids . . . on twins." Julie began to cry. "God, it's hard to . . ." She stopped and took a few deep breaths. "The staff had a nickname for Mengele: Angel of Death." More photos of children, this time in look-alike pairs, their brooding dark eyes staring into the camera. "Mengele's method was simple. He picked a set of twins, then chose one of the pair as his experimental subject . . . and injected a disease into the child. When the experimental twin died, he immediately injected chloroform in the other twin's heart. Instant death. Then Mengele performed autopsies . . . compared findings." Julie began to weep, slumped in her chair. She whispered, "Children . . . as laboratory animals."

Ben put his hand on hers.

After a moment, Julie pulled her hand away and wiped her eyes. She sat up straight and pushed photos of two little boys in front of Ben. "Hans and Erik Bok. Seven-year-old twins. Guinea pigs for Mengele's experiments. Unlike the others, they lived to tell about it. In 1999, a network television show described the medical abuses of children at Auschwitz, including Hans and Erik. Hans, by then the surviving twin, filed suit against Kabot, charging that the company supplied the experimental drugs."

Ben stared at the photos. "Julie . . . I want to believe you. But it . . . well, it doesn't track with what they tell us at work. With what my boss says."

"Why am I not surprised?"

"My boss said, 'From 1925 and the formation of IG Farben until well after World War II, Kabot didn't exist.'"

"I've read Kabot's press releases and the PR on their website. What they say, carefully worded, is the *legal entity*, Kabot, didn't exist during those years. Therefore, they add casually, since the company didn't legally exist, Kabot had no responsibility for what went on during the Third Reich. That's the party line." Julie felt her breathing quicken. A surge of anger brought her to the edge of her seat. "But it's *not true.*"

"I don't understand."

"Listen to me!" Julie slammed her hand on the table. The tea in their cups splashed out.

Ben recoiled. "I'm listening."

"Then hear this! IG Farben was formed in 1916. Legally formalized in 1925, right?"

"OK, right."

She tossed a photo in front of Ben, a nighttime photo of the office and laboratory buildings of Kabot's headquarters in Stuttgart. "Now see this!" Julie pointed to a giant electric sign, the Kabot logo formed by thousands of light bulbs. Like the company's logo on a pharmaceutical tablet, the lines of a square surrounded the word KABOT, printed horizontally and vertically; the lines intersected at and shared the letter B.

"In 1933, Ben, above its Stuttgart headquarters, Kabot proclaimed itself alive and well by erecting the world's largest electric sign, *the Kabot logo in that photo. In 1933,* eight years *after* the incorporation of IG Farben. Kabot hadn't disappeared. It remained alive and well. Within Farben, only at the very top, the most senior executive levels, had the member companies merged."

Julie handed Ben a photo of the 1939 Nobel Prize awards ceremony. "Here's Kabot scientist Wilhelm Brandt receiving the 1939 Nobel Prize for Medicine. Today Kabot brags that one of its own, Dr. Brandt, won the Nobel Prize. One of its own? In 1938, when there was no Kabot?"

"Maybe they mean he was a Kabot scientist after, or before, IG Farben and the war."

Her gut wrenched. Ben's tightly closed view of Kabot held in place. If this conversation had been a wartime battle, Ben would have repelled her attack.

Julie opened the file from her Cambridge meeting with Saslow, crammed with copies of routine business memos and letters. She handed one to Ben. "These are copies of documents from the Nuremberg Trials. In one of those trials, the Doctors' Trials, physicians charged with the inhumane treatment of World War II prisoners in medical experiments were brought to justice."

Ben leafed through the documents. An English translation of the German language memos and business letters had been inserted at the end of each document.

Julie pointed to the Kabot logo at the top of the memo Ben held. Then to another, and another. "The letterheads, Ben. Some are Kabot alone. Others are Kabot and IG Farben together. The business of Auschwitz: Buna Monowitz; buying and selling people for experiments; people as laboratory supplies. The Kabot letterhead is on every one of these documents. My question again, Ben: Do you really believe Kabot didn't exist during the Farben years?"

She handed a document to Ben. "In this memo Kabot managers wrote to inform Dr. Fritz Ronk of delays in the production and delivery of Kabot Preparation 3582. The doctor was conducting tests of Kabot drug 3582 on inmates.

"Here are prisoners on the receiving end of Dr. Ronk's drugs. He had injected them with typhoid-infected blood. His goal? To develop improved vaccines for German soldiers." The photos showed a typhus ward, prisoners lying on cots, orderlies and physicians walking among them. Then photos of gaunt-faced men, skin-and-bones prisoners, standing half dressed, blankets around their shoulders. They stared into the lens of the camera.

"Ronk was convicted and sentenced to death. Sent to Landsberg Prison in Bavaria and executed by hanging." Julie paused, waiting for a signal from Ben that he grasped the gravity of the story she had opened to him.

Ben remained impassive.

"Then there's Ludwig Von Freir. I said I'd come back to talk about him." She handed Ben a photo of Von Freir, handsome, middle-aged. "He planned and developed Farben's Buna Monowitz factory. Von Freir had been a chemist and executive in his family's chemical company. After Kabot acquired it, he became a Kabot senior executive. And not long afterward, a Nazi."

She handed Ben a photo of a Nuremberg courtroom. "Von Freir was among the men who faced charges in the IG Farben Trial at Nuremberg, the trial of Farben executives on charges of crimes against humanity, including enslavement, murder, and plundering.

"The prosecutor asked Von Freir, on the witness stand, whether he considered the medical tests on humans to be justified." Julie picked up a Nuremberg trial document and read aloud. "Von Freir answered, 'They were prisoners, thus no particular harm was inflicted, as they would have been killed anyway.'

"Von Freir was convicted of plunder and spoliation, and slavery and mass murder, yet sentenced to only seven years imprisonment. Then, like most of the convicted Farben executives, he served only three years. After his release, Von Freir returned to Kabot. He was soon elected to the company's senior board of directors, the supervisory board. In 1956 Von Freir became chairman of the supervisory board. *Chairman of the board*! The man who said, 'No particular harm was inflicted, as they would have been killed anyway.' Each year on Von Frier's birthday, Kabot honors him with a ceremony at his gravesite.

"For a half-century Kabot refused to recognize or honor the claims of concentration camp victims. In the 1990s the German government set up a fund for victims . . . Kabot paid 100 million deutsche marks into the fund."

"One hundred million? That's a lot of money!"

"Kabot paid into the fund. But without an admission of guilt."

In silence, Ben browsed the memos and photos.

Kabot's dark past—how else could Julie challenge him to accept its truth? To question it, to distance himself, even if just a little, from the ever-present company's view of itself? To take a small step on the road back to the chance for a life together?

Julie's thoughts leaped to imagine Ben in Kabot public relations meetings; executives talking about how to put a spin on the decision to rebuild and resume production using MIC. Debating what to say to families, the community, to people who, day after day, had to live with the lethal chemicals stored in tanks visible from their back yards? How could someone, Kabot, Ben, anyone, develop a PR spin so powerful it would override the risks that came with MIC? Kabot Agronomy's website flashed into her thoughts: The company's statement of values, "A trustful partnership with local communities; presenting the unvarnished truth." Trust? Truth? From the people who had nearly wiped out the valley, then tried to cover it up?

Julie recalled what her dad called 'the walk and the talk.' The talk: What people said about their lives. When investigating a case, he'd look at what people said and then look at how those people lived, behaved. What he called 'the walk.' He'd ask, 'Do they walk the talk?' And if not, in the words of a cop, 'How did they pull off the scam?' She remembered a college propaganda course. Her professor quoted Nazi Josef Goebbels, Hitler's Minister of Propaganda: "Repeat a lie often enough, and people will believe it."

The shrill ring of Ben's cell phone intruded. Ben glanced at the caller's phone number. His face changed from a look of defiance to one of concern. "Hi, Mom . . . you what?" He listened for a moment. "Sit tight." He listened. "I'll call the doctor. Be at your place in a flash."

Placing a phone call, Ben turned to Julie. "Something's . . . could be her heart." He turned his attention to the phone and placed the call.

"Hello, Bert? This is Ben Gruber. I'm calling for my mom. She had what, I don't know, irregular heartbeat, could be a heart attack . . . can you come? The address is . . ." A moment later Ben turned to Julie. "See you at Mom's?"

Julie's face flushed. "See you there."

Chapter 45

B EN AND JULIE JOINED DR. BERT COLLINS, Mary's doctor, in Mary's living room. Bert, a former neighbor and friend for thirty years, about Mary's age, sat beside Mary.

"Mary, come in tomorrow and we'll do some tests. The tachycardia you felt is a form of arrhythmia. Your heart has given you an early warning signal. What happened could've been worse. Your vital signs are strong. Tomorrow I'll get you started on a new medicine." He handed her a small vial of pills. "Here's something for tonight. Take one pill now. Another one if you have trouble sleeping. Just follow the directions on the label." He turned to Ben. "Can you bring your mom to my office in the morning?"

"Sure."

"Then I'll see you in the morning."

After Bert left, Mary said in a weak voice, "No need for you two to stay. I'm tired." She held up the vial. "Thanks for your help. With these, I'll be asleep soon. You two have things to do. Go on about your business."

Ben leaned over and gave Mary a kiss. "I'll check on you in the morning. Love you, Mom."

"Love you, Ben."

Ben turned to Julie. "Thanks for your . . . uh, instruction tonight, Jules. I'll give you a call."

As Ben went out the door, Julie lagged behind. Then she sat alone with Mary for a few minutes. She held Mary's hand.

Her voice little more than a whisper, Mary said, "Julie, can you hear me?"

"Yes, Mary, I hear you."

"Waiting for you and Ben . . . I thought, *Maybe this is it. I'll get to see Roger* . . . I will, you know, one of these days."

"Yes, you will. We all will, Mary. Some of us sooner than others. But we all will."

Mary's eyes drifted shut, then popped open. In a stronger voice she said, "I'm sorry about you and Ben. He's a good man . . . but so much like his daddy." Mary smiled. "Ben and Charles, father and son . . . what else should I expect?"

Julie returned Mary's smile. "You're right, he's like his dad. Dedicated to the plant."

"I learned to live with it, Julie." Tears ran down Mary's cheeks. "Sometimes I . . . wish I hadn't and," she hesitated and then spoke slowly, "I . . . hope you . . . won't."

"Mary, I want, at the very least, for Ben to see the light about Kabot. But maybe he won't. I don't know."

Mary's voice thinned. "Charles never did about Carbide, about the plant. And that took its toll . . . on him, on us." She squeezed Julie's hand and whispered, "Live your life, Julie."

"I will. I love you, Mary."

"Love . . . you . . ." Mary's eyes closed.

Chapter 46

O N CHRISTMAS DAY JULIE COOKED A MEAL for Mary and at noon delivered it to her apartment. They shared the meal and wished each other Merry Christmas. Julie gave Mary a gift, a colorful silk scarf. Mary gave Julie an opal pendant on a gold chain that had belonged to her mother.

Mary laughed. "I'll have two Christmas celebrations. This one with you, then later Ben is bringing Christmas dinner." During lunch Mary reminisced about Christmases with Roger. She cried as she recalled his handmade Christmas cards.

Midafternoon Julie returned home. She brewed coffee and sat down at her kitchen table, laptop computer in front of her. She wished herself Merry Christmas and felt nostalgic as a wave of family memories, and a sense of loss, swept over her. Julie counseled herself, "Hey, you're at a good place in your life. Give thanks for your blessings, your gifts from the Universe."

Julie opened files on the Kabot story and went to work. She gazed at the tall stack of articles on the table, articles she'd researched and printed. Each one carried significant facts for her Kabot stories. That stack, all her work on Kabot; somewhere along the way it had changed. From stories for the *Chronicle* to . . . she paused and thought, *to what?* A cause? The driving force in her life? When? How? Maybe it was Ben. Maybe it was Kabot Agronomy and the company's blithe announcement of plans to rebuild and restart MIC production without giving so much as the time of day to people living near the plant. The company's arrogance had stuck in Julie's craw. How could she handle that arrogance, find her path through her feelings? Do what her daddy used to do on his cases: write it out.

For her, the facts in her story, Julie's stack of articles, brought the story to life; transformed research into people and voices that awakened her in the night, pushed her to tell their story. Somewhere along the way she had lost her power of choice. Julie didn't know where or when, but it had happened. The story *had* to be written.

Julie wondered, had they, those voices, chosen her? Infused her with the story she had to tell? The story she wanted Ben, the people of the valley, to grasp and understand. She knew the odds on Ben's understanding it had become remote. He had become like his dad, a man who worked non-stop, slogged through sleepless nights, helped Carbide to sell itself and helped Kabot to buy the plant. *The Plant:* bigger than life.

Julie had researched years of work on Kabot by reporters who had gone before her. She had pulled together article after article, story after story, about the chemical and pharmaceutical industries. Newspapers, magazines. Some stories never used, filed in archives. But whether printed or filed, the stories sat there, like stranded travelers in an airline terminal, waiting, waiting. Each story told a part of the more than century-long tale of Kabot's history and culture. Each of them a dot on a page of history, dots that had been transformed into three-in-the-morning voices calling, "Connect us." They waited on Julie to do her job.

A light rap-rap-rap sounded at her back door.

Julie walked to the door and turned on the back porch light. She opened the door.

"Hi Don. What's . . . is it Flora?"

"Thanks, no. Flora's asleep. I saw your lights on. Can we talk for a minute?"

"Come in. I just made a pot of coffee."

A few minutes later Julie and Don sat at the kitchen table, each with a cup of coffee. They wished each other Merry Christmas.

Don said, "Your story on the workaround. Haven't seen it in the paper. You finished it?"

"Yes."

"When'll it be in the paper?"

Had that question brought him to her door? It seemed un-likely. She remembered her daddy's advice. 'Timing is everything. Just wait. Things happen.'

"It'll be out before long. A few days. I don't know. That's for the editor to decide."

Don leaned forward, his elbows on the table. "My name's not in it?"

"Don, do you want to read the story? Now?"

"If you don't mind. Sure, I'd like that." Don's face reddened. "No offense, but I'm still kinda worried."

Julie reached into her backpack and took out the most recent draft of the story. "I understand. I'd be worried, too." She handed the draft to Don. "I promised I'd keep your name out of it." She smiled. "You'll see, I kept my promise."

"I knew you would." Don sipped his coffee. "And I thank you. But that's not why I'm here." Don laid the draft on the table.

"Okay, what's up?"

"This morning on TV I watched a Kabot press conference. The big boss, Otto, said the company's investigating the explosion. A reporter asked him if any amount of MIC had been released in the explosion. He said, his words, 'After the incident . . .' Uh, I need to get this right. Lemme think, how'd he say it?"

Don looked away, then turned to Julie. "Okay, I remember. He said, 'After the incident, no MIC was detected on or off site.'"

Don looked away and took a deep breath. "Not detected? I yelled at the TV, 'Hell no! The MIC detectors had been turned off!' I was afraid I'd woke up Flora. But I didn't. Anyway, that's why I came over. What I want you to know, Julie, is this. The night of the explosion, the fence line MIC detectors had been turned off! Was any MIC released? Truth is, *we don't know*. Otto was tap dancing."

Don handed her a slip of paper. "Here are some names and phone numbers of people who work in the plant and in the main office. I told them I'd ask you to call early, before they left for work. They'll tell you about the MIC sensors on the fence line bein' turned off. I think they've already talked to one of the inves-tigators."

Julie awakened early and went for a run. She enjoyed the solitude that came with the darkness of winter mornings. By sunrise she sat at her desk at the *Chronicle* making phone calls.

At eight o'clock she walked into Harrison's office, a freshly revised workaround story in her hand. "I've made an important revision, an addition, to the workaround story."

Harrison looked up from behind his desk and scowled at her. "Revision? You're late. We're ready to go to press."

"Hold on. I think you'll find this is worth the wait." She handed him the printed story.

Harrison motioned for Julie to sit down as he scanned the document. "The beginning is the same." He turned the page. "So is page two. Where are the changes?"

"Turn to page four. Last paragraph. Continue through page five."

Harrison turned to page four and continued through page five, mumbling as he read. He scanned the end of the story. His eyes on the article, he said, "Powerful stuff, Julie." He looked up, "When this hits the streets . . ." Harrison barked a loud laugh. "By God, you're dangerous."

"I hope that's a compliment."

"Your source?

"More than one. Kabot insiders who're troubled by what the company has done. They're even more troubled by remaining silent."

"They may press us to name the people who talked to you. We could wind up in court. Are you prepared for that?"

Julie looked Harrison in the eye. "In court, under oath, I'll tell the truth as I know it."

"I mean your sources—what about your sources?"

Julie's voice rose. "I promised I'd protect them. I'll go to jail before I . . ."

Harrison held up one hand. "Okay, I understand. When this hits the streets, there may be an earthquake over at Kabot." He picked up his phone and dialed a number. "This is Harrison. Julie's sending you a revised Kabot story. Pull the one we were going to run tomorrow morning. Put this one in its place. Early edition, page one. Put it in our electronic edition, too, tonight. Chum the water. Send out an electronic announcement. 'New developments in the Kabot explosion . . .' You know what to say."

In silence, Harrison gazed at Julie. When he spoke his words came slowly, as if he'd reflected on each of them. "This is more than a revised story. It's a statement about withholding the truth. It's about who these people are."

Julie said, "Does anybody believe Kabot can be trusted? Do you think they worry about being trusted? Kabot reminds me of a colonial power in a third world country. They control the wealth and the resources. People in Academy, around the valley, too, are there to do what Kabot needs done."

Harrison said, "America was once known as Colonial America."

Julie slammed her hand on Harrison's desk. "Maybe this part of America is still a colony. And it needs to take political action, stand up and fight for its independence."

Harrison smiled. "Go tell that to our millionaire politicians, the governor, our senators and congressmen."

Chapter 47

JACKSON, WV, MARCH 5, 2009—At the Jackson airport, Julie boarded the last flight for Washington, DC. She reflected on the story she'd written a few years ago on the airport. How, in the late 1940s, it'd been built by leveling the tops of mountains. Airport passengers and employees drove up the mountain to the airport plateau. Local people took pride in the fact that, at the time of its construction, the airport claimed the distinction of being the world's largest earth-moving project. People chose to ignore the fact that by leveling mountain tops, engineers had made any future lengthening of runways impossible. "A demonstration of man's power over nature," a speaker at the airport's opening had called it. After writing her story, Julie wondered, did the region's pride in "man's power over nature" continue as coal companies blasted the tops off mountains?

For a long time, Julie wrote, executives in the airline industry had viewed the Jackson airport as economically marginal. Some of them called it a backwater airport—except for one route, the airport's cash cow: Jackson to Washington, DC. The frequent flights of business executives and elected officials and their staff members, as well as bureaucrats and executive branch officials, supported multiple flights each day.

Julie's flight, bumpy as they flew over the remnants of the day's snowstorm, landed at seven-fifteen. A couple of inches of snow had fallen that afternoon, a rarity for Washington. From the air Julie looked down on long lines of stalled rush-hour traffic. Surface travel had come to a near standstill. Julie traveled underground on the Metro from the airport to downtown.

200

After leaving the Metro, she walked a meandering route to the Willard Hotel. She first walked the few blocks to the National Mall, then walked to one end and the Washington Monument, then to the other and the Lincoln Memorial. She walked around the Reflecting Pond, now a smooth, dark rectangle of water surrounded by an expanse of white. Snow laced the branches of cherry trees. The lights of the mall and surrounding commercial and government buildings cast a warm glow over the snow.

She walked the few blocks from the mall to the Willard Hotel. A few days ago, when Harrison told her the paper had reserved a room for here there, Julie said, "The Willard? The paper's struggling to make ends meet and you put me at the Willard?"

"Easy, Julie, relax. For the paper, it's an operating cost, a business expense. And for you, well, you've been working hard. For one night, let the *Chronicle* treat you to a little luxury. You deserve more. But I'm glad we can do this. Enjoy."

Just inside the entrance to the hotel's lobby, Julie stood for a moment and remembered paintings and photos of the lobby of the original Willard Hotel's Victorian décor; its high ornate ceiling and chandeliers, a fire crackling in the lobby's massive fireplace. "Transported in time," she said to herself. "The Civil War; Lincoln, shot by Booth across the street at Ford's Theatre, then lying in a house down the street, dying. A large crowd, men in top hats, women in bustled dresses, milling around the lobby, the atmosphere buzzing with many forms of the same question: *would he live?*"

A bellman's voice shattered her private world. "Can I help you, ma'am?"

"Thanks. I would like to check in."

The bellman waved toward the registration desk. Privately Julie wondered, *Will the newspaper reimburse me for tips?*

As the desk clerk gave Julie her room key, he said, "Oh, Miss Brown, we have a message for you." He handed her an envelope.

Julie opened the envelope and read the handwritten note on Willard stationary. She took a quick breath. Her body tensed. "Join me for an early breakfast? The hotel's Café du Parc, 6:30? Ben."

Chapter 48

WASHINGTON, DC, MARCH 6, 2009—Shortly after 4 AM, Julie, dressed in winter running gear, walked out the Willard's front door. In bracing morning air, she ran along downtown streets. Snow had been cleared from sidewalks. She ran past the White House, then along the mall to the Viet Nam Wall and then to the Capitol. A storybook run, Julie thought, wishing she could continue. As she approached the Willard, the first light of dawn painted a rose hue over the city's cover of snow.

At 6:30 AM she entered Café du Parc, the morning's first customer. A moment later the morning's second customer, Ben, took a seat at her small table. He placed his laptop on the table. Frowning, and without a hello or good morning, he opened the laptop and turned its screen toward Julie. "Look at this!"

"And good morning to you, too, Ben." Julie looked at Ben's face. It remained unsmiling, stern and resolute.

"Uh . . . good morning." He nodded toward the computer screen. On it was the front page of the morning's electronic edition of the *Chronicle*, identical to the morning's print edition distributed throughout the valley.

Julie read the headline: "Cover up in Kabot explosion!" and beneath it, "By Julie Brown." Until now, most of the explosion stories had had two reporters in the byline. First, Bob Samuelson, the senior reporter, then Julie. But on this one, Bob insisted and Harrison had agreed that Julie alone deserved the byline. Don had sought her out. She'd done most of the interviews, worked long hours, probed sources with tough questions, and elicited revealing answers.

She read the first all-too-familiar paragraph of the story. "The *Chronicle* has learned from reliable sources within Kabot Agronomy that management deliberately withheld from Chemical Institute investigators important facts about last August's fatal plant explosion. Using a post-911 security law to justify . . ."

"I'm familiar with the story. I wrote it. So what is this, a reading test? I'm a high school graduate. And, oh I forgot, college, too."

"How do you, did you, know . . . what are you doing? Your story has changed everything. We had it all worked out."

With a note of sarcasm, Julie said, "All worked out? Sorry to mess up Kabot's plans."

"Do you want to destroy Kabot's presence in the valley?" His face reddened and his voice rose. "Are you another version of Samson at the temple, this time trying to bring down the walls of the company?"

Julie's inner voice counseled, "Don't say it," followed by another voice that said, "Oh what the hell, go ahead." Julie said, "How about David facing Goliath?"

"You and your slingshot. This story will hurt Kabot, the plant. Worst case, it could lead to Kabot's leaving the valley; jobs gone, huge economic losses. And for what? So you can complete a footnote on an already tragic event?"

Julie sipped her orange juice, then held her glass in front of her. With her other hand she rubbed its beads of condensation.

Ben stared at her. "Embarrass Kabot? Is that what you're up to?" His gaze remained intense, his face expectant.

She placed her glass on the table and twisted it in a circle. Then she stared at the condensation's wet ring. "This may be difficult for you and your friends to understand, Ben. Listen carefully . . . ."

"No, *you* listen carefully. Since four-thirty this morning, I've been on the phone with Kabot's senior people and company attorneys, reviewing what we did at the plant post-explosion. It was lawful. And right."

"Lawful? The people who wrote the law may have a different view. We'll find out this morning. And right? Right for whom? Whose interests are being served?"

"We had it all worked out. You say in your story that we with-held important facts. We withheld security sensitive, *classified* in-formation. It could not be disclosed."

"Classified? Could not . . .? Come on, Ben, how self-serving can you get?" She paused, then said, "Each time I think I know the an-swer to that question, Kabot does something more egregious. Kabot, looking out for Kabot's interests, classified all that infor-mation. Kabot put Kabot's interests, not the best interests of the valley, first, and withheld important facts about the blast. Security classification of the facts was used to cover up wrongdoing."

"Congress passed the 9-11 security laws. We were just obey-ing them."

"Obeying them? Can I rephrase that? How about *using* them to withhold . . ."

Ben closed his laptop, picked it up and stood. Then he sat again, this time on the edge of his seat, poised as if ready to spring away. "We had it *all . . . worked . . .* We could say, 'You passed the law, Congressman. We merely obeyed it.' *All worked out, Julie!*" Ben took a drink of water. "Then your article. Now what, cop a plea?"

"You'll find a way to spin it."

Ben exhaled as he leaned back in his chair, "Maybe." He hugged his laptop to his chest. "Kabot knows I'm connected to you. Otto's a masterful politician. He's told the corporate people I should've known about your article, should've warned them. Otto's hands are clean. They believe what's going to happen later this morning is my fault. Hey, Julie, got any ideas on spin control for Ben Gruber and his problem?"

Julie scooted her chair away from the table and stood. She dropped a five-dollar bill beside her orange juice.

Ben looked up at her. Julie remembered his forlorn expression from long ago when, just after Ben's tenth birthday, powerless, he had watched Roger's health worsen.

"You knew, Ben. But you weren't alone. Kabot knew, too."

"Knew what?"

"The truth about what led to that explosion. And those two deaths."

Julie picked up her backpack. "Enjoyed the orange juice, Ben. Fresh squeezed. Don't often get that in Jackson." She walked out of Café du Parc without a backward glance.

Chapter 49

A HOTEL COMPUTER'S MALFUNCTION DELAYED Julie's checkout from her room. Cars and taxicabs idled in snarled traffic. She walked at a brisk pace along Independence Avenue to the Rayburn House office building. The building's entrance pillars and its massive white marble presence, rising four stories, seemed daunting. She looked up at two ten-foot-tall marble statues on either side of the entrance, Spirit of Justice and the Majesty of Law. "Do you guys apply your principles to Kabot?" she asked aloud.

Julie passed through a security checkpoint, then in the main lobby found the directory of events and their respective rooms. After locating the room number for the committee hearing on the Kabot explosion, Julie walked beneath the ornate arches of the main corridor's golden ceiling, then down a less ornate side corridor to the committee's public hearing room.

Outside the entrance stood a sign: "Subcommittee on Oversight and Investigations, Committee on Energy and Commerce." Beside the sign stood a C-Span reporter holding a microphone. He looked toward a small red light above the lens of a television camera and spoke to viewers. "In today's hearing Hermann Gans, chief executive officer of the Agronomy division of Kabot Global, is appearing before the Energy Committee's Subcommittee on Oversight and Investigations. The committee is expected to ask Mr. Gans about the facts and circumstances surrounding last August's fatal explosion at the Kabot Agronomy chemical plant in Academy, West Virginia. We'll now take you inside the committee room. The hearing is in progress." The red light went out.

Julie opened the tall oak doors and entered the hearing room.

Reporters and spectators filled every seat, leaving standing room only. Many reporters, small laptops flashing, stood around the room's back wall. On a dais behind a long conference table across the front of the room sat the committee, ten men and two women. The members wore dark business suits. Only the color of men's neckties and women's neck scarves, along with members' nameplates, provided any touches of individuality.

Behind the committee sat congressional staff members, some of them leaning over the shoulders of congressmen and speaking in whispers. At the center of the committee table sat a handsome man in his fifties with graying black hair. On his nameplate was "Mr. Pachik, Wisconsin." Photographers knelt in front of the committee and snapped pictures; behind the photographers and facing the committee was the witness table; flanking the witness table were the television cameras and crews.

At the witness table sat a large middle-aged man, wavy gray hair combed straight back, with a wide smile. In front of him a nameplate read, "Mr. Gans, Kabot Agronomy." A man sat beside him.

Rep. Pachik said, "Mr. Gans, you are the chief executive officer of Kabot Agronomy, a division of the Kabot Global corporation. Is that correct?"

"Yes, sir, that is correct." The full and rounded tones of his bass voice signaled a man comfortable with public appearances and confident in his words.

The chairman smiled and said in a contrasting higher-pitched, sharper voice, one Julie likened to the honed edge of a knife's blade, "Thank you for braving the weather to appear at our committee hearing."

Gans nodded and flashed a pro-forma grin.

"Mr. Gans," the chairman said, "the Kabot plant explosion, danger and destruction, which were stunning," his voice became louder, "are dwarfed by the lawlessness of the company in hiding safety information necessary to protect workers and the town. Our committee staff, before publication of the story in this morning's *Jackson Chronicle,* had unearthed the facts the *Chronicle* has now published." He paused and referred to his notes, then continued, "We have evidence that Kabot identified over two thousand documents related to the explosion but withheld parts or all of those documents from Chemical Institute and local investigators. Kabot classified them security sensitive. Were they?"

Gans turned to the man seated beside him and conferred with him. Then he faced Rep. Pachik and replied, "Mr. Chairman, about eighty-eight percent of them . . . were . . . not."

Murmurs and whispers passed among the audience. People shifted in their chairs. Photographers on the floor between Gans and the committee snapped so many flash photos of Gans and Pachik that the front of the room resembled a fast-blinking strobe light show.

"Why were those documents classified as security sensitive?"

Gans again conferred with counsel. Then he turned and for a moment stared at Chairman Pachik as if carefully choosing his words. His words came slowly. "To . . . discourage safety investigators."

Julie imagined events at that moment in the offices and lounge at the Kabot Agronomy plant in Academy, and in Kabot's corporate offices: Executives and secretaries watching the televised committee hearing; lively discussions that only moments earlier had been laced with confidence in the company's post-explosion actions. Then following Gans's admission, stunned silence.

Julie imagined *Chronicle* editors and reporters gathered to watch the hearing in front of the TV in the coffee-break room, and at this moment dumbfounded, silent. Then she permitted herself an inward laugh, imagining them stumbling over each other to get to their desks and write about what had just happened.

In the hearing room, reporters ignored the bangs of the chairman's gavel as they spoke into cell phones, brought out laptop computers and began to type. Many jumped up and ran from the room, talking excitedly as they exited.

Julie wanted to yell, "Hey, not so fast. There's more to come!"

As quiet returned to the room, Chairman Pachik looked across the audience. "Please be advised, any further disturbances and I will clear the meeting room." He paused and referred to his notes. "Mr. Gans, Kabot has repeatedly claimed that none of the highly toxic chemical in use at the Academy plant, methyl isocyanate, MIC, the same chemical that killed thousands at Bhopal, India, in 1984, that no methyl isocyanate, MIC, was released by the plant explosion."

"Yes, sir."

The chairman held up a copy of the *Chronicle*. "A story in today's paper challenges that. Our staff investigators have raised similar questions. Sir, was MIC released?"

"Mr. Chairman, if I may make a slight correction to your statement, what we said was, 'We have no evidence that MIC was released.'"

"No evidence? Would you please clarify that?"

Gans' counsel leaned over and whispered to him. Gans then said, "Mr. Chairman, we do not *know* if MIC was, or was not, released."

"You don't know? Why not?"

"The MIC sensors on the plant's fence lines were not operating."

A buzz of whispers passed through the room.

Mr. Pachik asked, "Not operating? Why?"

Gans leaned forward, his arms on the table before him. "They had been turned off during the plant shutdown and remained off during the startup."

"Am I hearing you correctly: the sensors remained off when the plant started up again?"

"Yes, sir."

"Then you're confirming the *Chronicle*'s story? MIC could have been released?"

Gans shifted in his chair. "Could have been released? Perhaps. Could . . . or could not have."

Reporters spoke openly into cell phones. So many other reporters typed accounts of Gans' testimony on laptop keyboards that the clicking in the room sounded like an attack of grasshoppers on a field of grain.

A few minutes later, with a rap of his gavel the chairman adjourned the hearing. Julie walked out and retraced her steps along the corridor to the front entrance. Behind her, reporters jostled to get next to Gans. "Sir, would you care to comment . . .?"

A voice behind her said, "You and the *Chronicle* have created a God-awful mess, Miss Reporter. Congratulations. I hope you're happy. Maybe a big promotion is on the way."

She stopped and turned. "Just doing my job, Ben. Some people are interested in the truth."

"And shoot themselves in the foot. Maybe Kabot will move out of the valley."

"Maybe. But I doubt it. Assuming the plant stays, the real questions are, can we trust Kabot to operate a safe plant? Short of a shelter in place, how will we know?"

Chapter 50

JACKSON, WV, MARCH 7, 2009—Julie and Ben carried scones and coffee to a table in Henry's Books. During the night, light snow had fallen. Julie looked out Henry's front window. Beneath a still-dark sky, River Street's trees spread arches of lacy white branches. Snow peaked on top each of the turn-of-the-century street lamps. On an otherwise cold gray morning, the amber light of the lamps spread a warm glow.

As they sat down, other customers, relaxing on a Saturday morning, carried coffee and pastries to nearby tables.

Ben said in an accusatory voice, "Yesterday Otto climbed all over me. Word around the office is that corporate climbed all over Otto. Your story has derailed everything at Kabot, Julie."

"My story derailed . . .?" She laughed. "You've got it wrong, Ben. Kabot's faulty safety procedures and cover-up derailed Kabot."

Ben looked around the room and then in a softer voice said, "I used to think that my career, my future, was our future. Today I don't know . . ."

Her voice incredulous, Julie said, "You don't know? Where have you been?" She took a bite of her scone and spoke in an un-ruffled voice. "Ben, my future belongs to me. For better or worse, I'll create it. I'll live it."

"What our parents had, Jules. I want that. The life the plant gave to Dad. It's out there for you and me . . ."

"Stop. Your dad exchanged his life for what Carbide, then Kabot, gave him. Are you planning to do that?"

"Dad believed in the plant, believed in the company."

"And the PR woman, what's her name, Anna? Did your dad have an Anna on the side?"

Ben recoiled and sat erect. In a near shout, he said, "Leave her out of this!"

The couple at the next table turned and looked at them.

Julie shrugged. "Fine by me. You brought her in. You deal with her."

"I will . . . but . . ." Ben's voice trailed away.

"But?"

"But . . . us? What about us?"

Julie gave a brief laugh. In a good-natured tone of voice, she answered, "Us? There's no us any more, Ben. 'Us' is . . . how do they say *us is over* in German? *Kaput?*"

Ben put his elbows on the table, leaned forward and looked up at Julie. "My feelings haven't changed."

"Your choices have changed everything. Anna. Merchandising lies as truth. We define ourselves by our choices, Ben. And yours suck."

"Jules, I've been so caught up . . . the explosion . . . long days and little sleep. Anna means nothing to me. The investigation. What happened in Washington. It's all behind me, behind us. Now things will settle down. Please . . ."

"The train has left the station, Ben."

"But."

"No buts, Ben."

They sat in silence, sipping coffee, pinching off and eating small bites of their scones.

Ben shrugged and said, "OK, I guess I get it." He pulled out his handkerchief and wiped his eyes. "It's hard for me . . ."

Julie replied, "It wasn't easy for me. But I stayed on board the train, traveled to a new place."

"I'm still facing a rough time of it. Losing you. Trying to hang on at Kabot." Ben sipped his coffee and looked out the window. Then he turned to Julie. "Can you . . . for old time's sake, will you tell me what's next? I mean, what you're going to write next?"

"Is this your last chance to redeem yourself with Otto and Anna?"

"I just wondered," Ben muttered, and then added, "I probably shouldn't have asked. But it'd be nice to know."

"In the old days, it'd have been nice to tell you."

"Why not now? It would mean a lot. Is there a time . . . when *can* you?"

Julie looked out the front window. The flashing amber lights of a passing snowplow lit the street and blinked on the walls of the coffee shop. After the plow passed, Julie turned to Ben. "The truth is, I won't, I can't, tell you. Not now . . . not ever."

Chapter 51

BEFORE HER MORNING BRIEFING TO HARRISON on Monday, Julie and Harrison walked to the break room and poured themselves cups of coffee. Walking to Harrison's office, Julie said, "I enjoyed my short stay at the Willard. A rich history. I wish I could've seen the original building."

Harrison said, "Me, too. But the current one is comfortable. My former wife and I stayed there once; seems like that was in another lifetime. Did you know Martin Luther King wrote his 'I have a dream' speech there?"

"I read about that," Julie said. "Most everybody knows that Lincoln died just down the street from the Willard. But most people don't know this: Lincoln stayed at the Willard, in seclusion, immediately before his first inauguration."

"Include me in your everybody."

Julie sat on the other side of Harrison's desk, opened her backpack, and removed some documents.

"What's happening on the story from your Cambridge trip?"

"I'm working on it. First can we talk about the Washington hearing?"

Harrison sipped his coffee, then said, "Sure. The hearing has cranked up Kabot's PR machine. They're working overtime. Reminding everyone, the US, Germany, other countries around the world, of their charitable contributions, concerts and art exhibits they've sponsored. Bottom line: they say they're good citizens. Everywhere."

Julie replied, "It's what they don't say that troubles me. Yesterday I got an e-mail from a reporter in Paris. He'd read our electronic edition's coverage of the explosion. He asked if I knew about Marcel Giroux, a Kabot marketing executive in France."

"Did you?"

"No. Here's what he told me. A few months ago, Giroux blew the whistle on Kabot's bribing over two thousand doctors in France to prescribe Kabot drugs, including one drug that was known to have fatal side effects. Investigators filed charges against Kabot. Giroux was placed under police guard at his home. He was scheduled to testify in court two days ago."

"*Was* scheduled to testify? Did he?"

"Even though Giroux had police protection, the night before he was to give testimony, an intruder broke into his townhouse and stabbed him. Repeatedly. His wounds required seventy-seven stitches. The prognosis is he'll live. The Associated Press has picked up the story and is now circulating it."

"Write the story, Julie. Connect it to the explosion and some of the other things you've found. Review your story with Bob. We'll run the AP story as well. I'll tell Dan to hold space on page one, tomorrow's edition."

She handed Harrison three typewritten pages and a small computer flash drive. "Here's the story. Bob's already reviewed it." She paused and gazed at him, her face expectant. "Harrison . . . uh, aren't you overlooking something?"

"I don't . . . what?

Julie stood and picked up her backpack. "Will they come after me? Do you have some idea about how to protect me? My dad was a Jackson cop. I'm familiar with violence. But not when I'm the one at risk." Julie put down her backpack. Her voice rose. "The paper gonna protect me, Harrison? You gonna do that?"

"Until now, I hadn't thought about the need . . . of course, Julie, we'll protect you."

"Do you suppose that's what the Paris prosecutor and the Parisian gendarmes told Giroux?"

Harrison leaned back in his chair, his gaze locked on Julie's eyes. In a soft but firm voice he asked, "Do you want me to hold the story?"

"Run it!" Julie shouldered her backpack and walked to the door. "Then talk to the cops."

Chapter 52

OR THE NEXT THREE DAYS JULIE ARRIVED at the *Chronicle* early in the morning and stayed well into the evening. She spent most of her time in the archives, reading and making notes on stories related to Kabot and the plant. She electronically accessed archived stories from recent years. She accessed stories from the more distant past from spools of microfilm. She expanded her search by entering electronic archives available to the *Chronicle*, particularly the *New York Times* and the *London Times*.

After three days of mentally trudging through archives, Julie looked forward to her afternoon appointment with Delbarton. Brownie's at 1:30 PM. On her way to Brownie's, she stopped at home, removed a container of homemade lasagna from the freezer, and put it on the counter to thaw. "Real food," she joked to herself, trying to remember how many days had passed since she'd had a home-cooked meal. She gave up.

On her way to Brownie's, Julie found herself mentally returning to her stop at home: her walk through the house, opening the freezer, placing the container of lasagna on the kitchen counter, then back through the house and out the door.

Something kept pulling at her consciousness. Had she seen something awry, maybe something moved on the kitchen counter? Had someone been there? By the time Julie drove past the Kabot plant, she found herself repeatedly glancing into her car's rearview mirror. A late model gray Toyota had been behind her since she left her neighborhood. Soon the Toyota turned onto a side street. A red Ford sedan took its place.

Julie waited until the last possible moment, then, without giving a turn signal, quickly steered her car into Brownie's parking lot. The Ford slowed. When it passed, she saw a woman driving and two children in the back seat. Julie shook her head and laughed. She imagined Harrison saying, "Easy, Julie, easy." Then she again thought about walking through her house to get the casserole.

Julie joined Delbarton, already seated in the partitioned area in the rear of Brownie's dining room. On the floor beside him sat a briefcase. Helen brought them coffee.

From his flask, Delbarton added "spice" to his coffee. "I read your story on Gans' testimony."

"Thanks. Any thoughts about it?"

"The cover-up didn't surprise me. But the disclosures by Kabot employees to you, to investigators, must've surprised the hell out of top management."

"Kabot had it all worked out. They planned to have Gans push the whole thing back on the committee; say to them, 'We were just enforcing the law that you, Congress, passed.'"

Delbarton smiled. "No doubt they hoped the committee would ignore the neglected MIC detectors. See Kabot as a good corporate citizen. But it blew up in their face."

"John, tomorrow morning we're running a story on Kabot's pharmaceutical division. Some upsetting news has come to us from France. A sales executive, Marcel Giroux, turned whistle-blower. He went to the French authorities and revealed a Kabot program of under-the-table payments to over two thousand doctors to prescribe Kabot drugs."

Delbarton stirred his coffee, staring into it. "A long time ago, I knew Marcel Giroux."

"A few days ago an intruder scaled the back wall of Giroux's townhouse and broke in—even though he had police protection. The intruder repeatedly stabbed him. He'll live, but now he refuses to testify. Without him the government has, at best, a weak case."

"Kabot plays hardball."

"So people have told me."

Sipping his coffee, Delbarton said, "Their stock has taken a beating in recent months. The explosion. Disclosures in the congressional hearing. That citizens' group's filing legal papers, asking a federal judge to serve an injunction on Kabot to stop their use of MIC. My broker tells me some of his colleagues are changing their recommendations on Kabot stock from 'buy' to 'hold.'" Delbarton chuckled. "After the paper runs the story on Giroux, brokers may be changing 'hold' to 'sell.' How long do you plan to keep going after them?"

"As long as they keep putting us at risk." Julie paused and drank her coffee. "Do you suppose they've got me on the same list as Giroux?"

His face showing concern, Delbarton asked, "I understand if you're worried. I would be, too. Who knows about the *Chronicle*'s Giroux story?"

"Only a few people at the paper, people I trust. Tomorrow morning everybody'll know. On the way here I stopped at home and put a casserole out to thaw. Since then, I've kept thinking about my walk through my house. Something seemed . . . off-kilter, just a little off-center."

"Tell me more."

"After I left the house, driving here, I thought I was being followed." Julie laughed. "Turned out to be a woman with two kids in the back seat."

Delbarton laughed a deep belly laugh.

"John, I asked you to meet me because I need a favor."

"Sure, if I can."

"I need for you to confirm, if you can, some disturbing information about Kabot I've turned up."

"I'll do what I can." Delbarton took a long drink of his coffee.

"Let's start with honey bees."

In a surprised voice, John said, "I'd heard some buzz about that. Excuse the pun."

Julie brought a document from her backpack and showed it to him. "This article appeared a couple of years ago in the *New York Times*. All over the world, beekeepers and governments have complained about the collapse of bee colonies. As a consequence there've been major pollination problems for farmers. Loss of crops. Loss of income for beekeepers and farmers."

"I'm familiar with the problem. I read that in China thousands of peasants are hand-pollinating apple orchards. One tree at a time, one bloom at a time. Colony collapse has created big money losses."

"Much of the evidence points to pesticides. Kabot Agronomy pesticides."

"Kabot's response?"

Julie handed Delbarton a document from her backpack. "In a Kabot press release, the company said," she read aloud, " 'We continue to believe that . . .' "

Without reading the article, Delbarton completed Julie's statement, " '. . . when the evidence is viewed fully . . .' "

Surprised, Julie said, "Their exact words!"

"I've been there before. A standard company line. Sounds like they're using some of my old stuff."

Julie removed news clippings from her backpack. She laid photos of rice fields in Louisiana and Texas on the table. "In 2004, Kabot Agronomy contaminated US long-grain rice with genetically modified strains . . . Arkansas, Louisiana, Mississippi, Texas . . ."

As Julie added more photos to the tabletop, Delbarton said, "I remember. The European Union temporarily stopped US rice shipments. Japan and Russia put an outright ban on shipments."

Helen walked to the table and poured more coffee. Delbarton poured brew from his flask into his mug.

Julie brought out new documents and photos. She placed them on the table. "There's a lot more. Should I go on?"

Delbarton gave an affirmative nod, his eyes on the documents.

"Okay, let's shift to another part of Kabot Global. Pharmaceuticals. Their side effects and Kabot's full disclosure. Or, I should say, Kabot's lack of full disclosure. I'll start with Fluoroquin, a widely used antibiotic. In the 1990s it produced billions, *billions*, of dollars in sales for Kabot."

In the center of the table Julie placed a photo of an operating room. Members of a surgical team hovered over a patient. "Fluoroquin was widely used during surgery."

Then she showed Delbarton a photo of a commercial chicken farm with thousands of chickens crowded into pens too small for their number. "In addition, Fluoroquin has been widely used as a major antibiotic in the poultry industry." She pointed to the photo. "It's easy to understand why the industry needed an effective antibiotic, given these crowded conditions. After chickens from commercial poultry farms ingested Fluoroquin, the drug entered the food chain. Chicken dinners, sandwiches, chicken soup, chicken salad, KFC and other fast food chains. Meals in dormitories. Prisons and hospitals."

"I get it. A huge market."

"But," Julie said in a cautious voice, "consider this. Fluoroquin can cause," she read from a document, " 'heart problems, irreversible peripheral neuropathy, spontaneous tendon rupture, acute liver injury, severe central nervous system disorders . . .' "

"In chickens?"

Julie read faster, " 'Psychotic reactions, acute pancreatitis, bone marrow depression, interstitial nephritis and hemolytic anemia, loss of vision, irreversible double vision.' " She paused, then added, "In humans!"

Julie hurriedly pulled more photos from her backpack: Crowds demonstrating on Wall Street in front of the New York Stock Exchange.

"In 1999, on the day of Kabot's initial stock offering on the New York Stock Exchange, celebrities led a protest of Fluoroquin in the poultry industry." Julie paused and tapped her fingers on the photo. "Kabot's main competitor, Linden Products, stopped selling its version of Fluoroquin to the poultry industry in 1998. Kabot continued until 2003. Five years in the marketplace with no major competitor. Very profitable."

Delbarton remained silent, his eyes scanning the documents on the table.

"Then there's Cerivas—familiar with it?"

"I've heard of it," Delbarton answered.

"A popular, frequently prescribed statin. It lowers cholesterol. But with a dangerous side effect: muscle disorders. It's easy to forget the heart is a big muscle. Cerivas caused failure in that big muscle, and deaths."

Julie placed copies of news clippings on the table. "Kabot recalled the drug in 2000 . . . after confirmed Cerivas injuries to sixteen hundred people. And the deaths of one hundred. Kabot's defense? Doctors didn't use it as recommended. Germany's Minister of Health charged Kabot with holding back information on Cerivas' side effects."

Julie extended her coffee mug toward Delbarton. "I could use a little of that . . . share your brew, John?"

He smiled and poured a splash of whiskey into her mug.

Julie sipped her coffee mix. "The story gets darker." Julie placed copies of news stories and photos on the table. "Aprotin— a drug that prevented blood clotting. From 1992 to 2006, Aprotin was used in *one-third* of *all* cardiac bypass operations. In the USA alone, used in a half million bypasses per year. A lot of Aprotin. A lot of hearts."

Delbarton said, "I watched the story on a network television exposé."

"Then you may remember, Aprotin caused kidney damage, often leading to death. Kabot sat on knowledge of the drug's deadly side effects . . . *for fourteen years.*" Julie placed a photo of a network correspondent conducting an on-camera interview with a Kabot representative. "He confronted Kabot with hard data about Aprotin's fatalities." She placed news clippings beside the photo. "Aprotin sold for $1,300 per dose. All the while safer and more effective drugs were out there, costing under $50 a dose."

Delbarton said, "Former colleagues told me that in 2005 the FDA called a special meeting with Kabot to discuss Aprotin's safety. At the time of the meeting, Kabot had data on Aprotin deaths but didn't say a word about it."

Julie continued, "Finally, November 2005 . . . two years and *twenty-two thousand deaths* after an independent research team confirmed Aprotin's high death rate, Kabot pulled the drug. For two years, *nearly a thousand deaths a month*!"

Delbarton looked away and said, as if reading from a script long-ago memorized, "I quote, 'Kabot continues to believe that when used according to labeling, the totality of available data will support a favorable risk benefit profile for Aprotin.'"

"My God, Kabot's words, exactly!" Julie leaned back in the booth and looked Delbarton in the eye. "John, how many deaths does it take to support a favorable risk benefit profile?" She took a long drink of her now cooled coffee mix. Julie gazed at a couple with two young children who sat in a booth across the room. "How do you kill like that and never face charges?"

Delbarton poured more whiskey into his mug. "Incorporate yourself."

Chapter 53

A FEW DAYS LATER, IN THE LATE AFTERNOON Julie stood in the doorway of Harrison's office.

Harrison leaned over his desk making notes with a red pen on the document before him. He stopped and looked up. "Hey, Julie. Haven't seen you for a few days. Are you all right? You look tired."

"Not a lot of sleep the last three days. I'm trying to wrap up a draft of the Kabot and IG Farben World War II story. And I have some recent Kabot information on pharmaceuticals I'm turning into a story. Not pretty."

"Want to talk about it?"

"Yes, but later." She raised her arms and stretched. "Right now I want to go home. Get some sleep. Maybe tomorrow morning. A good night's sleep and a run should get me back on track."

"Okay. Get some rest. Take tomorrow off if you need to."

"Thanks. But I expect I'll see you in the morning."

~ ~ ~ ~ ~

SOUTH JACKSON, WV, MARCH 13, 2009—The next morning Julie rose early and put on her running gear. She strapped her cell phone to her waist and went out the front door. In the early March morning darkness, she watched the first traces of gold streak across the sky. Julie jogged along the streets of South Jackson, once again synchronizing her breathing to the rhythm of her footsteps. She inhaled the wisps of spring's moist air. Four steps to inhale, four steps to exhale. An eight-beat breath, she called it. Soon, three steps replaced four; six-beat breaths. Then, Julie's heart and breathing rate quickening, she moved into what she called "the zone." Two steps to inhale, two steps to exhale. Steady, repetitive, unchanging. In, in, out, out. Soon she reached what she called transcendence; her running and synchronized breathing carried her into another world. When she returned from it at the end of a run, as she approached her front yard, she knew only that she had done something that made her sweat a lot. And feel good.

Julie jogged out of the city on a two-lane country road. To her right was a craggy hillside, the blooms of redbud trees just beginning to color it. On the other side of the road on a precipitous ravine, the first stems of ferns had begun to spiral. A fox jumped out of the ravine and crossed her path. Then two rabbits. An occasional car went by. Julie reached her turn-around point, a church that marked a distance of two and a half miles from her home. She crossed to the other side of the road and headed toward home. In, in, out, out.

In the distance, Julie heard the steady drone of a motorcycle approaching. Suddenly a red motorcycle rounded the turn ahead of her. The rider wore a helmet with a dark visor, long hair flowing behind.

The cycle closed the distance to Julie. Just before it reached her, the cyclist surprised her with a sudden swerve across the road. Then, what she would remember as much like action in a slow-motion movie, the cycle came straight at her. The rider's left hand brandished a long iron rod, raised high. Julie felt frozen in place.

The cycle's roar became thunder, the rider's left arm and iron rod an arc in motion, aimed at her head. Julie leaped toward the ravine. In mid-air, the rod struck her shoulder. The cycle skidded, canted sharply toward the pavement, then, like a gyroscope, straightened and sped away.

Julie tumbled down the ravine, through brambles and the barren thorns of last year's blackberry bushes. At the bottom of the ravine she lay motionless, dazed but conscious enough to fear the return of the motorcycle and rider. She listened for the roar of its engine, but heard only, from deep in the ravine, the call of a red-winged blackbird.

For a few minutes she lay motionless. Dull pain spread through her body. Then Julie moved her left arm and attempted to stand. She lost her balance and fell to the ground. Finally she stood up, slowly. Sharp pains pulsed from her left shoulder. Blood soaked the left side of her jacket. Her bloody left knee protruded from her ripped running pants. Eyes closed, Julie lay on her back and gently extended each arm, then flexed her knees. Everything seemed to work. They didn't work well, and they creaked, but they worked. Her right hand, as if it had a life of its own, moved to her cell phone and uncased it. On her third attempt she accessed the phone's list of frequently called numbers. She touched Harrison's number.

"Hello?"

"Just got ambushed . . . motorcycle . . . someone tried to . . . aimed at my head . . . an iron rod."

"Julie—where are you?"

"In a ravine . . . they tried to kill me."

"Give me your location—can you do that?"

"On . . . outside South Jackson . . . Old Church Road . . . near the Exxon . . . couple of miles . . . a ravine, did I tell you, a ravine?"

"Stay in the ravine. When I call you, come to the road. Got that? Got that, Julie? Answer me!"

"Uh, yes."

"Stay put." His voice insistent, parental, Harrison said, "And what will you do?"

"Uh . . . wait . . . for your call."

"That's right. Stay where you are. I'll call 911. You wait on my call. Then come to the road!"

A half-hour later, one arm around Julie, Harrison helped her limp into the emergency room of Jackson Area Medical Center. "You're going to be okay."

Her voice weak, wavering, Julie laid her head on Harrison's shoulder. "I need a shelter in place."

Chapter 54

EARLY THAT AFTERNOON, STILL WRAPPED IN a down jacket, her left arm in a sling and a bandage on her forehead, Julie limped to Harrison's office and stood in the doorway. Harrison looked up from his desk. He quickly walked to her and opened his arms. She stepped into his embrace.

"Feeling better?"

She managed a smile. "Compared to when I started on my morning run, or when I found myself at the bottom of the ravine?"

He smiled and nudged her toward a chair. "Please, sit."

Julie sat down and extended her left leg in front of her. "Me and Giroux. We're both alive. For the moment."

"Take it easy today."

Harrison picked up the receiver of his office phone and dialed a number. "Hello, Suzie? I need some help." He listened for a moment. "Yes, I know what you're writing. And that story's important. But I have a more immediate problem, and I need your help. Keep this between us, okay?" He paused to listen. "Julie just survived an attack." He paused and listened. "She'll tell you about it. Right now I'd appreciate your helping her get settled over at the Jackson House Hotel."

After completing the call, Harrison turned to Julie. "This is my fault," Harrison said. "I should have called Al yesterday."

Harrison dialed another phone number. "Captain Billups, please. Harrison Wilde calling." He pressed a button that converted his desk phone to a speaker phone.

"Harrison, thanks for alerting us about that attack. I'll need to get more details. How's the reporter doing?"

"Al, the reporter, Julie Brown, is among the walking wounded. She's here in my office. I have the three of us on speaker phone."

"Julie Brown. I know that name. Any relation to Detective Harold Brown?"

Julie replied, "Yes, Captain Billups. He was my dad."

"I remember you as a little girl. Once in a while, your dad would bring you to headquarters."

"That was me."

"I looked up to your dad, Miss Brown. I hoped I could be half as good a cop as him."

"Thank you."

"Al, as you know, this isn't a social call," Harrison said. "Julie's working on a story about Kabot. And she's dug up some not-so-pretty facts about the company's past. Here are some details on the attack. This morning she went jogging. Just outside of South Jackson, on Old Church Road, she was attacked by someone on a motorcycle. Whoever it was aimed an iron bar at her head. She leaped away but got a nasty blow to the shoulder, then took a long tumble down a ravine. Just got out of the ER. I'm calling to ask your help to find out who ordered the attack and protect my reporter."

"Harrison, Old Church Road is outside city limits. I'll notify the sheriff; it'll fall under his jurisdiction. I'll assign some people to work with him. We'll need a photo of Julie, phone number and address. And her work schedule. You know, the basics. And Miss Brown, we'll need to know anything you can remember about the incident. The cycle. The rider. Anything."

Harrison looked at Julie and raised his eyebrows in lieu of a question. Julie nodded affirmatively.

"No problem. You should know that the paper is putting her up for a while here in the city. A temporary home address. I'll give that to your office directly."

"Good. In our jurisdiction. My people will place her under surveillance and blend into the woodwork."

"In a little while, Julie's going to check in."

"Okay. Julie, just hang out in your room until you get a call from me. I'll send a female officer to meet with you."

After the call ended, Julie said, "Harrison, yesterday I met with John Delbarton to confirm some facts my research on Kabot has turned up. I've been looking at pharmaceutical and pesticide operations . . ."

"We don't have to talk about it now, Julie."

Julie raised her voice. "Trust me. You need to know."

"Okay." Harrison leaned back in his chair.

Julie closed her eyes for a moment and then said, "Yesterday, on the way to meet with John Delbarton, I stopped at home. Afterward, I kept having an eerie feeling about my house. Something seemed out of place. I couldn't put my finger on it. Still can't." She paused as if to gather strength. "But something was awry. After I told John about it, I laughed it off. Now I believe my suspicion grew out of something, I don't know what, but something that I saw—maybe things on my kitchen countertop had been moved slightly. Someone had been there."

"Make sure you tell the officer who works with you."

"I will. I had lots of documents at home dealing with my story on Kabot's pharmaceutical products and my story on Kabot and Auschwitz." She took a deep breath and grimaced as she extended her left leg. "It would have been easy to photograph them . . . pass along the photos."

"You've been through a lot, Julie. Those stories are important. I just don't know . . ."

"Know what?"

"The best way to bring them to light."

Julie inhaled quickly as a needle of sharp pain radiated from her shoulder. "Aiee. That hurts." She gently massaged her shoulder. "Pesticides and pharmaceuticals are part . . ." She closed her eyes and again slowly rotated her shoulder, ". . . of Kabot's business today. IG Farben and Auschwitz is the context for that business, Kabot's living history."

"Julie, right now probably isn't the best time to talk about this."

"If not now, when? No, Harrison, now. There's a reason people read history. It holds lessons that are real, that apply to today! If you're afraid of what the publisher or shareholders will . . ."

"I've faced worse. But I have to deal with the fact that Auschwitz was seventy-five years ago."

"Seventy-five . . .? Who are you kidding? The Kabot way of operating . . . the culture, is alive . . . malignant and thriving, today. Did they ask anybody about restarting MIC production? Search for alternatives? *Profits über alles.*"

"Timing is everything, Julie. Right now I feel we have to move slowly. The *Chronicle* could look as though it has a vendetta for Kabot."

"And Kabot? Do they have a vendetta? Are they allowed to kill employees? Patients? To put their neighbors, mostly poor, many black, in harm's way? To put the whole valley at risk? Is Kabot allowed to attack anybody who ferrets out the truth?"

"You know that's not what I . . ."

Julie leaned forward, her voice angry and loud. "I know? I'll tell you what I know. Here it is, ready? *I know* I can't go home. *I know* I gotta go check in at Jackson House, thankful to be alive. And I *don't know* if my protection there will be any better than Marcel Giroux received in Paris."

Chapter 55

THE TWO POLICE OFFICERS ASSIGNED TO JULIE, Corporal Autumn Gilbert and Patrolman John Benson, met Julie at the front desk of the Jackson House Hotel. Julie remembered Autumn as a runner in local fun-runs and races. In the races she competed in an age group a decade older than Julie's group.

The small hotel's location, on River Street not far from the *Chronicle*, made it convenient for Julie to connect with staff. She liked the ambience. The hotel's architecture and lobby decor reflected the gilded-age styles of the late 1800s and the affluence of the region's economic boom years. The lobby and dining room had marble floors, high and ornate ceilings, leaded windows, and oriental rugs that complemented comfortable Victorian-era furniture. The guest rooms had been kept up to date, with modern bathroom fixtures, bedding, and lighting. Still, the rooms, including Julie's, carried a touch of the hotel's past in their wallpaper, artwork, and furnishings.

Patrolman Benson, the younger of the officers, helped Julie settle into her room while Corporal Gilbert walked through the hotel making notes of entrances and exits, fire escapes, the basement and roof. Corporal Gilbert then sent Officer Benson to retrieve files from Julie's home.

Aided by pain-relieving medication, Julie slept much of the next three days. Then she slowly began to alternate sleep and work. The period of work became longer a little at a time.

On the fifth day of her recovery, Julie removed the sling from her left arm and, accompanied by Corporal Gilbert, went for a slow early morning jog along the Vandalia River. They ran along the trail that had been cut into the hillside, not far above the water level. Above them, on Vandalia Boulevard, Officer Benson drove a police car, blue lights blinking, at the pace of the two joggers. After a short distance Julie slowed to a walk, then a limping walk as the pain in her knee returned.

"Enough," Autumn said. "Let go up to the street and hitch a ride with Benson. Go back to Jackson House."

After returning, Julie called John Delbarton. "Just checking in, John. Wondering if you're doing all right."

"More or less," he said in a slow, soft drawl. "Julie, for the past two, no three, days I've been trying to call you. No answer at home, and people at the paper didn't help any . . . they told me you were out of town. Did you turn off your cell phone?"

"I did. It's a long story."

"The truth is, I'm having a hard time. Otto's not returning my calls . . . I'm sorry, I needn't unload this on you. But there isn't anyone else to talk with."

"That's okay. If it helps, I'm here, ready to listen."

His voice suddenly eager, Delbarton said, "Could you . . . see me? Soon?"

"Sure. I'd like to do that." Even as she spoke, Julie wondered if she could go. What arrangements would have to be made for coverage? Police protection in a single space, a hotel room, had a simplicity to it. Following a working reporter added complexity and risk.

In a voice that Julie heard as approaching a plea for help, Delbarton said, "I have some photos and materials I'd like you to have. I think you'll find them, well . . . intriguing."

"Thanks. I'm sure I will."

"Can you come here today?"

"I'll need to check a few things first." Julie smiled, her first since the attack, and thought about surveillance cameras, patrol cars, Kevlar vests. "How about this afternoon, around three o'clock?"

"OK. I'm on the top floor of the Longview Building. Across the river from downtown."

"I know the building." Julie laughed. "But I never knew anyone rich enough to live there."

Delbarton remained silent for a moment, then replied, "Carbide and Kabot have paid me well. But I've learned that money has its limits."

"I apologize, John. Just trying to be light."

"No apology necessary. I'm having a hard time being light these days."

Chapter 56

JACKSON, WV, MARCH 20, 2009—Delbarton opened the door
to his apartment. The striking change in his appearance surprised Julie. He looked disheveled, his face pale. He held a drink
in one hand. "Come in." At first glance, his apartment appeared
as unkempt as he did.

Limping, Julie walked in. The large living room of his penthouse commanded a view along the river west of the city and
across mountains to the north. Julie quickly recognized that her
first glance assessment of the apartment had been correct.
Newspapers and magazines littered the room. Empty glasses sat
on dusty windowsills and end tables. Julie imagined how Bertha
could transform this place.

"Join me in a drink?"

"Thanks, nothing for me. Good to see you, John."

"You, too. But you're limping." He pointed at the bandage
on Julie's forehead. "What happened?"

"That's the long story I mentioned on the phone."

"I'd like to hear it." He pointed to a large Eames lounge chair
canted toward the windows. "Please, sit down."

Delbarton sat in a chair facing Julie. He placed his drink
alongside a stack of three empty and dirty glasses on the glass
coffee table between himself and Julie. Also on the table lay two
thick photo albums and a tall stack of file folders beside a telephone.

Julie recounted her attack. She began nearly a week ago, the
day before the attack, when she and Delbarton had last met. She
described her feeling that someone had been in her home. "The

next morning I went out for my early morning run. On my return route to town," Julie suddenly felt her breathing quicken and her heart race, "it happened." She described the motorcyclist's swerve toward her, the blow from the iron bar, and her fall into the ravine. She brought Delbarton through Harrison's rescue, her visit to the emergency room, then Harrison's call to the Jackson police.

"Are the police here? Now?"

"Yes, probably standing outside your door."

Delbarton gulped the remainder of his drink and, glass in hand, walked to the front door. He jerked it open to find a surprised Patrolman Benson.

"Everything okay?" Benson asked. He leaned in and looked beyond Delbarton, across the room. Julie smiled and waved.

"Yes . . . thanks, Officer."

Delbarton closed the door. He walked across the room to the bar, put cubes of ice in his highball glass, then poured a generous helping of scotch over the cubes.

"John, on the phone you mentioned you had some material you wanted me to have."

Delbarton pointed to the albums and files on the table. "All that stuff. You can take it with you. I won't need it anymore."

"Thanks, John. I'm sure it'll help me."

"Keep it. It's all yours, Julie." He looked at his wristwatch. "Whoops, I nearly let time get away from me." He picked up the phone's receiver and dialed a number. He gave Julie an apologetic look. "Give me a minute."

Julie nodded. She heard faint traces of a telephone ringing, then a distant and muffled voice.

"Otto Heidrich, please. Dr. Delbarton calling." He remained silent for a moment. "Otto? John here."

After listening for a moment, Delbarton said, "Yes, the weather has been nice. I'm pleased to learn you had a good trip to Stuttgart. And a good visit with your grandchildren." He paused and then said, "Otto, I'm following up on our discussion about my appointment . . . ."

Julie heard Otto's voice on the other end of the call, now loud and distinct. "Following up? There's more we need to discuss?"

"You said you'd contact me. . . ." Delbarton listened in silence. Otto's voice again became muffled.

Delbarton asked, "You don't want to meet?"

Julie heard Otto's voice, loud and clear. "That is correct, John."

John stood, walked to the window and gazed across the river. "Mmm, Otto, are you forgetting? This is John Delbarton. I can connect the dots, paint a picture . . . clear enough for even a cub reporter."

Otto's voice leaped from the phone, "And you forget, John. You're a failed executive. As well as, shall we say, a chronic imbiber. Your ramblings have no credibility. Nor will they . . ."

On his phone's screen, Delbarton touched the "End call" command. Otto's voice disappeared into cyberspace.

Why had Delbarton made that phone call in her presence? Julie wondered. Had he intended to signal something . . . ? Did he need a witness? If so, for what?

Chapter 57

D<small>ELBARTON TOSSED HIS CELL PHONE</small> on the table. In a brusque walk, he crossed the room to the bar, refilled his drink, then walked to the window. He pointed to a riverboat on the Vandalia, far below, squat and powerful, much like a harbor tugboat, pushing a string of empty barges upstream. "That boat, it's a twin screw push-boat. Pushes barges upriver as far as Vandalia Falls. Each boat, each barge, has a destination. Coal tipples. Chemical companies. In a day or two, they'll return, loaded, pushing their way downriver to a new destination. Sometimes as far as New Orleans."

Julie walked to the window and stood beside him.

He continued, "Unlike me. The only load I carry is guilt." In a whisper he added, "And I have no destination." He picked up the top file from the stack on the table and removed one page. "I'll keep this." He showed the page to Julie. "You can easily find the names and numbers."

Julie read the letterhead: Staff, Chemical Institute.

"I'll have to decide who to call. And when. But soon. Most of what I know will confirm what they're finding. But in investigative work, as you well know, confirmation is valuable. And who knows, maybe I'll provide a few of the puzzle's missing pieces."

Julie looked down at late-afternoon traffic moving along Vandalia Boulevard. Then her gaze lifted toward the northwest. A thin line of dark clouds had formed low across the horizon of the otherwise cloudless blue sky.

Delbarton pointed at the clouds. "Here it comes."

He and Julie watched the clouds rapidly expand in size and deepen their color, from gray to purple to black. Delbarton's voice carried a surge of excitement. "Thirty years of watching storms from this window. I've seen some spectacular lightning, heard thunder to knock your socks off. A showcase of nature's power. Today's show is on its way. And, Julie, we have the best seats in the house. Would you like to join me in a toast to nature's power?"

Julie gazed at the near-hypnotic undulations of the advancing storm's dark clouds, their bellies drooping near the tops of mountains. "Yes, just a weak one, please." From her bag she took out two pain pills.

Delbarton walked to the bar, refreshed his drink, and dropped a few cubes and a generous splash of scotch into another highball glass. He handed Julie her drink.

Julie swallowed her pain pills and watched distant needles of lightning, each followed by a roll of thunder, play across the dark sky. The lightning grew brighter and the thunder louder as the storm bore down on Jackson. Soon storm clouds covered more than half the sky.

Moments later a brilliant bolt of lightning arched from a low-hanging black cloud to the roof of a downtown Jackson building. An explosive crack of thunder came with it. Startled, Julie jerked upright, sloshing scotch out of her glass.

Against the rumbling thunder, in a quiet voice, Delbarton said, "There's another chapter to the Kabot story—one you should know."

"Thanks. I want to learn all I can."

"It relates to Charles' son, Roger. His illness."

"Roger? What about him?" With the energy of small animals suddenly released from the confinement of cages, memories leaped into her thoughts: Roger playing the piano, then in the back yard refereeing football; becoming, month by month, ever paler, weaker; then a weekly loss of strength as the red and brown patches on his face and neck grew larger; his confinement to bed. Finally, saying goodbye. Roger's last trip to the hospital. Mary, weeping, plagued with guilt. How she had prayed for relief from her burden. She hadn't protected Roger, she felt. She had failed as his mother. "What did I do wrong, Julie? *What?*"

Delbarton raised his voice. "Julie? Are you with me?"

"Sorry. I drifted . . . thinking about Roger. And his mom."

"In the late 1970s, what we now call the HIV virus and AIDS was diagnosed as GRID, Gay Related Immune Deficiency." Delbarton opened the folder he'd placed on the table. He lifted out photos of San Francisco street scenes, men holding hands, walking, laughing, enjoying the city's night life. "A mysterious disease, killing gay men. First in San Francisco, then in other major cities. LA, New York . . . then around the nation."

Delbarton took a long drink of his coffee mix. "In the early 1980s, the HIV virus jumped across gay-straight boundaries and began to infect heterosexual males. AIDS entered the larger population."

"In 1982 and '83—that's when Roger contracted HIV and AIDS."

He continued, "The Centers for Disease Control faced a major problem. A contagious disease was loose across the country, infecting ever larger numbers of people; a fatality rate of fifty percent. The CDC searched for a pattern, for links, for any possible way to connect heterosexual males with HIV. They zeroed in on a couple of possibilities. One, not surprisingly, came from HIV-positive drug addicts sharing needles with men who had not been infected with HIV. The second came as a surprise. A large number of newly infected straight males were hemophiliacs. Bleeders, like Roger."

~   ~   ~   ~   ~

Julie spent the next day at Jackson House poring through the photos and papers Delbarton had given her. Many dealt with Kabot's pharmaceutical division. The story John Delbarton told of how HIV/AIDS had leapt into the straight population kept replaying itself. Julie read the details of how the disease first came to infect hemophiliacs. How it had infected Roger. She knew now what Mary and Charles didn't know. In the absence of facts, Mary had blamed herself.

She had to share this with Mary. Ben, too. "Autumn, there are some things I need to do," Julie said.

In the voice not of a new-found friend, but that of a police officer, Autumn asked, "Will you need to go out?"

Julie realized that she had slipped into her old way of operating, making plans to move around town, doing what needed to be done. Autumn's question brought her up short.

"I've come across some important information. I need to share it with Ben. And with his mother, Mary."

"Julie, at least for now, your life has changed. Sit tight. I had a call from Captain Billups. They have a suspect who may have been the motorcyclist who attacked you. A conversation with Ben will have to wait. Mary, too. At least for now, you aren't an entirely free agent. We have to plan ahead. Cover your movements, even simple ones, like a trip to Henry's Books. You'll be able to do what you need to do within certain limits, but I need to know in advance."

Chapter 58

CORPORAL AUTUMN GILBERT RECEIVED an early morning call. She learned that officers had apprehended a man suspected to have carried out the attack on Julie. He had long hair and a red motorcycle. After bringing him into custody, detectives obtained a search warrant. In a shed behind his home officers found an iron bar with traces of what appeared to be blood and threads on it. They sent the bar to a lab for analysis.

Moments after Autumn passed the information along to Julie, Captain Billups called. "Julie, you'll now be able to go back to the office. But I'd like you to continue living at Jackson House for a few more days. We want to keep you under surveillance until we get this cleared up. At the paper, our officers will stay far enough away that they'll be invisible to you."

Julie spent the morning reviewing the documents Delbarton had given her. Then she made a list of questions to ask him, most of them dealing with Z-Factor. She called him, hoping to arrange to get together for another discussion, but he didn't answer. For the next two days, she left voice-mail messages. Her calls went unanswered.

The following morning she stood in the doorway of Harrison's office. Harrison looked up from his desk. He put down his pen. "Julie?"

"Harrison." The flat expression on her face matched the tone of her voice.

He eyed her from head to toe. "You look tired. Can you take a minute and bring me up to date on Kabot developments?"

She walked into his office and dropped into the chair on the other side of his desk. "Things are moving along okay. Well, more or less."

"Is something wrong?"

"It's John Delbarton. I've been trying to call him for two days. No answer. I've left voice-mail messages. No reply. That's unlike him."

"Any ideas about where he might be?"

"None."

"Any reason to believe something bad might have happened to him, like what happened to you?"

"I don't know. Possibly." She paused for a moment. A vague uneasiness, like a noxious odor from the plant, polluted her thoughts. "When I last visited with John, he called Otto Heidrich. John threatened to go to the Chemical Institute with insider stories about plant safety going all the way back to Bhopal."

"Whoa! That's pretty serious."

"But more than that . . ." Julie hesitated. She reflected on a concern that had nagged at her since her last conversation with John.

"More than that . . . what are you thinking?"

"At the end of our discussion, he gave me lots of materials. Photos and documents about the plant. And Bhopal, before and after the disaster. Some of it dealt with toxic leaks and safety failures relevant to the present explosion. Much of it went back to his early years at Carbide, then continued up through his time with Kabot."

"Was there a problem with his giving you the materials?"

"No. Except I hadn't asked for any of it. Some of the material duplicated what he'd already shared with me. Then, here's the odd part: he volunteered that he wouldn't need the materials anymore."

"That's a loaded statement."

"I thought so too, but not until later." Julie remembered standing by the window with Delbarton. "He lives in a penthouse apartment at Longview. We watched a river boat push barges up the river. He said, 'Each boat, each barge, has a destination.' Then he said, and I quote, 'Unlike me. The only load I carry is guilt. And I have no destination.' "

Harrison toyed with a pencil, then looked at Julie. "Deeply depressed?"

"I'd been so caught up in the story I didn't think about that. Now I wish I had."

Harrison picked up his phone. "Just to be on the safe side, I'll alert Al Billups."

A moment later Harrison said, "Al, this is Harrison. Julie Brown is here with me, and we've got you on speakerphone."

"Hi, Julie."

"Hello, Captain Billups."

"Al, since the plant explosion, Julie's been talking with Dr. John Delbarton."

Captain Billups said, "I know John. We're in the downtown Rotary Club together. Is something wrong?"

"All of a sudden she can't locate him. He's not returning calls."

"He's retired." Captain Billups laughed. "He's got time on his hands and plenty of money. Maybe he took a trip."

Julie said, "That's possible. But we've been working together and he never mentioned a trip."

Al said, "We get a lot of calls about people who are missing. Ninety percent of the time they turn up."

Harrison quickly replied, "But ten percent of the time they don't. After what happened to Julie . . . can you do me another favor and check around for Delbarton?"

"Okay. Send me a file photo. I can compose a brief description of John. I'll send the information out to the officers."

"Thanks, Al."

"Hey, just doing my job."

"Captain Billups," Julie said, "your officers have been great to work with. I appreciate their, and your, help. And about John Delbarton, you should know that he called Otto Heidrich, manager of the Kabot plant, and threatened to go to the Chemical Institute to give investigators inside information on plant safety."

"Are you sure about that?"

"Yes, sir. I was with him when he said it."

"That complicates things."

"To complicate things a little further, he seemed really down. Depressed and hopeless."

Chapter 59

SOON THE CHEMICAL INSTITUTE ANNOUNCED an open meeting to present the preliminary findings of its investigation of the explosion. The meeting would be held in the auditorium of the Student Union at Vandalia State, March 26th at 7 PM.

The evening of the 26th, Julie arrived at the student union shortly after 6 PM. She found the auditorium already filled. Reporters, television cameras and crews had commandeered the center of the room, along with an LCD projector. Most of the audience wore work clothes; they occupied virtually every seat. Some of the women held infants.

Across the front of the room, in front of a large projection screen, sat a wide row of tables end-to-end, and behind them were chairs. On the table in front of each chair was a tent-folded and hand-lettered name card for safety board members and plant officials.

A few minutes after 7 PM a middle-aged man, balding, wearing a sport coat and necktie, seated at the center of the table across the front of the room, stood and raised his hands for silence. As the chatter around the room subsided, he said, "Folks, please take your seats and we'll get the meeting underway." He turned to speak with people seated on his right, members of the Chemical Institute investigation team. On his left sat Otto Heidrich and three members of the plant's senior management team.

"I am Wade Ekland, chair of the Chemical Institute's investigative team for the Kabot plant explosion. This auditorium in which we're meeting," he paused and looked around the large space, "is designated as Vandalia State's shelter in place. I hope this space will never again have to be used for that purpose." A smattering of applause. "As you know, Vandalia State's next-door neighbor is the Kabot Agronomy chemical plant." He paused and gazed around the audience. "Many of you live near the plant. You worry about the well-being of your families, now and in the future. I share your concerns. And," he looked to his left at Otto Heidrich, "the Chemical Institute is deeply disappointed in Kabot's conduct. We will speak about that tonight. Now I'd like to introduce Fredrich Tormagen, who heads the team's on-site work."

Tormagen, in his early forties, stood. "Tonight's meeting will be a preliminary report. I'd like to emphasize that: it is a preliminary report. At the end of this presentation we will open the meeting for comments, discussion and further input from you. In the coming weeks we will conclude various parts of our investigation." He paused and checked his notes. "Then we will submit our final report to Dr. Ekland for review, and then we'll take the report forward."

The house lights dimmed, and Tormagen narrated the images projected on the large screen. The initial slides listed officials and plant executives who would speak during the meeting, then a list of investigative team members. "As a corporation, Kabot Global employs, world-wide, nearly twenty thousand people and operates in one hundred and twenty countries. Here at the Agronomy Division's plant in Academy, there are nearly six hundred employees. The plant's Desin Unit, where the explosion occurred, went into service in 1983."

Julie made notes. She would need to get hard copy of the slides after the meeting.

Tormagen's slides showed aerial views of the facility, then diagrams of the stages of Desin pesticide production, including the MIC and related methomyl production components. Then Tormagen presented a series of slides, each of them labeled "Incident Summary."

Julie's hastily typed notes, no time for corrections, on her laptop and attempted to keep up with Tormagen's presentation. The Incident Summary included much of what Julie had learned from her interviews. As the words and images of Tormagen's slides splashed across the screen, Julie heard the voices of people she had talked with.

The slides: Restart of the Desin Unit after an extended outage. First-time use of a new control system. Accelerated start-up to meet heavy international product demands.

"The shutdown can't end soon enough. Let's finish the training on those new controls. Turn on the juice. Get production going! We're losing sales. Maybe you can afford to give up your bonus, but I can't."

The slides: Adjustments and troubleshooting in controls and displays. First time use of a new tank, the residue treater.

". . . those old graphs, I knew them like the dashboard of my truck. The new pictures, icons, they call 'em, give the same information, but they're different. Remember when I bought my new GMC pickup truck? Well, this is kinda like drivin' that new truck. Everything's familiar, but it takes some gettin' used to."

The slides: Upstream equipment performance start-up issues. Residue treater: safeguards bypassed to raise temperature.

"Day shift fired up the kitchen. Desin soup's a heatin'. The residue treater's still slow to heat. Same old, same old. We got to raise the temperature." Then, *"Mix with the solvent. By God, that'll raise the temperature! Can't do it . . . not unless we override the safety interlocks . . . who's got the password? Okay, she's open. Temperature should perk up."*

The slides: Temperature climbing. Pressure unexpectedly increasing. Outside operator asked to check residue treater vent. Second operator asked to assist.

"Howard, Jim, can you read me?" And the answer, *"Loud and clear, Don."* Then Don's reply. Remembering Don's words, Julie felt herself wishing to change what he said, wishing she could alter a history now long past. *"Residue treater . . . temperature's goin' up fast . . . maybe a blocked vent. Take a look?"* Howard responded, *"Ten-four."* Then his last words, *"Oh, shit!"*

The slides: Residue treater ruptured: 2,500 gallons methomyl solvent suddenly released. Fire erupted.

Memories came alive:

A bright flash in the night sky. A shock wave shakes her house. On its back edge, the deep roar of the explosion. Julie and Ben grasp each other, jump up, run to the window and look toward the plant. The sky glows red.

The slides: The plant's delays in notifying state and local emergency officials about the blast, the chemicals involved, the threat to the valley. Fifty-nine minutes after the explosion, county emergency officials issued a shelter in place.

"I ask you, does MIC wait an hour to kill?"

The slides: Outside emergency responders not alerted to put on personal protective equipment. Emergency responders not decontaminated.

"Hey Curly, we need to decon . . . decontaminate?"

The slides: Kabot incident command did not use unified command structure. Shelter in place process complicated by lack of information. Gate guard followed Kabot communication procedures.

A large black SUV arrived at the front gate. Emergency responders gathered around it. On each of the front doors, in gold letters above an official seal, "State Fire Marshal." Marshal Bricker, beefy, tall, wide-brimmed Stetson hat, jumped out of the vehicle. First-responders, surrounded him, all talking at once. "Can't find out . . . another Bhopal? . . . get on 'em, Marshal . . . won't open the damn gate!" Bricker called the plant. "This's Marshal Bricker. What the hell's . . . ?" And the answer, "Sorry, Marshal, not authorized to . . ." Followed by, "Not authorized, my ass! Gimme your boss-man . . . hello? Hello? Bastards." Then the dispatcher's transmission, "We have reports of a dark cloud, moving west . . ."

The slides: Possible consequences: potential releases of toxic methomyl and toxic methyl isocyanate. Exposure symptoms: nervous system disruption, acute symptoms include blurred vision, tremors, nausea, respiratory arrest, coma, death.

Bhopal, 1984. In a large open field surrounded by a temporary fence, open sided pole tents extended to the horizon. Beneath the tents, bodies lay in rows. Along the fence, hundreds of pictures, all sizes, framed and unframed, Carbide's victims. Men, women, boys and girls; families, portraits, snapshots. Lives ended. Punctuating the pictures, sprays of flowers.

The slides: Was methomyl released? Possible sources of MIC release: broken piping and equipment, vent systems, methomyl decomposition.

Late night, Don at her back door. "Why I came over, what I want you to know, Julie, the night of the explosion, the fence line detectors had been turned off! Was any MIC released? Truth is, we don't know."

"Mr. Gans, the Kabot plant explosion, danger and destruction, which were stunning, are dwarfed by the lawlessness of the company in hiding safety information necessary to protect workers and the town . . . Kabot has repeatedly claimed that none of the highly toxic chemicals in use at the Academy plant, methyl isocyanate, MIC, the same chemical that killed thousands at Bhopal, India in 1984, that no methyl isocyanate, MIC, was released by the plant explosion." He held up a copy of the Chronicle. *"A story in today's paper challenges that. Sir, was MIC released?" And the reply, "Mr. Chairman . . . what we said was, 'We have no evidence . . . we do not know if MIC was, or was not, released . . . the MIC sensors on the plant's fence lines were not operating."*

The slides: The Kabot plant, the only facility in the US with MIC inventory over 10,000 pounds. MIC stored in above ground tank near explosion epicenter. An alternative to storage: produce MIC as used. An alternative to above ground storage: underground tanks, MIC pumped to production units daily.

"We were scared. The solution to our problem? We wanted Carbide to be like Kabot over in Germany. Maintain no stockpile of MIC. Make the stuff only as needed." He laughed. "Be like Kabot? The joke was on us."

The slides: Startup issues: equipment, fatigue, procedures. Twelve hour shifts, few days off.

"Meet your planned completion dates . . . stay on schedule!" Everybody worked long, sometimes eighteen-hour days. One Monday Don said to Flora, "Yesterday you got dressed up and headed out the door. I wondered where you were going. I didn't even know it was Sunday."

The slides: Procedure problems: new control system for residue treater. The workaround.

". . . like drivin' my new pickup truck . . . Howard, Jim, temperature's goin' up fast . . . take a look? Julie tried to block her memory

of Howard's last words, as if that would change what happened. Once again she heard, *"Oh, shit!"*

When the meeting opened for public comments, State Fire Marshal Bricker walked to the microphone. He looked directly at Otto Heidrich. "What were we dealing with?" He paused and then his voice boomed, "We didn't know! I called the plant. I called the gate. I got nothing but 'Not authorized' and other rehearsed replies. Hey, this wasn't my first rodeo. I called county emergency services; they didn't know. Forty, then fifty, then sixty minutes sittin' at that gate. Watchin' a fire rage in the plant. Billows of black smoke. Chemicals released? Did we need to protect people? From what? We couldn't get any answers!"

Then the county's director of emergency services walked to the microphone. He looked directly at the Kabot managers and said, "I learned more at the Washington, DC committee hearing than I learned from Kabot during or after the explosion." He paused, then said, "Going forward, anything like this explosion happens again, I'll not wait more'n fifteen minutes before I order a shelter in place!"

The audience burst into vigorous applause and continued clapping for a full minute.

Otto Heidrich walked to the microphone. "Thank you for coming tonight. The management of the plant shares your concerns." Across the audience, a murmur of whispers; the rustle of people shifting in their seats.

He continued, "The safety of employees and the community is my, is Kabot's, highest priority."

From the center of the room, a woman called in a sarcastic voice, "Oh sure, we believe you." A man said loudly, "The way you guys behaved showed that, right?" Scattered applause rippled through the audience. In the back of the room a man stood and yelled, "You lied to your neighbors!" Then loud applause punctuated with, "That's right." "Tell 'em!" "Bastards!"

Otto waited a moment. Ekland signaled for quiet.

Otto then continued, "We've already taken action to improve our 911 hotlines." He soon ended his comments with, "The layers of protection worked as intended. There is no indication that the blast released MIC."

A man near the front of the room coughed a loud derisive laugh. Others joined him.

Other speakers, professional engineers and members of the community, followed. Their comments included references to the Texas City and Bhopal disasters, further raising Julie's fears. A man beside her said, "That sure don't help me none. Hope I can sleep tonight."

A speaker identified himself as a safety consultant and said, "Safety starts at the top. If the plant's senior management is going to fix safety problems, they need to be candid about the truth. That includes bad news." A burst of applause.

Karen Hill walked to the microphone and identified herself as a member of the End MIC citizens' group. "We had a shelter in place in 1993. A plant explosion killed two workers, sent many to the hospital. I was sixteen years old. Home and alone. One of thousands of people in harm's way. I was scared, so scared. I ran to the basement. My hands shaking, I taped doors and windows. Then I prayed." Her voice slowed and wavered. "For my dad, who was at work at the plant. For my mom, who was running errands in town." She paused and wiped tears from her eyes. "And I prayed I would, we would . . . live through this nightmare. Those prayers were answered. Now, once again, the plant's history has repeated itself. Finally, with Congress breathing down the neck of management, I hope Kabot will take some action. But," she pointed toward the plant, "go out the plant's front gate, then follow the road along the fence around the plant. You'll come to a gate. Chained shut, padlocked. On the gate there's a sign, 'Evacuation route, keep clear.' Go look!" She paused for a moment and then continued, "Mr. Chairman, we need your help. We're tired of waiting!"

Applause erupted and continued until the chairman, Ekland, again raised his arms and signaled for quiet. He then made a few final comments. "We will continue to work on the investigation report. I'd like to thank you, the audience, Kabot employees, and public officials for being here tonight. We respect your concerns and appreciate your thoughtful comments. Our final report will include recommendations for your continued observations and input to plant management on assuring the community's safety."

A few people stood to leave. They stopped when a man near the rear of the auditorium stood and in a bass voice that boomed across the auditorium asked, "Mr. Ekland, would you live here?" The room grew silent. All eyes turned to the chair.

Ekland looked away for a moment and then said, "Well, I don't live here. But if I were asked to move here . . . I would have reservations."

Another burst of applause, mixed with cries of "Hear that, Kabot?" "What about us?" "How about you, Heidrich, you want to live in Academy?"

The meeting ended and people clustered and talked in small groups.

Julie made her way through the audience to Karen Hill. "Your statement was very moving."

Karen's dark eyes sparkled. She smiled and replied, "Thanks. I hope it helps. But it's not enough. We have to keep the pressure on. We're growing. Tomorrow morning, our group will be carrying signs at the plant's front gate. People are worried. But Kabot continues on its merry way."

"On its merry way?"

"They're re-building. Preparing to re-start the Desin Unit. And manufacture MIC. As if it's just another chemical. As if nothing had happened. Nothing's changed."

"Before the meeting, had anyone talked to you about Ekland's recommendation—to involve the community in safety efforts?"

"At END MIC meetings, we've talked about the need for community input to Kabot management."

"But nothing from Kabot?"

"The Kabot website talks about the management's commitment to honest and transparent relationships with the community. The truth is, Kabot talks only to Kabot."

"Think that will change?"

"Not likely. Unless they're staring down the barrel of a gun." Karen laughed, "Before you quote me, by barrel of a gun, I mean facing the legal firepower of the law."

Julie scribbled a note.

Karen continued, "Have Kabot executives, or executives anywhere, the people responsible for industrial deaths, *ever* faced criminal charges?"

Chapter 60

OVER THE NEXT WEEK, JULIE'S STORIES chronicled the plant's re-building and the growing fears of residents about the chemical risks they faced.

Walking to her car after work, Julie felt the warm sun of April. The moist earth and early blossoms of crabapple trees scented the air. She drove home slowly. Her car's windows down, Julie took a meandering route along the Vandalia River. There she noticed something out of place, a chalky white discharge on the surface of the river. She drove as close to the shore as she could get and parked. She walked upstream along the South Jackson shoreline and traced the chalky discharge to a stream feeding into the Vandalia. She took photos with her cell phone.

When she arrived home, Julie called Metro 911, identified herself, and asked about the discharge. She learned only that calls had begun coming in about 6 PM. Later she talked to a spokesperson at the state capitol's Office of Water and Waste Management. An on-duty officer said, "Most likely the discharge came from Lauton Chemical Company. Probably an accidental release. It happens."

After her call, Julie sat on her back porch. She inhaled the moist air of spring. Julie's thoughts turned to the small stream's chalky white discharge into the Vandalia, another flush of the chemical toilet. Got a problem? Wait until night, then flush. Who'll know? Would it never end?

She called Bob Samuelson. "Do you know anything about an accidental release from Lauton Chemical?"

"News to me. Keep me posted."

Julie called the county's office of emergency services. "My guess is it's a small amount of hydrocarbon," a man said.

"Hydrocarbon? Do you mean saturated hydrocarbons, alkanes? Unsaturated hydrocarbons, alkenes? Do you mean cycloalkanes? Or aromatic hydrocarbons? Which one?" Inwardly she smiled, proud of her new knowledge of hydrocarbons, of all she'd learned about the chemical industry in the past six months.

After a long silence, the duty officer said, "Probably doesn't pose any danger. But I'll have someone from Lauton Chemical call you in the morning."

"Can't you help me?"

"I've been here a long time. When I hear about a chemical spill, I ask the company, 'How's this gonna affect folks around here?'"

Julie sat down. "After what we've been through with Kabot, you believe what a chemical company tells you?"

"Lauton is a very well-monitored plant. They have experts on board. They know chemicals better than I do."

Julie called the Water and Waste Management spokesperson she'd talked to earlier. He said, "We only know about this because we received a lot of calls. But typically this sort of problem is controlled by applying a compound to the discharge on the river."

"You're saying, apply more chemicals."

"Right."

"In this case, would the applications remove the problem in a neutralizing chemical reaction, or just make it disappear underwater?"

The representative hesitated and then said, "Well, it depends, you know, on what it is. Sometimes the treatment removes the chemical. Sometimes it doesn't, and in that case, the treatment and the leaked chemical go underwater, drift downstream."

"That means," Julie said, "the treatment compounds the spill."

"Yes, it could."

The next morning Julie called Lauton Chemical's headquarters in Cincinnati. The company spokesman would not answer questions about the discharge. "But," he said, "go to our website. You'll find a prepared statement."

Later that day Julie met with Harrison. She briefed him on her discovery of the chalky discharge and calls to the state and to Lauton Chemical. At the end of the conversation she asked, "On the heels of what happened at Kabot, are we supposed to believe that the state trusts chemical companies to provide truthful information on leaks?"

Harrison smiled ruefully. "Can we trust the fox to guard the henhouse?"

Chapter 61

SOUTH JACKSON, WV, SEPTEMBER 1984—Late afternoon. The tips of Oak Street's tallest trees carried the first bright colors of 1984's autumn. Roger lay in bed, staring out his window. Dark splotches had spread over his cheeks and neck.

Charles returned home from work. After a quick hello to Mary, he went to Roger's room. "Hey, big guy, how you doing?"

Roger sat up in bed. "Okay, I guess," he answered in a weak voice. "Mom helped me with math. I heard the band practicing the halftime show." He looked out the window. "I miss our football games."

"I miss going to the games with you, Rog. Next year, we'll be there!"

In a near whisper, Roger said, "If they'll let me in."

Charles spoke with certainty. "They'll let us in."

"Uh, Dad . . ." Roger looked out the window, then turned to Charles, "sometimes I wonder . . . am I gonna die?"

"No! You're gonna get well, son."

"I've read about," Roger paused, his lips alternately ready, then not ready, to speak. He closed his eyes and continued, ". . . about . . . AIDS . . . and Ryan White."

"Son, your mom, me, Dr. Bennett, and Ben, too . . . we're gonna help you get well."

"Yeah." Roger's face became drawn.

"It'll come, Rog. It'll come."

Charles took Roger's hand. They sat in silence for a few minutes. "Do anything special today?"

"Practiced piano." With a self-deprecating laugh, Roger said, "Got tired after just a few minutes. Later, Ben and Julie came in. We played some games."

Charles glanced at the Monopoly board beside the bed.

Roger continued, "We talked about Carbide, the work you and Julie's mom do. I got to thinking . . ."

"And?"

"We're what they call a Carbide family, right?"

"Yep."

"When . . . if . . . I get better," Roger took a deep breath, "do you think Carbide would hire me?"

"If the New York Philharmonic doesn't hire you first." They laughed. Charles added, "Sure they'd hire you. Like me, you're a Carbider."

"And Julie's mom?"

"Yep, her too."

"What about Ben and Julie?"

"Them, too. We're all Carbiders."

~   ~   ~   ~   ~

A few days later, after supper, Mary sat at Roger's bedside.

"Mom?"

"Yes, honey?"

"Dad's a good man, isn't he?"

"Yes, sweetie, he's a good man."

"And the people who died at Bhopal, were they good people?"

"Yes, I believe so." She took Roger's hand.

"What about me, am I a good . . .?"

Mary interrupted, "Of course you are. Why're you asking?"

Roger made an unsuccessful effort to sit up, and then with a sigh of fatigue, lay back. "I just don't understand. Good people get hit with . . . what I've got. People say to get it, men, well, you know . . . they say it's not right . . . but I never did anything like . . ." He began to sob. His voice cracked, "I swear . . ."

"I know you didn't, sweetie." Mary hugged Roger and sobbed.

"So how can I have AIDS . . . I mean, how did I . . .?"

"Honey, there are things none of us understands. I pray, and trust in God."

"Me, too." Roger gazed out the window. "Do you think God hears our prayers?"

"Yes, I know he does."

"I wish he'd say something. . . ."

Chapter 62

JACKSON, WV, APRIL 26, 2009—At her early morning meeting with Harrison, one month after the public meeting at Vandalia State, Julie brought with her two multi-page documents. She handed one to Harrison.

"Here we go, Harrison. Hot off the press. Hard copy of the Chemical Institute's preliminary report. I gave Bob a copy. He's looking it over."

Harrison asked, "How long will the report be posted and open for comments?"

"Thirty days."

Leafing through the report, Harrison asked, "And then?"

"They'll take another month, possibly more, to review comments."

"Any initial reactions, Julie?"

"Right from the beginning, the report is a show stopper."

"Show stopper?"

Julie sat down, opened her copy and read aloud. "The first section of the recommendations is for the director of the Vandalia-Jackson health department. The CI recommends that the director establish a Hazardous Chemical Release Prevention Program, one that enhances the prevention of accidental releases and optimizes responses in the event they occur. Local authorities should study and evaluate applicability of similar programs around the country."

Harrison leaned back in his chair. "Has Vandalia County ever done that?"

"Not to my knowledge. Other places have. For example, the CI cites Contra Costa County in California and says that county has a program that could help here."

Harrison read from his copy. "Ensure that the new program implements an effective system of independent oversight and other services . . ." He read more slowly, ". . . to enhance the prevention of accidental releases of highly hazardous chemicals." He looked at Julie, his eyebrows raised. "Independent oversight?"

"Independent, Harrison. Not under the control of the company being reviewed or its handmaidens in government." Julie laughed. "Possibly under the control of those obnoxious folks out there called 'citizens.' God forbid, they might find that Kabot is putting the valley at risk. And then they might want to see some changes, risk reductions. Changes the company might not want to do. Or pay for. Hey, Harrison, what's a life worth?"

Harrison grinned. "The plot thickens." He read from the document, "The program is to facilitate the collaboration of multiple stakeholders in achieving common goals of chemical safety." He looked up. "Fancy language, cooperation across multiple stakeholders. Who are the stakeholders?"

Julie said, "All the people affected by a company. Not just shareholders. Shareholders are only one kind of stakeholder. Stakeholders include employees, and neighbors who want to live in safe, non-toxic neighborhoods without fear of toxic air and water, without fear of explosions."

"And Kabot is supposed to collaborate with them? They've never done anything like that before. Why should we believe they'll start now?"

Julie walked to the window and looked out. She turned to Harrison. "And what if they don't? What if, five years from now, little, if anything, in this report, in these recommendations, has been done? What's the county, the state, going to do? They haven't done much up 'til now."

"The report also says," Harrison read aloud, "Ensure that the new program increases the confidence of the community, the workforce, and the local authorities in the ability of the facility owners to prevent and respond to accidental releases of highly hazardous chemicals."

Julie said, "Right now, community confidence in Kabot has got to be at an all-time low. Granted, Kabot has nowhere to go but up. But increasing confidence is not like marketing pesticides. People have to believe Kabot has their interests at heart. And Kabot's done damn little to demonstrate that. Kabot has to walk the talk. Something they haven't ever done."

"Can they do it?" Harrison asked, and then answered his own question, "Maybe." He looked at Julie. "But will they?"

"Can a groundhog fly?"

Chapter 63

JACKSON, WV, MAY 26, 2009—Four weeks later the report of the Chemical Institute became official. The board posted the final version on its website.

On an unusually warm June first, Julie returned to Vandalia State's Student Union for an evening meeting of the END MIC group. On a bulletin board near the building's cafeteria, Julie saw a small hand-lettered sign. "Will we celebrate May Day with another Shelter in place? Where are your children?"

Entering the meeting room, she found every desk occupied. People stood around the back of the room. Julie found a space to stand near a rear window.

At 7:30 Karen Hill said, "Welcome, everyone. Tonight's meeting is special. We have a lot to talk about. There are two items on our agenda. One, maintaining our presence at the plant's front gate, keeping our bucket brigade going. We're growing. We need to stay organized, keep the pressure on. I'd like to delay that part of our meeting until later.

"I'd like us to begin with the other agenda item, an opportunity to take a step forward. A giant step, a discussion of possible legal action we could take. With us is attorney Warren Massey." She pointed to Massey, early forties, athletic, wearing jeans and a khaki shirt, seated in the front row. He stood and nodded to the audience, then sat down.

Karen continued, "Warren practices law in Jackson. Some of you may know him, perhaps have worked with him. He has practiced law here since he finished law school up at WVU nearly twenty years ago. I asked Warren to join us tonight to help us think about a course of action to deal with Kabot and

MIC. And as you know, since the explosion, and without any discussion with the community, Kabot has moved forward with the rebuilding of the Desin Unit and its use of MIC. They are doing that now, as we speak."

A man on the front row said, "You'd a thought that public meeting woulda slowed 'em down."

A woman seated behind him said, "A neighbor's child was just diagnosed with cancer. They live two streets from the plant."

Karen said, "I have it from insiders that nothing has changed. The re-building of the Desin Unit is going forward according to schedule. When it's done they'll have the same operations they had before the explosion. And re-building will be wrapped up soon."

An older black woman said, "And MIC . . . it'll be running through those pipes again?"

"Yes," Karen answered. "Unless we're able to mount a way to stop them. In the board's final report they make some strong recommendations to Kabot. But Kabot doesn't have to follow them. As things now stand, once construction is completed, and Kabot does some system tests, MIC will again be used in Desin production. I'm told orders are stacking up. Around the world, growing seasons are coming. Mother Nature won't wait on us."

Side conversations buzzed around the room. A man in the audience said, "Well, Warren, got any ideas?"

Karen laughed and nodded to Massey. "That's a perfect opening for you, Warren. What might we do?"

"Thanks, Karen." Warren stood and faced the audience. "I'm glad to be here. Thank you for coming tonight, for supporting END MIC. I have the same concerns you do. I worry about the safety of my kids, my family. Many of us have friends and family who work at Kabot. Good people, but caught up in Kabot's way of operating."

He paused and walked across the front of the room. Julie imagined him making his case in front of a jury. Low key, personal, organized and to the point.

Warren continued, "Ideally, our friends and family who work at Kabot and take issue with the company's actions, or fear the risks associated with an unsafe plant, might walk away. Refuse to work for a company they don't trust. A company that's committed acts like Kabot has, then tried to cover it up.

"But we all know life is not that simple. People can't easily replace one job with another. Replace one retirement plan or health plan with another. For most people, that kind of change puts a lot at risk. Some employees have kids in college. Others have family members who are ill, or who need continuing medical care."

A woman said, "We have to do *something*. MIC is a dangerous neighbor."

A man beside her asked, "Warren, what's your proposal?"

"My proposal's not simple. But with your support, I'm willing to develop a legal action to enjoin, stop, the restart of some parts of production at the Kabot Agronomy plant. We would petition a court, a judge, to stop the restart of production using MIC, unless and until Kabot and state and federal agencies certify that they have implemented the recommendations of the Chemical Institute. I'm referring to the recommendations recently issued after the board's investigation of the explosion at the plant."

"We're just a bunch of local citizens, Mr. Massey. We don't have a lot of money. Legal fees add up fast. Kabot knows that. They've got platoons of lawyers, nearly unlimited funds. They could drag us into a long court proceeding we couldn't afford. They would win by attrition."

"I appreciate that. Costs are a major concern. Legal fees add up fast. And you're right, they have a large legal staff. Kabot can reach into deep pockets. But I'm prepared to do pro bono work to get us started. And there may be other attorneys who will join us. Looking at the legal action itself, I have a path in mind that could avoid protracted legal proceedings."

Karen asked, "A path? What are you thinking about, Warren?"

"With your agreement and support," Warren waved an arm toward the audience, "I will develop a legal brief on risks the Kabot plant poses to the valley. I'll cite the recent explosion, past toxic releases and deaths. Cite the immediate and continuing threat we face from plant operations using MIC. Then include that brief as part of a petition we present to the US District Court in Jackson. We will petition the court, the judge, to issue a restraining order to stop Kabot's use of MIC."

A man laughed and said, "A restrainin' order! Why didn't I think of that? A woman at my church got a restrainin' order and had it served on her no-account husband. Took that woman about two seconds to get the order. The restrainin' order calmed that ol' boy down right fast."

The room burst into laughter.

Red-faced, the man said, " 'Course, she didn't go to no *federal* court. I think a justice of the peace was all she needed."

Karen stood and faced the room. "How do you all feel about Warren's proposal? Should we go down that path?"

People smiled as conversations buzzed around the room. Many of them said in loud voices, "Let's do it." "Yes." "Right thing to do."

A woman said, "I move we support the legal action Warren has outlined." A man yelled, "Second."

"Any further discussion on the motion itself?" Silence followed Karen's question. She waited a moment, then said, "All in favor, please raise your hands." The hands of everyone in the room went up.

"Those opposed?" Karen looked around the room and then said, "Seeing none, the motion passes." She laughed. "Warren, you have your marching orders. How soon can you have something for us?"

"Give me a couple of weeks."

"Thanks. Everyone, let's plan on meeting on this two weeks from tonight, here."

Smiles passed around the room and people shifted into side conversations. Soon the whole room buzzed with chatter.

Karen rapped her knuckles lightly on the white board at the front of the room. "Hey, everybody, thanks. Now let's talk about the front gate and the bucket brigade, keeping the pressure on."

The next day, Julie's story, "Citizens group backs legal action against Kabot," appeared on page 2 of the *Chronicle*. A photograph of more than one hundred sign-carrying demonstrators at the plant's front gate ran next to the story.

Then, three weeks later, the *Chronicle* carried the headline, "END MIC files legal action against Kabot. Asks injunction to stop MIC," front page, with a story bylined, "Julie Brown."

Chapter 64

JULIE HAD DEVELOPED A ROUTINE of calling Mary once or twice a week. "Just checking in," she usually said. Mary welcomed her calls. Julie and Mary's connection had strengthened as Ben had become more deeply involved in the plant after the explosion. Mary said to Julie, "Ben tells me about all he's doing at the plant, and I can't help thinking about Charles. His commitment to the plant. What it took away from us, from the boys. The example it set for Ben.

"Now," Mary continued, "Ben is . . . well, he's becoming his dad. And he's right in the middle of what you've written about, Julie, the plant's withholding information, covering up, getting ready to re-start MIC. I'm Ben's mom. I want to take pride in his work. But it makes me sad every time I learn more about it, more about Kabot."

Mary's first heart attack, four years ago, accompanied by a minor stroke, had left her with a partial paralysis of her left arm and leg. She had undergone a sudden transformation from a woman enjoying vibrant older years to a frail senior citizen. Mary walked more or less normally, but her movements had slowed, as had her speech. Every word, every hesitant step, became a statement about her new life of uncertainty.

With a lot of Julie's assistance, and considerably less help from Ben, she had sold her home and purchased a two-bedroom condo in a building for senior citizens. When friends asked Mary how she liked her new condo, she usually replied, "I'm doing well. I'm very comfortable. And I have many friends in the building." Julie often heard her add *sotto voce*, speaking more to herself than to anyone else, "But I doubt I'll be here long."

It had been a few days since Julie had talked to Mary. Sitting at home in her small study, Julie picked up a framed photo of Roger performing at the Bicentennial Concert. She dialed Mary's phone number. Mary answered on the second ring.

"Hi, Mary, it's Julie. I saw that you'd called earlier. Are you doing okay?"

"Hi, honey. Yes, doing well. I had a dizzy spell earlier; that's when I called. But it went away. I'm okay now. I probably shouldn't have called."

"You know better than that. Please call. Anytime."

"I didn't want to bother you, honey. You have work to do."

"*Mary . . .*"

"I know. It's just . . . well, some days memories of Roger weigh on me. Today's one of them. I keep asking myself what I might've . . . you know, done differently." Mary laughed. "I made the mistake of a picking up a photo of Roger performing at the Bicentennial Concert, staring at it. Remembering."

"Mary, you did every . . ."

Mary interrupted, "Yes, I keep telling myself that. Trying to reassure myself, I suppose. But I always . . . well, then comes the question I can't answer: why AIDS? When, where, did I fail? He was just a boy."

"Mary, please believe me, it *wasn't you.*" Julie wanted to tell Mary what she had learned about Z-Factor. But not on the phone, not now. "You did all you could. You nursed Roger, gave him love."

Mary's voice dropped to a near-whisper. "It wasn't enough."

"Please, get some rest. I'll come over tomorrow and we can talk."

"It'll be twenty-three years . . . tomorrow, since Roger left us. . . ." Then in a faint, wistful voice, "Twenty-three years."

"Tomorrow. I should've remembered." Julie picked up the photo of Roger performing at the Bicentennial Concert and gazed at it. "With the explosion and all, I've had a lot going on."

"I know. Even to you, I'm sure Roger's become ancient history. I didn't want to bother you."

"Mary, I'm glad you called." Julie paused, then said, "Hey, tomorrow can I take you to dinner? Just you and me. We'll remember Roger. Celebrate his life. Okay?"

"Thanks, sweetie. Maybe that's what I need."

"Great! I'll pick you up about six. I love you, Mary."

Hanging up, Mary said, "I love you, Roger."

Julie replayed Mary's parting words and stared at the photo. Then she began to weep. Soon she gasped wrenching sobs. Tomorrow at dinner she would tell Mary about Roger's contracting AIDS; how it had happened. And that, she hoped, would lift Mary's burden of guilt.

Chapter 65

Early the next morning, Julie knocked lightly on Harrison's office door.

"Hey, Julie. How's it going?"

"I'm having lunch with an attorney, a clerk in Judge Robinson's office. He's about my age. Also a runner."

"Business or pleasure?"

"I met him a while back at a fun run. I'm not certain, but I believe he thinks our getting together is ninety percent pleasure, ten percent business. For me, the percentages are reversed."

Harrison laughed. "The sign of a good reporter."

Julie didn't laugh. Her face showed a mixture of fatigue and seriousness of purpose. Since the explosion, the stress of her work had begun to etch lines in her face. Each morning when she looked in the bathroom mirror Julie noted them, imagining the lines' progress since the day before. Did they foreshadow her face a few years from now?

~ ~ ~ ~ ~

At noon Julie found an empty table at Kaufman's Deli on River Street. She placed her backpack on the table to claim it as occupied and then walked to the counter to place her order. "Tuna salad sandwich, wheat bread, please. And a Diet Pepsi."

The overweight clerk, wearing a chef's hat, asked, "Y'all want potato chips or cole slaw?" Julie ordered slaw, then paid for her lunch.

As she walked toward her table, Keith Burwell, a law clerk to Federal Judge Robinson, entered the deli.

"Hey, Julie, where are you sitting?"

She pointed to the table. "I've already ordered."

Keith, about Julie's age and with the lean body of a runner, placed his order and joined her at the table. Julie recalled meeting him at a local fun-run a couple of years ago. Though his running speed put him back in the pack, his height, well over six feet, and blond hair made him stand out.

"Thanks for joining me, Keith."

"Hey, my pleasure. Ever since I watched you win that Turkey Trot race, I've wanted to get acquainted."

Julie and Keith exchanged the kind of small talk that runners enjoy: training run schedules, preferences in running shoes, plans for entering upcoming spring races.

"I've been following your stories on the plant explosion, Julie. Nice work."

"Thanks."

"Can I ask you a few questions?"

Julie laughed. "That's what I was going to ask you. I understand Judge Robinson is handling the legal action filed by the citizens' group."

"Yes. The citizens' group filed papers yesterday in federal district court. Judge Robinson expects to make a decision soon. I'm doing some background work."

Julie smiled. "Sounds familiar. I've been doing lot of that."

Keith spoke slowly, as if weighing each word. "Judge Robinson wants me to sift the facts, define the truth in the case, and make a recommendation to him. No later than the close of business today."

Surprised, Julie asked, "How can I help?"

"I'm reviewing the facts about MIC and the real and potential dangers it poses to the community. The citizens' group cites MIC as a clear and present danger. Kabot attorneys do not contest the fact that MIC can be dangerous. But, they say, Kabot has well-engineered control systems."

Julie laughed. "Did I miss something? Wasn't there a fatal explosion?"

Keith continued, "They say reducing the use of MIC is feasible, but would be costly."

"Costly? What's a life worth?"

Keith said, "Kabot has presented voluminous engineering reports concluding that once the work is completed, everything will be under control."

"The evidence says otherwise. MIC caused a lot of death and suffering at Bhopal. If the flight path of that exploding residue treater had been a few degrees to the right, it would've done the same here. And I've learned that inside Kabot there are engineering reports pointing to dangers: local, catastrophic dangers posed by MIC."

Keith leaned forward and looked Julie in the eye. "I have to answer the question, what are the true risks presented by MIC? Do you know what they are?"

For a moment his question took Julie aback. She reflected on it as she took a bite of tuna salad sandwich, then sipped her drink. She wished she had the power of a character she remembered from a sci-fi movie. In the movie the character could leave her present world and Earth-time, travel through the universe for an extended period, then return to the present and find that in Earth time, less than a second had passed. She wished, she wished. If she had that magic capability, she could quantify all the risks that MIC presented.

Julie said, "Chemists may have complex answers to that question. But for me, the answer has to be simple, and real. There's just life, and the ways we live. When I bring all the evidence together, I see a pattern. Sort of an answer to your question."

Keith raised his eyebrows. "And that is?"

"Our past behavior predicts our future performance."

Keith flashed a look of surprise. "That's it?"

Julie pulled a document from her backpack. "I'll say it in another way." She read aloud. "In 1985, seven months after Bhopal, after spending millions to upgrade chemical and safety controls, the plant had another major toxic chemical spill. Another shelter in place. There were 135 people hospitalized. In 1993, a chlorine leak. In 1994, an explosion killed one worker, shelter in place; another worker died later. Also in 1994, sulfur dichloride leak, shelter in place. Then in 1996, toluene leak and fire, shelter in place. In 1997, high winds blew out an incinerator flame, and traces of MIC leaked. In 1996 a phosgene leak; another shelter in place. In 2001 a chloroform leak; ten workers needed medical treatment. These events generated a high level of community fear *before* the explosion. And now it's worse."

Julie removed a thick pack of documents from her backpack. "Here are," she paused and flipped to the last document in the pack, "thirty-seven pages of toxic spills in the USA by Carbide and Kabot. One after another. Single spaced. In some of them workers died. In others, workers were injured and disabled. Some later died of injuries. The reports make no mention of untold community illnesses and deaths caused by chemical releases and spills."

She handed the documents to Keith. He leafed through them, pausing occasionally to read. When he finished, he handed the documents to Julie. Keith looked at his wristwatch. "Uh-oh. I've got to get back. I'm meeting with Judge Robinson at three o'clock. And I have things to do before then."

Julie laughed. "Keep the documents. They might be helpful. Sorry, I kept you from eating your sandwich."

Keith laughed. "You've given me a lot to digest." He gave her a warm smile, stood, and tapped his fingers on the documents. "Thanks, Julie. See you on the running trails."

Chapter 66

JULIE AND MARY HAD DINNER AT THE MANOR, a restaurant in what once had been a large old home high on the mountain overlooking Jackson. The chef specialized in seafood dishes. Fresh seafood was flown in daily from the Maryland shore. Julie and Mary had ordered today's special, sea bass.

A small jazz combo, piano, bass, guitar, played at the front of the room. "Satin Doll," "Just You," "You are Too Beautiful" and other standards; the Ellington songbook, the Johnny Mercer songbook; songs from Mary's era, lovely tunes.

Julie ate heartily, but Mary picked at her food. Her thoughts seemed to be elsewhere. She asked Julie about life at the plant. She wondered how Charles would find the place today.

"Today? New technology, some new operations. But the same buildings, with maybe a few additions here and there. Charles would know the place."

"He worked so hard, cared so much." She leaned back in her chair and sighed.

"Ben often said his dad set an example for him."

"Example?"

"Yes. His dad's commitment."

"Commitment . . . to his work. To the company. But," Mary sipped her water, put the glass down, then picked it up and sipped again, "his commitment at home? To us?" Mary's eyes teared. "When I needed him, he wasn't . . . oh, he loved us. We loved him. But the plant, *that* was his life. Then he began to lose weight. The doctors discovered pancreatic cancer, and poof! Before I knew it, he was gone."

"He lived his commitment, what he believed in."

"To a fault. When he lost Kabot . . . he lost a big part of himself. Those days after they sold the plant, sold with his help, he withdrew from everyone. Some days I hardly recognized him. That's about the time Roger went downhill."

"Ben and I were around nine."

As if she hadn't heard Julie, Mary continued, "Those days I hardly recognized Roger, either. Often I would sit alone, listen to the recording of his Bicentennial Concert . . . try to remember the beauty of that night. A little kid with the grin of a proud artist." Mary began to weep. Then she clutched the tablecloth, took deep breaths and said, "Julie, uh . . . uh, I need to . . ." She began to stand up, stopped, her eyes closed. She toppled to the floor.

Julie rushed to her. People at nearby tables stood. A man brought a glass of water. A waiter elevated her legs with an infant's seat. Julie grabbed her jacket from the back of her chair, folded it as a cushion, and placed it under Mary's head. Should she call an ambulance?

Mary opened her eyes and looked up at Julie. Julie held the glass of water to Mary's lips. "Here you go, Mary."

Sipping the water, Mary glanced at the waiter and patrons staring at her. She gave them a gentle smile and a small wave of dismissal. With Julie's help Mary slowly stood, then again sat at their table.

"Sorry, honey. I'm okay now. But I'm embarrassed." She aligned her dress and touched her hair as if to put it in place. "All day I've been thinking about Roger; haven't eaten anything."

"How about some soup? Might help."

In a whisper, Mary said, "Mmm . . . *soup*, good idea."

Had she waited too long? Julie had struggled with when and how to tell Mary the truth about Roger. Now, with a growing sense of guilt, she admitted to herself that after her talk with Ben, she had hoped he would tell Mary about Z-Factor's transmitting HIV to Roger. Get her off the hook.

But it hadn't happened. Julie couldn't continue to wait, avoid what she felt she had to do. She also worried, *What if Ben did tell Mary?* Might he distort the truth? Where were his loyalties?

Soon Mary pushed away her soup. "Julie, I can hardly keep my eyes open. I need to get to bed. I'm sorry to end our dinner. I hope we can talk more, maybe tomorrow."

After she took Mary to her apartment, Julie returned home. She took a half-pint carton of milk from her refrigerator and sat down on her couch. "Now, I must call Ben. Now!" She opened her cell phone to place the call, then stopped.

Julie dropped her cell phone on the couch, opened the carton of milk and gulped it down. "Why is this so . . . difficult?"

Chapter 67

SOUTH JACKSON, WV, SEPTEMBER 1985—Through the weeks of September 1985, leaves turned red and gold. The air mellowed with scents of leaves. By early October, mornings had become crisp and cool.

Mary often reminded Charles, "Autumn's my favorite season. The rich colors on the mountains. Harvest time, the last apples and pumpkins picked."

The passing weeks of autumn brought ever more barren trees and declines in Roger's health. By mid-November, like the few leaves clinging to branches, Roger's hold on life had become tenuous. The morning the trees became bare, Roger needed hospital care.

In Roger's hospital room, Charles, Mary, Ben and Dr. Bennett stood near Roger's bed. Mary held his hand. With the other hand she wiped away tears.

His breathing shallow, Roger looked at Mary. His eyes seemed to ask the question again, "Why?" Moments later his eyelids fluttered and closed. His breathing stopped.

Dr. Bennett placed his stethoscope on Roger's chest. He listened for a moment and then folded the instrument.

Weeping, Mary leaned over Roger and kissed his forehead. Charles put one arm around her and laid a hand on Roger's forehead.

Ben fell forward over Roger and wept. "No, Rog. Wake up . . . wake up! C'mon, Rog, wake up!"

~   ~   ~   ~   ~

Roger's funeral took place at the red brick United Methodist Church in South Jackson. Beneath the sanctuary's high ceiling, its large stained glass windows transformed sunlight into ribbons of bright colors. Roger's coffin, closed, sat in front of the sanctuary's dais. Seven-foot-tall banks of autumn flowers extended from each end of the casket to the sanctuary walls. The room's air carried a rich mix of the scents of roses and chrysanthemums.

Mourners filled the church's pews. In the front row sat Charles, Mary, and Ben. Behind them, Julie, Arlene and Harold, Roger's teachers and school staff, including Mr. Holmes, students, John Delbarton and Charles' colleagues from the plant, neighbors and friends. The sanctuary resonated with a recording of Roger's bi-centennial performance of "Rhapsody in Blue."

The service was brief and simple, a prayer followed by remarks from friends. Roger's friends spoke of his passion for music, his skills. They described his love of sports and his willingness to serve as a backyard football game's referee, just to be part of the action.

Ben walked to the front of the sanctuary, placed one hand on Roger's coffin, and read the Twenty-third Psalm, "Yea, though I walk through the valley of the shadow of death . . ." At the end of the reading he paused, looked at the casket and said, "Rog, your courage, even when you hurt real bad, will stay with me. I won't forget. One time you said, 'All I have, all we have, is today. We must live it. Appreciate it. Tomorrow never comes.'" Ben's voice wavered. "There's only today." Ben paused, cleared his throat, and then added, 'Each morning when I wake up, it's just like you said, Rog, there's another today. This morning I thought about some-day awakening on the other side. And you and me starting an-other day, together. Bye for now, Rog. Wait for me. We'll play, celebrate another today. . . . I love you."

After the funeral, everyone drove to the cemetery and gath-ered at Roger's gravesite. Large snowflakes began to fall, drifting languidly over the cemetery and graveside mourners. Soon the snow painted the cemetery white and softened sounds from the world beyond the gravesite.

The minister led the group in prayer and then said, "Memories of Roger's ever hopeful presence, and his music, stunning, beautiful, will remain with us. His passing is a great loss. But we are richer because he was here."

Mary sat in the front row, overlooking the open grave, the casket poised above it. She stood and turned to the graveside mourners. Grasping Charles' hand, her knuckles white, she said, "Losing a child, burying a child, is every mother's worst nightmare." She paused and took a deep breath. "Since we learned of Roger's illness, that fear has been at the center of my life, day after day." Mary paused. When she spoke again, her voice weakened and began to quiver. "And now the thing I feared has come to pass. Please know the love you've given Roger and our family has sustained us . . . sustained me. From my heart, thanks to all of you for helping me, helping us, bear our burden." Mary paused. When she spoke again, her voice became resonant. "When life was at its darkest, you helped me remember, I am not alone."

Julie, seated between her mom and dad, held their hands. Quiet tears, then breathtaking waves of grief shook her body.

Chapter 68

IN THE DAYS FOLLOWING ROGER'S FUNERAL, Charles joined the Union Carbide team in its final negotiations with the German corporation Kabot Global. Kabot proposed to buy the entire corporation. Kabot's Agronomy Division would own and operate the Academy plant.

In December, then in January and February 1986, Charles made multiple trips to Union Carbide's headquarters in Connecticut and to Kabot Global's headquarters in Stuttgart, Germany. In March, Carbide and Kabot made a joint announcement. The boards of each corporation had provisionally approved the purchase of Union Carbide by Kabot Global. Final approval would await completion of legal and financial due diligence efforts and approval by each country's respective government agencies. Privately, executives in both companies said, "The deal's as good as done."

Immediately after announcement of the sale, sign-bearing demonstrators, many of them from India, walked slowly in front of both the Academy plant and corporate headquarters. "Bhopal survivors—no justice," "Will Kabot make us whole?" "Carbide made us sick—Who will make us well?" A woman carried a sign: "I am mother of sick Bhopal Baby. Hear us, Kabot!"

After completion of the purchase, Charles' seven-days-a-week patterns of work continued as the former Carbide management adapted to Kabot. For Charles, that meant modifications of accounting and financial systems and his learning to become part of the new Kabot management team.

The sustained demands that Carbide and then Kabot put on Charles began to impact his health. He contracted and slowly recovered from a disabling strain of the flu. During his recovery he worked only three days a week. Then, shortly after what seemed to be a full recovery, Charles began to suffer from gastrointestinal illnesses. He missed work for increasingly longer periods. Two years after the completion of the sale, he accepted early retirement.

In 1995, shortly after the end of Ben's freshman year in college, Charles had a dramatic loss of weight and soon died of pancreatic cancer.

At Charles' funeral, former Union Carbide and current Kabot executives eulogized Charles. His tireless dedication, first to Carbide, then to Kabot, received hearty praise. Otto Heidrich, Kabot's new managing director of the plant, described Charles as "an exemplary model for all of us." Hermann Gans traveled from Stuttgart for the service and eulogized, "Charles was like a father. We shall never forget him. Nor shall we see his like again."

Ben spoke briefly. His last words were, "I hope and pray I can be half the man my father has been."

As Ben finished, Mary wept . . . shaking her head, *No!*

Chapter 69

JACKSON, WV, JUNE 2009—When Julie arrived at the *Chronicle,* she went to the break room. She poured a cup of coffee and, arriving early, had her choice of doughnuts from an open box on the counter. Then she went to her desk.

Soon Harrison joined her. He wore a look of nervous anticipation. Julie had seen that look—a mix of concern and excitement, usually right before important events unfolded.

"Hi, Harrison, what's up?"

He laughed. "What makes you ask?"

Julie liked that about Harrison. The joy he found in events, in the news, good and bad. "Your face is like a text message announcing itself. I hope you don't play poker."

"I just got a call, a tip. Judge Robinson is expected to issue a decision on the END MIC petition today. Maybe before noon."

"Should I go over there now?"

"Sit tight. I expect a call before anything happens."

An hour later Harrison called Julie. "Okay, hurry over to federal court. Judge Robinson's ruling will be issued in about a half hour."

She walked the few blocks to the federal court building, then found herself delayed in a long line of people waiting to go through building security. Julie had seen many of them at the END MIC meeting.

Julie entered a crowded courtroom and found a place to stand along the wall on the right side. The session had already begun, Judge Robinson presiding. Kabot attorney Martin Bean and the END MIC attorney, Warren Massey, stood before him.

On one side of the front row sat Karen Hill, beaming a bright smile, and on the other Otto, Anna and Ben, looking glum. Behind them sat a large audience, a full house.

Chief U.S. District Judge John Robinson's face had a stern look. He said, "I am aware of the history of safety violations at the plant and the catastrophic dangers presented by the production of the chemical known as MIC.

"In this court's opinion, the residents who have sued Kabot are likely to win the case on its merits. Further, without relief from this court, they are likely to suffer irreparable harm. I am also aware of allegations of Kabot's misrepresentations to the public about prior incidents at the plant. I hereby issue a fourteen-day restraining order on the plant's use of MIC, an order that is in the public interest."

Across the room, Julie saw Keith Burwell standing along the opposite wall. They made eye contact. Keith mouthed the words, "Thank you."

Judge Robinson concluded the session, saying, "Later today my office will issue a written order. This court will meet for a full hearing on this matter two weeks from today. At that time I will consider a request for a lengthier injunction."

The judge then rose and left the courtroom.

Cheers and applause erupted as many spectators jumped out of their seats and gathered around Karen and Warren.

Julie made copious notes. At one point she looked up from her notebook and saw Ben glaring at her. When her gaze met his, Ben turned away.

Chapter 70

ARLY ON A MOIST AND BRIGHT JUNE MORNING, during her run Julie planned her talk with Ben. Then she planned her follow-up talk with Mary. About Z-Factor and Roger's AIDS. She would call Ben that evening after work.

When time to call Ben arrived, her breathing quickened. On the first ring of Ben's phone, Julie realized she'd called Ben's landline at his apartment, not his cell phone.

A woman with a German accent answered. "Allo?"

Without thinking, Julie said, "Anna?"

The voice replied, "*Ja*. Und who is this?"

Julie felt as if her stomach had fallen into her intestines. "Julie ... Brown. Is ... Ben available?" Her hands shook. Julie slowed her breathing. In an effort to control her turbulent insides, she began to count with each in-breath and out-breath, "In, one-two, out, three-four, in, one-two ..."

Then she heard Ben's familiar, "Hey ..."

"Ben, I need to talk with you. Can we have coffee tomorrow afternoon? Won't take long, I promise you. I'll come to Academy, meet you at Brownie's. You pick the time."

Ben hesitated, then said, "No offense intended, Julie, but why do we need to get together? We haven't had much to say since your last lecture on Kabot."

"Roger, Z-Factor, and your mom. That's what I need to talk to you about."

"Roger? Okay, I'll figure out a way to do it. I've got a busy day tomorrow. Meet about 4 PM?"

"Good. See you then."

After ending the call, Julie thought about Ben and Anna. Then she remembered sharing everyday life with Ben. Their making love. She waited on an expected tidal wave of jealousy, perhaps anger. It didn't come. Once she got beyond the surprise of Anna's answering Ben's phone, her insides had calmed. Julie counseled herself, "Ben will do what he will do. And so will I."

~   ~   ~   ~   ~

At four o'clock, Julie and Ben sat in the portioned area in the rear of Brownie's dining room.

Helen served them coffee. "Good to see you again. Where's John been keeping himself?"

Julie smiled at Helen. "Thanks. I don't know about John. But good to see you, too, Helen."

His face flushed, Ben ignored Helen. He leaned across the table. "I can't believe what you and your friends have done. The discovery documents we're producing? A huge number. For what amounts to . . . Kabot on trial, can you imagine it? Right now we're working overtime to meet discovery requests for 200,000, maybe 300,000 pages of documents. If there's a document we object to producing? Hey, they can ask the judge to make us produce it. For the last two weeks an army of Kabot's people have . . . well, that's all they've done."

"Are you finished?"

"No!" Ben gazed at Julie for a moment, then sighed and sat back in his chair. "I mean, yes, I guess I am. For now."

For a moment Julie reflected on her life with Ben. She remembered childhood play, high school, the joy of falling in love. Becoming first-time lovers. Later, talk of marriage. It seemed as if one morning she had awakened and discovered they'd changed from lovers to adversaries. How did it all happen?

"Knock, knock. Hello? Julie? Are you here?"

Julie shook her head and gave Ben a nostalgic smile. "Sorry, I got lost in thought." She paused, then said, "Ben, those are not my friends. I'm a reporter. I report. Yes, I'm sympathetic to their cause. But I'm not part of END MIC. They are local people, frightened, trying to protect themselves from a company that's putting their lives, their children's lives, at risk. A company who hasn't listened to scared people"

"It seems unfair. All the work. The expense. We have engineers who know how . . ."

Julie held up one hand, signaling him to stop. "Ben, it's me, Julie. I've seen what your engineers have done. Leaks. explosions. Deaths. And what they haven't done—build underground MIC storage. I've watched engineers, senior executives and Otto avoid doing at the plant what Kabot did a long time ago in Germany, that is, produce MIC only as needed. Now the house may come tumbling down."

"Okay, okay. Enough. Why are we here? What is it you want to tell me?"

"I talked with Dr. John Delbarton. He used to work with your . . ."

"I know who he is. He worked with Dad. I'm told he's been a pipeline of insider information to the *Chronicle*. Some Kabot people would like to teach him a lesson or two about loyalty."

"What would they do, Ben? Take him out? The same thing they tried to do to me?"

"I didn't mean . . ."

"That motorcyclist who attacked me? Who could very well have killed me? Tell your Kabot friends the police have him in custody. They plan to indict him for assault, maybe attempted murder. Will he point his finger at somebody you know? Did Kabot hire him to do their dirty work? For all I know, Otto gave the order."

"But you don't know."

"The prosecutors will find out."

"I'll ask again, why are we here?"

"Roger. AIDS. How it happened. Who's to blame."

His voice accusatory, Ben smirked and said, "This better be good."

"Good? No, it won't be good. But it'll be true."

A few minutes later photos and documents from Julie's back-pack covered the table. She pointed to photos of institutions. "The Arkansas prisons. For twenty years they harvested prisoners' blood . . . sold it to commercial labs. The blood money from the sales generated a stream of income for the prisons and the prisoners. Everybody enjoyed the revenue. Even the taxpayers."

"What the hell's this got to do with Roger?"

Julie answered, "A major buyer was a division of Kabot." She pointed to a photograph. "Plasma from prisoners' blood went into the company's drug for hemophilia, Z-Factor."

"Roger was on Z-Factor. I remember when he started treat-ment. How hopeful it made Mom and Dad."

Julie continued, "The prison blood donors were unscreened. Many were HIV positive."

Ben's face fell. He exclaimed in a whisper, "HIV pos . . . my God!"

Julie spoke softly, "Much later, labs developed a heat treat-ment that eliminated HIV. But by then, contaminated Z-Factor had already been sold. Around the world. It infected thousands of hemophiliacs . . . including teenagers like Ryan White."

On the table she placed photos of Ryan White; news stories about his campaign to deepen awareness and understanding of AIDS, then stories of his death. "When Mr. Holmes asked your mom and dad to keep Roger out of school, he cited the precedent of the Kokomo, Indiana, schools and what they'd done to Ryan White.

"Z-Factor infected Ryan White. And it infected Roger." Julie's thoughts raced to Roger's hospital room and memories of his emaciated body, blotched face and hands; hands that had once mastered piano keyboards and produced stunning music.

"How could they allow that to happen? Why didn't . . ." Ben's voice trailed off.

"After looking over the links in the chain of HIV and Z-Factor evidence, a veteran medical investigator said, "These are the single most incriminating documents I've ever seen in the pharmaceuti-cal industry."

"Hard to believe." Ben shook his head and looked away.

Her voice forceful, Julie said, "The FDA stopped US sales of untreated Z-Factor. But Kabot continued selling it overseas. Until their warehouses emptied."

"That's scary. They couldn't have."

"It's the truth." She tapped the documents on the table. "Years later, Kabot began payments to victims. At first a flat $100,000 per claim. Then the company paid six hundred million dollars into a victims' fund."

"But Mom and Dad never knew . . . never received . . ."

Julie began to gather the photos and documents from the table-top. "Kabot PR kept the scandal out of the American press. Who knows how much they spent hushing it all up? Big league spin control by your colleagues, Ben. And Kabot didn't go searching for victims."

"Roger was just a kid. How could they let him take infected . . .?"

"How could *they*? Who is *they*, Ben?"

Ben slumped forward, his head in his hands.

Julie leaned close to Ben. "I haven't heard any remorse from Kabot. A trial lawyer told me, 'Any admission of guilt by a company, even indirectly, opens the floodgate to lawsuits for damages.' Is that what Kabot's silence is about?"

Ben sat up. Tears ran down his cheeks. "Mom . . . she's got to stop blaming herself. . . ."

Julie touched Ben's hand. "Spin control, Ben. It's what Kabot does. Is it what you want to do with your life? Is that your future?"

He jerked his hand away. "Quit pushing me! You know as well as I do, I work in the Agronomy division. It's just one part of Kabot. We're *separate* from pharmaceuticals, Z-Factor."

Julie jerked back her hand. She sat upright. In a voice of dis-belief, she said, "Just one part of Kabot?" Her voice rose. "We're separate from . . . *we*?" She stared at Ben and slowly shook her head.

Julie stood and picked up her backpack. "Ben, *your company killed your brother!*"

Ben gasped. His eyes widened and he glared at Julie. The sud-den ring of his phone intruded. "Hello?"

Julie could hear the loud voice of the caller. "Mr. Gruber?"

"Yes. Who is . . . ?"

"Will Vincent, Mr. Gruber, Vandalia County Emergency Services. Your mom has had a heart attack. We're on our way with her to Jackson Area Medical Center."

"See you there." Ben pocketed his phone and jumped up. "They're taking . . ."

Julie said, "I heard him. Let's go!"

Chapter 71

BEN DROVE TO THE HOSPITAL, Julie seated alongside him. He burned two caution lights and narrowly missed a collision when he ran a red light. Blaring horns sounded behind them. During the trip, Ben and Julie remained silent.

Julie wiped away tears. Her last trip with Ben? Would there be an opportunity to tell Mary about Roger, about Z-Factor? "Dear God, please forgive my silence. Give me time; help me tell Mary the truth. Please."

Approaching the hospital, Ben said, "By the way, Miss Reporter, Otto is being recalled to Germany. I'm told it's permanent. Thanks to you."

"Because he failed to take me out? Is Otto one step ahead of the law, Ben, avoiding arrest?"

"Shut up!" Ben screeched to a stop near the emergency room entrance.

The antiseptic smells of the intensive care ward reached Ben and Julie in the corridor, well before they passed through the ward's oversized swinging doors. Once inside, the quiet patter of intercom announcements, a doctor needed here, a nurse needed there, gave a steady rhythm to the ward's mini-dramas of life and death.

They found Mary's room and walked to where she lay in bed amid electronic equipment that signaled her vital signs. Ben and Julie whispered their hellos. Mary's eyes opened.

Ben took her hand. Julie kissed her cheek. Mary slowly raised her arms and opened them. They both leaned over, and Mary hugged them. Then her arms fell to her sides.

"You're going to be all right, Mom," Ben said.

Mary's eyes intermittently opened and closed. "Maybe my time's . . . Roger . . . what'd I do, what'd he do . . .?"

Ben gently touched her lips with his index finger. "Hey, shh . . . we'll talk later."

Julie leaned over and hugged Mary. "You're going to be okay. I love you."

Slurring her words, Mary said, "I love . . . Julie, d'you suppose Roger . . . still plays . . ."

The shrill ring of Ben's cell phone startled Julie and Mary. Ben answered, "Otto . . . this is not a good time to . . . okay, okay."

Ben walked toward the door. "I'm sorry to hear you're . . ." His voice faded as he passed into the corridor, and behind him the door quietly closed.

Julie took Mary's hand and asked, "Can you hear me okay?"

Mary gave a slight smile and a gentle nod.

"Mary, there's something you need to know."

Mary's eyes widened.

Julie spoke in soft, clear tones, "I learned something about Roger's drug, Z-Factor."

Mary whispered, "About Roger's . . ."

"The Z-Factor drug prescribed for Roger was contaminated."

"Contam . . ." Mary's face became apprehensive.

"Yes. Contaminated with HIV. Z-Factor caused Roger's AIDS."

"No! But Kabot . . . Charles' company . . ."

"Kabot didn't test the blood plasma in the drug."

Mary squeezed her eyes shut, then opened them wide. "Charles kept telling me . . . I didn't cause . . ."

"He was right. Roger's AIDS came from the drug, from Kabot."

Mary again closed her eyes. Opening them, her face relaxed into a small smile. "Then I . . . didn't . . ."

Julie squeezed Mary's hand. "No, you didn't. Nothing you did caused Roger's AIDS." Then Julie leaned over and hugged her. Mary wrapped her arms around Julie. Inside herself, Julie whispered, "Thank you, God."

Julie looked at Mary and felt joy in the sudden lifting of Mary's burden, the visible change in her face.

Julie sat up as Ben came into the room. Mary beamed a weak but warm smile at Ben.

Julie said, "I told her about Roger and Z-Factor"

Mary flashed a grin and whispered, "It wasn't me, Ben. *It wasn't me!*"

A nurse entered the room. "I'm sorry to ask you to leave, but Mary needs to sleep. I thought her sedative would've worked by now."

"It'll work . . . now," Mary said, still smiling. Her eyes drifted shut.

Julie and Ben walked through the emergency room's waiting area. The rays of an orange sunset colored the walls of the room. The screen of the room's television set carried a repeating banner across its lower section. "Kabot ends legal fight to restart MIC production . . . Kabot ends legal fight to restart MIC production . . ."

Ben pointed to the screen. "Look!"

They stood in front of the TV screen. Julie read aloud in a voice of disbelief, "Kabot ends . . ." Then added, "My God!"

Ben shrugged. "I kept thinking, that bunch can't pull this off. Not a snowball's chance in hell."

"Looks like hell may've frozen over, Ben. And I've got the final chapter of my story."

"That reminds me." Ben hesitated, then said, "Before you wrap up that story, turn it in, do you suppose . . . well, do you suppose you could give me a copy? You know, so I can give Kabot a heads-up?"

"So you can *what?*"

"I need a break. My job's on shaky ground. Mom's hospital bills will be coming."

"You need money, Ben? Sell your magic pen!"

Julie walked away.

Ben caught up with her. He waved his arms and in a pleading voice said, "I know I've made mistakes, Julie, but we can still put things back together."

Approaching the front door, she said, "Why don't you talk that over with Anna." Julie went out the door and then began to jog across the parking lot.

Ben yelled, "Hey, Julie, wait up! Where're you going?"

Over her shoulder she said, "Not with you!"

Julie picked up the pace and headed down the street. She glanced behind her and saw Ben standing in the entrance.

Two blocks away she slowed her pace and looked behind her. Along an empty street, cedar and pine trees waved in a light breeze. No sign of Ben's car. She continued running for three blocks, then stopped. She took out her cell phone and called Harrison.

When he answered, Julie said, trying to talk and catch her breath at the same time, "I'm heading down Second Avenue, west of Jackson Area Medical Center. Need your help . . . please, please, get me out of here?"

"Be there in a jiffy."

She again jogged along the street. Soon Harrison's sedan pulled alongside her. Julie got in.

Harrison took her hand. "Are you okay?"

She took quick and deep breaths, and then gradually slowed enough to say, "I'm okay. Just closing a chapter in my life. Looking for a shelter in place."

They rode in silence. Julie leaned her head against Harrison's shoulder. Images of Roger's Bicentennial Concert rushed through her thoughts; Gershwin's "Rhapsody in Blue," Roger's solos; the audience's standing ovation. Under the night's dark clear sky, the notes of Roger's solo soared to join crystal points of starlight.

Harrison's voice ended her flight of thought. "There are a couple of things you need to know, Julie."

Julie felt overloaded. She didn't want to know more. About anything. At least not today. On the other hand, she trusted Harrison. He knew her well. She nestled her head more snugly on his shoulder, and her body relaxed. "If I have to."

"First, last night a body was found in the river below Jackson. It has been identified as John Delbarton. This morning the police found a suicide note in his apartment."

Julie gasped. Sudden sadness washed over her. She began to cry. "I'm sorry . . . but not surprised. I hope he has found peace."

They remained silent. Julie remembered her last conversation with John Delbarton about the documents. "I won't need them anymore."

A few minutes later Julie wiped her eyes and asked, "What's the second thing?"

Harrison hesitated for a few seconds, then said, "I didn't want to tell you. Trying to protect myself, I guess. That's unfair to you. The second thing is . . . an editor at the *New York Times* called. He's been trying to reach you."

Julie's eyes narrowed. "What about?"

Harrison hesitated again. "He would like to talk with you about an opening at the *Times.*"

At another time, Julie thought, she would have jumped out of the car and headed straight for the airport. But now she felt empty, her batteries drained, emotionally flat. Her voice soft, she said, "Thanks for telling me. I'm honored. But right now, I don't even want to think about it."

Harrison slowed the car, drove to the side of the street and stopped. He turned to her. "Leaving the *Times* aside, Julie, I don't want to lose you." They sat in silence until Harrison said, "Now, where to? I mean, where would you like for me to take you?"

Julie repeated his question slowly, "Where to?" How to answer? Since the explosion there'd been little other than, well, the explosion. Oh yes, except Auschwitz; breaking up with Ben; surviving an attack on her life; Mary's illness; learning the truth about Kabot, AIDS, and Roger. Through it all she had come to value Harrison's presence, his unending support, his thoughtful counsel. His voice had become part of her waking thoughts, even her dreams. She imagined conversations with him, testing a story line or an approach to an interview. Some mornings, arriving at their meeting, she felt an eagerness to see him, share with him, something she hadn't felt since high school. A Broadway melody came to her. "I've become accustomed to his face, he almost makes the day begin . . . ."

Julie placed one hand on Harrison's cheek. With gentle pressure she brought his lips to hers. They kissed lightly. Then her tongue traced his lips.

Harrison put his arm around her and gently pulled her next to him. Their kiss deepened.

Since the explosion her life had been in an emotional straitjacket, now suddenly removed. She had been released, freed! Julie felt the power of Harrison's presence, her connection to him. Joy!

She ended their kiss and whispered, "Where to? Don't you live near here?"

"Yes, a few blocks."

"Got a fireplace?"

Harrison laughed. "Yes. As a matter of fact, I do."

"This evening's a little chilly for June. Let's go to your place. Build a fire." Julie looked at him and smiled. "And sit in front of it . . . then see what happens."

About the Author

Dwight Harshbarger is a native West Virginian. He is the author of two previous novels, *In the Heart of the Hills: A Novel in Stories*, 2005, and the award-winning *Witness at Hawks Nest*, 2009. Dwight holds a Ph.D. in psychology. He has served as a professor of psychology and professor of public health at West Virginia University, and as executive director of the Cambridge (Massachusetts) Center for Behavioral Studies. He is a fellow of the American Psychological Association and the Association for Psychological Science. Dwight has served as a senior executive in two corporations and has done extensive organizational consulting in the USA and Asia. He is currently an adjunct professor of public health at West Virginia University.